I0619403

shattered

Aubrey Coletti

ESCAPE ARTIST PRESS

ESCAPE ARTIST PRESS
Milton, Massachusetts

Shattered
Copyright © 2013 by Aubrey Coletti
All rights reserved. Published 2013
Printed in the United States of America
First printing

ISBN 978-0-615-89270-2

This is a work of fiction. Names, characters, places, and incidents are either the
product of the author's imagination or are used fictitiously, and any resemblance to
actual persons, living or dead, business establishments, events, or locales is entirely
coincidental.

No part of this book may be used or reproduced in any manner whatsoever without
written permission except in the case of brief quotations embodied in critical
articles and reviews.

Designed and typeset by Joshua Langman
JL TYPOGRAPHIC DESIGN

This book is set in Alegreya, designed by Juan Pablo del Peral in 2012.

DEDICATED TO

WHOSE FIRE KINDLED THE INSPIRATION
THAT SET THIS TALE ALIGHT.

PROLOGUE

The Headmistress opened her personal files and began typing.

Evolution stems from extremes. Adaptation only
occurs when nature must deal with a challenge.
Humanity has become lazy, stunted in our
growth by our dominance of the planet. Our
minds run in the same tired circles. Technology
and innovation have allowed our senses to fade,
and our bodies to stagnate. Only when humans
are forced to cope with the most extreme kinds
of trauma and experience do we see forward
progress in evolution. Only when we are pushed
beyond all conceivable limits do we discover
that our ability to conceive can expand in the
most incredible of ways. But to push forward,
sometimes we must push our current moral
boundaries as we

The Headmistress' phone rang. She saved and closed her personal files, and slid her phone open.

"Yes? Oh ... now ... no, that is very interesting. Yes. Yes, I will be right over."

CHAPTER ONE

TONI WHITE TAPPED HER PENCIL SOFTLY ON HER NOTE-book, her hazel-green eyes blinking heavily as she took down mindless notes. She played with one of her curls as she tried to look attentive. If her history teacher, Mr. Alderman, glanced at most of the other students and decided they weren't paying attention, they would get a sharp comment and most likely detention. If he decided Toni was not paying attention, she would be far more severely punished.

It would just be completely shocking. Totally electrifying. I'd just sizzle with excitement. God it's good I find myself funny.

Toni resisted the urge to touch the wires or the connected bits of cool metal, irritating against her skin. It would be so easy to just pull off the wires, so easy to free herself.

And then get shocked into oblivion for doing it, Toni thought wryly. She could so easily rip the skin-shock device from her skin.

I could also call Mr. Alderman a pathetic, lonely, xenophobic old zombie again. Because those four rounds of 'therapy' down in Discipline were just so much fun.

Toni bit her lip and sat up straighter in her chair as Mr. Alderman scanned the class. At J. Alter Academy she couldn't risk even minor infractions. The skin-shock device, which consisted of a small backpack linked to innumerable wires and round metal disks placed all over her bare skin, marked her out as one of the high school's problem boarders. Toni was a serious threat to herself and others, according to her parents, her school, and her records. Someone who justified the use of extensive, aversive therapy. Someone who deserved to be controlled.

Except they haven't, thought Toni, suppressing a defiant little grin. *I chose to be here. I chose to stay, when I could have run. And I'm choosing to keep my bad, bad, nasty juvenile behavior in check for my own reasons.*

Toni waited until Mr. Alderman's gaze was focused on a student asking a question, and then she glanced over into the next row of desks. The blonde who occupied the seat near the aisle shifted. Toni caught a glimpse of her sharply carved face, somewhat blank without the dramatic lip gloss the girl usually wore. Ann Cost tossed her ponytail and sat up primly when Mr. Alderman seemed inclined to look her way, the picture of a perfect student. Toni kept another vicious grin from making its way to her face, a skill she had developed over the past months since The Incident.

Ann can look like a regular church angel when she puts her mind to it, Toni thought, knowing that when her blonde friend did so, it meant her mind was on things of a less than angelic nature.

"So I expect your five page paper by the end of this week, no extensions, no exceptions," Mr. Alderman said, dismissing the class with his usual, oddly contented grin. Toni took as deep a breath as she could manage without being obvious. This next action would have to be careful, delicate, so subtle that none of the multiple cameras which monitored J. Alter Academy could detect it. Toni rose as nonchalantly as she knew how, moving with what she hoped was a careless air across the room to conveniently rub against Ann as they moved towards the door.

The brush pass was light, brief. One minute she was side-by-side with Ann, the next the other girl had exited through the door. If Toni hadn't felt into her jacket pocket for the tiny pill, she probably wouldn't have registered its presence. In two, quick, innocuous seconds, both girls had practiced their greatest act of defiance since The Incident.

"Toni."

Toni's head shot up, her heart racing so fast it ached in her chest, her stomach plummeting with fear. If she were caught now, the entire plan was ended before it was begun — the plan they had all spent months slowly crafting through glances and passed notes, any form of communication small enough to slip past the constant surveillance under which they all lived.

But it wasn't a teacher who was staring at Toni now. The big, liquid brown eyes set in a small, pale face which blinked up at Toni were those of a friend. This girl's hair was matted and twisted; unhealthily skinny, all she wore was an oversized hospital gown.

Charlie. The name formed in Toni's mind, but before she could form and speak the words another student moved between them, and Charlie was gone.

"Are you alright, Ms. White?"

Toni's body seized up when she felt the sickening pressure of Mr. Alderman's hand on her shoulder.

"No, nothing Mr. Alderman," Toni said, through gritted teeth. "I'm fine. Just . . . dizzy for a second."

"Well, then I suggest you hurry up. You don't want to be late for your next class," the history teacher admonished.

Toni nodded, and began moving out the door, propelled back into action by the churning disgust in her stomach.

Great, so now I'm hallucinating too, she considered wryly. *Not really a fucking surprise. If nothing else, we're all definitely proof that crazy is catching.*

Joseph Valdez leaned back against the bleachers, feeling the metal of the seats heat under his fingers. Sweat covered his bronze skin, and his gleaming amber eyes were hooded in pent up rage. His rising body temperature made the disks attached to his skin even more uncomfortable than usual. He swallowed hard, forcing himself to breathe through his anger.

But seriously — I just got fouled by a fuckin' sociopath. This is my life. It's a goddamn miracle I ain't burned up from the inside when every day it feels like I got acid for blood.

Seth Dryer, the tall, handsome, utterly compassionless cause of Joseph's rage shot him a wide, nasty grin before turning back to the basketball game. Joseph's knee ached, but he knew it would be of no use to complain to the gym teacher. Mr. Protus taught physical education along with Spanish now, and he had despised Joseph since the first day he'd laid eyes on him.

"All right, one more goal and then we'll call it a game," Mr. Protus bellowed. The boys in his class struggled to get in a final basket, some of them winking and grinning at the cluster of girls who had formed to watch at the gym's left door.

Joseph bit his tongue and sucked in his breath when he located the tallest girl in the group. Ann's head was tilted to the side, a sly grin playing around the edges of her lips. Joseph tried to catch her blue-green eyes without success, and fisted his hands against the singular combination of anger and desire which always made an appearance when she ignored him.

Fine, wanna be that way, fuckin' be that way, Joseph thought. He lined up when Mr. Protus ordered the class to fall in, walking directly past the girls without a glance. For a moment, out of the corner of his eye, Joseph wondered if maybe he saw Ann move towards him, trying to catch his eye. He forced himself to continue into the locker room, his gaze focused on the floor.

Don't understand why she does this, Joseph grumbled inwardly as he stripped off his gym clothes. *And I'll probably never fuckin' understand.*

He was removing his shirt when he felt it. Dipping his hand into his pants pocket, Joseph located the tiny, oblong pill and closed his eyes for a moment, a half-smile on his face.

Nope. I'll never fuckin' understand her, and she's always gonna drive me insane. But God, I love her.

Ann Cost slid into her seat cautiously, placing her tray down on the table. She braced herself to devour a meal of cold carrots, undercooked chicken, and an uncertain grey mess, which was alleged to be mashed potatoes.

The dark, muscular girl across from Ann let out a half-suppressed laugh.

"Something funny, Lieutenant?" Ann said under her breath after a quick look around their table determined that the other two girls present were deep in conversation about someone named Roy.

"Yeah," Amina 'Lieutenant' Jackson acknowledged, a mocking sideways smile on her horsey face. "That Catholic schoolgirl look you workin' is crackin' me up. S'like when Britney Spears walked 'round tryna convince everyone she was a virgin. It's funny and creepy at the same time."

"Ha, ha." Ann rolled her eyes, spearing one of her carrots with a fork. "Like that Amazon-warrior princess thing you try for is so much better."

Lieutenant shivered, shaking her head. Even within the strict dress code they had to abide by, Lieutenant still managed to have her own style, with a tie wrapped around her collar, her hair braided into a sideways bun. "Amazons had that thing where they'd cut off one breast to make it easier to fire their arrows. I ain't checkin' for that, that's all pain."

"Pain is the name of the game," Ann mused.

"Oh, please do not," Lieutenant begged. "You start tryna rhyme and I will have to change my name and pretend I don't know you."

Ann grinned back at Lieutenant and started to flick a carrot at her friend. She stopped up short when she remembered that they couldn't risk any behavior which could be construed as too hostile between them, or too friendly. Ann could see the realization on the other girl's face as well. Both looked down at their food.

"How's Melvin?" Ann asked, cutting up her chicken with her right hand as her left inched forward under the table. She cast a glance across the busy cafeteria at the spiked black hair which was all she could see of their friend.

"'Bout the same," Lieutenant said, taking a bite of an apple as she leaned to the side, her right arm disappearing under the table as well. "He goes up and down. With parents like his, I still can't believe he does as good as he does. I woulda gone Lizzie Borden on 'em way before now."

Ann snorted, looking down at her plate again when her hand touched Lieutenant's own. She passed the two pills to her friend quickly, both moving away from each other as soon as it was done.

"What about you?" Ann said in a tone even more hushed. "How you handling everything?"

"Me, I'm fantastic. You know me," Lieutenant stated. "I could jump off the roof and fly with my magical fairy wings."

"Thought Melvin had those?"

"I borrowed 'em," Lieutenant explained. "Gets tiring bein' a vampire. Hard to get vitamin D, and this town ain't got enough virgin blood," she joked.

"Well I could have told you that," Ann said, tossing her hair. The two girls shared a grin before focusing back on their food.

"No, but how are you doing about . . . him?" Ann asked carefully. She could practically feel her friend stiffen from across the table. She made sure not to look up either at Lieutenant, or towards the tall, dark boy in question, three tables over.

"I don't think about him," Lieutenant said shortly. "None of us should. Best to just say . . . a word we ain't allowed to say, and move on."

"Yeah." Ann nodded, wishing she could reach out for her friend's hand again, knowing she could not. "Probably best."

"I can see him. I can see him. See, free, me . . ."

"Tighten the restraints. We need to keep her arms down."

"But I can see him," Charlie Persan said earnestly to the chemistry teacher working on the bonds that held her to the cold steel table. "I really can. And he saw me."

Mrs. Waters simply shook her head and turned to the woman moving up to flank her. "Are we just going to leave her like this?"

Mrs. Carter, the principal of J. Alter Academy, tapped her

heels lightly on the floor, her chin-length black hair framing a delicate, thoughtful face. "What else would we do? We have to wait until she calms down and is no longer a danger to anyone before we can release her."

"Sophia approved the use of tranquilizers to calm her if we felt there was no other way," Mrs. Waters reminded carefully.

"But we don't feel there is no other way," Mrs. Carter said while continuing to examine the disturbed girl lying on the table before them. "We are trying to keep from overmedicating these children. We just need to give her a chance to relax and come back to her senses naturally."

Charlie bit her lip hard, drawing blood. Her skin was sallow and cold, her breathing feverish. The harsh florescent lights illuminating the white room glinted off the bright steel of the equipment and instruments around her. It made her head swim, and she closed her eyes against the painful sensory rush to her brain.

A cool hand touched her forehead.

"Do you think she may be sick? Physically sick, I mean?" Charlie heard Mrs. Waters ask.

"I don't think so," Mrs. Carter replied, "but we'll keep a close eye on her. We certainly don't want to miss anything."

Charlie let the blood dribble into her mouth.

"Charlie, stop biting. You are hurting yourself."

Concentrating through the haze in her mind, Charlie managed to release her bottom lip.

"Good, good, you see?" Mrs. Carter said soothingly. "You're already getting better."

The principal removed her hand from Charlie's forehead. The overwhelming scent of her perfume retreated, allowing Charlie to breath more easily. The voices of the two teachers continued, becoming more and more indistinct as Charlie faded into sleep.

But before drifting off, Charlie made sure to silently slip the key card she had stolen from Mrs. Carter under the back of her hospital gown and out of sight.

CHAPTER TWO

"SHE KNOWS WHAT YOU ARE PLANNING, YOU KNOW,
snow."

Charlie swallowed hard, keeping her eyes focused on her algebra textbook.

"Shirk, shirk, shirk, you can't do homework!"

The fading light of the setting sun streaming in through the wide glass windows of Mrs. Carter's kitchen was so bright, Charlie wanted to scream, and rage, and dance. The last thing she had wanted was to be placed in the principal's house for monitoring. The sparkling marble floors, the fresh scent of the cinnamon plug-ins in each room, the pristine rugs and carpets and sheets, all melded together in Charlie's mind. The house seemed to her an extension of Mrs. Carter herself. Pretty and neat and beckoning on the outside, but full of darkness and strangeness within. Charlie's friends knew about the cameras placed in all of the homes to watch them — regular hidden cameras during the day, thermal imaging cameras at night.

But they don't know about the sensors in the wall, Charlie thought, as she pressed her pencil pointlessly against the checkered paper of her algebra notebook. *They don't know about the scanners that can see through your whole body, that come around every day at five. And they need to be told about the nanobots, the little buggy wuggies, that are in your blood. Mud, blood, dud —*

"Are you alright, Charlie?"

"Yes, ma'am," Charlie answered Mrs. Carter automatically. The principal smiled in the gentle way she did whenever Charlie used that proper title. It wasn't a phrase Charlie normally used — it had simply popped out one day. Mrs. Carter hadn't minded, so Charlie continued using it. "Just working on algebra."

"That's good. Try not to force yourself to concentrate too hard. Just take it problem by problem," Mrs. Carter advised. Charlie nodded, using the smile she'd practiced in the mirror as an answer.

"She's going to find out and kill you, will you, let her? She needs to be taken care of."

Charlie ignored The Voices. Today was a good day. Today she knew they were The Voices, stemming only from her mind. When The Voices took on bodies, or seemed to come from lamps, or couches, or shadows, it was harder to fight the desire to answer them back. And talking to things no one else could see or hear was an instant trip to Discipline.

Of course, sometimes that suits me just fine, Charlie mused with an inner smile as she wrote down some random number for an answer to a math question she hadn't bothered to figure out. *Because no one suspects a poor little looney toon of lifting the key card that gains access to any house containing a boarder right off the principal's very body. Oddly.*

Charlie shifted just slightly, feeling the tiny plastic card rub against the skin of her inner thigh where it was hidden inside the nylons she wore under her skirt. In her left pocket was the tiny pill Ann had slipped her in school.

Everything's ready, Charlie let herself realize. *Our first big act of defiance since The Incident. If we can all sneak out safely, meet quickly, and get back in time without getting caught, we'll have really done it. Wow, that's a lot of ifs.*

Charlie sniffed the air as Mrs. Carter's movements in the kitchen brought the scents of oregano, dried pasta, and olive oil to her sensitive nose. Charlie would have to move, soon the smells and sounds of cooking would send her into sensory overload.

Load, abode, foreboding . . . Charlie swallowed painfully.

And yeah, add one more if to that list — if I can keep my mind from going completely mad.

Let's be honest, there is no such fuckin' thing as a 'good girl.' The sweetest girls on the outside during the day are the dirty, nasty sluts of the night.

Ann smiled sweetly at herself in the bathroom mirror as she pulled her blonde hair into a ponytail atop her head. She stretched, happy to be free of the skin shock device, which she no longer had to wear to sleep. She smiled less sweetly as she filled up the plastic bottle of water that she was allowed to have on her nightstand with boiling hot liquid.

No glass for big bad Ann, of course, she thought, padding across the carpeted floor of the bedroom she shared with Katrina Vaglienty, another boarder. *We wouldn't want her to cut herself again, oh no. No, causing her pain and physical harm is the Academy's job. Because that makes sense.*

"Sleep well," Ann said to Katrina as she swallowed the pill dry. She then surreptitiously slipped the bottle into her bed by her side.

"You too," Katrina responded, rolling over and lying still.

See Katrina sleep, thought Ann. *See Katrina smile. See Katrina make pills to leach out your body warmth into piled pillows and sheets, to fool the hidden thermal cameras into thinking you are still in your bed, so you can sneak out and fuck your boyfriend. Bad Katrina, bad.*

Ann lay down under her bed's comforter and worked on bunching the sheets and her pillow together so that it would resemble her body. She had to work quickly, so that, when the pill's effects kicked in, she would be correctly positioned.

I still can't believe this works, Ann thought wryly, finally settling and waiting, one eye on the electronic clock that was the only illumination in the room. When she had first been assigned to a new house with Katrina as her roommate, Ann had been in despair of ever seeing Joseph again. With it known beyond a

20

doubt that they had had sex, the Academy intended to make sure they never had any chance to repeat the act again. Ann had lost her glass privileges when she smashed one and used the pieces to cut herself after being shocked for passing him too closely in the hallway.

Ann suppressed a shiver and resisted the urge to touch her rapidly cooling skin.

Never thought I'd be sitting here thanking a god I don't believe in for Katrina, Ann smiled wryly. When Ann, for her part in The Incident, had been reassigned to a new supervisor and gotten Katrina as her new housemate, she had been furious. The last thing she wanted was for J. Alter Academy's star reformed boarder to be breathing down her back night and day. The last thing Ann expected, when crying in her room over her situation, was for Katrina to sit down beside her and refuse to leave even after repeated threats and cursing. Even more surprising was when Katrina offered to lend her some of the pills she had developed to sneak out past the cameras and see her own boyfriend. Ann felt for the bottle at her side. Its boiling heat also helped to fool the cameras.

She sneaks out to see her boyfriend, and I sneak out to see mine, Ann thought, a glance at the clock telling her she had only a few more minutes to wait. *We'd better not get fuckin' caught tonight, or Katrina will kill me in my sleep for ruining her newest trick to see her boy.*

Hell. I'll kill me in my sleep for ruining her newest trick to see my boy. Ann let out a slow sigh and turned once more to the clock.

11:23 PM.

Joseph closed his eyes and focused on his breathing to keep his body from protesting its rapidly dropping temperature. He'd taken the second pill sooner than he usually did on nights when he went out to meet Ann — his nerves had gotten the better of his willpower. It was frustrating not to be able to go until exactly the right moment, but they had all planned this out carefully.

None of them could afford to be caught. Not when things were finally cooling down since The Incident.

Coolin' down. Fuck, why is my damn body like this? If I had to choose a superhero to be, it woulda been Spiderman or Batman, not the Human Torch.

There was no help for it. As desperate as he was to go and sneak out the door, down to where he knew Ann, and this time Charlie, would be waiting, he simply had to wait.

I hate my body. Bein' a pyro ain't a power, it's a fuckin' inconvenience, is what it is.

Joseph had to wait while his abnormally hot body cooled down enough for him to slip undetected past the cameras. Even with two pills, his body temperature still went back up to normal far faster than Ann's did. He would have just enough time to use the key his supervisor, Sherry Nearson, hadn't wanted to report as stolen, to get out the door.

There's advantages to havin' a drug addict as a supervisor, Joseph thought darkly. *Not many, but enough.*

11:24 PM.

Just one more minute. I got five minutes to sneak downstairs. Joseph desperately tried to control his body's urge to leap up and run for the door. *We got ten minutes to get to the middle of the woods, and then fifteen minutes to get our meetin' over with. That gives me and her, what, ten, twelve minutes together?*

Fuck math, that ain't enough time.

Joseph forced himself not to think about Ann. If anything could make his body heat, and ruin their carefully put-together plan, it was thinking about Ann.

11:25 PM.

Time to go. Joseph gently placed his hands on the headboard of the bed and skillfully used his arms to drag his lower body out from under the sheets. Whoever was viewing the cameras would see movement, but it would appear to simply be his body shifting under the sheets. His heat signature was bound up in pillows and blankets stuffed to resemble his body shape. Those watching would view it and assume he still slept innocently. His own bottle of burning hot water lay in the center, helping to give off a constant, steady heat. Joseph was now a ghost.

Ann's right, Katrina came through on this one, Joseph mused as he placed both feet firmly and gently on his bedroom floor. He moved as lightly as he could towards the door. *She's been playin' the good girl act, and all this time scopin' out the cameras, mixin' up drugs, and using it all to run off and get laid. And helpin' others to do the same. That right there puts her on the fast track to sainthood in my book.*

Joseph reached the door. Now came the tricky part. A small change in temperature could be seen on the cameras as movement. He had to open the door as slightly as possible, so that it minimized his chances that those watching would notice. His advantage was that they would be looking at his heat form in the bed, if they were paying close attention at all.

Joseph touched the doorknob tentatively, turning it without breathing as he positioned himself in front of the door. The dim bathroom light cracked through as he tugged it open. Joseph pulled just a little bit more before swiftly and smoothly slipping through the tiny opening. As fast as he dared, as quietly as possible, he closed it behind him, leaving his room unheard and unseen.

Toni waited for a cautious moment after she closed her bedroom door. Her new supervisor, Augustine Booker, wasn't exactly a heavy sleeper, and she couldn't afford to be caught tonight.

None of us can, she mused, as she decided it was safe to proceed. She moved as swiftly as she dared, down the hall and to the stairs.

Breathe. Trying to breathe steadily and quietly despite the cocktail of excitement, anxiety, fear, and apprehension churning inside of her, Toni made it to the bottom of the stairs.

Augustine Booker's house was a maze of shadows at this hour. Toni had to squint and blink until her eyes adjusted to the darkness enough to navigate her way past the living room couch and coffee table, through the foyer, and to the front door.

Toni waited. Augustine Booker kept the key to the back door around his neck at all times, but all of the houses containing boarders had been fitted with an electronic lock. This lock, along with opening to the supervisor's key, opened to the principal's key card, so that she had easy access to any of the boarder homes at any time.

Which meant that, with Charlie's theft of said key card, they had their first chance to meet up together since The Incident.

Only if Charlie got it, Toni couldn't stop herself from thinking. *Only if everything worked out and she got past Mrs. Carter, and Joseph managed to get out, and Ann, and Melvin, and —*

There was a soft buzz, and then the door was pushed open. A small, pale face peeked over the side.

"How's it flyin', Foxy?" Charlie whispered.

Toni blinked. "Fine, Charlie."

"Good." Charlie nodded, as if it answered a very important question. "You'd better come, or they'll hear us. The bugs, you know. The nanobots."

"Right," Toni agreed. "That would be bad."

"Is it really a good idea to meet in the same place?" Joseph asked as he helped Ann over a fallen tree. It was very nearly pitch black, save for the dim glow of the moonlight through the trees. The forest ground, frosted over with the chill of early winter, crunched as the crew made its way to their base of operations. The only light for the small band came from a tiny laser pointer Melvin had lifted from his father's study. Lieutenant moved methodically through the trees, pushing branches aside with a practiced hand for Toni, who followed quickly behind her.

"It's only for tonight," Charlie explained. Leading the group along with Melvin, she walked easily, avoiding stumps and thorns as if it were broad daylight. "It doesn't matter tonight, because if they know or suspect, well, we're screwed anyway, no matter where we meet."

"Yup, that's a happy thought." Joseph chuckled wryly as they finally emerged from the woods and began to trudge across the field to the old abandoned house. "You'll be able to run all the lights in a fuckin' house for a year on us if we get caught."

"Then we better make sure we don't," Ann said, flicking him on the ear.

"Ow," Joseph said loudly. "Don't bite my head off for sayin' an opinion."

"Come on, you two," Lieutenant said as they reached the shaky old house. "Keep the foreplay to a minimum until we're all done with this and safely outta range, m'kay?"

She opened the door and stopped short, causing Toni to bump into her back.

"What," Lieutenant fumed dangerously through gritted teeth, "the everlovin' fuck is he doin' here?"

"Wait, okay, everyone wait." Charlie squeezed past the furious girl and into the house, holding her hands out calmingly. "Just come in and please, please listen."

"I can't see —" Joseph pushed through, making way for Ann. Melvin and Toni followed him around Lieutenant into the damp, creaky room. At the center a tall, dark boy blinked at them in confusion.

"Anton," Toni said, breaking the silence. "Charlie, why the hell is he here? Why the hell would you bring him here?"

"Why don't we ask him?" Lieutenant snapped. "Then he can try and tell me why I shouldn't turn this shit into a real life horror movie."

"Okay, does someone want to explain what the fuck is goin' on here, or are me and Ann s'posed to just guess?" Joseph demanded loudly.

"You mean you don't know?" Melvin's voice cracked. "He turned us in! He's the one who told the Headmistress everything. He's the reason we got caught!"

"He didn't turn us in," Charlie said quickly. "If you guys will just listen —"

"Nah, nah." Lieutenant was shaking her head. "I got no reason to listen to him. If you brought us out here for this shit, to bring him here "

"I don't even know why I'm here," Anton said, his flint-like eyes darting from Melvin to Ann.

"You're right, you shouldn't be here," Lieutenant snapped at him. "You shouldn't be here, you shoulda never come out to face me."

"I didn't come here to face you," Anton said, looking to Charlie and Joseph and Toni.

"Then why the hell did you come, mutherfucker?" Lieutenant yelled.

"I don't know! I don't know how the fuck I got here!" Anton hollered back, finally angry enough to get up in the tall girl's face.

"Of course you don't," Charlie said in the wake of the heated silence. "I asked Anthony to come."

Joseph raised an eyebrow. "What's the difference?"

"Anthony and Anton are two different identities," Charlie said. She reached out to touch Anton's shoulder gently, to pull him away from Lieutenant: the two were still staring daggers at each other.

"Like an alter ego?" Joseph asked.

"If by alter ego you mean one that can completely take over the body and do things the others aren't aware of?" Charlie answered. "Then yes, that kind of alter ego."

"You're saying he has dissociative identity disorder," Toni whispered.

"He has what now?" Joseph raised both eyebrows.

"Dissociative identity disorder, multiple personality disorder," Toni explained. "It's when someone has different identities living in one body."

"So which one of those personalities betrayed us like a pathetic lil' rat? Anton or Anthony?" Lieutenant snarled.

"Neither," Charlie answered. "Ant did."

"But it's still him though." Ann gestured towards Anton, who turned away.

"No, no it isn't." Toni stepped forward. "It's not like with Clark Kent and Superman, where he becomes stronger or faster in one identity, and then goes back to himself remembering everything. It's like . . . if Clark Kent were writing an article for The Daily Planet, and all of a sudden he's at home with Lois Lane and she's like "Wow, you really mean it? You want to marry me?" And he's like "But, wait, I was just at work a second ago!"

"So his Superman identity could take over, and his Clark Kent self wouldn't know at all?" Joseph said, frowning.

"Exactly," Charlie said. "It's a whole identity change. When one identity is in control, the other isn't. The other doesn't even know. When Superman is running things, Clark Kent is just kinda . . . gone. He could be walking down the street and then, all of a sudden, he's somewhere else. Like he's —"

"Lost time." Anton spoke the words roughly.

"Yeah," Toni said softly. "And that whole time Superman's been in control."

"So, basically . . . " Ann tried to put it all together. "What you're saying is . . . you're all enormous geeks."

Joseph chuckled, Toni and Charlie grinned, and Anton cracked a hint of a smile.

"So then who betrayed us?" Lieutenant asked. Her voice was hard, but the tension in her rigid body was beginning to fade.

"Ant did," Melvin said. The others turned to him. "Remember? On the tape — they showed the rest of us a tape," he explained to Ann and Joseph, "of Anton — of Ant telling the Headmistress where we were, about our plans."

"So who the fuck is Ant?" Lieutenant said, crossing her arms.

Charlie swallowed, turning to Anton. "I talked with Anthony about coming here. He's the one I slipped the note too. Could we . . . talk to him?"

Anton took a step back, scowling.

"Anthony?" Toni said, moving up to flank Charlie. "Anthony,

are you there?"

The vein on the left side of Anton's neck bulged, and his body stiffened. Then the anger in his eyes faded, and his face visibly relaxed and brightened, although his expression stayed sober.

"Hey," Charlie said, smiling.

"Am I here?" Anthony asked, looking around.

"Yeah, you made it," Charlie assured.

"Whoa." Anthony chuckled, glancing around the room. "I ain't the most popular guy right now, huh?"

"We've been trying to figure out what's going on," Toni said.

"Yeah, me too." Anthony laughed.

"So do *you* know?" Joseph asked, narrowing his eyes at Anthony. "About you and Superman?"

Anthony blinked.

"We are great big geeks," Charlie explained, "but I think they get it now. Mostly. Maybe."

"Wait, I thought the . . . Supermen couldn't know about each other?" Melvin asked, nose crinkling.

"Usually, they don't," Toni explained, "but sometimes they can . . . meet up I guess, learn they exist."

"So you, what, organized a play date with your three personalities?" Ann asked, wincing at the very thought. "Suddenly I feel way more sane than I should."

"I've been tryin' to put it together in my head for a while now," Anthony said, with a heavy sigh. "Kept losin' time. I just . . . fuck, man, I thought that was how everybody was. Start goin' one place and end up in another with new shoes you know you wasn't wearin' when you first walked out. After . . . everything went down, they put me in a room alone, and I started talkin' to . . . the others."

"Now my head hurts," Joseph lamented, rubbing his neck.

"Okay, so . . . Anthony's here now, and Anton was here before," Lieutenant said with difficulty. "What if this — *Ant* fucker pops up and turns us all in again?"

"He won't," Anthony promised. "I can talk to him. He was

confused when he did that. Scared. Didn't know where we were, thought we were . . . back home. You ain't have to worry about him."

"We do have to worry about getting back, though," Toni said suddenly, touching her wrist. "How long does this stuff last?"

"According to Katrina, about an hour," Ann answered. "Whoa, wait. Anthony . . . Ant . . . Superman, whatever, how did you get out here?"

"Hey now, hey now." Anthony put up his hands and waved them in defense. "Now, everybody just stop lookin' at your boy like we about to do some replay of *Deliverance* here. I already don't feel safe at creepy ol' houses out in the woods. I ain't tipped anybody off. I got the camera that goes to my bedroom to freeze on an image of me still there."

"How?" Lieutenant demanded.

"I don't know, L," Anthony said, smiling at her sadly. Lieutenant glanced away. "Just figured out a couple weeks ago I could do it, and told Tiny here —" he nodded at Charlie "— that I could make it out. The backyard door opens for me too, if I just kinda concentrate. They'll notice the shit is frozen by mornin' but by then we'll all be snug in our beds."

"Not if we don't hurry, we won't," Ann said. "Charlie, if we wanna do this again, you've gotta get everybody else back before it wears off."

"What about you?" Melvin questioned. Ann grinned, digging into her pajama bottom pocket and revealing a tiny key. "I've got the old fashioned key home," she stated. "Katrina lets me use the one she stole — sorry, the one that 'went missing' — when I wanna go out. In exchange, I cover for her if our supervisor comes in when she's out with her boy. And Joseph has the key to his house that I stole from Sherry way back when this all started."

"Oh, the things we do to get laid." Lieutenant shook her head.

"Who said anything about sex?" Ann stated, at the same time that Joseph said, "Oh, yes."

Ann whirled around to glare at him. "Excuse me? You made

some decision I don't know about before we even got here?"

"Aaaannnd that's our cue to go," Melvin said, moving to the door.

"Wait, why is she mad?" Charlie asked, as Toni tugged her outside. "He was joking, right? Or am I wrong?" *Wrong, gong, gongs from Honk Kong, it's all a matter of chopsticks . . .*

"Don't even worry about those two," Lieutenant said, smiling finally. "They'll be *fiiine*, m'kay? They'll have their little fight, get it outta their system, and then you just put on some Barry White and back away, back away."

"White is the absence of color, but absence is a clue to the existence of the five central polygraphs, which are key to understanding the oscillation of the grid, if you are to escape it," Charlie said earnestly.

"Um, yeah, that's real good," Lieutenant said, patting Charlie on the shoulder. "Let's get you home, a'ight?"

"Don't look at me like that, like you don't understand!"

"I don't fuckin' understand, Ann!" Joseph yelled. He quickly looked around and brought his voice down. "Will you be quiet? You're gonna get us caught!"

"Oh, and you wouldn't want to be found with me, would you?" Ann demanded.

"What the hell are you talkin' about?" Joseph spread his arms in confusion. "If we wouldn't fuckin' pay ten times over for it, yeah, I'd love to be found wit' you!"

"Because it would help your reputation, right?" Ann snapped. "Of course it would. You're the guy, so it's fine for you to be found with a whore."

"When the fuck did I call you a whore?" Joseph backed away, stunned.

"You didn't have to. It was obvious right back there." Ann gestured furiously. "Talkin' like it's a done deal we're gonna have sex."

"Well we have, almost every other time we come out here!"

"Oh, so that means you get to expect it!?"

Joseph shook his head. "You're tryna bite my head off 'cause I acted like we was gonna have sex? Well fine, we won't have sex."

"No, that isn't the goddamn point," Ann practically shrieked.

"Then what the hell is?" Joseph screamed back, reaching his breaking point. "I make a fuckin' joke, and you freak out on me? Why you always wanna start a fight over bullshit?"

"So that's what my feelings are to you now?" Ann's eyes flashed. "Bullshit? That's it, that's what they are?"

"Oh my God, are you serious?" Joseph rubbed his hands over his face. "Are you serious? Do you even *know* why the hell you're so mad?"

"Yes!" Ann hissed at him. *No.* "I know exactly why I'm mad!" *But not why I always get so mad.* "It's you — you make me fucking angry! Maybe if you knew what the hell to say I wouldn't have to remind you not to be a prick all the time!"

"Well good!" Joseph snapped back, stomping over to get up in her face. "I'm glad I make you mad! 'Cause you drive me up the fuckin' wall, so I'm happy to return the favor."

Unable to put her rage into words, and in reality unaware of why she even felt it, Ann shoved Joseph back with all the force she could manage.

I want to stop. Make it stop. I wanna get off. "I hate you."

Joseph's eyes dimmed with pain, and then he moved over to shove her back, one-handed. Hardly rough, but enough to make his point. "Yeah, I hate you too."

"Good." Ann pushed him again, just enough to force him to take a step back.

"Fine," Joseph retaliated, moving back in to fill the heated space between them.

"Well great, I guess you can just —"

His kiss saved her from having to create a reply, and she returned it heatedly, throwing her arms around his neck and letting her fury find another outlet. Joseph wrapped his arms around her lower back, and they stumbled together until they hit one of the rotting, creaking walls.

"Ow," Joseph whimpered against her lips, and Ann laughed recklessly, kissing his cheek, his chin, his nose, his neck. Arching and groaning into her assault, Joseph slipped his hands up under her shirt and grinned when she moaned. Moving back to capture her mouth again, his breath hitched when she drew her nails down his chest.

"So . . ." He panted between kisses. "You still . . . mad . . . at me?"

"Mmm-hmm," Ann purred, pulling him closer. "So mad. Hate you . . . hate you so much . . ."

"Good," Joseph said as they sank together to the floor. "Hate . . . hate you too."

I'm so close.

Toni swallowed hard as she moved to open the door to her room. She heard a sound and froze.

Don't let this be Booker waking up. Please, just let this be anything except Booker waking up.

The door of her supervisor's bedroom opened. Toni held her breath and tried to imagine herself small and dark and invisible.

You don't notice me . . . don't notice me . . . please don't notice me . . .

The bathroom was directly down the hall from where Toni stood. If Booker walked into it without seeing her Toni could try and sneak quickly back into her room. Of course, that movement could also alert him to her presence.

But if I wait and let him come back out, he has a chance of seeing me, Toni evaluated, her lower body aching with stress and fear. *Please, please, please be one of those gross guys who spends way too long in the bathroom doing things no woman ever wants to know about.*

Booker shut the bathroom door with an audible click, and Toni put her hand on her room's door knob. It was cooler now.

No, she realized, shivering. *I'm warmer now. It's wearing off.*

Toni closed her eyes tightly, turned the knob, and rushed into her room. She pulled the door shut behind her. Rushing over to her bed, she slipped under the covers as gently as she could, and adjusted so that her body was over the pile she had left in her place.

It's still a little warm, she thought, trying to calm herself. *Maybe they didn't see. I'm sure they didn't see. Please don't let them see.*

"Charlie, have you seen a key card around here?"

Charlie looked up from her cereal and blinked at Mrs. Carter. The principal was already smartly dressed in a navy blue skirt and cream-colored silk shirt. The morning light glinted off her silver jewelry, making Charlie want to squint and duck away.

"No, ma'am," Charlie replied. "What does it look like?"

"Just a small card with my picture and name on it," Mrs. Carter explained, her voice soft, but her eyes searching.

"Like a driver's license or something?" Charlie continued, trying to control her blinking.

"Yes, very like," Mrs. Carter responded.

"I'll keep an eye out for it," Charlie said. Mrs. Carter held the young girl's gaze before nodding and turning away.

Charlie looked down at her cereal, which this morning appeared free of strangeness.

No messages in the milk today, she thought in an internal sing-song voice that hardly sounded like her own. *But the writings on the wall if she doesn't fall for it, the pretty principal, pernicious vicious villainess, find it, find it, find it . . .*

"Oh, here it is."

Charlie tried not to jerk her head up at Mrs. Carter's relieved voice. The principal waved the card briskly. With a light smile, she slipped it back into her pocket. "Must have just missed it."

Charlie nodded and blinked.

CHAPTER THREE

"CAN SOMEONE LIST THE MALE SECONDARY SEX CHAR-acteristics for me? Ann?"

Ann answered Mrs. Waters' question with wide eyes. *Joseph's hands, muscled and strong ... but gentle, nervous. How does he always know just where to touch?* "I . . . I'm sorry, could you repeat the question?"

Mrs. Waters closed her eyes for a moment in a sign of weariness. "The male secondary sex characteristics."

Ann looked left and right, and a blush ran up her cheeks. *His hands on my legs, my thighs. Last night lasted longer, so good . . .* "What about them?"

There was a series of titters and scattered giggles around the class before Mrs. Waters frowned deeply, bringing silence. Ann made sure to keep the same expression of doe-eyed innocence she had been using over the past months pasted across her face. She felt a twinge of sympathy for Mrs. Waters, having to teach the male and female reproductive systems to a class of awkward, hormone-addled teenagers.

Well maybe if they weren't so fuckin' scared of us — gasp! shock! — having sex, that they actually could teach us what we really need to know, then I wouldn't have to sneak Katrina's do-it-yourself morning-after pills and pray to Christmas and the Eater bunny that I don't get pregnant every other day, Ann thought wryly. She stole a glance over at Katrina, who was wearing the same cloying look of pre-

34

tend shyness and innocence.

"Can you list the male secondary sex characteristics?" Mrs. Waters asked Ann again with more iron in her voice.

Joseph's back, his stomach, the way his muscles move when they react to my fingers ... guy sex characteristics versus girls, uh ... the way he's smooth and hard and so different from me where I'm soft and warm ... uh, right, question, characteristics, guys ... does the way he always closes his eyes and bites his lip to try not to whimper when he comes count? Ann swallowed against the rising warmth of her blood and tried to shut off the faucet of memories.

"Can you name me *one*?" Mrs. Waters interrogated, her lips pursing.

The way he looks when he's straining, the way he groans when I kiss over his chin ...

"They need to shave?" Ann replied. Someone in the back of the room snorted, but Mrs. Waters seemed satisfied.

"Yes, facial and body hair," the teacher stated, writing it on the board. "Does anyone else know any others?"

Lieutenant raised her hand, and it seemed to Ann like she was breathing rapidly.

"Yes?"

"Other male secondary sex characteristics include a larger, more muscular stature, deepened voice, broad shoulders, and the development of an Adam's apple," Lieutenant listed, her eyes bright and glistening as if she had held them open all night. Ann frowned slightly, zeroing in on how the other girl tapped the desk repeatedly with the fingers of her left hand, her right scribbling away, even as her gaze was fixed upon Mrs. Waters.

"And what," Mrs. Waters said, as she continued to make her list on the board, "is responsible for causing these changes?"

"Androgen," Lieutenant said, this time without raising her hand or waiting to be called on. "Also known as androgenic hormone, or testoid, which is just a general term for any compound that stimulates or controls the development of said characteristics in vertebrates, which it does by binding to androgen receptors. They were first discovered in 1936, and y'all might know of them in the form of anabolic steroids, or as the very important ingredient in makin' all you little boys into men — testosterone."

The words poured out of the tall black girl in a rush, and Lieutenant's lips curved into a small smirk as she ended with a flourish of her head. Mrs. Waters had frozen with her back to the class, her hand stopped on the 'o' of androgen.

Lieutenant's eyes were darting wildly around the room. Ann managed to catch them for a brief moment and shake her head in warning. Lieutenant answered her silently by raising one cocky eyebrow.

Don't, Ann thought at her friend as hard as she could. *Just stop, don't do it. Hold it in, hold it back . . .*

Lieutenant's confident expression vanished, and for one horrified moment Ann was worried she had spoken aloud, until she realized the taller girl's gaze was focused over and behind her head.

Ann turned around just in time to see a flash of red hair through the window.

"Now do you all think you can manage that?"

"Yes Mr. Protus," the gym class responded in unison to the beefy teacher, who grunted and nodded. Joseph frowned, eyes scanning the obstacle course he had to complete for his fitness test. It included ten hurdles, fifteen sets of cones he had to dodge back and forth between, a small wooden climbing wall he had to scale by use of a series of shaky old pegs, and finally a one hundred yard sprint across the gym to the finish line where Mr. Protus would be waiting with a stopwatch.

And I gotta do it all with this *on me,* Joseph thought darkly. His hands clenched into fists to keep from touching the wires on his arms or fiddling with the backpack containing the device for the skin-shock system that Mr. Protus never hesitated to utilize. *Whatever. They can write me down as failin' at fitness. Probably better for them to think I'm weak and underestimate me.*

Joseph felt a heavy clap on his back, and he whirled around, his hands coming up in defense.

"Calm down," chuckled Seth, backing away mockingly. "I was just wishing you good luck. Seems only fair, what with, uh . . ." The handsome blonde nodded towards the apparatus visible on Joseph in his short-sleeved shirt and shorts. Seth raised his eyebrows with a grin as he danced his fingers up and down his own bare arms. For his part in helping the Headmistress during The Incident, Seth no longer had to wear the skin-shock device.

Joseph felt the slow burn of rage begin in his stomach and flow out through his chest, down his legs, into his arms, and around his face. He smiled with rage. "'Yeah, 'cause you all about what's fair, huh?"

"I like to reach out to the less fortunate," Seth said, inclining his head magnanimously.

"Please do not reach out for me in any way," Joseph said flatly. "I —"

Fuck! Joseph doubled over as the shock hit him. He glared over at Mr. Protus once his eyes cleared: the stone-jawed man had his left hand behind his back. The aids and teachers who handled the device were instructed to keep the control mechanism out of sight so the recipient student couldn't prepare themselves in advance.

"You two should not be talking," Mr Protus said heavily. "And you know this. But I'm feeling charitable today, so I will take this as you both volunteering to go first. Come up to the head of the line."

Joseph swallowed down the blood from biting his tongue and moved to put his foot at the starting line. Seth moved in beside him, his eyes trained on his own row of hurdles.

I have to kill 'em, Joseph thought as he took in deep breaths to ready himself. *That's gotta be what this is. God is tryna tell me to kill these two mutherfuckers. Or to off myself, but if I do that, I'ma take 'em both down wit' me.*

"Mark," said Mr. Protus lazily. "Set." He blew the whistle.

Right away Joseph could tell the backpack would be the reason he lost the race. His muscles screamed and strained just running to the first hurdle, and getting its weight, plus that of this own body, over the obstacle was almost as physically painful as a shock.

He could tell by the scattered cheers behind him, quickly silenced by Mr. Protus, that Seth was in the lead. Over the pounding of his heart and the burning in his stomach, Joseph soared over the last hurdle, and hurriedly zigzagged through the line of cones. He sped to catch up with Seth who was already scaling the wall.

His shirt soaked in sweat already, Joseph grabbed the nearest peg he could find and hauled himself up by both hands, his feet searching for the next peg after the fact.

Joseph grinned up at Seth who was shooting nervous glances down at him, speeding up as he began to gain traction.

That's right, Joseph thought, his fierce and furious joy sustaining his body despite the pain that had almost reached numbing point. *I'm comin' for you.*

Joseph's fingers clasped at the top peg and, with a stifled yell, he began to pull up the rest of his groaning body. He blinked sweat out of his eyes, looking upwards just as Seth's foot slammed down into his face.

Joseph let out a full-throated scream when he hit the ground, his back protesting the violent landing. Mr. Protus blew his whistle, and Seth dropped easily down onto his feet beside Joseph. With a sly smile, he offered him his hand.

"Fuck you!" Joseph slapped the other boy away. "I said don't try to touch me. You —"

Jesus! Joseph seized up as the shock hit him. He grit his teeth and stood up as Mr. Protus came striding over.

"All right, all right," Mr. Protus grumbled, drawing abreast of the two boys. "The two of you clearly have some trouble with the wall —"

38

"Yeah I had trouble. I had his foot in my fu— face." Joseph gestured towards Seth.

"I don't care to hear your whining, Valdez," Mr. Protus said firmly. "You two have one last chance to run this course, or you're both headed straight for Discipline."

Both boys shot each other lethal glares before looking down and away. Mr. Protus nodded. "Start again."

Joseph's chest was burning when he put his left foot on the starting line again. The rest of his body had a strangely numb quality, and he could feel his heart skipping beats as it raced.

"Mark," Mr. Protus called out. "Set." He blew the whistle.

Joseph raced over the hurdles, landing painfully after each jump, his knees threatening to buckle. He made up the distance between himself and Seth during the cones, and the two boys reached the wall at the same moment. Joseph scaled the wall in a fury, not stopping even when he was unable to breath for a solid thirty seconds.

I just gotta win this, he told himself, pushing over the top of the wall and dropping into a crouch on the other side. *Breathing comes later.*

His pack bashed heavily into his back as Joseph began the final sprint. He could hear Seth drawing up behind him, could feel his heart skip again. Joseph's breath caught, and his gaze clouded over for a moment. When it cleared, he could see Seth pulling ahead of him.

No, fuckin' God damn it, NO! Joseph screamed to himself. *Get the fuck off my back and away from me!*

His anger gave him the needed boost of adrenaline. Joseph pushed himself past Seth, skittering across the finish line and staggering to a halt.

Panting, he caught the look of anger and surprise and disgust on Seth's face as the boy stumbled across the line after him. Joseph was just opening his mouth to laugh when everything went dark.

"Mr. Levant, what is your answer to question seven?"

Ms. Donelle waited for the boy, upon whom her eyes were fixed, to respond. He simply stared ahead, his eyes almost too white in his dark face.

"Mr. Levant, I would like an answer please."

The boy glanced from left to right as if looking for someone.

Ms. Donelle clenched her fist as if steeling herself and delivered the shock. The boy jumped and then faced her.

"Mr. Levant," she queried again. "What is your answer to question seven?"

"Uh ... seven ... right. X equals the square of four," Anthony stated, his body still quivering from the aftereffects.

"Thank you," Ms. Donelle said, shaking her head a little. "Really, that didn't have to be so hard, did it?"

"I don' know," Anthony muttered under his breath once Ms. Donelle had moved on to another student. "I wasn't here."

"Drink this."

Joseph took the glass of water that was handed him and let it rest on his lap. The room he'd awoken to find himself in was viciously white. He had to squint to make anything out over the harsh lights, and the space possessed an overly sterilized smell that wasn't doing his headache any favors. He could feel the IV in his arm, nestled in amongst the apparatus of his shock system.

Great: more wires. They can barely fit 'em on my fuckin' arms. I look like a really enterprisin' heroin addict, he thought with a grim twist of humor as he tried to hold onto the slippery wet glass. "Thank you."

"Thank me after you drink it, Joseph," the woman said smartly. She sat down in the chair placed opposite the table where Joseph was half reclining and propped up by an uncomfortable plastic pillow. She was tall with skin that had not yet wrinkled, though it gave the impression that it was stretched over the proud bones of her face. Her lips were tight, but her grey eyes were not unkind.

40

She was dressed in a black and off-white suit, which served to make her drastically red hair pop. Joseph's eyes widened as he realized who sat before him. He swallowed.

"Honestly, with all due respect," he answered the Headmistress carefully. "I think if I tried to drink right now, I'd just cough it back up. My throat feels kinda dead."

Sophia Valentina smiled as if amused, and pulled a file from under her arm and opened it. "Do you know the average core human body temperature, Joseph?"

Joseph bit his lip. "No, I can't say that I do, ma'am."

"That's all right. It's a bit of a trick question," the Headmistress said, conciliatory. "It varies in different parts of the body; cooler in some, hotter in others. Generally, the internal body temperature lingers around 98.6 degrees Fahrenheit, 37 degrees Celsius. This will fluctuate during the day, and increase due to different activities, or illnesses, or environmental factors or ... hormonal changes."

Joseph tried very hard not to look away from Ms. Valentina's gaze and worked to affect a respectful tone. "Okay ... so, now I know about that. I'm ... glad to learn somethin' new."

The Headmistress let the comment go without a response, allowing a silence to hang so long that Joseph could hear the ticking of the hands on the clock on the wall.

"Your internal body temperature averages out at 106 degrees Fahrenheit, 40 degrees Celsius," she stated at last, one bare fingernail tapping the inside of the file. "Your core body temperature, on average, is two degrees higher than that of a person suffering from life-threatening hyperthermia. You are a walking heatstroke victim. When you collapsed, your temperature measured out at around 140 degrees Fahrenheit. By all rights, you should be dead."

Joseph searched around for a reasonable answer to the Headmistresses information. "Well, I guess I should count myself lucky then, right?"

"Lucky is a word for it." Ms. Valentina looked down at the

open file on her lap and turned over a few pages. "Your organs should be cooking in their own juices. Instead, they seem to have adapted very nicely to your . . . situation."

"Uh . . . should I be apologizin' for this?" Joseph raised an eyebrow. "I mean, I ain't tryin' to be a walkin', talkin', human stick a' dynamite. Be a *lot* easier for me if people *couldn't* toast marshmallows on my skin."

The Headmistress smiled, closing her file. "Have you heard of flashover, Joseph?"

"No," Joseph said again. "Gotta say I haven't."

"When certain materials are heated, they undergo thermal decomposition," Ms. Valentina recited. "If they reach their autoignition temperature, they release flammable gases. In the real world, this means that if a room is especially hot — perhaps from, say, a fire in one corner — it may cause certain materials in another — let's say, baking grease — to ignite."

Joseph met the tall woman's grey eyes with his own golden ones. "Well . . . the more you know, I guess."

"Indeed." The Headmistress stood up. "Well, with what you've learned, I hope you try to cool things down a bit from now on. You can only run hot for so long before you reach a breaking point, and you have one Joseph, even if it is higher than the rest of us."

She stood up. "Now, are you going to drink that glass of water?"

Joseph raised it to his lips.

Toni waited while Melvin settled himself across from her. The constant buzz of conversation during lunch might allow them to speak, if they were very, very careful. She made sure to let a few minutes go by before glancing over at her friend. His black hair, normally so carefully jelled and spiked, was unkempt and tousled. His tray of beets, grilled chicken, and a red mess she couldn't identify sat untouched. Peeking out from under his shirt at his neck and wrists, Toni could see the red burn marks which

42

came from repeated skin shocks. The welts were not limited to the areas covered by the personal apparatus he currently wore. She looked down into her water.

"Why'd they bring you down this time?" she questioned out of the side of her mouth. A visit to the lower Discipline levels to receive extra shocks was something they had all been trying to avoid.

"To heal me," Melvin responded. Toni didn't need to see him to know he wore a bitter smirk. "'Cause nothing makes the pain go away like more pain."

"They honestly still think they can torture you out of being depressed?" Toni stabbed her plastic fork into the oily chicken skin on her plate.

"According to my Mom it's because I'm ungrateful and if I were just more grateful, and *tried* to be happy, she'd be able to love me as her son again," Melvin whispered, his musical voice achingly dry. "That's not even a freakin' joke, that is verbatim. *Verbatim*. If I'm sick it's because I inherited it from her. She's a lunatic, and she should be locked up in here with us."

"You're preachin' to the fundamentalist Mormon choir," Toni murmured back, glancing to the side to make sure no one was catching their stolen conversation.

"I don't know if I'm gonna last a lot longer, hun." Melvin sighed.

Toni looked up sharply. "Now don't you even."

"I'm being serious, babe." Melvin shrugged and pulled back his shirtsleeves enough to show the deep scars imbedded in his right and left arms. "I don't wanna get you guys in trouble — or hold you guys back, but I'm breaking here."

Toni looked down as an aide moved past their table. "We will get out of this," she whispered once the aide had passed. "Okay? We will. We just need some more time and you just need to hold on "

"I don't know if I can —"

"You can," Toni interrupted sharply. "I know you, and you are not weak. You are funny, nasty, and brutally honest, and we need you on this earth. Capiche? You are not allowed to leave. The consequences to the fate of the world would be dire. Also, I would be sad."

Melvin smothered a laugh, while covering his damaged flesh. "I'll try, hun."

"We'll find a way out," Toni promised. "We just need a little more time."

"May I go to the bathroom?"

"No, Ms. Persan. You've just gone."

Charlie lowered her hand and bit her lip, hard. She had stayed as long as she dared in the bathroom the last time, holding her head in her hands and taking refuge in the quiet. Here in the classroom the air buzzed with the white noise of thoughts, feelings, images, and snippets of knowledge that she knew were not her own. They tore at her mind's ragged edges, threatening to drown what little of Charlie was left inside.

"Now, if the coefficient is x," her teacher was saying, scribbling on the whiteboard, "can anyone tell me . . ."

Charlie kept her head down. The jumble of numbers and letters and graphs always played tricks on her, wove themselves into meanings only she could see. She tried to explain them on paper and so her tests and quizzes were always marked in damning red, unambiguous Ds and Fs circled at the top.

Everything is so loud, but so quiet, Charlie thought, rocking back and forth slightly to take her focus away from the ache in her skull. *So loud, everything so confused, misused . . .*

Charlie stopped up short, stilling as if she'd been blasted into ice. Suddenly, all of the haze and fog faded away into one clear, simple, recognizable sound.

"Hello, Alice." The tall redhead now standing in the door smiled at Charlie's math teacher. "So sorry to interrupt. I'm here to borrow one of your students."

The Headmistress looked directly at Charlie and smiled.

CHAPTER FOUR  looking

IF CHARLIE COULD THINK OF ONE THING TO THANK THE
Headmistress for, it was that the shock she felt at being pulled
out of her class had numbed her mind into silence at last. She
followed the tall redheaded woman down the echoing halls of
the second floor and into the teacher's wing. She blinked in the
florescent lights as the Headmistress opened the door to her
office with a small copper key.

"Here we are," the Headmistress said lightly.

Charlie swallowed, hesitating as the woman waved her inside.
"Well, go on."

Charlie nodded, moving into the new space like a tense cat.
The room was centered around a mahogany desk covered with
gleaming trinkets that instantly drew Charlie's eye — golden
fountain pens, an abacus that looked genuinely aged, a series of
black and white photographs, and a clear crystal sphere placed
upon a hollowed out piece of quartz.

The shelf behind the desk was near overflowing with books
that seemed to have no particular unifying theme. All of the
available copies of the *Diagnostic and Statistical Manual of Mental
Disorders* stood propped up against the *Egyptian Book of the Dead*,
journals of forensic and neuroscience lay beside books on weap-
onry and ammunitions, which were stacked besides volumes on
musical theory, theoretical physics, and the traditional forms
of horse breeding in Saudi Arabia. On the wall, an elaborately

carved cuckoo clock ticked maddeningly away.

"Please sit." Ms. Valentina bustled into her chair and gestured to the seat opposite her. Charlie settled herself slowly into the indicated seat, as if at any moment it might explode.

"I've been away," the redheaded woman said brusquely, holding up the set of black and white Polaroids. "The Maghreb. I go there when I need to clear my head."

Charlie swallowed, and then, feeling in the ensuing silence as if she should say something, replied, "Yeah ... clear my head. I would like to clear my head." *Head, dead, red. They all go together so perfectly, like lilies and roses and baby's breath ...*

"Oh, Charlie, Charlie, Charlie." The Headmistress shook her head then propped her elbow on her desk and rested her head in her hand. "Well! You seem to be responding well to your treatment, and that is good news."

"Treatment." Charlie nearly shook with the force of the word. "You think this is treatment?"

"You objected to being on medication," Ms. Valentina answered.

"The doctor put me on haloperidol," Charlie said, voice low and stony. "I would have preferred a medication from this century, thank you." *Thank you, bank you, she has all the money, doesn't she know it will be demanded by the seven gods who govern greed when the world ends? It's coming so soon, she should be able to smell it, tell it, tell ...*

"Well, Charlie," the Headmistresses' said, her voice softening as she folded her hands, "after your doctor tried risperidone, Seroquel, Abilify, and thioridazine, there really were no other options for your age group. Your condition doesn't normally come to one so young."

Charlie's lip trembled. "Chronic," she whispered, her voice losing its previous fire. "Acute, chronic, untreatable, and hopeless. I came here because there was no hope and no point."

"Now, that I do not accept," Ms. Valentina said firmly. "There is plenty of hope for a bright, young, gifted girl like you."

"Yes," Charlie said with pained sarcasm, "A bright young

schizophrenic. The world is just an oyster for girls like me." *You eat oysters while they're alive, like me, like how I will be eaten from the inside if I don't hide . . .*

The Headmistress turned her head slightly, narrowing her eyes, and it came to Charlie that she had the gaze of a surveying serpent, still and silent in the grass. When the bite came it would be impossible to predict. "And is that all you are? Hmm? Just schizophrenic?"

"Well, we thought I might be lactose intolerant a while back, but it turned out it was just my mother's cheesecake."

Ms. Valentina laughed. "Oh, a sense of humor will keep you alive even when your heart has given up beating — remember that. No, Charlie, I think you know what I mean. The line between madness and brilliance is so very thin. Isn't there anything about you that you think may have crossed it?"

Charlie tried to take deep, calming breaths. "I'm sure that sentence sounds really romantic to you, but I'd exchange any brilliance I get from this for the chance to be whatever normal is."

"Never say that!" The vehemence in the tall woman's response made Charlie pull back, and it seemed to her that a low cackling filled the office. The Headmistress noted Charlie's terror and let out a small sigh. "I'm sorry. I only meant that you should try not to think that way. You can never change who you are and so, to deny your gifts is to deny what was given to you to make your life livable. You are hardly the only one to struggle with a mind a little too finely calibrated."

"Somehow I doubt anyone else has *my* kind of . . . calibrated," Charlie said in a heavy voice, dripping with despairing sarcasm.

"Oh?" The Headmistress smiled slowly, her unadorned lips curving into a secret-holding smirk. "Don't be so sure."

The older woman held Charlie's gaze until Charlie opened her mouth to speak. Just then, Ms. Valentina looked over her head and nodded as the door opened. "Yes, Ms. Donelle, you can take Charlie back to class now."

Charlie tried to catch the Headmistresses eyes once more, but the woman was opening her glossy white laptop. Pulling her limbs inward, Charlie stood up and turned to go, shuddering as her senses made every step she took echo in her sore ears. She closed her eyes and shook her head to try to jolt her mind back into some semblance of order.

Her mind's eye cleared, and suddenly it was as if she could zero in on any sound with perfect clarity; the ticking of the clock, the uneven breathing of Ms. Donelle, the tap of the keyboard as the Headmistress entered her password. And then another sense of clarity came, and with it, knowledge.

"Charlie?" Ms. Valentina's voice tugged her back to earth. "Is there a problem?"

Charlie turned to glance over at the head of the school and wondered if she knew. "No. No problem at all."

"I'm really not sure we should be meeting this many days in a row."

Toni glanced over at Lieutenant, who shrugged, holding her faded army coat tightly to her in an attempt to keep out the cold night air that breezed through the drafty old house. Melvin stood beside her, his eyes appearing almost hollow in the dark. Ann leaned against Joseph, who had one hand wrapped around her waist. The other hand balanced over the tiny fire they had built in the abandoned fireplace, keeping the flame low. Anthony — he had informed them he was Anthony today — stood opposite Lieutenant, casting surreptitious looks her way.

"Well, Tiny called the meetin'," Anthony reminded, nodding to the smallest member of their group. Charlie was crouched near the fire, shivering, but at his words she stood up.

"Yes I did," she said, clearing her throat. "I know we said we'd be careful about how many times we met here, but I think we have a chance to figure out why we were brought to this school once and for all."

The others shifted, glancing around at each other. "Well, don't keep us in suspense," Lieutenant said. "How?"

"The Headmistress," Charlie said in a low voice, as if the woman herself might hear them if they were too loud. "If anyone had a reason and a plan for bringing us here, it's her."

"Thought we knew why we was here." Joseph snorted. "So they could fix all our naughty, naughty behavior and make us good little citizens."

"Well they sure as fuck failed at fixin' 'naughty behavior' with y'all two," Anthony cackled, earning himself a flash of Ann's middle finger, and a disdainful, mimed kiss from Joseph.

"No, I think Charlie means why those of us with 'special abilities' were brought here," Toni said quietly, and Charlie nodded.

"Exactly. Mrs. Carter might think this is just about fixing our behavior, but the Headmistress didn't bring a pyrokinetic, a psychic, a telekinetic, and a walking, talking interference machine to this school by accident."

"I am offended at my description." Anthony sniffed. "Note how deeply offended I am. Witness it."

"You can witness my foot up your butt. Let Charlie talk," Lieutenant joked, and for a moment the two shared a grin, before the tall girl looked away.

"She called me into her office today," Charlie shared, her small, plain face intense.

"What did you do?" Joseph asked immediately.

"Nothing," Charlie answered. "She just called me in."

"Oh," Joseph replied. "See, when she called me in it was 'cause I'd collapsed after a race with Seth."

"Why were you racing Seth?" Melvin asked.

"Why didn't you tell me you'd collapsed?" demanded Ann.

"He probably wanted to keep up his manly impression on you," Anthony surmised.

"Aw, baby," Ann cooed. "You should know by now you don't have to pretend to be manly for me. I knew what I was getting myself into."

"Ha. Ha. Ha," Joseph said through gritted teeth. "*Anyway*, after I woke up in the nurse's office, she was there, and she said somethin' about my body temperature bein' higher than the average person's and that that leads to flashover or somethin'. That explains how I'm able to do what I do."

"Faint?" Ann suggested sweetly.

Joseph scowled at her. "Make you feel pretty faint, don't I?"

"Okay!" Toni made the time-out sign with her hands. "Back to business. Remember business? Not that kind of business. The more respectable kind."

"Well, what I have in mind isn't exactly respectable," Charlie said with a side-grin. "We need to figure out what the Headmistress knows, and to do that we need to get into her office and onto her computer."

"Right, and so, what, we just ask Joseph to use his incredible charm to get her to let us take a look?" Lieutenant scoffed.

"I'll have you know I am the fuckin' epitome of charm," Joseph huffed. "Next to 'charming' in the dictionary is a picture of yours truly."

"Yeah, with the label 'See antonyms'," Toni replied smartly.

"C'mon, let's be serious," Melvin pleaded. "Okay Charlie, what's your plan for getting us in? We know you have one."

"Well, we know we can't let them find out at all that it's even happened. Not before, and not after," Charlie said, threading her fingers together. "If they even suspect something has happened, they'll instantly blame us."

"Ain't we a lucky bunch," Anthony quipped.

"So we'll need to steal her keys *after* she's closed up the office and break into it the same night," Charlie continued. "That way, if she notices they're gone she'll think she lost them at the school, and when she comes back in, she'll find them, and it will be like it never happened."

"Assumin' we can pull it off," Lieutenant reminded.

"I think I could snatch her keys," Ann said thoughtfully. "I've gotten pretty good at that kind of thing, living with Katrina."

"I wouldn't put it past the Headmistress to dust her computer for prints every day before she opens it," Lieutenant remarked. "I ain't touchin' that thing without gloves. Actually . . . " She tapped the outside of her mouth with a finger. "I think I could get them from science class."

"Great," Charlie agreed. "Now, since they changed to thermal cameras, we should be able to be basically invisible if we take Katrina's pills. But we can't risk getting onto the school grounds by cuttin' the wires or stealing any of the guards' keys because that would definitely get us noticed, and they've made sure not to leave anything parked high enough near the fences for us to be able to climb over ever since the last time we did this."

"So we gotta go in right after the guards switch shifts," Anthony noted, his clever mind catching on. "My supervisor is a guard. I'll find out when he does his night shift, and we can plan for that day. We gotta go in right after he does. A'ight, Tiny, if you such a mastermind, how we gonna actually get *inside* the Academy?"

"We can't steal a key to get inside. Even if it wasn't noticed, they'd see the door opening and no one opening it," Melvin reasoned. "I guess we could start a rumor about ghosts. I've seen the people they've hired recently, they're about as dumb as a sack of bricks. They might fall for it."

"Yeah, but Mrs. Carter and the Headmistress wouldn't," Toni stated.

"I would offer to use my, ahem, *skills* to open a window for us," Joseph said, waggling his fingers over the tiny fire. "But they'd see the temperature change on the cameras."

"Yeah, and I can't disrupt 'em like I could the other ones" Anthony said. "I am *not* tryna learn that lesson again," he reminded them, shivering. "I couldn't lie on my back for days after they caught me last time I tried sneakin' anywhere on campus without those pills."

Charlie's bright eyes met Toni's, and the darker skinned girl grinned. "Oh, but they don't have cameras on the hall where the Headmistress and Mrs. Carter have their offices," Toni said softly. "We're not the only ones who don't want people watching what we're doing. If we get in through the window on that floor, they'll never pick it up."

"So this all sounds like a hell of a fuckin' plan, Charlie," Joseph drawled. "But once we get inside the Headmistresses office, how we s'posed to get on her computer? She's gonna have it protected."

"Oh," Charlie said, archly, "didn't I mention?" She grinned. "I know her password."

Joseph's heart pounded as he watched Ann check her book bag. She was the picture of nonchalance. The Headmistress stood only a few feet away, boots tapping the cool, hard hallway floors, deep in quiet conversation with another teacher. He looked away, trying not to stare at Ann. She had been trailing the Headmistress for the past three hours, in and out of classes. Joseph couldn't understand where she found the time or how she'd picked up the skill. He wasn't entirely sure he wanted to know. He certainly wasn't going to ask her and start another fight about him 'prying' into her past.

Why the fuck won't she trust me enough to just tell me about it? Joseph thought, fingering the edge of his locker in frustration. *I've trusted her enough to tell her about mine.*

Ann was moving now, and Joseph bent down to pretend he was tying his shoes as she glided past the Headmistress, barely pausing. He blinked. *Did she miss again?*

Ann turned to him and winked. He suppressed a smile.

Oh, she got it.

Toni glanced over at Melvin who caught her eye for only a second before they both looked away. Lieutenant's science class was due to pass by them at any moment, returning from a lab. If she looked over into the room, it meant she had gotten the gloves. If she didn't, it meant they had missed their chance. And if she wasn't in the line at all, it meant she had gotten caught.

We can't afford to get caught anymore, Toni noted, looking over at Melvin. Even when he smiled now, he had the look of someone barely holding on. *None of us.*

Melvin stiffened, sitting up straighter. Toni's eyes immediately shot to the door. Lieutenant passed by, staring straight forward. Toni felt her stomach begin to drop when the tall black girl cast a quick glance their way — the sign that her part of the mission was complete.

So we're really doing this, Toni thought on a long, drawn out breath. *We'd better do it right this time.*

Charlie tasted blood and slowly managed to make herself stop biting her lip. She went back to poking her lunch with her plastic fork, turning it around and around in her beef and carrots and blood —

Blood?

Shaking her head hard, she stared at her plate again. Just bland beef, carrots, and a watered down brown sauce. Not blood. No blood.

Charlie counted to ten as she looked away and scanned the lunchroom for any of her friends. *I've been good,* she thought, her head beginning to ache. *I've been so good. I just need to . . . to keep trying. Push it to the back of my head, and focus, focus . . . locusts, most of us, gross and blood and guts and lies and the world inside my head.*

Anthony got up from a seat across the hall and moved down the aisle. Charlie kept her head down, her ears picking up the cheery whistling he made as he passed. She zeroed in on his hands. As he shifted his tray from one hand to the other, he pointed three fingers downwards.

Tonight, Charlie thought, the single word sending off a babble of chatter in her mind that she did her best to ignore.

Oh please, please, she prayed, whether to some vague, benevolent god or to her own mercurial mind, she wasn't sure. *Please just let me stay as sane as I can through this. Please. This is my plan. If it fails, it's my fault, and everyone goes down.*

My fault.

CHAPTER FIVE  glass

"AND THAT'S THE LAST ONE, RIGHT THERE."

Toni settled down, kneeling low on the cold ground, the leaves crunching wetly beneath her knees. She breathed in the frigid night air and nodded at the others crouched beside her. Hidden at the edge of the tiny woods that bordered the wire fence surrounding J. Alter Academy, the seven friends stayed still and quiet as they surveyed the gateway.

"When's your supervisor coming through, Anton?" Ann whispered, blinking down at the lights gleaming from the guards patrolling the grounds.

"About another five minutes," Anton replied, rubbing his lips in anticipation. "But I don't know how it helps us unless we can all get through without them seein' us."

Lieutenant narrowed her eyes and nodded. "We will. When Anton's supervisor drives up and inside to park, he'll block the guard's vision long enough for us to get inside. And see right there?" She pointed. "That's a blind spot. We can all fit into that space, by those bushes, there. They won't be able to see us for a whole round."

"Yeah, but then we gotta get across the field without bein' seen before the guard comes back around," Joseph noted.

"Well, if we're gonna even get inside we gotta do it now," Melvin whispered. "The car's coming!"

The seven friends fell silent as a beaten down grey sedan came into view. Exchanging glances, they waited for Lieutenant. She raised her hand in the signal to move, and in single file, heads down, the seven sprinted away from the cover of the woods and down the incline. They slowed with stifled gasps as they drew level with the car.

Toni's heart was beating like a steel drum as they tip-toed, hunched over, to the left side of the car as the vehicle slowly ground through the gate. She kept her eyes fixed on the bushes, refusing to glance over towards the guard patrolling the field. She held her breath as, one by one, they darted out and into the bushes; first Lieutenant, than Anton, Charlie, Ann, Joseph, and Melvin. At her turn, Toni's throat constricted painfully. Desperately praying to be spared a panic attack, Toni practically dove into the bushes, wincing as she hit someone's foot. The car stopped.

I don't think any of us are breathing, Toni thought dully as she put her head down. Someone's unnaturally cold hand brushed her face. Collectively they waited — either the guards would miss them, hidden in the dark under the bushes, or they would find them. There was nothing they could do.

Seconds, minutes passed, and still Toni didn't draw breath. Finally the car moved through the gate fully, turning to park in the school lot. She took in a little air.

"We have to go now if we gonna go," Lieutenant murmured. "The guards are almost at the points where they ain't likely to see us."

"And if 'likely' don't work out?" Joseph muttered.

"Well then I guess we all betta pray we become masochists real fuckin' soon," Anton noted. "Let's go!"

"You ready for this, Lighter Boy?"

Joseph scowled at Ann. Bent down with the others at the side of the school where the offices of the principal and headmistress were located, he shook his head despairingly. "That was terrible.

Just terrible. Feel ashamed. Feel very ashamed."

"Why don't you feel my —"

"If we get caught 'cause y'all screwed this up," Lieutenant warned calmly, "they will never find your bodies."

"A'ight, I'ma need somebody to stabilize me if I'm liftin' you," Anton whispered, crouching down on one knee, his back firmly against the wall.

"I got you," Lieutenant confirmed, grabbing his right hand. Toni took his left, and Anton nodded for Joseph to step onto his shoulders.

"Fuck." Anton grunted as the other boy clambered on. Anton balanced himself and slowly stood up.

"Can I start?" Joseph whispered, grabbing the windowsill and pressing the lighter, which Ann had lifted from the local drugstore two weeks ago, against it.

"Not yet," Melvin warned, squinting out over the school grounds. "The guard is just rounding the corner to the right side. When he does, then you can start."

Gritting his teeth, Anton held. The seven waited in silence for the tiny figure carrying a gleaming flashlight to turn the corner around the edge of the field and out of sight.

"Go!" Lieutenant ordered, and Joseph flipped the lighter on, pressing it against the glass and willing it to burn. For a few, dreadful moments he worried that he'd lost it as the flame seemed to have no effect. Then the glass began to darken and finally to warp. The knot in his stomach loosened as he went to work.

"Whoa, whoa!" Melvin started after a few minutes of tense silence. "He's coming back around. Stop, stop!"

"I'm almost finished." Joseph grunted, moving his lighter steadily to the final corner of the window and ignoring the bits of hot melted glass dripping onto his fingers.

"Joseph, stop!" Ann snapped. "Turn off the light. He's gonna see you!"

"I just got it," Joseph said, pushing at the edges of the window, catching it as it fell sideways, and turning it to slide it through and down onto the floor.

"He's searching with the flashlight," Charlie whispered, eyes wide. "He's gonna make us."

"Can you get inside?" Toni called up to Joseph as quietly as she could.

"Yeah, just gimme a sec . . ." Joseph winced and grunted, trying to avoid the more jagged edges of the window he'd opened as he pushed himself inside and stumbled down onto the darkly carpeted floor. "I'm in!"

"Get down, everybody!" Lieutenant directed, and they all dropped to the ground, laying as flat as possible as the round circle of light traveled over the broad side of the school.

Joseph stayed on his back, blinking in the darkness of the teacher's hallway, the cold night air abrasive against his burning hands.

Finally he heard Lieutenant softly whistle the all-clear. He shuffled painfully onto his knees and moved to the window.

"Who's comin' up first?" he whispered down.

"Mel, why don't you go," Lieutenant suggested. Melvin nodded, clambering over Anton's shoulders with a wry grin.

"Seriously, there are some really choice jokes I could make right about now," Melvin informed Anton, using his hands to steady himself as Anton stood upright.

"Yeah." Anton grimaced. "And then you'd get a really choice drop on the head. Get yo' ass inside."

"I got you," Joseph said, grabbing the other boy's hand and helping Melvin through the window

"A'ight, whoever's next, let's move it here," Anton said hurriedly.

"I'll go," Toni volunteered. "Sorry if I'm heavier than everybody else —"

"Now don't even start that shit," Anton said, not unkindly. "Just get up."

Toni wavered slightly on the taller boy's shoulders, but Joseph and Melvin each grabbed a hand and helped her through the gaping hole in the window.

"A'ight, your girl is comin' up next," Anton informed Joseph as Ann crawled onto his shoulders.

"If I fall I'm blamin' you," Ann informed Joseph as she nimbly gripped his forearm and was hoisted up.

"Yeah, sure you are," Joseph acknowledged, gently guiding her inside.

"You next, Tiny," Anton said, nodding at Charlie.

"Oh, okay." Charlie boarded her friend nervously, swaying and shivering when Lieutenant put a hand on her back to prevent her from falling. Charlie put both her hands on the red brick wall of the Academy and tried to reach up her hand as Anton stood.

"I can't reach her," Joseph whispered, stretching his arm down as far as it would go. His hand was inches from Charlie's.

"Hang on a minute," Anton said, arching his back and standing up onto his toes. Charlie gasped and her legs trembled, but Joseph and Melvin latched onto her hands.

"Now use your legs to climb up," Lieutenant instructed. Charlie nodded, scraping her feet against the wall while trying to get her footing. After a few tense minutes, she was able to get high enough for the two boys to pull her inside.

"Your turn, G.I. Jane." Anton grinned at Lieutenant, surprising her into a genuine smile before she cleared her throat and mounted his shoulders as professionally as possible. Able to reach the edge of the window with her hands by herself, she pulled herself up and over into the school, landing as quietly as possible.

"Show off," Ann said, rolling her eyes, and Lieutenant chucked her in the shoulder.

"Wait, how is Anton getting up?" Toni questioned.

"Jus' be ready to grab my hand," Anton whispered up, as he backed away from the school wall. Joseph and Lieutenant leaned slightly out of the window as Anton readied himself. Letting out three sharp breaths, Anton sprinted towards the school, taking a leap and running up the side of the wall just far enough to reach his friend's hands. Each catching an arm, Joseph and Lieutenant pulled as they stepped back and slid the final member of their company inside.

"Maybe after this we should try and break into her office," Joseph proposed darkly, glaring at the door emblazoned with 'Evelyn Carter, Principal' in gold lettering.

"If there is an 'after this'," Lieutenant muttered, taking Joseph's shoulder and tilting him towards the opposite door that bore the inscription 'Sophia Valentina, Headmistress'.

"I wonder if that's her real name?" Ann narrowed her eyes as Charlie moved to the doorknob and placed the key in the hole.

"I guess we'll find out," Anton whispered, his face dark and intense.

The seven teens let out a collective breath as the door swung open.

"Should we turn on the lights?" Toni questioned, blinking into the dim room.

"Nah." Joseph shook his head, flipping on his lighter. "The less light the better."

"Well, we ain't gonna get anywhere standin' in the door," Anton reminded. "Let's do this and get out."

They spread into the room slowly, Joseph's lighter flame casting shadows around the office, gleaming off glinting desk trinkets and coming to a pause on the white computer.

"I don't know about this," Toni whispered.

"About what?" Melvin questioned.

"The computer is just there, all plugged in," Charlie answered in a low, shaky tone. "Like it's waiting for us."

"Is that what you were gonna say?" Lieutenant questioned Toni as she pulled out the white gloves she'd stolen from the science lab and passed them to Anton.

"Yup," Toni confirmed. "You should know by now that me and Charlie are the same person, except that we're different and she's white."

"Well, we're here, and we got in, so are we gonna fuckin' do this or not?" Joseph demanded, rubbing his arm. "We got less than an hour till Katrina's pills wear off."

Charlie glanced at Toni and nodded. Toni shrugged. "We're here. We might as well. If we're gonna get caught we should at least learn something from it."

"Test a' truth then," Anton remarked as he opened the computer carefully, his gloved hands gentle as he turned it on. "C'mon Charlie, you got the password."

Charlie nodded, swallowing, and joined Anton at the desk. The others gathered around them as the screen blinked into life, the background a starry violet and blue scene of deep space. A small white block asked for the password.

"Your turn, Tiny," Anton said, pulling off the gloves and handing them to her. Charlie pulled them on quickly, glancing around at the others before looking to her task.

"Okay," Charlie said, biting her lip. "Here goes nothing." Gloved hands trembling, she typed the seven letter password and clicked enter. Charlie and Joseph closed their eyes as the computer processed it, while Ann and Anton stared intently as the screen. Lieutenant looked to the door.

"One of us should stand guard," Lieutenant decided. "Assumin' we're workin' under the assumption we ain't already caught."

"I'll stand watch for you Philistines," Melvin offered, walking over to the door and positioning himself half-way in and half-way out. "Call me if my file says anything other than 'depressed' and 'gay.'"

"We will," Toni murmured. "Look, we're in."

Charlie opened her eyes, heart ramming against her chest harshly, ears humming slightly, to see the screen filled with tiny files and folders. "Um, okay. What do we check first?"

"Right there." Anton pointed. "Try that one, 'J. Alter Profiles.' Gotta be us."

Charlie obeyed, her gloved fingers fumbling slightly on the

60

mouse pad as she clicked on the folder. It opened to reveal eight files.

"Cost, Valdez, White, Persan, Jackson, Levant, Stavos, and Vaglienty," Ann read off. "That's us. Who wants to go first?"

"You broke us in, Tiny," Anton said. "You want first crack at it?"

Charlie shivered. "Actually, I'd kinda like to . . . to go later . . ."

"Hey, take your time," Ann soothed, putting her arm around Charlie's shoulder. "No pressure."

"A'ight, I'll go," Anton said, his voice calm, though the vein in his throat throbbed. He cast a rapidly withdrawn glance at Lieutenant, before nodding at Charlie to click on his file.

"There's a whole set of them," Charlie said as a number of options presented themselves. She scrolled through the file's many pages. "Medical profiles, academic profiles, psychological profiles . . ."

"*Antoine* Michael Levant," Toni read. "Eighteen years old, 6'1, 155 pounds, birthday October 14th . . . diagnosis: Dissociative Identity Disorder."

"Guess you were tellin' the truth on that one," Lieutenant remarked.

"Yeah, I was," Anton replied sharply.

"Known alters," Toni raised her voice slightly, reading the psychological profile, "Anton, Anthony, Ant. Anton; male, around eighteen, capable, intelligent, in control, mature, a 'fighting' alter, likely a trauma identifying alter. Anthony; male, around eighteen, mature, amiable, possibly trauma identifying. Ant; male, between thirteen and fifteen, insecure, trauma identifying . . ."

Anton's hands began to shake, and Charlie pointed further down on the file. "Look, under Psionic profile, it says known *abilities* include electrical psychokinesis, most likely due to an increase of electrical energy overall, stemming from the presence of multiple identities. Case history; born in Terrebonne Parish, Louisiana —"

"Yeah, yeah, yeah. We can move on now," Anton said, clearing his throat. "Who's next, Toni?"

"Sure, I'll go," Toni said, eyes moving between Anton and Lieutenant. "Bring it up, Charlie."

Charlie clicked on Toni's name and began to read down the file. "Toni Ciara White, fifteen years old, 5´4, 147 pounds ... diagnosis; panic disorder, generalized anxiety. Psychological profile and case history —"

"You can skip those for me too," Toni mentioned as lightly as possible.

"Well, aren't we all a trusting little bunch of precious flowers," Melvin called from the door.

"We're openin' yours next, Sparkles," Lieutenant threatened.

"Go ahead. I am ashamed of nothing."

"Melvin Johan Stavos," Toni read. "Fifteen years old, 5´4, 149 pounds ... Hey Mel, your file says 'dangerous lack of respect for authority.'"

"Damn right it does," Melvin acknowledged.

"It also says severe depression and lists two separate suicide attempts," Charlie whispered.

"You guys can move on, now," Melvin said back to them, scanning the hallway. "We should get all the information we can, as soon as we can, and get outta here."

"Go ahead and check mine," Lieutenant offered. "Quick though. Mel's right."

"Got it," Charlie said. "Amina Laverne Jackson "

"Laverne?" Joseph snorted.

"I know so many ways to make you scream in pain," Lieutenant mused. "So very many."

"That's nice, but I'm loyal to my girl here," Joseph bragged, putting his arm around Ann.

"Age seventeen, 5´7, 148 pounds, diagnosis; bipolar disorder ... Psychological profile ... oh here, Psionic profile; known abilities include psychokinesis likely due to increased energy from subject's mania and focused through ... ooh, look, she's got a diagram of your brain and a bunch of possible places she thinks might have adapted to explain how you can do it."

"That's real," Lieutenant acknowledged, considering the file. "Okay, that's somethin'. I don't need to hear my case history. I know my own story."

"Yo, try mine," Joseph requested, and Charlie selected his name.

"Joseph Nathaniel Valdez," Ann read off, pushing in between Charlie and Toni. "Age fifteen, height 5'6, weight 135 ... diagnosis is ADHD, explosive disorder, impulse control issues ... Psychological profile ... 'Joseph in many ways typifies the classic at-risk adolescent male.'"

"Psionic profile," Joseph said, overriding Ann, who rolled her eyes as she continued to silently read his psychological profile and chuckle. "Here we go. Psionic abilities over fire, due to increased body temperature manifesting as flash over, and/or a psionic ability to increase the vibration of molecules in the general vicinity. Case history ... crazy Mom, absent abusive Dad, blah fuckin' blah," Joseph dismissed. "Ann, your turn!"

"We gotta hurry it up. We don't have much time left," Lieutenant reminded.

"Annabelle Jean Cost," Joseph read as Charlie opened her file. "Fifteen, 5'5, 130 pounds, diagnosis; borderline personality disorder ... Psychological profile —"

"I don't have any abilities so there's no point in reading mine," Ann said swiftly. "Charlie?"

"Look at this folder." Charlie pointed, eyes narrowed. "'Treatment, Procedures, Protocols 5.'"

"Now that might help us know what they got in store for us," Anton surmised. "Go ahead, Tiny."

Clicking on the folder, Charlie's eyes widened.

"Look. There's J. Alter Academy," Ann said, pointing.

"Yeah, and a fuck ton more," Anton remarked, his face growing taut. "St. Sylvan's, Trent Academy, Jefferson High ..."

"Guess we got a lotta friends out there," Joseph murmured.

"Look at treatment models under J. Alter Academy," Toni said. "Let's find out what dastardly plans they have in mind for us."

"Nah, not today," Joseph said, feeling his skin. "We only got a little more time until the pills wear off. We gotta get back."

"Dammit," Lieutenant swore. "Okay, quick. Exit outta everything."

"I am, I am," Charlie protested. "Am, spam, pan, plans from the man to control, control . . ."

"What?" Toni frowned.

"Nothing!" Charlie squeaked. "Okay, I'm turning it off . . . closing . . . done!"

She shut down the computer and closed it quickly with her gloved hands, praying the sweat wouldn't seep through and leave a trace.

"Shit!" Melvin whispered.

"What?" Lieutenant demanded.

The boy's dark eyes locked onto hers. "I think someone's coming."

"Fuck." Joseph ran out of the office and headed for the window, followed by Ann and Toni, while Lieutenant and Anton went to kneel beside Melvin. Charlie pulled the door closed behind them, fumbling as she inserted the key into the lock.

"You guys comin' or what?" Joseph whispered urgently over his shoulder as he helped Ann lower Toni down and out of the window. "Charlie, c'mon."

"Not so loud," Lieutenant warned, hurrying to the window and helping hoist Charlie over the broken sill. Leaning out to let the younger girl fall gently to the ground below, Lieutenant's eyes scanned the dark before pulling sharply back. "We gotta make sure we don't forget the guard outside."

Lieutenant moved as Anton crouched down besides them. "I don't know if we have that time," Anton said, rubbing his lips anxiously.

"You want me to go over or not?" Ann demanded. Lieutenant and Anton exchanged looks.

"Go," Joseph said finally, helping her climb over and avoid the harsh edges of the window. "Then we'll wait for the guard to pass around."

Ann paused, gripping his forearm. "You're starting to feel warm," she said, meeting his eyes. Joseph grinned it away.

"Tell me that later when we're alone," he said, before letting her drop. She rolled over to lay flat on the ground besides Toni and Charlie.

"We've got guard!" Toni called up, and Lieutenant, Anton, Joseph, and Melvin pulled away from the window. Lieutenant put her head down over her knees, slowly counting the moments out on her fingers. Joseph swallowed hard, digging his nails into the grey carpeted hallway floor. Anton scowled in frustration and Melvin just lay back, leaning his head against the wall.

"Clear," Ann said softly.

"Okay, Mel next," Anton ordered. Lieutenant and Joseph took the boy's arms as he grunted while backing out of the window. Dangling for a moment, he let go with a grunt and fell heavily besides Toni.

"Y'all should start runnin' while we do the window," Anton whispered to Lieutenant as he took her left arm. Lieutenant gripped Joseph's left hand with her right, eyes moving between the two boys. "You know Ann ain't gonna agree to that."

"We'll follow," Joseph supported, as they helped the tall girl over the sill.

"No you don't." Lieutenant snorted. "I ain't havin' either of you tryna play hero. You'll get caught, and Ann will kick my ass. We all go together."

Joseph shook his head as Lieutenant let go. "What happened to impressionable women who liked a heroic male?"

Anton shrugged, holding onto Joseph's left arm with one hand, carefully passing him the windowpane through the square frame with the other. "Guess we just had the misfortune to draw the 'interestin' woman' card," Anton surmised.

Joseph nodded sagely in agreement as he handed off the glass pane to Ann, who moved out of the way as he jumped down. Anton set his hands on the outside sill for balance and propelled himself through the window opening with a sideways leap, falling hard to the ground.

"Quick, on my shoulders." Anton motioned for Joseph to climb him, kneeling down as the other boy scrambled up, the window pane under his right arm, lighter in his left hand.

"And again — I could make many comments," Melvin remarked.

"We got, like, two minutes before the guard comes back around," Lieutenant warned Anton as he stood up. Joseph balanced precariously as he fit the windowpane back in place. "Just gimme one and a half. I should be able to do it," Joseph promised.

Ann chewed her nails harshly as she sat in the cold earth, until Toni forcibly pulled the blonde's hand out. "He'll be fine," Toni assured her.

"Did I say anything?" Ann responded defensively.

"You were doin' somethin' with your mouth," Lieutenant mumbled. "Okay, less than a minute left!"

"Don't rush me!" Joseph demanded. He winced as he used his fingers to spread the melted glass more evenly into place, burning himself. If anyone looked closely at the edges of the windowpane they would be able to detect some unprofessional pockmarks and bubbles, but only if they were looking for it.

Hopefully, Joseph thought. A glimmer of light shone down the hallway, and Joseph dropped his lighter, biting back a curse as he fell and just missed Anton. He managed to slap the ground and roll, narrowly avoiding breaking his leg.

"Joseph!" Ann snapped worriedly.

"M'fine," Joseph coughed.

"Did you finish?" Melvin questioned.

"There's a light," Joseph whispered, and all seven compatriots flattened themselves to the ground, suppressing grunts and cries of pain as they bumped into each other. Pulling their black hoods and shirts up over their heads, they held perfectly still in a concerted attempt to remain unseen.

Charlie, face in the hard, frozen dirt, glanced up through

her hair. She watched the flashlight pass over the evergreen shrubs — the only barrier between them and the guard whose boots could now be heard crunching the frosted grass.

John Hollinger moved his flashlight carefully over the north facing wall of J. Alter Academy, squinting at the shadows cast by the evergreen shrubs and bushes. His walkie buzzed.

"Anything on your side?" the voice on the other end asked.

"Nah," Hollinger answered the other guard. "Nothing here. You sure you heard something?"

"No, but if we miss anything Mrs. Principal will have my ass for breakfast, so I'm takin' no chances. Check around the back, would you?"

"Sure thing."

Toni waited in the frigid silence until there was no sound but the combined breathing of her friends. Then she turned, just slightly, towards the dark area where she knew Anton was. "Do you think they know we're here?"

"I don't know," Anton practically growled. "But if they call our supervisors to check and we ain't there, we fucked."

"Then let's go," Joseph exhorted.

"Hold on," Lieutenant said, grabbing his shirt tightly, rising up, and then wincing. "Dammit."

"What?" Charlie questioned, her voice trembling.

"There's five guards at the entrance," Lieutenant revealed, digging her nails angrily into the dead, icy grass. "We ain't gettin' out that way. We need a contingency plan."

"Do we have one?" Joseph asked.

Anton and Lieutenant exchanged looks.

"Wait," Ann said, inching forward and turning to survey the corner edge of the Academy's main building. "They've been doing landscaping on the edge of the campus next to the dining hall, right?"

"Yeah," Lieutenant confirmed. "They've been transplantin' bushes around the whole east side of the fence, so we can't dig under it without them knowin'. How does this help?"

"Because they had to stop for the winter and didn't finish — there's a whole foot or so where they dug up under the fence to change the soil," Ann explained. "They've finished with most of it, except that one little part, but it should be enough space for all of us to crawl under if we do it one at a time."

"Uh huh," Anton responded. "But then our clothes'll be covered with dirt, and if our supervisors find 'em they'll know what we been up to."

"Then we make sure we do our own laundry," Toni suggested. "Either that or hope we don't get caught trying to run past three guards."

Anton bit his lip, considering, and then nodded curtly. "A'ight, let's break."

The flashlight bobbed and blinked as the guard rounded the eastern edge of the fence, his breath making little trails of steam behind him as he paced through his rounds. J. Alter Academy's dining hall lay just a few feet away. Hidden in its shadows, Toni pressed herself closer to the wall besides her three friends in an attempt to seem smaller, gaining scant warmth from Anton's black sweater. She cast a glance to the right where she knew Joseph, Ann, and Melvin were crouched in an alcove. She could barely make them out in the dark, which gave her hope that the guard would miss them as well. Still she held her breath until the footsteps crunched away.

"'Kay, I'll check first," Anton informed them. Rising up onto the balls of his feet, the tall dark boy half-ran, half-crawled out from their hiding spot, across the small stretch of grass, and to the fence. Toni squinted in the dark, able to make out only slight movement.

"He's pulled the fence up," Charlie whispered, her eyes held wide as she leaned out to see. "Lieutenant, he's saying come."

"Well you first then, girl," Lieutenant said.

Charlie gulped loudly, shivering as she ran, forgetting to duck down but making it to Anton without detection. Charlie's little form seemed to disappear under the ground and then reappear behind the fence. For a few moments she seemed to be wavering. Then she sprinted towards the woods.

Lieutenant waved two fingers and gestured her arm to the right. Joseph emerged from the shadows to take off for the fence. It took a few moments, but then he too appeared on the other side of the fence and was off to the trees.

Toni felt the familiar tightening of anxiety in her lower abdomen as Lieutenant pushed Melvin out. She closed her eyes as the boy struggled under the fence, stumbling as he ran for the trees.

"Toni? Toni, time to go."

The steady pounding waves of adrenaline emanating from her chest surged up into Toni's throat as she forced her body to run. Looking to the left and right as she crossed out into the open grass where she could be seen, feeling as if her steps were loud as battle drums, she nearly careened into Anton when she finally reached the fence. The older boy pulled her arm to bring her down, and Toni's hand scraped painfully against something sharp and cold.

"Feel," Anton ordered, directing her hands. Toni obeyed, moving them around in the dirt. "The hole is right here. I'ma pull up the fence as much as it goes, and you gotta crawl under."

Toni tried to respond but found her throat constricted. Leaning down she found the depression, half-falling. She coughed violently as the dirt turned under her hands and got into her nose.

Making herself flat, Toni crawled on her belly, clawing and pulling and pushing. The tips of her fingers brushed grass, and she scrambled for it, rushing to make her way out.

Her shirt snagged, and Toni gasped and fought for breath as the fence raked down her back. "Anton," she rasped. "Anton, pull it higher."

"Someone's comin'," Anton said, and Toni tried to process his words. "Coming?"

"A guard."

A guard. Toni almost laughed as the fear bled from her center out to her legs and arms. "Pull it higher, get me out!"

"I can't, he's comin' too fast." Anton sucked his teeth. "Lie flat, just get down and pull your hood over your hair."

Toni shook as she lay her face flat, her emotions a mixture of terror and resignation.

They're gonna catch us, Toni thought numbly. *They're gonna catch us and shock us, and we'll all have the devices put back on, and they'll try out fun new treatments, and there'll have been no point to any of this. Oh well. The pain is only incredibly painful for the first few weeks.*

Unable to see behind her, Toni could only imagine what the guard would do as his footsteps grew nearer. He could walk past them, if he were tired, or lazy, or simply not the watchful type. If they didn't move, and they were lucky. More likely he would pass his flashlight over them and catch them. Catch Ann and Lieutenant hiding in the shadows, and trace out Joseph, Melvin, and Charlie's involvement by way of default.

Please just walk past, Toni prayed, feeling sure he would spot her wisps of breath escaping, despite her best efforts, from between her shaking lips. *Just be lazy, just be tired, think about your wife, your kids, your football, gambling, drinking, hookers, your Chia pet, anything — just keep moving, keep moving . . .*

The steps continued, and the cold, hard fist squeezing her insides began to loosen. Toni allowed herself to swallow the bile building up in her mouth.

The steps stopped.

Oh no, Toni pleaded, the tears seeping out of the sides of her eyes, hot against her cold skin. *No, no, no, just keep walking, why can't you keep walking, I'll do anything, God, just keep walking —*

There was a clank, a hollow bang a few feet ahead, and Toni

70

could hear the guard change his stance.

"Who's that?"

His voice was reedy and slurred as if he might have the beginnings of a cold, and Toni bargained with the universe, promising to wish Reedy Voiced Guard a speedy recovery if only he would walk on.

There was a sound that could have been him clearing his throat and then hurried steps. Toni smothered a cough of her own, closing her eyes. *Away, away, away . . .*

There was a rapid flurry of movement behind her, and Toni felt someone grab her leg. She let out a choked sound of defiance.

"Toni, shh, quiet. It's us!" Ann said quickly, her hands somewhere along the other girl's back. "You're tangled, hold still."

Toni let her head fall against the ground, all of the adrenaline flooding her system screaming for release. "The guard . . ."

"Ann threw a rock up ahead," Lieutenant explained. "Okay, got it. Go, go!"

Toni didn't need to be told twice. She writhed, and flailed, and crawled, ignoring the burn in her knees and elbows as she fought out from under the wires. Once clear, she whirled around to see Ann grappling her way through. Taking the blonde's hand, Toni helped heave her out.

"Thanks." Ann gasped as Lieutenant immediately followed, wiggling her way under in a matter of seconds and holding up the fence for Anton as soon as she was free. The tall boy maneuvered his way through after a few moments of problem and joined the other four panting teens.

"So?" Anton managed between deep, lung-filling breaths. "What y'all waitin' on? Break!"

Nodding, Toni and Ann pushed themselves onto shaking legs as Lieutenant hauled Anton upright. They raced for the woods, Joseph and Melvin becoming discernible as they reached the trees. The boys helped them avoid the fallen logs at the edge as they entered the enfolding darkness.

"This way." Charlie's voice came from a little way ahead. Quivering, gasping, giddy with fear and euphoria, the seven escaped back into the shadows.

Charlie stared down at her Monday schedule. Fourth period. Spanish. *Outlandish.* 12:45. It was at this time that the Headmistress would be coming by to enter her office.

Nothing happened so far, Charlie reassured herself again as she opened her locker and pretended to check her pale face in the tiny mirror. *No extra checks, no call to the principal's office, no new meetings. If she'd found her key missing, if they suspected us, they would have done all or at least some of that. I think.*

Charlie folded and unfolded the edge of her schedule. The truth was she didn't have a strong sense about what the Headmistress might or might not do — not in the way that she was steadily coming to have about almost everyone else. Save for the one clear moment which led to the entire plan, Sophia Valentina was an unknown element.

Speak of the redheaded devil. Is she a demon? Do demons wear such nice shoes? Sure they do. It must be part of the complex.

Charlie bit down hard on her already chapped and scared lips, forcing that bizarre train of thought to the back of her mind as the Headmistress moved down the hall, weaving past students with a smile, making her way to where her office lay nestled. Charlie didn't dare glance at the woman for fear that it would tip her off. They still had one last part of their plan to put into play.

Ann was handling the drop. Without being seen or suspected, she needed to deposit the key somewhere on the floor close enough to the Headmistress as she passed by to make the woman believe it had fallen out of her purse or pocket. Charlie shivered.

Ann moved into Charlie's line of vision and winked before sallying down the hall.

"Ma'am, I think you dropped this."

Charlie froze like a rabbit spotting a recoiling snake as out of the corner of her eye she watched the guard handing the little gold key to the Headmistress. The ruler of J. Alter Academy took it slowly, her expression obscured from Charlie's view. Then, as if she had suddenly remembered her purpose, the Headmistress strode to her door, inserted the key, moved inside, and snapped it shut behind her.

Charlie blinked. *We did it*, she registered, feeling oddly empty in victory.

CHAPTER SIX  **hear**

"WELL, NOW THIS IS A NICE LITTLE ADDITION TO MY DAY."

Toni couldn't keep down the shudder that arose at that cold male voice, and when she met his disconcerting eyes she could tell by his satisfied expression that she'd given him the reaction he wanted. She carefully laid down her plastic fork and spoon, her appetite for lunch quite gone.

"Seth, you are the literal definition of a bad day," Toni said, as calmly as she could manage. "Also the poster boy for sociopathy. And douchbaggery. Really, you should look into getting endorsement deals for all three."

Seth laughed good-naturedly, leaning back in his cafeteria chair while the three other girls, clustered at the end of Toni's table, shot the handsome blonde teen admiring glances. "You were always my favorite, you know. You've got wit and charm. It makes me feel this connection to you."

Toni shook her head, putting up both her hands. "Stop, really. It's embarrassing to watch now. You're wasting your time if you think you have any shot at manipulating me."

"Oh, you're not still mad about that whole thing are you?" Seth tilted his head to the side and put on an appearance of contriteness. "I really didn't mean for anyone to get hurt."

"You didn't mean for anyone to get hurt when you had us make bombs to blow up the school, and then snitched on us to the Headmistress, and got us all caught and punished for weeks,"

Toni said musingly. "Wow. Well, now that you put it that way, of course I believe you only had our best interests at heart. However could I have doubted you?" Rolling her eyes, Toni turned to get up. Seth grabbed her wrist.

"Wait, wait," he requested, his vivid blue eyes appealing. "C'mon, sit down. Just talk with me. It gets so boring around everyone else here," Seth explained, lowering his voice and casting a quick, significant glance down at the three girls giggling at the end of the table. "I just need to talk to someone stimulating."

"Because you're a sociopath who needs constant excitement to make up for the inner life you'll never have," Toni stated, pulling her arm away but lowering herself back into her chair.

"Oh, don't recite psychology to me," Seth chastised, tsking. "I can get that from any book. Besides, if I'm just programmed this way, can you blame me for what I do? I'm just like some animal, right?"

"Animals don't prey on other animals just for the joy of causing pain," Toni snapped, her nails digging into the cheap metal edges of her tray.

Seth smiled lazily, folding his arms. "It really burned you that you didn't see it coming, huh? I know our friend Madame Schizo told you what I was way before, so that means you must have not wanted to believe her. Which means," Seth elaborated, leaning forward on his elbows and taking a small breath in as if he'd caught the scent of something delicious, "that you must've wanted to see something good in me."

"And that's what I get for being a slave to my own compassion," Toni noted wryly. "Don't worry though, I'm usually only an idiot once."

Seth raised an eyebrow, shifting in his black J. Alter Academy Panthers jacket, his gaze intent. "Maybe not. Maybe all I need is someone to believe in me. Maybe the ultimate thrill for me would be trying to feel something I don't usually."

Toni blinked at Seth as disdainfully as possible. "Okay, now? Now I am just offended. I made one bad call, but I haven't got permanent brain damage from shock treatment just yet, thanks. I do still know the difference between Harlequin romances and reality. I'm not gonna risk my sanity and health playing the virginal young maiden who tries to save the soul of the rakish Lord Psychopath."

Seth grinned. "Virgin?"

Toni picked up her tray determinedly. "Good bye, Mr. Dryer. It was horrible seeing you, as usual. Please don't stick around."

Seth tipped an imaginary hat to Toni. "See you around, oh brave, bonny lass."

Toni did not answer, already moving through the crowed cafeteria, her body pulsing with strangely charged sensations she couldn't place. Nearing the exit, she chanced a quick glimpse back, and saw Seth seating himself at another table, beside Melvin.

Fuck, I like animals. Biology should not be this hard.

Joseph bit his lip, trying to memorize the cell cycle for the sixth time and tapping his pencil rapidly on the desk between his index and ring fingers. Mrs. Waters sat at the front of the class, intermittently looking up at him over the papers she was grading to make sure her single extra-help student was behaving. Joseph was mouthing out the process of mitosis when he felt resistance to his pencil and turned to see two white fingers with carefully manicured red nails gripping the eraser.

"I'm sorry to interrupt your studying," said the red-haired woman who smiled down at him. "You seem to be making a lot of progress."

Joseph's insides froze, and he stuck his tongue into his cheek, nodding to buy time as he tried to remember how to lie. *Shit, she knows,* he couldn't help saying to himself over and over. *Fuck, we thought we got away with it.* "Not really, I'm kinda stuck."

"Maybe you need a break," the Headmistress posited. Joseph tried to read the the smiling, rather sallow face, but he kept getting distracted by the colorful table of the elements poster behind her head. She seemed to take his silence as agreement. "Wonderful. You can leave your things here. We'll be back for them later."

"Where are we goin'?" Joseph questioned, narrowing his eyes.

"Just down to a lab," Mrs. Waters supplied, motioning for him to stand. Joseph followed the two teachers out a side door and down two flights of stairs. They reached a small white hallway with no windows and stopped. Mrs. Waters took a ring of keys from her pocket and opened an unlabeled door.

Joseph hesitated as the Headmistress stepped inside. Mrs. Waters placed a gentle hand on his shoulder, and Joseph was obliged to follow her within.

The room was relatively small, consisting of a few shelves, an old sink filled to the brim with ice water, and a table lined with three hot plates and what appeared to be some kind of large burner. The burner was on, and its fire leapt steadily, heating a solid black container filled with something that bubbled and smoked.

"What is this, a science experiment?" Joseph questioned, his body flooding with adrenaline, his eyes scouring the room for any means of escape.

Ms. Valentina smiled as she danced her fingers above the handleless coffee pot, the glass vial, and the metal bowl on each hot plate. "Yes, exactly. Science is too often a case of reading dry books and looking at little Petri dishes. Experiments should be experienced." The Headmistress stopped and laced her hands together in front of her. "Joseph, could you please pick up the coffee pot?"

Joseph started. "Uh, ma'am I ..." Joseph glanced over at Mrs. Waters, who was taking deep breaths. "Do I have to?"

"No," Ms. Valentina answered simply. "This is our experiment. You're not a guinea pig. You choose."

Joseph shifted from one foot to the other. "And if I say no?"

"Then we walk you back to your classroom, and you continue

deciphering your biology homework."

Joseph moved towards the table, and the Headmistress stepped aside. He lifted his hands, let them fall to his sides, and lifted them again slowly. Joseph took a quick breath and swiftly placed both on either side of the pot, lifted it, and put it back down. "Anything else?" he asked.

The Headmistress raised her eyebrows, bemused, and inclined her head at the other three items. Joseph picked up the glass vial with his fingers, and raised the metal bowl slowly, wincing at its weight.

"Too hot?"

Joseph turned to Mrs. Waters, who seemed to be clenching every muscle in her body. "No, it's heavy," Joseph answered honestly. "I mean, I guess it's hot too," he amended. "I mean, obviously it's hot, it's just . . ."

Joseph swallowed as he trailed off, and Mrs. Waters looked to the Headmistress who was standing by the dark container on the burner. Ms. Valentina displayed a small glittering key, which she then tossed into the container.

"Could you please retrieve my key for me, Joseph?"

Joseph took a step back. "That water's gotta be boilin' by now."

The Headmistress gave another tiny smile. "The choice is still yours, Joseph. You don't have to do this. But please understand, I would not ask you to do something if I were not sure you could."

Joseph ground his teeth. "And do I really have a choice in this?" Joseph asked, unable to keep the cynicism from his voice. "Really?"

"There's always a choice," the redhead answered.

Sure there is, Joseph laughed inwardly to himself. Striding forward he plunged his hand into the container, wincing at the heat and feeling around for the key. "I can't find it . . . I . . ."

"You can take your hand out!" Mrs. Waters exclaimed, and Joseph jerked it back, eyes widening at the shimmering substance clinging to him.

"Put it in the sink," the Headmistress instructed. Joseph flung his arm into the water, shaking it and using his other hand to wipe the rapidly hardening substance off his skin. Mrs. Waters joined him as rolls of steam rose up, blurring his vision.

"Are you all right? Are you all right?"

Joseph shook his head, feeling at his arm and pulling it out of the water to squint at his reddish skin. "Yeah, I'm fine, I guess . . . that hurt. I'm sorry, I don't think I can get your key," he apologized to Ms. Valentina, who nodded.

"Of course not," she accepted. "It's almost certainly melted by now, anyway."

"What was it?" Joseph demanded, still feeling his tingling arm. "What is that?"

"Silver," the Headmistress stated. "Molten silver."

"Does she honestly think she looks good like that?"

Ann didn't bother to keep from rolling her eyes, and she simply shifted in her seat, adjusting her brown turtleneck so that it was pulled tighter around her chest. She knew, despite their whispered tones, that the girls behind her expected her to hear. Situated at the back of the class, they knew they could take chances, especially since Ms. Donelle's hearing was going.

"You know she's had sex with, like, every other guy in her grade, right?" whispered Ariel, the skinny brunette sitting in the desk behind and to the left of Ann, who always seemed to be talking about someone else's alleged sex life.

Ann turned her head just enough to cast a glance at the gossiping girls. She threw them a self-satisfied smirk to let them know she was reveling in the scandalized and offended gasps they shared with each other.

"See, she's proud of it," said Rachel, the auburn-haired, snub-nosed junior who was retaking geometry. "That's so wrong."

Ann finally rotated enough to remark in a low, drawling voice, "I'm just flattered that you're inflating my numbers, sweetie."

"Oh, so you didn't bang the Hispanic boy from the gang?" Rachel questioned boldly, pretending to work on an equation in her unicorn embossed notebook.

"He's not from a gang," Ann began and then sighed and gave up, turning back to try and puzzle out Ms. Donelle's latest lesson on the whiteboard.

"That's why her parents sent her here," Ariel said softly, voice dripping with disdain. "I know if my parents found me doing any of that stuff they would have been ashamed and thrown me out too."

Ann felt the words penetrate her mind like a physical sting. She inhaled and felt herself rising, weightless. She exhaled, and the fury settled in her stomach and spread through her limbs giving her a shot of adrenaline, and a feeling of incredible power and energy.

Whirling around, she slapped Ariel, hard. Laughing in the girl's terrified face when she started to cry and pitifully fight back, Ann pushed Rachel aside when she tried to aid her friend. Ann let out a moan that grew to a scream and echoed around the room as she hit at the little brunette again and again.

She could barely feel anything when she was finally restrained, two guards securing her arms and legs as they pulled her off the other girl and dragged her out of the classroom. *I'm empty*, Ann thought with mild amusement as she was taken down the halls to the stairs. She knew her feet were moving. She knew they were taking her to Discipline. When they opened the door to strap her down, she knew it was her legs and arms being held down, and that soon it would be her body feeling the shocks. *Doesn't feel like me though*, Ann noted dazedly, and she laughed again, this time at the ridiculousness of trying to hurt a girl who was no longer confined to her body.

Charlie's history textbook was full of leaping words.

Why does this always happen when I'm trying to focus? Charlie bemoaned internally. *Focus. Locus. The axis mundi is in here somewhere, and if I can just locate it I will win a Nobel Prize.*

She shook her head, trying to dislodge the idea, but the thoughts remained, perfectly rational; if she could find the axis mundi, the center of the world, she would win a Nobel Prize.

Causes behind the passing of the Sherman Act, Charlie repeated to herself, sure that she should remember something about the passage she had just re-read for the fourth time. The scent of strawberry from the air freshener Mrs. Carter used in the living room was overpowering. Charlie rubbed her fingers into the soft velvety texture of the maroon couch, upon which she sat, begging for her senses to pull her back to earth and fill her head with reasonable thoughts.

"But I am responsible for what happens here, all the time!"

I'm responsible? Charlie frowned, looking around the room for the source of the whispers. She saw movement at the edge of her vision and leaned forward in her seat to see Mrs. Carter in the other room pacing, the phone to her ear. Charlie went stiff, and everything around her heightened. The scent of strawberries was now suffocating, the feel of the couch under her hands pricked at her skin, irritating it, and her ears ached with the sounds of two voices. One was Mrs. Carter's. The other, filtered through the phone, was a distinctive female tone that made Charlie shiver with recognition.

"Evelyn, I can assure you that, just like you, I take responsibility for our students and see to it that they are carefully monitored during all situations," the Headmistress soothed.

"Punishments need to be passed through the appropriate channels and approved before they are permitted," Mrs. Carter insisted heatedly.

"But there was no punishment," Ms. Valentina replied with laughter in her voice. "It was simply an exploration geared toward discovering useful information pertaining to the treatment of our more behaviorally challenged students."

"Oh?" Mrs. Carter seemed to practically choke on her response. "Any information which you could share?"

"Yes. I think we need to hire a new replacement company to

upgrade the windows of the school," the Headmistress answered dryly. "The chemical composition of the air emitted from Lake Amiszi is softening all the glass within a 200 mile radius around the school. It leaves them . . . vulnerable to pressure, of various kinds."

"And you got this from interrogating one of my students?" Mrs. Carter prompted.

"I got it from continued observation, careful testing, and interaction with *our* students," was Ms. Valentina's silky answer. When next Charlie heard her speak, it was more gently, to ease the tense silence. "Evelyn, we have the same goals in mind. We are both working in the best interests of the children. We simply have different roles."

Charlie swallowed hard, unable to tell whether her anxiety was her own, or if it emanated from the two women currently locked in argument.

"I expect I will see you for our meeting this Thursday?" Mrs. Carter finally spoke.

"Of course, Evelyn," the Headmistress responded.

"Wonderful," the principal said shortly and with the click of a phone being hung up the conversation was ended. Charlie waited until Mrs. Carter had stormed upstairs and was safely out of range. Then, mind shocked clear of fog, she furiously began thinking.

"We gotta be careful 'bout meetin' so often," Lieutenant warned as she seated herself next to Melvin on the dilapidated floor of the abandoned house. Melvin was breathing on his hands to warm them as the cold, harsh breeze invaded through the many cracks in the old building. Ann snuggled into Joseph, sharing his coat, while wrapping her arms around her legs. Charlie was fidgeting erratically, her fingers twitching as if pricked by needles. Her eyes darted around their dim hideout as if she could track the pace of some rapidly moving fly. Anton sat, cross-legged, his

82

hands under his chin. His dark face alternated with extreme expressions of deep emotion and a blank, empty stare.

"It was necessary," Charlie murmured, eyes still roaming about the room. "We have news."

"We do?" Melvin prompted. "Or *you* do?"

"We," Charlie said with certainty after a moment's thought. She turned to Joseph, who shifted as the focus of the group turned to him.

"Charlie, exactly how much do you see in your psychic moments?" Joseph questioned uneasily.

"The sky. The universe. The truth behind rocks," Charlie replied. "Oh! You mean like personal stuff, like naked times? I . . . try not to think about it." Charlie glanced guiltily over at Ann, and Joseph wrapped his arm around his girlfriend.

"Now, now, what we do in our dungeon," Joseph said primly, "is . . . the subject of an FBI investigation. And also, our business."

"I never needed to hear that," Lieutenant lamented. "I coulda gone my whole life never hearin' that."

"Let's not joke about dungeons," Ann grumbled. "Not until the shock burns on my arms heal. "

Toni's eyes widened. "You got shocked? Why? Did they . . . find out? About us?"

"No, this one was all on me," Ann acknowledged, taking on a cavalier tone. "I took issue with some of the more insufferable, gossipy members of our student body."

"What did you do?" Joseph demanded.

"Stopped suffering them," Ann replied sweetly. "Don't worry," she added, noting the anxious, angry look on Lieutenant's face. "It was about them insulting me, ya know, the 'whore' routine, blah blah. Not about our last adventure or anything."

"They called you a whore?" Joseph growled.

Ann smiled. "Everyone here calls me a whore," she soothed. "It's a small town, so they have to make me more interesting than I actually am. I'm the only real homegrown scandal in recent years besides Melvin coming out of his dark, glittery closet." She blew a kiss to the black-haired boy in question, who caught it and mimed crushing it in his hands before shrugging with a wry grin.

"She's right," Melvin ceded. "Once you've got a label, everyone sticks to it. She's 'The Bitchy Whore', I'm 'The Flaming Gay' and anything that contradicts that they just toss in the trash. For example, my ability to recite all the actors who've played *Doctor Who* in succession in under a minute means nothing to these savages."

"Have I told you lately how much I love you?" Toni said dreamily.

Melvin cooed, pulling her into a tight hug. "No, but I'm always open to praise."

"I hate to break this up, but Charlie's right," Joseph confessed. "I got pulled outta extra help by the Headmistress and Mrs. Waters yesterday. They took me down to this room I don't remember seein' before, and she had me ... do this test."

"Dare I ask what the test involved?" Melvin dared.

"She had me stick my hand in melted silver," Joseph stated flatly. "First she had me pick up some hot containers, and then she tossed a silver key in this big black ... I stuck my hand in melted silver," Joseph repeated, the muscles in his throat contracting, "and it ... it didn't scar me, it ... the burn is almost *gone*."

"Why the hell didn't you tell me this?" Ann scolded, busily examining his arms, pulling up his shirt sleeves to caress his skin, and peering closely at the red marks which remained.

"I wanted to tell everybody," Joseph answered. "I just ... I kinda can't believe it."

"I can," Lieutenant volunteered. "Silver's meltin' point is 1,763 degrees Fahrenheit. Glass has one that's even higher, and you been meltin' your way in and out of the windows here for a minute now."

"Soft glass," Charlie murmured. When the others turned to her, she elaborated. "That explains the conversation I overheard between the Headmistress and Mrs. Carter on the phone. Mrs. Carter was upset about the Headmistress 'experimenting' —

84

which must have been Joseph — and all she would tell Mrs. Carter was that the experiment proved they needed to replace the glass in the windows, because it was being weakened by chemicals or something coming from the lake."

"But doesn't that mean she knows?" Toni asked, voice rising. "If she tested Joseph, and she said they need to fix the glass, do you think she found the window and noticed?"

"But then why not tell Mrs. Carter?" Charlie wondered. "I mean, she really wanted to know, but the Headmistress was barely telling her anything."

"It get heated?" Anton asked.

"It did, actually," Charlie replied, and the dark eyed boy nodded.

"So she's testing us," Toni said urgently. "Well, *you* guys," she amended, swallowing. "So, is that what this is? A big experiment? Seeing what we — what you guys are?"

"Or gettin' us ready for somethin'," Lieutenant proposed darkly. "Maybe she's tryna mold us into some kind of weapon, and gettin' ready to sell us off."

"You would think that," Melvin noted cynically.

"Well it ain't as crazy as half the rest of the shit that happens here!" Lieutenant snapped.

"Hey, hey, hey." Anton put up his hand. "We ain't gonna know her reasons for sure 'less we get more information. Now, I'd bet money if I had it that we all goin' in one of these rooms for 'testin' soon. I'd sure like a look around *before* I go in and play guinea pig. How 'bout y'all?"

"Mrs. Waters is a part of this," Joseph asserted. "She was there the whole time durin' my 'test'. She's probably got access to those lower floors. If we can get her keys, we might be able to get into some of 'em. I think I can remember the way once we get inside."

"If we get into the school again through the window, and if the Headmistress is already suspicious, she might make us," Lieutenant evaluated, cracking her knuckles as she tried to think. "We're gonna need another way in."

"If the Headmistress is suspicious, I don't know if we should risk anything," Toni advised. "The tiniest little thing, and she'll know it's us."

"Unless she doesn't think it's us doing the snooping," Melvin said slowly. His eyes bright above the dark circles under them, he surveyed his friends. "Charlie said it — Mrs. Carter wants to know what the Headmistress is doing as much as we do." He picked his nails archly. "Maybe she decides to pursue some underhanded tactics to find out."

"You got some tactics in mind?" Anton asked. Melvin smiled a predatory, devious smile.

"More than a few."

CHAPTER SEVEN

JOSEPH COPIED THE DIAGRAM OF THE PROCESS OF

photosynthesis from the white board into his notebook, taking careful, measured breaths, while trying to keep his face as blank as possible. Above all, he avoided looking to his left, towards the supply closet.

If Melvin's right, he recalled, trying to look interested as Mrs. Waters continued to explain the reason for varied pigmentation in plants, *then there's been a camera blind spot at the entrance to the closet ever since the Headmistress took over. Someone sneaky don't want to be seen takin' things from it. Naughty them, lucky us.*

The click of expensive heels just outside the classroom door sent a sensation like electricity down Joseph's back. For the past few days, Mrs. Carter had been passing by Mrs. Water's classroom and office — sometimes to talk with her, sometimes just to check out her lessons. During these instances Mrs. Waters cast constant, uncomfortable glances towards the principal, and gave short, snappish answers to student's questions. Joseph surmised that if anything in Mrs. Waters' office — or the supply closet — were to show evidence of having been inspected after one of Mrs. Carter's little visits, the paranoid science teacher would have no trouble suspecting the principal.

It was easy, Joseph marveled, staring down at his bronze hands, the soft pads of his fingers molded by his tight handling of his pencil. *A few months ago I got caught for graffiti by a fat cop* with two weeks 'til retirement, and now I'm plantin' a false trail like it's my job.

Joseph erased part of the sketch he was absentmindedly working on, blowing away the pencil shavings and starting over deliberately. The cool metal of the desk's legs were irritating against his hot skin. Slipping from the bathroom and into the supply closet had been easy — he'd managed it right before class and wasn't even missed. Finding something he could leave out or take, to make Mrs. Water's suspect Mrs. Carter, had been the tricky step. After a few tense moments of reading labels he only half understood, he'd spotted a small black notebook shoved behind some cans of fertilizer. Pulling it out, Joseph recognized it as a log book used to keep track of inventory. He'd flipped through a few pages before leaving it open and slightly to the right of where it had been before. If Mrs. Water's was getting as paranoid as they'd suspected, she'd instantly notice it had been moved.

There was a squeak, and Joseph looked up to see the principal turn on her heels and exit the classroom. Mrs. Water's body visibly relaxed, her voice becoming less shrill.

So that's my part of the operation completed, Joseph thought, a laugh bubbling up in his throat but dying on his lips. *So, maybe after I get out of here — if I ever get out of here — with what I'm learnin', I can apply for a job at the CIA.*

Assuming the Academy don't have 'em dissect me first.

"Charlie? You can stand up and go outside. Just pack up your things."

No, you bitch, witch. I see through your connection. I know your true meanings, and you can't make me! Charlie shivered at the vehement thought. *But I didn't think it. I didn't!*

Charlie opened her mouth to explain to her new English teacher, Mrs. Taylor, that someone, or something else had spoken through her. Then, blinking, Charlie realized that if she had actually spoken aloud, the stumpy, grey-haired woman dressed in upsetting shades of orange and beige would have been looking at her with shock and fury, not merely annoyance. Charlie's eyes traveled past the shelves, filled with bent copies of abridged Shakespeare and new editions of *The Great Gatsby*, to the half opened classroom door. The Headmistress smiled, not unkindly, and beckoned.

And now it's my turn, Charlie thought, looking quickly away so the red-haired woman couldn't read her mind through her eyes. Gathering together her messy notebook with words scaling the margins and coming into confused swirls on the main page, Charlie shoved pencil nubs and chewed erasers into her green plastic holder. Then, hoisting her backpack bravely over her shoulder, she took the slow, agonizing walk to the door.

To your doom, your doom, the peeling letters pasted on the upper parts of the classroom walls whispered in a frequency just a few decibels lower than Charlie's heartbeat. Ms. Valentina placed a firm, long hand on Charlie's shoulder and steered her down the half-empty halls.

"I..." The words kept getting stuck in Charlie's throat, clotting it with terror as she tried to explain how she had to stop and hop on every single one of the black tiles on the hallway floor — avoid the blue ones, avoid the blue ones — or terrible things would happen in Ghana, and in Paris. Tornadoes and typhoons, all her fault, all her fault.

"Don't worry," the Headmistress soothed. Charlie nearly snapped her neck in whirling to look up at the tall woman's face, but a kind look animated the woman's otherwise arresting, metallic features. "You'll get course credit for this, and I think you'll even have fun."

"Fun is a frequency, frequently one hears, but only when I focus," Charlie babbled. "You see it's hard to discern which of the messages is — down."

Charlie stopped as Ms. Valentina took a step down a small, nondescript staircase. Charlie looked around at the little alcove which harbored it. She could have sworn that it had not been here every other time she'd walked these halls.

"Yes, down," the Headmistress said, and with a slight push to Charlie's shoulder, she made the girl's legs shoot out and take the steps with an almost automatic rhythm.

It's like I'm a puppet, and she's holding my strings, Charlie thought as she was guided down a small darkened hall, housing an out-of-order vending machine. *No,* she realized, her mind darkening with every dim buzz of the slowly dying hall light above. *It's like I'm a corpse, and she's found the right nerve to prick to make me jerk.*

"Here we are."

Charlie's aching eyes went to the keys in the woman's right hand, but the Headmistress merely knocked upon the unlabeled white door. It opened to reveal Mrs. Waters, clothed in a white lab coat that caused Charlie's lower body to lose all sensation.

"Everything is ready," Mrs. Waters assured the redhead, as Charlie was gently pushed inside. The lighting here was clear and bright, making the contents of the room horribly clear.

"No, not a chair," Charlie moaned. The chair inclined backwards and was complete with a headrest, armrests, footrests, and straps. It dominated the center of the room. To the left was a large, circular machine, like a donut propped up on its side, the hole within emitting a low, blue gleam. It was aligned with a long white table supporting a sterile cushion, as if someone were meant to lie with their head in the machine's gaping mouth. Beside it stood a table with the legs nailed down. It supported a computer opened to a program comprised of brightly blinking graphs and dots.

In the upper left hand corner of the room was a giant screen angled toward the chair. Facing opposite the chair was a booth enclosed in darkened glass. Charlie could just make out the glow of computers within.

"Please, Charlie, have a seat."

The Headmistress' words seemed to echo over and over in Charlie's ears like a bad transmission, but it took her a moment to realize what they meant. By then, she had been steered by the two teachers into the cold metal chair. "I'm being punished," Charlie said dully.

"Not at all," Ms. Valentina said brightly, coming around to bend over in front of the chair and face Charlie clearly. "We're doing this together — with you, not too you."

Charlie started to nod and then realized Mrs. Waters was wiping a paste that felt like glue and smelled of alcohol, in her hair. Twisting, she felt Mrs. Waters steady her neck.

"Just relax. This won't hurt," the science teacher soothed. Charlie stilled as Mrs. Waters attached a number of tiny electrodes to her hair and clipped two onto her ears. She was trying to follow the course of their little wires to the computer when Mrs. Waters began pulling the straps tight around her arms.

"You can't move when the test is happening," the Headmistress explained at Charlie's terrified expression. "But you won't need to."

"There," Mrs. Waters announced when Charlie could no longer move. "All done."

"Wonderful," Ms. Valentina approved. "Now, Charlie, do you know what these are?"

Charlie squinted at the series of cards the redheaded woman held up to her face. "Those are Zener cards," Charlie exclaimed, her eyes running repeatedly over the five cards — the star, the circle, the square, the plus sign, and the three lines curved like water.

"And if you know what they are," the Headmistress continued, answering the young girl's unspoken question, "you know how they are used. So. Mrs. Waters is going to remain in the room here with you. I am going to go behind the screen. When I have chosen a card, the light above the booth will flash red, and I just want you to say aloud which one you think it is."

Charlie swallowed, her heart doing hummingbird exercises. "And if I get it wrong?"

Ms. Valentina just gave an unreadable smile and folded the

cards as she walked into the booth, closing the door securely behind her. Charlie glanced over at Mrs. Waters as much as her eyes would allow. The science teacher was holding a black notebook, pen at the ready.

Does this mean she knows? Charlie thought, her dirty fingernails grazing the cold, unfeeling metal armrests. *Knows, goes . . . I should lie. I should try to not guess right at all. Just say a card.* Charlie moistened her mouth anxiously. *But if I score below chance, she'll know I'm actively trying to not guess, and she'll know I'm hiding something.*

The light above the booth flashed red. Charlie waited to see if inspiration would strike, and when it didn't, she furrowed her brow and concentrated on imagining the woman behind the booth. *Booth, truth, loose . . .* She closed her eyes, trying to clear away the clawing fog. Suddenly it was as if her mind pinched itself and then relaxed. An image swam into view.

"Water," Charlie said aloud. "I mean . . . the squiggly lines. That one."

She waited, almost expecting a reaction, but Mrs. Waters merely logged down Charlie's answer in the notebook, and after a few seconds the light flashed red again. Charlie licked her lips, keeping her tongue at the edge of her mouth, and tried to recapture the sensation from before. It reminded her slightly of the few times she'd tried meditating and felt anything close to success: focus that mostly hurt, and then a few precious moments of clarity before her mind started filling up with thoughts and sounds again. She took a few breaths and tried for that.

"Star," she said, somewhat surprised at the strength in her own voice. Mrs. Waters made another mark in the notebook, and the light flashed red again.

With each new answer, Charlie felt herself gaining a strange confidence, which made little sense, as she had no idea if any of her choices were correct. *It's fun,* she realized, almost bouncing in her seat with the rush of enthusiasm that jolted through her. *No voices, no Badness, no fog — just nice and clear and squaresquaresquare.*

"Square," she giggled aloud. Mrs. Water made a note.

When the Headmistress finally came out of the booth with her own notebook, Charlie actually felt disappointed. "Is it over?"

The two women looked up from consulting their respective records. "It's been forty-five minutes," Ms. Valentina informed her. "I think that's long enough for now."

"Did I … get any right?" Charlie questioned, trying to appear as if she didn't care, knowing she was failing.

"Oh, I would say so," Mrs. Waters muttered. Charlie blinked.

"The better question is — did you get any wrong," the Headmistress said as Mrs. Waters moved to undo the attachments to Charlie's forehead.

"Well did I?" Charlie asked. Mrs. Waters stopped, looking over to the Headmistress who was tapping the pages of the two notebooks. "Hmm?" She looked up and located Charlie, as if lost in thought. "Oh," she said casually. "No, actually. Not a one."

"Zimmerman, Danvers, Valdez, you're in!"

Ann glanced over from her seat on the rough plastic bleachers to the other end of the spacious gym where the boys' class was playing basketball. Joseph adjusted his jersey and strode onto the court, wincing at something on his arm. Ann strove to catch his eye.

Unfortunately she only succeeded in drawing the attention of Drew Zimmerman, a particularly loud, particularly vulgar sophomore who grabbed his crotch and tapped his friend's shoulder.

"Hey, I think the Wildcat, kittycat, wants to come play. Am I right?" he jeered. Ann waited until the other boys had also turned to throw up both her middle fingers. Some of them started to catcall. Ann rolled her eyes and then seized as she was hit with a shock. She glared at Mr. Protus as Zimmerman and his friends exploded into laughter then quieted slowly when Mr. Protus barked for them to get into places for a scrimmage match.

Ann waited until they had turned their backs to her and their attention to the game, to rub her aching arm.

Call a girl names, oh that's just boys being boys, but the girl defending herself back? Oh no, we can't have that, Ann fumed. Zimmerman caught the ball and spun it in his hands in a bit of showmanship before pivoting to shoot. Suddenly he was howling and doubled over, and Joseph was leaping up to cast the ball into the hoop.

"What is it? Move outta the way. I said move. Move!" Mr. Protus bellowed, barreling through the cluster of teens to find the sandy-haired boy rolling on the ground, whimpering pitifully with his knees drawn up.

"C'mon Zimmerman. You're young, it can't hurt that bad," Mr. Protus huffed, motioning for the half-wailing sophomore to get on his feet.

"It was him!" Zimmerman bawled, throwing a vicious look in Joseph's direction in-between moans.

"Yeah, I'll bet it was," Mr. Protus grumbled. "Valdez get off the court, now, and don't think I'll forget this."

"Pendejo," Joseph muttered.

"What was that?" Mr. Protus snapped.

"I said, with pleasure," Joseph offered, as he lazily moved backwards off the field. Lounging down on the bleachers, he leaned nonchalantly to the side, just far enough to look over his shoulder at Ann, and mimed a kiss.

That's my boy, Ann mouthed back, feeling a warm flood of heat extend outwards from her stomach. She tried not to smile too widely at the little thrill of excitement running like static electricity over her skin and making her shiver. *It's like the instant before and after a jump — the anticipation and relief all at once, combined with the warm, dizzy, easy feeling you get from alcohol,* Ann thought. She pulled her legs protectively up to her chest as if the other girls near her would feel the heat radiating off her skin and know, and by knowing, somehow make the sweet emotion less her own. *It makes boring things interesting, and funny things funnier, and —*

"Kerins, Cost, you're up!" shouted Miss Saunders, the sturdily built, frizzy-haired female gym teacher.

And clearly it makes me think I'm suddenly Lieutenant, pretending I can be poetic, Ann considered with a hidden smile as she pulled her ponytail tighter and jumped down two steps of bleachers to join the other members of her class on the volleyball court.

"I can't believe he did that to Drew," fussed Courtney, a lanky, blonde junior who was nursing an obvious crush on Zimmerman. She sneered at Joseph as she moved to her space on the court. "He's just so violent for no reason."

"It's a culture thing," added Courtney's friend Valerie, a wispy sophomore in ill-fitting pink sweatpants. "That's just how they're raised, to like *attack* people if they think they've been disrespected or something. I don't think it's fair to the rest of us to bring them here if they're not even gonna try and change."

"Cost," Miss Saunders announced, tossing Ann the volleyball. "Your turn to punt."

Oh, now but if God wanted us to change, Ann thought, feeling a very different kind of delicious feeling bubbling up in her now, *He wouldn't make it so, so easy to be bad.*

Ann tossed the ball into the air, jumped, and punted it so hard into Valerie's face that the girl stumbled and fell onto her backside with a resounding smack.

"Foul!" Courtney declared, and Miss Saunders blew her whistle. "Cost, get back on the bleachers, now. Right now!"

"With pleasure," Ann replied just loud enough for Joseph to hear and look up. She met his amber eyes with a wink and a smile that was thoroughly inappropriate for school.

Toni cut up her meatloaf very carefully as Melvin slid in next to her, his tray just bumping hers and the milk carton on the edge wavering dangerously. Toni waited until the din of the cafeteria reached an especially high point before allowing herself to ask, "Anything to report?"

"Yeah. I think the theme behind lunch today was, 'Foods

That Were Edible Back When People Washed Them Down With Eye-Blinding Homemade Whiskey'," Melvin noted, squinting at the contents of his tray suspiciously. "Oh, and Mrs. Waters and our dear principal were in her office for like ten minutes, and when they came out one of them looked like she'd been crying."

"So I guess that's good, for us," Toni said slowly, twirling her fork around in the juices of her lunch.

"Uh-oh," Melvin said. "Don't tell me you're having one of those annoying, God what do you call them ... oh yeah, 'consciences' again."

Toni risked a look in Melvin's direction. The boy's eyes under his floppy black hair were cynically disapproving. "You sound like Seth when you say that," Toni said before she could stop to think.

A number of emotions flashed over Melvin's wan face before he finally shrugged. With a voice full of resigned, amused bitterness, he replied, "Well. He was the one who won last time."

"You can't think like that," Toni warned urgently, placing a hand on Melvin's cold, calloused one. "We screwed ourselves over because we followed him last time and the last thing we need to do is take a page from his book."

"Honestly, doll?" Melvin sighed, pushing his food away. "I'll take a page from anyone who can find a way to live with this."

Toni followed Melvin's gaze to the table where Seth sat. The handsome, arrogant blonde was laughing with some friends and enjoying the admiration of the girl beside him who was batting her eyelashes at him lovingly.

"Being like him would mean shutting down everything that makes you human," Toni argued. "You'd have to strip away everything that lets you feel and just be empty."

"I know you want me to say that sounds horrible, hun," Melvin said, adjusting his backpack straps. "But shut down and empty sounds pretty nice right now."

"Okay, so what you're saying sounds like —"

"Toni, no offense. You know I love you, but I don't really need you to shrink me right now," Melvin said, piling up his uneaten food and swinging his backpack over his shoulder.

"I'm sorry," Toni said, annoyed but attempting to keep her voice gentle. "I was just trying —"

"No, it's fine. I'll see you tonight," Melvin dismissed, squeezing her hand clandestinely to let her know there were no hard feelings, though his face remained shadowed. "I'm on full bitch mode right now, I need to be somewhere else." He shot another look over at Seth who was in the midst of telling what appeared to be a hilarious joke.

Yes, Toni thought as Melvin strode tossed the contents of his tray harshly into the trash and strode away. *I really think you do.*

"You gonna drop straight through the floor you keep doin' that," Anthony warned Lieutenant who was pacing around the old abandoned house like a caged tigress. "They're comin', L. Relax."

"Can't," Lieutenant explained, shaking her head, her hands moving erratically over her body, rubbing her pill-chilled skin, and fingering her braided hair. "Shit's too quiet. No birds, no bugs, no owls — it's creepy."

"It's the winter, girl," Anthony said. He grinned up at her from his comfortable position on the rough floor of the house. He rested his head against the fraying wooden wall, then shifted to avoid being stuck with a stray nail. "Birds, and bugs, and cute lil' bunnies have all gone to sleep or left. They're smarter than us."

"Or they die," Lieutenant said, pausing only for a few seconds to look for the rest of their party through a crack in the boarded up windows before going back into motion.

"Yo, can you sit down?" Anthony requested, squirming. "Makin' me nervous."

Lieutenant laughed — a fractured, uncomfortable sound. "Wrote a new poem. Just now," she informed Anthony.

"That's nice, L. I guess ..." Anthony began hesitantly, but Lieutenant barreled forwards, reciting in a wild, rhythmic cadence.

"Crazy like a creepin' shadow comes,
Not unlike an army in the night,
To the sound of ever risin' drums.
Slowly, slowly, then suddenly,
The shooters circle 'round,
Then steadily, steadily, completely,
You go down, down, down."

"Yeah, that was creepy, L," Anton stated flatly.

"I feel creepy," Lieutenant answered, her whole body persisting in uncomfortable motion. "I am creepy. Creepin', creepin' ..."

Anthony pushed himself deftly to his feet and grabbed Lieutenant by her shaking shoulders, forcing her to look at him. "You gonna be able to do this? 'Cause we can put this shit off if you need a minute."

Lieutenant braved his look, staring up into his glinting black eyes, her own hands coming up to rest over his. "I'm fine," she said, more slowly. Anthony raised a brow, and Lieutenant raised one saucily back. "Yo, I'm straight. I can do this." Then, softer, "I promise."

A noise from behind broke their tenuous silence as Joseph and Ann pushed their way through the creaking, resistant door. "The troops are here," Joseph announced brightly, helping Ann in by the hand. Charlie and Melvin squeezed in after them, and Toni picked up the rear.

"Do we know exactly what we're doin'?" Lieutenant asked brusquely, folding her hands behind her back and planting her legs firmly. "Mel?"

"The boiler room doesn't have cameras near it," Melvin went over aloud. "Ann stole the keys from one of the guards, so if we can get there without them catching us, we should be able to get inside. From there, there's a door to the lower levels. We'll be right where we need to be."

"I also lifted Mrs. Waters' keys," Ann said, pulling them out of her pocket and tossing them to Lieutenant. "Hopefully they'll be able to get us into some of the rooms."

"Good work," Lieutenant praised. "Joseph? You think you can remember where the room she took you to was?"

"I think so," he said, nodding. "The general area."

"Nice," Lieutenant affirmed. "A'ight, so when we get there —"

"There's a stranger in the hen house. Fox. Scared little furryfurry," Charlie said suddenly, her head jerking to the side, her eyes wide. "Uh-oh. Uhohuhohuhoh."

"What the fuck is she talkin' about?" Lieutenant snapped, her body moving into a ready stance and her hands up.

"Calm down, chill. I'm sure she's fine," Toni eased. "Charlie?" She put an arm around the smaller girl's shoulder. "Charlie, are you okay?"

"Fine. Dandy. Spifferiffic. But it's not me," Charlie said, swaying while Toni tried to steady her. "It's him."

"Who? Seth?" Melvin rushed to the window to scan the outside.

"No — the birdie," Charlie said, her eyes drifting to the back of the house. Slowly, shaking, she raised her finger and pointed.

Each member of the group turned to the direction she indicated, looking around for the 'him' that was meant. After a long, long silence, realization slowly sunk in.

"Anthony?" Lieutenant questioned, taking a step toward her friend. The tall dark boy blinked. "Anton?" Eyes widening, Lieutenant pulled slightly back. "Ant?"

Finally registering that he was being spoken to, the object of Lieutenant's queries faced her, quizzically. "I'm sorry," he said in a soft, feminine voice. "Who?"

CHAPTER EIGHT  white

THE SIX TEENAGERS WATCHED THE TALL BOY SMOOTH
his closely shaven hair back with shaking fingers then delicately
touch his shirt. "Well, this is not me at my best, but I suppose
I can fix that 'ish later," he said in a lilting, high-pitched voice.
"This will definitely have to go."

"Um." Toni swallowed, and stepped forward. "I'm sorry. What
are — *who* are you?"

"Oh!" The new addition gave a little laugh and extended her
hand. "So sorry, honey. It's like my manners flew out the window with my fashion sense today. I'm Leisha. Leisha Deveraux."

"So you're a . . . girl?" Joseph asked gingerly, body angled towards the door as if worried he would succumb to a change
himself if he got too close.

"Lady. I'm a lady, or you can call me a woman," Leisha said,
putting her hands on her thin, flat hips. "None of this 'girl' stuff,
all right honey? Men need to show respect, and we gotta demand
it of them."

"No."

Leisha turned to Lieutenant, whose fingers were curved like
claws as she glared at the body that had been Anthony until
moments ago.

"No?" Leisha raised both eyebrows and tsked. "Honey, if we
give 'em an inch they will take a mile, and if you don't know that
you ain't lived long enough."

"I haven't lived . . . you know what, no." Lieutenant pursed her lips and waved Leisha away with her hand. "No, no, no. I ain't dealin' with this shit. Either send Anthony or Anton back, or I am fuckin' outta here."

"With an attitude like that it's no wonder your men left you," Leisha said tartly. "That 'keep it real' thing you tryin' to pull is probably what's drivin' 'em away."

"Real?" Lieutenant snapped, and Joseph and Melvin took several steps back in the face of her rising fury. "Real? *Real?* Look, I don't know if you're Anthony's drag queen fetish or Anton's, but the *last* fuckin' thing you are is *real!*"

"Lieutenant." Melvin put his hand on the muscular girl's arm and placed himself so that she didn't have a clear shot at Leisha. "Just calm down."

"Calm *DOWN?*" Lieutenant screeched. "Anton is gone, Anthony is gone, and now we got this bitch personality to deal with instead!"

"Oh, now, do not disrespect me, or you'll have to deal with my mutherfuckin' ice pick," Leisha snapped, stepping up to Lieutenant.

"Bite me, Ru Paul!" Lieutenant challenged. Leisha snapped her fingers in Lieutenant's face, and the latter lunged for Leisha's throat.

"Okay, stop!" Toni yelled, striding in-between the two furious females as Joseph worked to hold Lieutenant back and Ann jumped in to block Leisha. "We all need to stop, 'cause if we're any louder, we'll all get caught, and then we can fight over this while we're being lit up like Christmas trees," Toni reminded.

"The mission is fuckin' ruined now anyway," Lieutenant practically spat, and Leisha sneered her disdain.

"We're not actually in the army, remember?" Toni reminded Lieutenant. "The 'mission' isn't more important than your friend."

"*That* is not my friend!" Lieutenant yelled, pulling out of Joseph's arms and gesturing violently at Leisha. "That's . . . I ain't know what that is. Anton is my friend — Anton, Anthony, you remember him?"

"Anton and Anthony aren't even the same person," Toni tried to explain as Leisha dusted off Melvin's shirt and fixed his collar. "They're both separate identities, too."

"Well which one is the *real* person then?" Joseph asked as Leisha rolled her eyes.

"They all are," Toni emphasized, frustrated. "They're all as real as each other. Leisha's got her own likes, dislikes, and background. Right?"

Leisha realized she was being spoken to and pressed both hands to her chest. "Oh, yes, me? Well I was born in New Orleans, I went to school at Tulane, and I currently work as a cake designer in the French Quarter. My favorite colors are pink and turquoise, and if I have to brag, my homemade cream is as close to divine as any of y'all are gettin'."

"Right," Toni said, blinking. "Right. But okay, see, she's here for a reason. She was created to help deal with whatever made the split happen, to protect a mind that was being shattered by abuse, and torture, and trauma."

"Protect who?" Joseph asked, his eyes moving to Lieutenant, and Leisha, and back again. Toni opened and closed her mouth as she turned to Charlie who was grabbing at the air as if it were full of tiny flies.

"Antoine," Ann said at last, looking up and around at her friends with excited realization. "Remember? In his file it said his name was Antoine. That must be the name his parents gave him. His first name. So Antoine must be the ... I don't know ... the original? The actual him?"

"I am *actually* here right now, and I can *actually* hear you, with my *actual* ears, you know?" Leisha said smartly, and Ann looked away.

"Sorry," she muttered, looking to Toni for help.

"But we've never met Antoine," Melvin said. "I mean, we know Anton, Anthony, Ant, and now Leisha. Do the original ... does the original person just go away? How does this work?"

"No." Toni shook her head, her eyes on the floor as she tried to understand. "No, we should have met Antoine. Antoine might be kinda flat, like with not a lot of personality. Not much affect, but he should be in there."

"I don't know any Antoine," Leisha said, putting up her hands. "Sorry."

"Charlie." Toni turned to her small friend. "You got any ideas here?"

"The lights keep us from seeing, but we can understand the equation if we focus on the unseen," Charlie said clearly, staring at her hands with unfocused eyes. "Buggies. Little bugs that crawl under the skin and send the signals. Comprehension comes with freedom, and freedom comes when you cut, cut it away, stay, away, today, today is tomorrow is all one in the great experience of quantum locality."

Leisha pointed with her thumb at Charlie and looked to Toni. "That one? Now she's crazy like it's her job."

"FunSize?" Ann asked, worried, as Charlie traced her fingers over her left forearm. "Are you okay?"

Charlie mumbled unintelligibly under her breath and moved to squat down and feel around the floor with her right hand. "Buggies. The bugs are the part of the conspiracy we didn't see. But they're right there, under the skin. Fin, wing, bird, and fish."

"Oh this is fun," Lieutenant said, gesturing furiously, helplessly around the room, her voice speeding up so that her words almost blended together. "Anybody else wanna have a breakdown while we're at it? Make it an even three?"

"I ... think that might make it four," Ann said cautiously. "L ..."

"Buggies need to come out," Charlie shared, narrowing her eyes as she lifted her right hand above her left arm. "Outoutout."

"She's right, buggin' is exactly what's happenin' here," Joseph noted dryly while rubbing Ann's shoulder as she stared worriedly at Charlie.

"I shoulda known," Lieutenant muttered to herself, pacing violently back and forth now. "Shoulda known. It's my job. I gotta command everybody. Gotta keep straight, gotta stay on target ..."

"Buggy comes out," Charlie said, raising her arm.

Ann's eyes widened when she noticed the dull bit of iron Charlie held in her hand. "Charlie, no!"

Blood spurted out of Charlie's arm as she plunged the nail in and Leisha screamed. Charlie twisted the nail. "Buggybuggybuggy."

Lieutenant and Ann rushed to grab the nail from Charlie's hand as Melvin supported the swaying girl. Joseph pulled off his coat to wrap it around her bleeding arm. "Charlie, what are you doing?" Toni asked urgently.

Charlie's eyes were wide, giving the impression of a sleepy owl, as she held up a tiny, blinking piece of glinting machinery in her bloody hand.

"What the hell is that?" Melvin whispered.

"Buggy," Charlie said, her smile bright and proud before she wavered and half-collapsed in Melvin's arms.

"Is it?" Joseph asked, squinting at the tiny piece of thin metal. "I mean, can she hear us now?"

"No," Lieutenant said softly, her frantic energy settling slightly as she focused and pinched the 'bug' out of Charlie's willing hands. "I think it's some kind of trackin' chip or device."

"So the Headmistress knows we're here now?" Ann practically squeaked.

"Where is here?"

Lieutenant whirled around at the familiar deep voice. Anton shook his head once to clear it and quickly sized up the other six members of the group. "Did we do it?" he asked, moving forward cautiously, his eyes narrowed. "Yo, is Tiny okay? What's that? Did we get it from the school?"

"From Charlie's arm," Toni answered when no one else volunteered to speak. "No, we didn't get into the school. You ..." She trailed off, unsure. "You weren't here."

"Coulda gone without me," Anton offered, shooting a smile at Lieutenant. "I know how much this means to our commander over there, wouldn't wanna hold her back."

Lieutenant closed her eyes and swallowed perceptibly. "I think we're startin' to run outta time for the pills. We should all head back."

"What about that?" Joseph indicated the tiny device Lieutenant held in her hands. "I mean, do we all have one? Doesn't that kinda mean the Headmistress knows where we are now?"

"She would've punished us already," Melvin figured. "It must just alert her if we try to leave. Or maybe it just monitors our vitals. Or maybe it will shock us to death if we try to run."

"Maybe," Anton considered. "What you think, Tiny?"

Charlie plucked her 'bug' from Lieutenant's chilled hands and cupped it in her palms like a butterfly. "I think," she said slowly, "that we're her little buggies right now, in her Petri dish. And while we pick, pick, pick at each other, she's standing above, watching us squirm."

Mindfulness meditation, Toni thought to herself as she worked quietly with Melvin to set up their lab station, setting down the components of the mixture they would need to make to extract DNA from their strawberry. Taking a deep breath, she tried to recall the meditation training she'd taken to deal with her anxiety. She conjured up images of soft carpets and a small, jade Buddha statue seated on a doily-covered shelf. *I need to be more calm, more relaxed. I was close to a panic attack again this morning, so if I can focus my awareness on just . . .*

"Mr. Dryer, if you could supervise table five, thank you," Mrs. Waters said, assigning the grinning blonde senior to Toni and Melvin's table with barely a glance as she continued to write out the steps of the lab on the whiteboard.

Kill, kill, killing, killing him, bash, bang, head, hammer, kill, kill, cancer, die, fire, kill —

"I remember this experiment," Seth said, rolling up his sleeves to reveal his strong, wire-free forearms and resting the palms of his hands firmly on the table. "Isn't biology fun?"

"If we ignore it, it might just crawl away and go spread disease somewhere else," Melvin suggested without looking up while carefully dipping his Q-tip in the bottle of rubbing alcohol.

"Now that's just immature and hurtful," Seth chastised. "Not to mention dehumanizing."

"You're a sociopath. You don't have any humanity. That's the whole point," Toni said impatiently, mashing their strawberry with purpose.

Seth placed his hand gently over Toni's, and she froze at the cool touch. He pried the plastic spoon from her hands and set it down besides the paper cup. "How can you give me a diagnosis when you haven't done a thorough examination?" he purred.

Toni and Melvin turned to share a look at the exact same moment. "I really shouldn't have eaten lunch," Melvin joked dryly.

"Hey, at least you didn't have it touch you," Toni jibed back. Seth's face hardened, his knuckles boring into the edge of the table, and Toni moved in closer to Melvin.

"What makes you so sure you know what I am?" Seth challenged through gritted teeth, his veins pulsing at his neck under his uneven skin. "What, because I hurt you guys once? Because your schizo pal got scared trying to read my mind?"

"Yeah, those would be two key reasons on a very long list. And our 'schizo pal' was the first one to notice what you are, so I'm going with her, thanks, " Toni shot back.

Seth captured her eyes with his unnervingly blue ones, his thin mouth working before he finally argued, "Look, you're all different, not typical. You're right. Your friend, Charlie? She's not just crazy, she does see things. Muchacho can melt glass with a lighter. Who knows what the rest of you can do. Mel here can stand up against an entire town that's got more than a few homo haters and that's gotta be a superpower," he said almost affectionately, shooting a winning smile at Melvin, whose face remained stony. "So why can't I be more than just some psychopath?"

Toni brushed her fingers against the blank page where the results of their experiment were to be catalogued. When she answered her voice was soft to conceal her own bitterness. "Not all of us are special. Some of us are just normal little worker bees like me, so there's no reason to think you're anything better than a style-deprived Patrick Bateman."

"No," Seth denied, ducking down to catch Toni's gaze again then tilting to the side to meet her unwilling eyes. "Don't sell yourself short and pretend. I know when someone is more than normal, and believe me, you are nice and wrong."

God, where is she?

He waited, impatiently, pacing back and forth and rubbing his hands on his ragged blue jeans despite the fact that no sweat came from them. He scuffed the ground with his shoes, the baggy sweatshirt he wore no comfort against the cold of the old abandoned house.

Joseph swallowed, wondering if she'd been caught, or worse, decided not to show. *It's been a whole two weeks since we had a fight,* he assured himself. *She ain't mad. Just relax.*

Two weeks since a fight, said the nasty, reasonable part of his mind he worked hard to ignore. *That means one is fuckin' comin'. Get ready for the storm, buddy.*

Growling in frustration, he slunk down on the splinter-prone floor and pulled up his knees, wishing he had something to draw on. *She ain't comin'. Fuck, if she ain't comin' . . .*

Joseph heard a noise and moved up onto one foot and a knee, ready to run, ready to fight. Slowly the door, making sounds of protest, opened enough for the pony-tailed blonde to slide through. Ann smiled, her hooded eyes both mocking and inviting. "Is the place taken?"

"Nah, I think I could make room for one more," Joseph answered, with a smile of his own, holding out his hand. Ann took it and then smothered a yelp when he pulled her down into his lap. "Hi," he said, resting his forehead against hers and making his voice squeaky and his eyes bug to elicit another laugh from her.

"Hi yourself," Ann said, sticking out her tongue and poking one of his eyes.

"Ow!"

"Sorry," Ann apologized, snuggling into him and wrapping her arms around his neck. "I didn't mean it."

"Yeah, right." Joseph scoffed. "You just enjoy seein' me in pain."

"You would look totally cute with a broken arm," Ann considered. Joseph's eyebrows shot up.

"Um, yeah, time out, time to go. I'ma just slip out the back . . ." Joseph made a motion as if to leave, and Ann grabbed him by the collar and pulled him into a quick kiss. "No going anywhere," she ordered when she broke it. "It's so cute that you think you have things like freedom and stuff, ya know?"

"Well not here, that's for fuckin' sure." Joseph snorted. "How you doin' where they placed you?"

"Fine, I guess." Ann shrugged. Joseph narrowed his eyes, and Ann felt a chill go up and down her spine at being the center of that intense gaze.

"C'mon, there's somethin'. I can tell."

Ann rubbed her neck, twisting up the side of her lips in a way Joseph knew meant he was touching on something she would rather keep hidden. "Nuthin'. Just . . . not really sleeping. Nightmares, ya know?"

Joseph leaned back on his forearms. "I thought they was gettin' better?"

"They were when we were sleeping — when I wasn't sleeping alone," she amended quickly. The tug of a smirk at his lips let her know he hadn't missed her slip up. "Oh, shut up," she pouted.

"*Te extraño, hermosa,*" he drawled.

"Are you making fun of me?" Ann snapped.

"No," he laughed. "I just said that I missed you, and I called you beautiful."

"So you say," she challenged. "You could have just called me an ugly humpbacked whore. I wouldn't know."

"Shh." He pressed a finger to her lips. "You can't tell everybody 'bout my fetish, it's a secret. I told you that shit in confidence."

"Oh, you're so funny." Ann rolled her eyes, but she was smiling.

Joseph's grin became a smirk and his eyes drooped as he drawled, "Yeah, you think so. Why don't you come a little closer and tell me about it. I'll scare any bad dreams away."

She shivered at the warm, intoxicating sound of his voice and leaned in. "Think you're a magician, huh?"

"Magic touch, baby, magic touch," he bragged as she moved both her knees around his hips and crawled further down over him. She pushed up his shirt and moved her mouth just close enough to kiss then pulled back to feel the gasp caught in his throat as his desire began to get the better of him. "Yeah, I actually remember nightmares bein' in your file," he recalled, sneaking his hands around her neck. "Think it has somethin' to do with your family?"

Ann jerked back. "Why the fuck would you ask me that?"

Joseph frowned, surprised. "I'm just makin' conversation, askin' you 'bout your day. What's the problem?"

"What, you think asking me about nightmares and my family is supposed to get me hot or something?" she snapped, pushing him down hard and extracting herself from his grip.

"Yo, what the fuck just happened?" Joseph asked, shaking his head in confusion as he pulled down his shirt and stood up. "Hello? Back here on planet earth I'm kinda lost, so if you could, anytime you feel like explainin' ..."

"Oh shut the fuck up," Ann snapped, rubbing herself all over. "Just don't talk for a minute. The sound of your voice is just in-fuckin'-sufferable right now."

Joseph opened and closed his mouth twice before biting his tongue and laughing angrily. "Wow. All fuckin' righty then. I'll make sure not to talk to you like you're somebody I care about next time and just fuck you. Is that better?"

"Oh, right, call me a whore, is that it?" Ann exploded. "We're back to that? God, I hate you, you know that?"

"No!" Joseph yelled, furious now. "No I don't! Maybe this whole jump made sense to you, but I'm lost, and the only conclusion I got is that you felt like bein' a bitch!"

Ann saw black at the edges of her vision and slapped him, hard. Joseph stumbled back, his body tightening and becoming defensive even as his eyes registered shock and hurt.

Oh God. What am I doing? Against the pain and anger in Joseph's face, she had no words. His gaze was too accusing, too raw for her to apologize, so she drew herself up haughtily and made her voice cold. "Don't fuckin' call me that. Do not."

Joseph's mouth twitched, and he nodded slowly. "Don't worry. I got plenty of other names in mind."

"Fuck you."

"Is that why you gotta come at me physically?" Joseph laughed with as much cruelty as he could muster, considering the pain in his face and the part of his chest where he knew his heart was supposed to be. "'Cause you're too fuckin' stupid to say what you mean? Go ahead, hit me again, and you can learn Spanish by countin' how many ways we got to say *massive cunt*."

I'm sorry. I'm sorry, please stop. "And how do you say *over*?" Ann said aloud, practically spitting the words to keep from wavering.

"In this case?" Joseph shot back. "I think a plain old English *fuck off* is just right for you."

"Fine!" Ann said boldly. "Enjoy yourself. I hope you find a nice dumb bitch stupid enough to let you touch her."

"Oh don't worry. I'll send you a picture," Joseph called back as Ann stormed out of the room, covering her face with a hand to keep him from seeing her tears. Biting his mouth to keep in a scream, Joseph drew blood. As soon as she was gone he released the animalistic sound of rage as he punched his fist through the rotting wall.

The Headmistress folded her arms solidly over her chest, her expression one of disengaged bemusement. Mrs. Waters was not so calm. While gripping her clipboard tightly, her eyes flickered between the redheaded woman and the defiant young girl who sat strapped to an upright metal chair, shivering with energy and anger.

"This can end whenever you want it to, Amina," Ms. Valentina offered sympathetically, her voice ringing around the small, grey room that was silent save for the undertone of its buzzing computer monitors. "Either after you have complied, or after the allotted time is up."

Lieutenant's muscles tensed, the wires attached to her dark brown skin twitching. Mrs. Waters moved to adjust the arrangement of the equipment to which they led. The Headmistress waved her down with a slight, firm movement of her hand.

Lieutenant glared up at her tall, pale adversary, her body practically shaking as she spoke through gritted teeth. "I can't move a chess piece if you got my hands tied down."

The Headmistress raised one gingery eyebrow, glancing almost carelessly at the plastic table a few inches in front of Lieutenant. The queen, which adorned its center, was delicately carved out of bone-white stone. "I think we'll both save ourselves time if we admit we know that isn't true."

Mrs. Waters' nails dug into the hard cardboard in her hands, making a softly crunching sound as she observed Lieutenant's very visible struggle to keep herself contained. Pressing her pencil to the page, Mrs. Waters endeavored to take her notes as quietly as possible.

Subject exhibits severe difficulty in controlling outward expression of mania. Her attempts appear to put great strain on her physically, as well as mentally and emotionally, and it is likely that prolonged exercises in willfully restraining responses which —

The queen began to sway, tremble, and careen from side to side. The Headmistress drew in an anticipatory breath and leaned in ever so slightly closer as the piece graduated to shaking, twirling, nearly bouncing . . .

And then it was still. Ms. Valentina waited patiently and then nodded politely to the sweating black girl. "Well, I think that's —"

There was a sickening sizzle and crack as one of the computer monitors shot violently off of the right hand counter, snapped free of its connecting plugs, flew across the room, and slammed into the opposite wall with a resounding crash. Mrs. Waters pulled back with a high pitched cry, and Lieutenant screamed in release, laughing uncontrollably, the manic sounds cascading like a backward, out-of-tune symphony around the room. The awful noise reverberated and echoed throughout the enclosed space until the Headmistress pressed a needle into the teen's arm. The sounds faded to a broken gurgle as the liquid in the syringe drained and Lieutenant collapsed into unconsciousness.

Fie, fee, fees for services, I serve mankind, man and kind, but we never are, are we? Can truth come from love, or is it all a question of quotes, which indicate the conspiracy in the books, thousands of words to sort through every day, must be sorted through or the fate of all can be damaged . . . I must meditate on my navel, my novel, the realizations that are entrusted to me. It all makes sense if I focus, but how can I faux-cuss when swearing isn't allowed?

"Swearing isn't allowed," Charlie said, dribbling her fingers on the oaken dining room table. The soft flower-printed placemat before her was a riot of bright colors that made her eyes ache. She giggled in triumph. "I said swearing isn't allowed aloud!"

"Yes, that is true," said Mrs. Carter, carefully folding her violet woolen sweater and laying it over the high back of one of the chairs as she seated herself across from the young girl who was pulling at her matted hair. "Charlie, have you had your shower today?"

"Shower, shower, flower, flows . . . swearing isn't allowed, if you swear you will be punished, which is a pun, a bit of the secret code, see I know which way is down," Charlie argued, her nose twitching like a rabbit as she picked at the placemat with nervous fingers.

The principal pulled the placemat away and set it aside,

smoothing a bit of her own black hair behind her ear before taking Charlie's wandering hands in her own and holding them still. "Charlie. It is important that you stick to your schedule and keep yourself clean. To be healthy."

"Healthy, healthy . . . wealthy and wise, Benjamin Franklin frankly didn't understand electricity all that well," Charlie confided to the older woman and looked around as if the man himself might burst into the well-scrubbed, floral-themed dining room to defend his honor. "If he had been in on one of the Headmistress' experiments, *she* could have gotten the truth out of him. Mark my words, mark them down, right there, on that little piece of paper . . ."

"Experiments?" Mrs. Carter shifted forward in her seat, her platinum heart necklace swinging erratically and catching Charlie's roving, riveted eyes.

"It isn't what you think. Just an object," Charlie noted, moving her head to meet the rhythm of the heart charm.

"Experiments, Charlie," Mrs. Carter questioned, pulling one hand away from the girl's to wrap it around her necklace protectively, forcing Charlie to blink. "What experiments are you talking about?"

"The electrodes, of course," Charlie said impatiently, shivering in the light blue shirt that clung loosely to her rail thin body. "The ones she attaches to your head when she and Mrs. Waters take you downstairs "

"Mrs. Waters?" Mrs. Carter interrupted. "She's there?"

"Both of them, two by two, put on the wires and ask you questions, in the lower rooms, where everything is locked and only they have the keys. Keys. Do with them what you please, just like they do, when they probe at your mind and find all kinds of dirty, nasty, naughty evil things, bad, bad, bad . . ."

Mrs. Carter sat back stiffly in her chair, the blue and white plaid cushion tickling her thighs as Charlie's mutterings became even less coherent. "Look what she's done to you."

"Done to me, done right, I'll need more basting before I'm

finished, obviously."

"I promise I'll see this whole thing settled properly," Mrs. Carter avowed to the half-cognizant teen.

"Promise, promise ... promises are always made to be broken into the pieces, the sharp little pieces," Charlie murmured, laying her head down. "Tired. So tired."

Mrs. Carter brushed aside Charlie's greasy hair and laid a warm palm to the girl's forehead. "Why don't you go upstairs and have a nice shower before dinner? Then you can rest," the principal suggested.

With the laborious and unsteady motions of someone having to remember what to do, Charlie pushed herself to her feet and gave a dull-eyed nod. "Shower. Nice. Nice and clean."

"Yes, that's right. I'll see that everything is fixed," Mrs. Carter promised again, her voice taking on the kindly patronizing cadence used to coax a small animal. Charlie shambled out of the room and up the curved staircase, tip-toeing to minimize her impact.

Fixed. Yes, it is all fixed now. The trap is fixed, and you are the bait this time. See, even the craziest little buggy can weave a web fixed and fit to capture a spider.

"Are we ready this time?"

Lieutenant surveyed the small assembly — everyone was dressed in the blackest clothes they owned. Joseph and Melvin had their sweatshirt hoods pulled up over their heads and Ann and Charlie had their hair pulled tight into ponytails. They all crouched down close to each other for warmth in the frigid abandoned house.

"As ready as we'll ever be," Melvin volunteered.

"Be sure," Lieutenant demanded. "The only way this works is if we're perfect."

"Perfect," Charlie said, rocking back on her heels slightly, "takes a lot of work."

114

Ann put an arm around Charlie's slight frame. "You okay, Fun Size?"

"I'm gray," Charlie explained. "It's like I'm looking at everything through a tunnel. I feel heavy and weighed down." She looked up at Lieutenant's measuring expression. "I'm not psychotic. I got Mrs. Carter on the scent, trail, the —" Charlie closed her eyes and counted silently to control herself. "I told her what we wanted," she finished firmly. "She'll do exactly what we want. And I will too," she added defensively.

"You'll do fine," Ann said supportively, her look to Lieutenant a warning.

"We're all loose cannons anyway," Joseph said, his chest rising and falling. "If we can't do this as friends and stick wit' each other, why do it at all, ya know?"

Lieutenant did not look at Anton, but still he nodded. "We got a job to do," he asserted. "We'll do it."

Lieutenant slapped her hands on her thighs and pushed herself to standing, a smile finally emerging on her wide lips. "Oo — fuckin' — rah, then."

CHAPTER NINE knight

IN THE ICY NIGHT OF WINTER, THE HEAT FROM THE J.
Alter Academy boiler room bled out into the immediately surrounding area. Crouched into the small, crumbling red-brick
stairs which led down into the source of the school's heating
systems, Anton waited for any sound, and then he moved up
just enough to motion with his hands the all-clear.

There was a low, nearly imperceptible grating noise as chain
fence links were pushed up, and then a swift shadow was moving,
low to the ground, towards him. He grabbed the shadow's hand
and helped Lieutenant leap down into the stairs and land quietly.
She placed a finger to her lips and held the silence, counting to
three on her fingers, before standing up and making the all-clear.

Both teens crouched close to the wet brick bottom step, bits
of dead leaves and dirt clinging to their fingers as they propped
themselves up against the stairs, tense and ready to flee. Lieutenant winced at the inevitable crunching sound as Joseph leapt
down to join them with skillful dexterity. The air warmed around
the three as Lieutenant again counted, stood up, and signaled
the next member of the group.

Ann's arrival created an increase in sound as Joseph's breathing sped up to match hers once she was safely tucked in beside
the others. In their close quarters it was impossible to keep
personal space, and excitement and anticipation were shared
evenly without any need for words.

116

Lieutenant's signal for Charlie to join them was cut short when a light flashed around the corner of the building. Lieutenant rapidly gestured for Charlie to fall flat and freeze. Anton pulled Lieutenant down before she could see if Charlie had followed her instructions. Lieutenant's eyes watered as she tried to maintain absolute stillness despite her shaking. The four exchanged glances of helpless, immobile fear, not needing to see each other's faces clearly to communicate their similar emotions.

The light skimmed up over the staircase, and Anton pulled Lieutenant closer to the ground as Joseph and Ann tried to make themselves small. There was the discernible sound of heavy footsteps, and then the light bobbed around the opposite corner of the building where the guard had come.

Lieutenant counted to five on her fingers before rising up and signaling for Charlie. The short girl made the last leg of her trip stumbling and trembling, but she joined their party without incident.

Melvin made the journey in fast, loud bounds that made Lieutenant crack her knuckles, but he left enough time for Toni to follow almost immediately after him. Once the curvy, curly-haired girl was reunited with her friends, she tightened her ponytail and shifted to allow Ann to come nearer the door.

Fumbling with fingers stiff and numb from the cold, Ann extracted the small key she'd lifted from the guard, and she inserted it into the keyhole. She felt a pain as she wrapped her right hand around the knob and turned. The metal burned against her chilled palm, and the others behind her leaned back as she slowly, slowly pulled the door open, just enough for her to slip inside. Charlie followed, with Joseph and Melvin squeezing through with some difficulty. Lieutenant waited until everyone was within to enter, pulling the key out of the hole and holding the lock mechanism in to shut the door with barely a click.

Lieutenant rubbed her hands together impatiently while the rest warmed themselves by pressing near the active hot water pipes that were invasively filling the concrete room with banging sounds. Lieutenant wrapped her knuckles against the floor — the sign to move out.

The group maintained their no talking policy as they found their way by touch across the boiler room floor. Lieutenant's long hands slid up the doorframe to find the knob, opening it only once everyone was together.

They filed through the door and into pitch black, bashing into each other and releasing quickly smothered cries as the door closed behind them.

"Fuck, that was my elbow, man."

"That was *not* my elbow, Joseph."

"Well, I apologize —"

"Guys, guys, guys. I found the door," Toni said, loud enough to break up the squabbling couple. She felt blindly around, biting her lip as someone heavy stepped on her foot. Somehow she found the knob and ran her finger down to locate the keyhole. "Ann, the keys."

"Here." Toni felt a cold palm on her face and moved her left hand up to pull the other girl closer. "Can you feel where I'm touching?"

"Hey-oh."

"Shut up, Melvin," Lieutenant ordered as Anton chuckled.

"Yeah, I got it," Ann confirmed, and there was a jangle and click as she tried to find the right key. "Almost there . . . yup, here we go."

The door swung open and Ann groped at either side of the walls within until she found the light switch. "Huh. Looks kinda like a hospital."

"Is that an fMRI machine?" Toni questioned, moving inside and nodding to the large donut shaped contraption on the left side of the room.

Charlie peeked over the other girls' shoulders' and shuddered with recognition. "This is my room," she mumbled, turning red and looking away.

"You okay, Tiny?" Anton asked kindly. Charlie just swallowed, and Lieutenant motioned for Ann to give her the keys. "Keep the door open and the light on, and we'll check the other rooms to see if we find anythin' we ain't seen before."

"I'm pretty sure ..." Joseph jogged further down the hall, into the shadows where the light didn't pass. "Yeah, I'm pretty sure this door was mine. Wasn't much in here, it was more what she ... wasn't much here."

"None of these doors are labeled," Toni muttered, mostly to herself. In the dim light from the one open room, the hall itself looked small and dingy. There were doors to four rooms on the left hand side, the entrance to the boiler room was on the far right end, and the door to the upper levels of the school was roughtly in-between.

"What about this one?" Melvin suggested, tapping on the door nearest to the boiler entrance. Lieutenant tossed the keys from one hand to the other as she strolled over. She bent down to try a few of them in the lock, then hissed with pleasure as the knob turned. "Success," she bragged, brushing off her shoulder.

"Yeah, you black ops now," Anton joked, earning himself a shove more playful than angry. The group hurried inside, their whispered voices now tinged with the giddiness of high strung nerves.

"Turn off the other light," Lieutenant instructed. Joseph flipped the switch and closed the other door as Lieutenant clicked the newest room into bright illumination. The group crowded around the threshold as if a wire might trip should they step over too soon. Joseph let out a long whistle.

"Now this," Melvin said, taking the first, brave step inside, "is going to haunt my nightmares."

"You and me both, buddy," Joseph agreed as the group filtered steadily into the arrestingly arranged space.

The floors, walls, and ceiling of the lab were of old stone. The room was formed almost like a bunker with the roof sloping towards the far end.The long, sleek, modern operating table system in the center was clearly a recent addition to the space, as was the surgical mobile X-ray generator which curved over it. The cabinets, which lined the walls on the right and left, were made of new plastic, and the jars, bottles, vials, and instruments within showed signs of recent use. Three large computers rested on two separate desks in each of the far corners of the room. Toni zeroed in on the strange contraption that hung above the operating table, suspended from the ceiling, its wires drooping down over the headrest like electronic wisteria.

"Yo, there is no way this can be legal," Joseph said, almost pleading while treading delicately around the operating table as if the equipment might swallow him whole should he get too close. "Right?"

"I'm sure we can file a complaint," Toni deadpanned, examining the X-ray machine.

"I'm drawing upon the Jewish prerogative of my mother's side of the family to say this is giving me major Mengele vibes," Melvin announced, peering at the neatly stacked bottles of pills through the glass windows of one of the cabinets.

"Oh, don't say that," Charlie piped up, her eyes wide. "It's not that bad. No, no, no."

"I'm just saying what we're all thinking," Melvin defended, shaking out his spiky hair.

"I agree with Charlie," Joseph supported. "That comment was kinda outta mein kamfort zone."

There was a beat of quiet, and then Lieutenant extended her arm without looking to Ann. "A'ight, slap him. Once, hard, just so he learns his lesson." Ann gave a non-committal, uneasy laugh, and Toni didn't miss the stinging glare Joseph cast in the blonde's direction.

"It goes on your head," Charlie said abruptly, pointing to the hanging contraption. "See? It circles around, and then you tighten it with the screw. Those little spaces are for vials, and the needles go right inside your skull."

"I'm really startin' to hate it when you're right," Lieutenant informed the smallest member of the group as she angled herself to look under the headpiece. "Half this stuff ain't in any decent hospital, and I know, I been in plenty. She musta had this made special for us."

"Somehow I don't feel flattered," Melvin said. "I don't care how much you hate children, at what point does this become okay, even for our dear principal?"

"It doesn't," Toni responded plainly. "There's no way Mrs. Carter knows about all this. She likes to think she's helping us, and this would just blow her little paradigm to pieces."

"Paradigm, nice word," Lieutenant complimented as she tried to read the handwritten list of ingredients on an angular glass vial filled with a soupy red liquid.

"Thanks. I try," Toni accepted.

"Buggies!" Joseph and Melvin jumped when Charlie pointed emphatically to the small, clip-sized devices on a shelf besides a pair of matched scalpel blades and see-through speculums. "See, see? Just like inside! She has her little messengers, keeping tabs and controlling the tabulations, up and down and in the little zigzags as they go —"

"Calm down, FunSize," Ann soothed, putting a hand on the twitching teens back.

"But it's the buggies," Charlie repeated. "Just like the one I pulled out. She has more, many, many, many more. And look, she has all she needs to put it under the skin."

"She's right," Lieutenant said darkly, coming over and tapping the cabinet windows. "Look — forceps, retractors, injection needles, probes, calipers, staplers, even drills. It's a fully stocked surgeon's kit, and somehow I don't think our lovely Headmistress has this place tricked out just to dissect frogs and chipmunks. This is for us."

"So she's gonna bring us down here?" Ann gripped her stomach and squeezed, fighting for breath, her eyes on the specula. "What is she gonna tell our parents?"

"Probably nuthin'." Joseph snorted, trying to ignore the sick feeling rising in his throat. "They didn't care before, why start now?"

"They'll care when she starts this," Toni asserted, an extra edge to her voice. "This is human experimentation without consent, on minors. This is massively illegal. When she starts this —"

"What if she already has?"

Anton's question cut through the room like a razor blade, leaving a bloody trail of silence in its wake. "What if she's already done it?"

"We'd know," Ann stated, crossing her arms over her chest protectively, as if any one of the sharp edged implements might rise from their place to begin their morbid work. "There's no way we would forget that. Right?"

"Like Tiny said," Anton continued inexorably, "we already got those bugs up under our skin. I ain't remember volunteerin' for them to get put there. I got no difficulty believin' one a' these lil' bottles is full of somethin' that can knock us out for hours without us knowin' and have us wake up in our beds like it's all been a bad dream."

Toni shook her head, and Anton raised an eyebrow at her. "Don't believe me?"

"No," Toni said stubbornly. "I would know if I'd missed out on whole hours of my life."

Anton smiled his crooked grin, and Toni colored in embarrassment after a moment. "Sucks, don't it?" he said. "Havin' time taken outta your life that you just can't get back?"

"What do the rest of you say about this?" Lieutenant asked in a voice half-hard, half-appealing.

Anton swiveled his neck to consider. "I only talk to Anthony," he admitted. "Never knew there was anybody else 'til recently." His grin returned. "Hey, I just found out I'm sharin' my head with who knows how many people. Ain't really surprised to have one more tryna push inside."

"Jesus," Joseph whispered, stepping backwards and then stumbling. "Ouch, fuck." Turning down to glare at his aching toe, Joseph's eyes widened. "Yo, check this out." He waved Anton over as he knelt down and pulled upright the heavy iron handle he'd tripped over. Lieutenant bent over to scrape at the sides of what, upon inspection, was a trap door hewn into the stone ground, eddies of dust and dirt just visible at the edges.

"Great. She's got a basement. A 'through the floor, into the ground, shortcut to hell' basement. Awesome. Peachy. Guys, I am not going down into the basement," Toni stated flatly, backing away significantly.

"Can't anyways," Anton muttered as he and Joseph heaved together on the iron handle.

"Locked," Joseph confirmed. "Or stuck."

"So even in her mad scientist lab, there's stuff even she don't want to be able to open?" Lieutenant whistled. "This is beyond fucked. This, this is space, the final frontier and *beyond*, beyond fucked. I'm in favor of us all dippin' outta here now."

"Need more time," Charlie said. She was still at the cabinet where she'd found the bugs, her nose pressed up against the glass case, her eyes traveling over the unmarked vials and bottles of the third shelf as if she could sense their contents with enough focus. "Need to put all the pieces together."

"We'll just have to do it later," Lieutenant dismissed, putting her hand around Joseph's warming wrist. "We gotta get back before the pills wear off. Anton?"

Anton sat, his hands still clinging to the iron handle, his eyes on the trap door, riveted and yet unseeing.

"Anton?" Joseph nudged the boy, and Anton yanked himself roughly upright, his chest heaving. "Anton? Anthony?" Lieutenant asked, rising slowly, watching the dark boy carefully.

"Anton," he repeated to himself, and after a second he met Lieutenant's eyes solidly. "Fine. I'm fine. We gotta go. Break. Now."

Steve Berman frowned, pausing in his rounds at the edge of the lawn nearest the west end of the Academy. He scanned the area between the back exit of the cafeteria, and kitchen, and

the buildings which housed the heating systems and generator. There, if he narrowed his eyes and focused, Berman could
detect movement.

Taking out his walkie talkie, he spoke softly to the guard
who was situated at the front gate. "David? Yeah, it's Steve. I
think we're seeing some movement on the west lawn, near the
cafeteria. Yeah. We could definitely use some backup if this is
anything like before."

"Wait, wait, wait!" Ann grabbed Joseph's arm before he could
sprint from the shadow of the red brick building to the spot at
the fence where they could slip through. When Lieutenant gave
her a fiery look, which Ann could see even in the dim light the
waning gibbous moon provided, Ann gestured harshly to the
figure standing only a few yards away. Lieutenant squeezed
Anton's shoulder, and he passed the movement down the line
to Charlie, Toni, and Melvin, who all froze accordingly.

The guard stood in the same spot for a few more seconds before walking on. Lieutenant eased her hold on Anton's shoulder
slightly as he moved, and then she squeezed involuntarily again
when the guard stopped almost exactly in front of their escape
point under the fence.

Charlie started to shake, Toni's breath becoming the loudest
sound nearby as it increased erratically. Anton pivoted to face
the others, his face impossible to read, he so nearly blended into
the dark. He stayed low as he began to half-crawl around the
right side of the building they pressed up against. Lieutenant
grasped his forearm tightly to hold him back. He used his other
arm to reach over and touch her lightly, comfortingly under her
chin before carefully extracting himself. He scoped out the path
that wound around the east side of the school, past the gym, and
around the main building to the front gate.

Ducking back into the shadow near his friends, he tapped
Lieutenant on both shoulders with two fingers and jerked his

head in the direction of the front gate. Charlie started to make a sound like a protest, but Lieutenant nodded, the motion perceptible to the others, and signaled for them to follow Anton's lead.

Hurrying on tiptoes and using their fingers for balance on the cold ground, the seven friends scampered along the side of the building which housed the cafeteria. They paused as Anton lifted his hand when he reached the gap between the shrubbery at the building's corner and the open space before the back entrance to the gym. Lieutenant pointed out the guard strolling leisurely through the walkway lined with small, bare trees that led towards the main building. The teenagers covered their mouths, as Lieutenant demonstrated, to keep their breath from being seen as clouds in the cold air, and waited until the man moved out of sight.

Toni nearly cut her head falling on the slippery walkway as they raced through the silent night to the cover of the alcove near the front of the main building. Joseph and Melvin stopped to pull her upright. Without a word, they half-carried her the rest of the way.

Panting loudly and trying not to, Toni's chest heaved as her curls blew, unbound, around her face in the brisk breeze, stinging like so many pins and needles.

Anton pulled Joseph and Lieutenant closer with either hand and indicated to the front gate to the school, which was half-open. Two guards were conferring as they partially jogged away, leaving the gate unprotected.

Lieutenant swallowed audibly before tapping her chest with a fist to alert the others, and then saluting briefly before Anton tapped her back. She rose, and Charlie had to bite her lip to keep in a shriek when the tall girl fled across the wide open lawn between J. Alter Academy's main building and its front gate. Joseph lurched when Anton tapped him on the back, and he almost shoved the other boy before he realized he was meant to do the same. He started to look back for Ann, forced himself to stop, and then shoved off from the ground with his hands.

He sped out through the dark, disappearing as Lieutenant did when he reached the gate and could no longer be thrown into relief by the reach of the Panther Field lights.

Anton had to practically pull Charlie to her feet to get her to start running, and Melvin grabbed her hand to drag her along and get her up to speed as they strove for the gate. Ann and Toni were ready on the balls of their feet when Anton finally tapped them. Toni only cast a quick glance in his direction before trying to match Ann's pace and gasping at the pain in her lungs from the influx of cold air. She heard Anton draw up behind her as they raced for the front gate.

"There's nuthin' here."

"I know I saw somethin'," Berman insisted, shining his flashlight over the cafeteria building again. "I swear."

"I'm not doubting you," the other guard assured, rubbing his hands together to heat them. "We've got raccoons and all that, especially near the trash cans on this side."

"Nothing on your end?" Berman asked, and the other man shook his head. "Not before we left."

"Wait, you mean there's no one there now?" Berman questioned, incredulous.

"We came here because you called," the other guard replied testily. "We're gonna head back now. We'll call if we see anything."

"What about backup? I thought you asked for more guys?" Berman said, frustrated.

"We did," the other guard said stiffly. "No go. Higher ups said it wasn't necessary. Hey, I'm sorry. I know you're jumpy since the last time, but don't let it get to you. They got the kids here on an even tighter leash this time. They won't get away with pulling a stunt like that again."

"Yeah, yeah," Berman acquiesced. "Sure, sure."

CHAPTER TEN talk

CHARLIE BALANCED CAREFULLY ON THE TURNED DOWN toilet seat, her hands on the cool metal of the stall walls, trying to grab and hold onto just one of the thoughts that churned through her mind like a riotous sea.

If you can keep your feet off the ground you can hold your head up long enough to log the logarithms and find the equation that will even out the balance . . . balance, balance . . . turn the screw and cut the corners and the whole tripod comes crashing down, and we can't have that, no, no, no we can't . . . There is something to be known, and only I can know it, but I can't put my finger on it . . . I should be able to see the way through the mirror, it's only bent glass anyway!

The sound of the bathroom door swinging open on creaky hinges was like nails on a chalkboard to Charlie's over-sensitized ears. She clapped her hands over them, wobbling on her perch. The feet which came into view made the tiny girl freeze as she tried desperately to stop breathing, stop moving, stop taking up so much space lest the person just outside her door come in and discover her before she could answer the final question.

"Charlie?"

Oh Gods, they know my name!

"Charlie? It's Ann. I'm pretty sure I saw you duck in here."

Ann, fan, Mississippi goddamn . . . Charlie pinched her ears with stubby nails, before recognition came, sluggishly, to the forefront of her chaotic awareness. "Oh, Ann. My friend. I know you."

"Um, yeah, I hope so," Ann said with dry but gentle amusement. "You're not getting multiple personalities like Anton, are you?"

"He's not well," Charlie stated. Ann snorted as she opened the door to the stall beside Charlie's and copied her position on top of the toilet. "Yeah, he's not well, and neither is he," Ann joked.

Charlie chewed on her lip. "I'm not well."

"No?"

"No," Charlie repeated. "I'm thinking crazy. Maybe."

There was a pause. "Wanna talk about it?" Ann offered in the calm voice she so rarely used on anyone else.

"I kept getting every single one right," Charlie said, her bony limbs rubbing together painfully as she rocked unconsciously on her seat. "Star, water squiggles, square . . . not one wrong, the whole time."

"Do . . . the star or squiggles mean something?" Ann probed, and Charlie gave one, short, wry bark of a laugh.

"You think I'm just talking crazy," Charlie surmised bitterly. "Oh, God. I wish I was. No, the cards don't mean anything. They're just cards. The Headmistress asked me to guess the ones she was thinking about without my seeing them. Star, water, square, circle, plus sign . . . for forty minutes, she asked me again and again. Every single one I got right. Every one."

"Well, that's amazing," Ann said with a hitch of awe in her voice. "I mean, we knew you were psychic, but —"

The toilet seat on which Charlie balanced began to rattle as she shivered, and Ann held up her hands, forgetting that the other girl couldn't see her. "What, what's wrong?"

"Not amazing," Charlie said harshly. "It's awful. It's the very, very worst thing. I'm psychic — I was right. And it's so very not good."

"Why?" Ann questioned, trying to shove down the twinge of jealousy which reared its viperous head at the thought of her own paltry collection of 'skills.'

"Because I'm a paranoid schizophrenic," Charlie said, her voice finally rising above a pained whisper. "I see things that aren't there, I hear voices that don't have people attached, I think I need to save the world, and I know people are listening to my thoughts. And if that was all, it . . . well it's bad, but I could at least know what I know, which is that I'm crazy, and it's all not real. But I was *right* all those times. Sometimes I *can* see into people's minds, or I *do* know when something is coming." Tears leaked down Charlie's face, weaving clean little lines of water across her dirty cheeks. "How am I supposed to deal with being psychic *and* paranoid? How am I supposed to live when I can't even be sure that the most insane, awful thing I think I see isn't actually there? How am I ever going to not be afraid, when I know that the monsters I see might actually be real?"

Charlie listened desperately for a reply, as if Ann might truly have the answer, despite knowing that, of course, she could not. "Well, I guess that's why we have each other," Ann said finally, putting her own feet on the ground. "To help tell each other if we see the same monsters."

There was a quiet rustle as Charlie hopped down and leaned against the side of the stall, parallel to her friend. "What if the monsters are inside us?" Charlie asked, laughing a little with Ann at the trite sound of the question.

"I don't know," Ann said, her smile fading as the whisper of shame and fear in her own mind tried to compel her attention. "I guess we'll have to be really good to each other when that happens, and try not to kill each other by mistake."

I hate her. I seriously just fuckin' hate her.

Joseph picked at his unappetizing salad with angry thrusts of his fork as he shot glances across his cafeteria table to the one just behind it. Seated in full view, Ann was tossing her hair and giggling loudly enough for him to hear while stretching her back in her baggy grey turtleneck to pull it tighter around her chest.

Yeah, laugh it up, holmes, he thought at the relaxed brunette who leered at Ann as he let out a laugh disproportionate to the paltry joke she had made. *Won't be so damn funny when she's shovin' you into a wall and slappin' you, 'cause, well, it's Wednesday, and she needs to fill her bitch quota.*

"I wish I could see more of you. You're really funny," said the overenthusiastic brunette, shooting a sly wink to his friends huddled at the other end of the table.

Ann rewarded him with a smile that made Joseph want to commit felonies. "Well, I've never really thought about a career, but maybe stand-up is my calling."

And she's usin' her ventriloquist talents to make sure *I can hear her,* Joseph noted. The burning anger in his throat helping to mask the sting in his chest and abdomen. It made him want to curl around himself like a wounded animal, the physical effects of his emotional pain temporarily making his head swim. *God, I hate her. I do. I really just hate her.* Ann brushed a strand of hair unconsciously out of her face and pulled her sleeves down over her hands, sticking them between her legs as she cocked her head to the side and nodded, her eyes just slightly hooded. Joseph assassinated a cherry tomato with his fork and then pushed his dish away, the unstable, empty feeling in his stomach making him even less hungry. *I hate her.*

Ann was moving as close to the other boy as she could without attracting the attention of the aides. Joseph looked down, rubbing the cross tattoo on the inside of his wrist. *What did Jesus say 'bout beatin' the hell outta the man hittin' on your girl?* Joseph tried to remember. *I'm sure he said somethin' . . .*

Ex-girl, he reminded himself, trying to wash down the lump in his throat with his lukewarm water as Ann nodded again at the brunette. *So it doesn't matter. She could fuck him, and it wouldn't matter. I don't care. I'ma stop listenin', right now. I'm done.*

"Your sister is coming into school next year, right?" the brunette asked Ann, and Joseph's eyes shot over to the other table. Ann had stopped smiling and nodding, and was angled away from the over-eager boy. "What do you mean?" she asked slowly.

"Like, she's coming in, right?" the boy asked again.

Ann's scowl deepened. "Yeah, so, why?"

"I'm just saying, if she's as much fun as you, it'll be great," the brunette said, and his friends at the end of the table snickered.

Joseph could have warned the other boy about what was coming. Ann's blow resonated throughout the entire left side of the cafeteria, and the brunette had to pull away fast to dodge another punch, shoving his tray aside and stumbling away from the table. "What the hell?"

"Don't ever fuckin' mention my sister again, or I'll kill you," Ann threatened, smacking her own tray off the table in fury.

"You're crazy. God, don't worry." The brunette spat, touching his bleeding lip. "If your sister's anything like you, I'll stay away."

Ann lunged, and Joseph was on his feet, catching her around the shoulders before she could reach the other boy again. "Yo, calm down, calm down! Stop, you gonna get us both —"

Both teens screamed and buckled in pain as they were hit with multiple shocks. Blinking, shaking his head, and trying to clear his vision, Joseph felt it as Ann was pulled roughly away from him. When she emitted a muffled cry of pain, Joseph's fist snapped out. The aide, who was trying to subdue a struggling Ann, took the hit to his chin and was forced to release her.

The entire cafeteria was filled with raucous shouts and cries of "fight, fight, fight!" Three guards raced towards the two teens as the sounds of clapping, cheering, and fists and cutlery banging on the tables swelled to a roar.

Joseph swerved away from one guard, a particularly heavyset man, only to find himself locked into a pain compliance hold by another guard who bent his arm harshly behind his back. Joseph was forced onto his knees, and watched helplessly as Ann was hit with another round of shocks before she too was subdued.

"All right, get up. You know the drill," grumbled the guard behind Joseph as he pulled him to his unwilling feet. Wincing in pain, dizzy, and disoriented by the noise, Joseph's eyes found Ann's, and they held each other's gaze until they were dragged completely out of sight.

"Yes, I only need to borrow Toni for a few minutes."

Toni cooly closed her English notebook, arranged her pencils, and waded through the desks. She stepped over hastily-moved-aside feet and legs to draw abreast of the tall, redheaded woman in the starched grey pantsuit. The Headmistress patted Toni genially on her shoulder.

"We'll have you back here soon, don't worry," she promised, leading them on a brisk pace down the hall, making Toni nearly jog to keep up. Toni kept her hands in her pockets so the Headmistress couldn't see her dig her nails into her sweaty palms.

She can't want to bring me down to The Room, Toni assured herself, trying to get logic to cancel out fear. *I don't have any special talents. There's nothing she can do with me, I'm useless.* Then, with a combined burst of excitement and dread, she wondered, *What if that's the point? What if she's gonna bring me down to that lab and see if she can splice DNA from the others into me, use me to see if she can make a power potion and inject it into me?*

Jesus Christ, I might actually just be in a shitty comic book movie. Help, please.

Toni felt both relief and disappointment as her theory was put on hold when the Headmistress merely took them to her office. Opening the door courteously for Toni to walk through first, the redhead gestured her to the finely carved seat before the desk. Toni took it, trying not to let her eyes drift too much around the room. Her gaze was naturally pulled to the large masks which adorned the walls, and to the stark black and white photographs that placed Sophia Valentina in jungles, deserts, and atop a mountain.

"I'm a collector," Ms. Valentina said, and Toni blinked, meeting amused grey eyes. "All of the things you see around you," the redhead explained, waving to them with her strong hands. "I travel, and I pick up something from just about everywhere I go."

"You've been to a lot of places?" Toni said, judging that the Headmistress was inviting queries.

"Yes," the older woman said animatedly. "There are few better ways to learn about people than by meeting many of them, in their own habitats."

"What are the others?" Toni asked bluntly, boldly. A pale eyebrow was raised at her.

"Other ways to . . . ?"

"Learn about people," Toni said, her brief burst of confidence sinking at the knowing grin playing around the Headmistress' lips.

"By taking them out of their environment, presenting them with challenges, and observing what choices they make," Ms. Valentina said, drawing one scarlet painted finger over the binder of a small photo book. "That is what makes college such a telling time in the lives of people in this country — they finally have the freedom and the burden of dealing with all their challenges more or less alone for the first time. "

"So why not run a college?" Toni asked, and was rewarded with an almost praising smile, as if she had gotten the right answer to a quiz.

"Oh, because there is nothing quite like the boiling kettle of hormones that is adolescence," the Headmistress shared, relaxing into the high back of her chair. "We all start to wake up when become teenagers, and that process is deeply interesting to me."

Toni nodded, rubbing her thumbs into the polished wood armrests of her chair. The Headmistress pushed the book of photos towards her. "This is a collection of pictures I took while I was in the Serengeti. I think you may find them interesting. Obviously college is the next step out of high school for an exceptional girl like you, but you may want to consider traveling first."

Toni snorted, and then covered her mouth in apology, meeting those magnetic grey eyes again. "Sorry, just . . . exceptional. Not sure that's how anyone would describe me."

"On the contrary, it is exactly how I would describe you," the Headmistress said, with just enough emphasis on the pronoun to make her personal opinion clear. "Choices are the steps we take towards evolution — no matter how great or small we think our natural gifts, our choices are always our chance to set ourselves apart, to change the game."

Toni swallowed, trying to think of something bright and meaningful to say in response, and then wondered at herself for wanting to impress this woman. Before she could say anything one way or another, the Headmistress stood up and handed the book to Toni, who took it and rose when the tall woman tilted her head towards the door.

"Thank you," Toni said, as they walked back down halls now crowded with students as the bell rang for the end of third period classes.

"Of course," the Headmistress said briskly, pausing to deliver Toni to the door of Mr. Alderman's room. The history teacher waved her inside with his upsetting smile, and Toni took a seat as far away from him as possible. When she looked up to the doorway, the Headmistress was gone.

Ducking down behind the bushy brown hair of the girl in front of her, Toni surreptitiously opened the small book of photos. It sprang open easily, the first page revealing a circular black twist of cloth. Toni picked it up and turned it around in her fingers, expecting it to be some kind of exotic item. It was only on the third round that she recognized it as her own scrunchy. The scrunchy that she'd lost somewhere on the school grounds the night of their mission to the labs.

"Where are they?"

"Calm down, Toni," Lieutenant eased, putting a hand on the shorter girl's shoulder and motioning for her to take a deep breath of the cold, musty air inside the crumbling old house. Toni shook her head, and Lieutenant frowned. "What is it?"

"Everyone needs to be here," Toni said, pulling her grey woolen sweater tighter to her shoulders. "Once Ann and Joseph get here, then I'll tell everyone, all at once."

"That bad?" Melvin questioned, pausing in his whittling of

a broken piece of floorboard with a rusty nail. Toni just looked down, but Charlie nodded. "Yes, bad."

"A'ight, they better show up fast then, 'cause this suspense is makin' me itchy," said the tall black boy scratching his back on the chipped wall nearest the fireplace.

"You gonna literally die of splinters, Anthony," Lieutenant asserted. "And I'ma make a ballad to it at your funeral, and everyone will laugh."

He stopped mid-rub, straightened, and announced, "Nah, I'ma be around for a while yet, best believe."

"It's Anton now," Charlie said, her hands clumsily tying and untying the frayed tips of her hair. Anton nodded. "Yeah, that's right, Tiny. You catch on quick."

Lieutenant turned away.

"Toni, seriously, sit down," Melvin pleaded. "I'm tense enough already. Our favorite person decided to sit at my table again today."

Toni did stop at that. "Seth?" Melvin nodded darkly.

Lieutenant's eyes widened. "Oh shit, Toni, you ain't gonna tell me he knows again?"

Charlie's head shot up, and she bounced on the tips of her toes. "Coming, coming!"

Lieutenant, Anton, and Melvin all fell completely silent, eyes veering between each other in fear.

"Yo, you guys there?" Joseph whispered, pushing at the dying door to work his way inside. Lieutenant let out a huge sigh, glaring at Charlie. "Don't do that again," she chastised. Charlie made a sound like a sadly mewing cat.

"It's just us," Ann said. Her hand was in Joseph's as they entered the house, and she leaned on his arm when she stumbled over the remains of a decaying broomstick. "We had to be careful coming out. They've been watching us pretty closely since Tuesday."

"Yeah, I heard about the cafeteria riot," Lieutenant noted dryly. "You get fed up with the food?"

Ann pursed her lips, and Joseph shrugged it off. "Nah, just the company. We're good now though. Just the usual round a' shock therapy."

"Looks like it's the right kinda therapy for you two then," Lieutenant said, nodding at their entwined hands. "Guess next time y'all break up we can ask 'em to try the leather straps."

"Sounds kinky," Melvin pointed out immediately with a wicked smile.

"Oh, you think she hasn't tried that on me already." Joseph waggled his eyebrows. Ann nudged him in the stomach with her elbow. "Like you would complain if I did," she responded tartly back.

"A'ight, a'ight," Anton said, snorting his laughter into a closed fist. "Toni called this 'cause she said she has somethin' to tell us all that's real important. You got the floor, girl."

Toni fought the impulse to lie, to say it was nothing, anything to hold onto a moment when she was simply a girl with her friends. "It's . . . I was called into the Headmistress' office. She had my . . . I could tell from what she said that she had figured it out."

Anton, Lieutenant, Melvin, Ann, and Joseph all stared at her blankly, but Charlie let out a whimper. "Oh, no. No, no. She's made us. She laid down the moths under the light and let them test their wings out, and they thought they were flying towards the outside but the light was only for inspection the whole time."

Lieutenant rubbed her temples. "I think my brain is gonna burst out my head if I try to make sense outta that. Toni, you got a translation for us?"

"What she's saying is that she knows," Toni said plainly. "The Headmistress knows. She knows we're meeting together. She knows we're working together."

There was utter and complete silence for a split second, and then Lieutenant lunged at Anton. Expecting the reaction, Toni had just enough time to pull him out of the line of fire before Joseph grabbed the ranting, struggling black girl around the waist.

"You!" Lieutenant accused, practically spitting in anger, her eyes boring into Anton's. "You fuckin' did this!"

"I didn't tell her anthin' L, I swear," Anton said in a lower voice, trying to bypass her high pitched screams. "I promise. I know I didn't."

"One of you did, one of your selves, probably a bitchy gay self, or, or a mad scientist self, or a wannabe gangster murderin' self, you piece of shit," Lieutenant raved, pulling at Joseph, who was perspiring already in his attempts to hold the muscular girl back.

"Lieutenant, calm down," he groaned, trying to wrestle her arms behind her back.

"Like hell," she growled, breaking his hold with a rapid twist and shoving him back. She stormed up to Anton, who stood, solid, against her fury.

"He didn't do it," Toni tried to explain, coming up just in front of the tall boy and blocking Lieutenant. "It wasn't him."

"How do we know, huh?" Lieutenant demanded, swerving to keep her eyes trained on Anton's. "We don't know how many mutherfuckers he's got up in there. Maybe he's got a really insecure snitchin' countess in there who doesn't like our manners, and decided to get buddy-buddy with Sophia."

"She doesn't know because anyone told," Charlie said, her voice rising and falling unevenly. "She knows because she's letting us. Little pieces on a board, push them around, see them rise, see them fall. Adapt. This is the game."

Lieutenant rolled her eyes, scowling at Anton, but finally looking somewhere else when she faced Charlie. "Charlie, I love you, for real, but this trippy, *Alice In Wonderland* cat talk is straight drivin' me to drink, and we ain't got alcohol. Could you translate it for me, please?"

"I knew the password to her computer because she thought it to me as hard as she could," Charlie said clearly, finding her breath as she spoke. "It was ... a test.

Lieutenant glanced at Ann, who turned to Charlie.

"Uh ... Charlie," Ann said delicately, "look, if you think ... I know you sometimes feel like people are following you, or giving you thoughts, but remember earlier today, when you asked me —"

"And she gave me back my scrunchy," Toni interrupted, moving to place a hand on Charlie's back as the little girl frowned with a trembling chin at the skeptical expressions of her friends. "She called me into her office today, gave me some cryptic conversation about evolution and high school and kettles of hormones, and then she slipped this," Toni said and held up her black scrunchy, "into a book of photos she gave me. I had this in my hair the night we went down to the labs, and I lost it sometime when we were running out of the boiler room. She called me into her office to give me this to let us know that she knows what we're doing."

"Why?" Joseph demanded, practically spitting. Lieutenant pressed her fingers to her temples and shook her head, as if to will the reality away. Anton jammed his fists together as he bit his lip, rage evident in the tight muscles of his neck. "Fuckin' why? If she knows, why is she lettin' us do this?"

"She's a scientist," Toni said wryly. "And we're her guinea pigs. This is her experiment. This whole school. She wants to see how far she can push us. She wants us — I mean, you." Toni swallowed. "She wants you to develop your ... abilities."

"But why not just ask you, then?" Ann argued. "I mean, she could just say 'Hey, you have telekinesis. Wanna come to a school for mutants and learn how to use it?' Why make us into enemies of the school?"

"Because," Joseph said after a long, drawn out silence, "then if we saw something we didn't like and wanted out, we could go and tell our parents." Joseph smiled, laughing softly with bitter realization. "We could go to police, to the press. We could expose things they ain't want exposed. But if we're crazy, problem children who try to hurt ourselves and blow up schools, who needa be restrained ..."

"Then our credibility is gone, and no one will believe us even if we do try and tell," Lieutenant finished.

"Tell what, though?" Ann asked. "That she's experimenting

on us?"

Lieutenant met Anton's eyes, and he shook his head, his face stormy. "Nah," he said darkly. "There's gotta be more to it. Her doin' experiments is one thing. She might be worried about that gettin' out, but all this ... this goes deeper. Bigger."

"But she knows now!" Melvin exploded, throwing a piece of an old, rotting chair against the wall. "If she fuckin' knows, then why are we even bothering? She's engineered everything. Wow, great, we're just her little dummies. Even if we fight back, we're doing exactly what she wants."

"What she wants is us, here," Toni tried to reason out. "If Seth told her about us before, when we tried to wreck the school ... that means she let us get all the way inside and actually set the bombs, before she told Mrs. Carter. She let us do everything except —"

"Except get out." Lieutenant caught on. "Toni's right. Whatever she wants us for, she wants us here. If we wanna move against her, we gotta break out."

"Great, we're back at square fuckin' one!" Joseph threw up his hands. "How do we get out, if Her Redheaded Majesty knows what we're doin'? She's been one step ahead of us this whole time. She's got files on us, she's been testin' us. How the hell are we supposed to outthink her?"

"And even if we do get out," Melvin added dully, "she'll just come after us. The police, our parents, maybe even some secret army they keep in one of the basement rooms — they'll all be out after us. How can we ever get away?"

Anton met Lieutenant's eyes, and she turned away. Joseph bit his inner cheek, and Ann leaned into him, rubbing her head. Toni pulled on her curls, frowning.

Charlie flopped down onto the floor in a cross-legged position and rocked backwards and forwards, slowly. She paused and chuckled, drawing the attention of the others.

"What is it, Charlie?" Toni asked.

"Melvin's right," Charlie said, still smiling. "We can't ever get away. They'll come after us again and again, maybe for as long as we're alive. They'll never stop hunting us, not with what we know."

"Oh, so nice to hear," Joseph said with false brightness. "So we just resign ourselves to bein' lab rats 'til we fuckin' die. That's encouraging, Charlie."

Charlie continued to smile. "It is," she answered with real enthusiasm. "It's very, very encouraging."

backwards

"MELVIN? YES, PLEASE COME HERE, IT WILL ONLY TAKE a few minutes."

Toni gripped the pale boy's hand under the lab table. His sweaty fingers squeezed hers tightly before he straightened, shook out his gelled black hair, and strode as bravely as he could over to the waiting Headmistress. The tall redhead, dressed in a basic black suit and wearing a burnished gold collar around her solid neck, nodded to Mrs. Waters with a satisfied smile. The science teacher, her brown hair barely held down by a series of hair clips, pinched her lips and reshuffled her stack of tests.

She's picking us off one by one, Toni thought, trying to ignore the whispers and looks from the other students in the class as the door clicked shut behind her friend. *So she knows, and now she knows we know she knows. And we're just playing cat and mouse with a six foot tall redheaded Dr. Strangelove, which is neither funny nor sexy, and therefore sucks.*

Toni pressed down hard on her paper, writing her notes as if the pencil tip could pierce through the table. The tip broke. "Sh — urgh," she garbled away her swear, inwardly cursing the handsome blonde senior staring down at her with over exaggerated concern.

"You think our experiment is Strangelo?" Seth read Toni's notes as he leaned over the table. She hastily erased her unthinking comment.

"No, I'm just trying to work out the final paragraph, and then we'll be finished," Toni said significantly, taking a step back to move downwind of the musky scent of the senior's cologne.

"Oh, c'mon." Seth drummed his fingers impatiently on the table. He pushed aside the miniscule test tubes, his expression alluring and interesting even in its petulance. Toni fought to summon up the same hatred and fear that had worked so well as a ward against Seth's natural charm for weeks now, but it was difficult when he so closely resembled an abandoned child. "You never used to be so . . ." His upper lip twitched in consternation.

"Disgusted with you?" Toni chuckled with scant humor, checking her notes to make sure her final conclusion was supported by all the evidence.

"Don't." Seth's tone was harsh and unrelenting, and it took all of Toni's willpower not to shoot her eyes up at it and meet the senior's demanding gaze. "Don't pretend you don't understand. You're not like the town drag queen over there, or Senior Valdez and his little kitten, or your other little friends . . . you're like me. Embrace it."

"No, now *you* don't," Toni whispered, setting her pencil down with fingers as steady as she could manage. Glancing around to see if anyone else was listening, she leaned in to answer Seth fiercely. "You did the same thing with Ann — trying to get her to believe you have some *connection*, that she's special because of it, and that you're the only one who understands her . . . I'll even bet you do that to most of the people you manipulate, girls *and* boys." Toni smirked, narrowing her eyes derisively. "Well a trick only works on me once, and I do not appreciate being treated like an idiot, which is what you clearly think I am if you think I'd ever feel anything but disgust for you."

Seth balanced his fists on the table and leaned in so that his nose nearly met Toni's — daring her to come forward, daring her to move back. "See?" he whispered. "That right there is what we have in common. You don't have special abilities like your little super powered friends, do you?" The tension in Toni's throat gave Seth his answer, and he nodded, his expression somehow both mocking and sympathizing. "No. But nature doesn't make mistakes, not here, and if you don't have that, then you have something else to compensate. You're right. I'm really good at getting people to do what I want them to do. And you're really good at resisting. People underestimate you, even me. I don't make the same mistakes twice either, and there's a reason *you* are the one I singled out, out of all of your friends."

"Because you think I'm the weakest," Toni surmised, raising her eyebrows in skepticism. Seth tsked.

"No, no," he declared, grinning now and enjoying himself. "The weakest one is the fairy who just left. He's barely got enough balls to put on his eye makeup and thong in the morning, and it's obvious. In the wild, the animal that loses its will gets eaten first, because part of it wants it."

"Don't threaten my friend," Toni warned, her hand clenching and unclenching, readying for a punch she knew she couldn't throw.

"I'm not." Seth took his hands off the table to hold them up in a protest of innocence. "I'm just saying what I see —"

"Which is?" Toni interrupted, aware that she was pushing now, hoping he would break and show the demon she knew lurked behind the perfectly sculpted planes of his face. Seth turned his head a little to the side, waiting. Toni's skin prickled in fear and another more pleasant and more dangerous sensation.

"Not everyone survives," Seth said finally, no discernible guile in his voice. "It's a fact of existence, man, just is. I respect strength where I see it, and I see it in you. You want to make the most of things? Then you drop the extra weight and take only what you need to get out."

Toni started a sharp answer and then realized what he was saying with his last word. "Out?"

Seth nodded, his gaze level. "Out."

The bell rang.

"What is your name?"

The tall, lean boy's face remained dark and closed, the whites of his eyes stark against the black of his irises. With his head, wrists, ankles, and chest bound firmly to the upright operating table, he could make no sudden movements that might wrench the tightly clenched apparatus cinched to his head. Its attached wires pulled taut as Mrs. Waters carefully monitored the computer to which they led. She wrote her notes down manually, eyes darting between the results on the computer's screen and the subject himself. The Headmistress kept her eyes upon those of the boy.

"Anton," he answered with some difficulty, his jaw hampered by the confining bands of the headdress he wore.

"And where we you born?" the redheaded woman queried.

"New Orleans, Louisiana."

The Headmistress paused and glanced over at Mrs. Waters, who looked up, nodded, and made a note. The redhead continued, "And who are your parents?"

"I ain't never met 'em," Anton replied, meeting his interrogator's gaze head-on. "I grew up in Waldo Burton Boys' Home."

"And when were you born?"

Anton narrowed his eyes. "My birthday's in May. The twenty-seventh. Though I don't doubt you know that already."

"And in what year were you born?"

Anton blinked, his lips coming together into a scowl. "I don't know. I'm around nineteen, I think."

The Headmistress leaned in, bending over the table and examining the thin, sharp facial features of the male before her. "What year?"

"I. Don't. Know." Anton bared his teeth like a cornered dog. The Headmistress pursued.

"Have you ever been to Terrebonne Parish?"

Anton's muscles tightened, and Mrs. Waters wrote quickly, distributing her glances between the readings on the computer and the reactions of the boy on the table. "Mighta been. Once or twice."

"And what did you do while there?"

The computer screen flickered. "Sophia…" Mrs. Waters began, but the Headmistress threw up her hand for silence and pressed on. "Anton, what did you do in Terrebonne Parish?"

The thin plastic mattress upon which Anton lay crinkled as his form stiffened. "I had business there."

"Business?"

"I visited a friend, sometimes," Anton snapped. "When I had the chance."

"A friend?" The Headmistress nodded, considering. "And what was this friend's name?"

"Why? So you can go and pick him up and bring him here too?" Anton countered. Mrs. Waters made another note.

"What was his name?" The Headmistress repeated.

Anton swallowed. There was a sound like a sizzle, and the screen flickered again. "Sophia —" Mrs. Waters began.

"What was your friend's name, Anton?" Ms. Valentina insisted.

Anton's nails dug into the plastic mattress, and he closed his eyes, straining against the heavy leather straps. "Not your business."

There began to be a smell like smoke in the air, and Mrs. Waters stepped away from the computer, which was now blinking and flickering. "The computer —"

"Do you remember his name?" The Headmistress's voice was urgent and prevailing, and she placed her arms on both sides of the operating table, her gaze trained on the prone figure laid upon it. "Try. Try very, very hard."

Sparks leapt from the wires attached to the computer as it emitted thoroughly unhealthy sounds. Mrs. Waters backed further away, clutching the notebook to her chest.

"I … ain't …" Anton held his eyes shut, his face working.

"Do you remember his name?"

He hissed, trying in vain to twist his head against the weight of his bonds.

"What is the name?"

There was a zapping snap and a boom as the lights in the room went out. Illumination came from the sparks shooting from the board where the wires connected to the computer. The computer made a popping sound as it died, leaving the lab smelling like the air before a thunderstorm, full of electricity and the hint of smoke.

"Have I mentioned that this is a terrible fuckin' idea?"

"Yes, about a hundred times, Joseph," Ann said, rolling her eyes and laughing. She pulled him by the hand through the dank underbrush and past the breaking sticks hanging in their line of sight, to expose the path to the edge of the still, silent lake. "C'mon, we need a new place to meet where they won't find us, and it's our duty to check it out and make sure this one is safe."

"Yeah, right, safe." Joseph scoffed, crossing his arms as he followed Ann onto the gritty sand and mud at the edge of the lake, the softly lapping water one of the few sounds in the winter night. They had met at the old abandoned house, but Ann insisted that they find a new place for the group to meet the next night.

You'd think I'd a' learned somethin' 'bout what happens when she wants to go 'explorin'".

"The lake that is makin' glass melt and frogs grow four heads? Sure, that's real safe to be beside." They cleared the forest and found themselves standing on the last of the dry land before the mud and sand led into the wide expanse of water. The steady lapping on the shore was broken only by the sound of a far off howl.

"Not beside," Ann said, smiling deviously and extracting her hand from his. She was lightheaded from the cold night and the thrill of her idea. *C'mon, smart boy, you can work it out.* She winked at him and waited for comprehension to dawn.

Joseph frowned, then paled under his caramel skin. "No, you are not."

"It's not frozen yet," Ann pointed out, slipping off her hood and shaking out her mane of blonde hair. "That should tell you something."

"Yeah, that this might be a portal to hell," Joseph said, scowling. Ann responded by undoing her sweatshirt zipper in tiny increments.

"You are not."

Ann began delicately pulling the sweatshirt off.

"Oh my God, she is." Joseph looked away, shaking his head and covering his eyes. "You insane, you know that right?"

"I know," Ann said over her shoulder. "It's been brought up before."

"You gonna freeze to death," Joseph warned. "You gonna seize up into a damn block of ice and die of hypothermia. It's gonna look like murder." Joseph glanced around, and muttered, "And they're gonna think I did it."

In the fading light of the moon, Joseph had to squint to see Ann's form as she shimmied out of her pants.

"Well, then you're gonna hafta come in and keep me warm like a good boyfriend."

"I go in there naked like you into that weird ass water, I'ma come out with two heads."

"That could only be an improvement."

"Hey!"

Ann just snickered as she discarded her last bits of clothing. Joseph groaned loudly as he pulled off his shoes. "I'm gonna regret this."

"Now you know how I feel every other night," Ann needled, jumping to dodge Joseph's tossed aside shirt, her feet squelching in the muddy sand. Folding her arms and tapping her bare wrist, Ann waited impatiently as he shrugged out of his jeans

147

and boxers. "C'mon, hurry up."

"Why? The water ain't gonna get any colder," Joseph argued, shivering at a gust of wind and resisting the urge to pick his clothes back up and cover himself in one very specific area.

"No, but I might," Ann challenged, skipping to the water's edge. She smothered a gasp when her feet hit the icy ripples, and flipped Joseph off when he laughed at her. "You better get in this water with me," Ann demanded, steeling herself and backing into the lake. Bravely, she pushed herself to wade in deeper, the smooth rocks slippery beneath her feet.

"You are so fuckin' lucky you're sexy when you demandin'," Joseph informed her, grudgingly following her lead and biting his fist as the cold water broke against his already cooled skin.

"You're lucky you're cute when you're uncomfortable," Ann countered, already in the water up to her waist. Feeling out with her toes, she could tell where the sand bank fell away into deeper waters. She took a moment to collect her courage, then pushed off and let herself sink fully into the dark black liquid. She surfaced, gasping and shrieking, and shaking out her hair. "Shh, quiet, quiet, fuck!" Joseph hushed, yelping as he shoved off into the deeper waters himself, treading to keep his head up. He covered Ann's mouth with both palms. "Jesus, I'm freezin' my fuckin' balls off here."

Ann pulled his hands away and wrapped her arms around his shoulders. "That's because you're too far away."

Joseph found her waist under the waves with his half-numb fingers and wound her into his front. At the touch of her body to his, he shivered in a way that for once had nothing to do with the temperature. "Oh, yeah?"

Ann nodded, the glint of moonlight on the water throwing her bluing lips and narrowed eyes into relief. She ran her nails over Joseph's slick upper back and touched the edge of her nose to his. "Guess what's funny?"

Joseph shook his hair a little to free it of a wet leaf. "What? What's funny?"

Ann met his amber eyes in the dim light, her eyelashes almost brushing against his own. "I love you."

"Yeah?" Joseph's smile was slow and soft as he tried to play down the triumph and glee rising up from within his chest. He found her legs and drew her up, holding her in his arms, so that she was nearly resting on the top of the water and able to flick the surface with her toes. "Well I love you too, so there."

Ann swallowed, and the vibration of it carried down their entwined bodies. "When we get outta here, I don't know what we're gonna do."

"We'll find somethin'," he promised, spinning them around lazily, drifting towards the area on the water where the moon's reflection shone brightest, so that he could meet her gaze. "I could work as a graphic designer or somethin'. You could, I don't know . . ."

"Work as a ventriloquist?" Ann snorted. *I got no real talents,* she thought, insecurity nibbling at her core like a starving creature. *Not like him. What the hell will I do when we get out? If we get out?*

"Hey, you could bring back the circus," Joseph joked, laughing when she splashed him. "Nah, but you know . . . we're in this together. We'll figure it out. We got our whole lives to do it. Ain't gotta plan our kids names out or nothin' yet."

"Definitely not Ernest," Ann insisted, crinkling her nose.

"Why the hell would we ever name a kid Ernest?"

"That's my point!"

Joseph laughed and continued laughing until he brought his lips to Ann's, and then he kissed her deeply, steadily, hungrily. Ann whimpered at the sweet, sharp pain spreading out from her chest through to all her extremities as she pressed herself shamelessly against him. His hands on her body were a steadying point in the constant motion of keeping above water. Ann wrapped her legs around his waist, needing to be as connected to him as possible. Joseph kicked back until his feet touched the sand bank and used the leverage, in addition to the buoyancy of the water, to support their weight. Ann drew her palm down his damp cheek, her eyes meeting his as their bodies uncertainly, insistently, sought to find a way to join. With her heart fluttering like rapids, Ann's hair made a curtain around their faces as they spun in the silent, cold lake, their passionate, desperate noises the only sounds for miles.

All's well, hall's fell, open the well and find the secrets she does tell . . .

"Don't tell her! She'll catch you!"

"What's the point in hiding? You know she can read your mind, you dirty demon."

"Charlie, Charlie, silly little girl with the buggies under her skin."

"Charlie?"

Charlie swayed, her hands fumbling on the smooth polished armrests of the chair in front of the Headmistress's desk. She tried not to slip off and fall onto the floor and break into a million pieces under those calculating grey eyes. Ms. Valentina's office was only slightly cooler than the classrooms in the Academy, but to Charlie even the slight change in temperature was too much for her fragile form. Her brain woozy and clogged as if by so much dust, Charlie was kept awake only by the sporadic and abrasive chants of the voices and her own stimulating fear of slipping up and letting the redheaded woman know the game.

Game, fame, shame, she's come to claim your mental processes . . .

"I hear from some of your teachers that your work has been slipping," the Headmistress stated, thumbing a sandy-colored file which seemed to double and melt in and out of the mahogany desk before Charlie's blinking eyes. "We both know you are above average in intelligence and that the work they have you doing is something you could do with both hands tied behind your back, so there must be another reason for your lack of initiative." The Headmistress laced her fingers together over the folder and smiled briefly. "How have you been feeling lately?"

Lately, stately, gods I'm tired, sleepy . . . "I've been tired," Charlie replied, slurring.

"Is there a reason you haven't been sleeping?" the redhead asked delicately, brushing a strand of copper hair aside to display a twinkling gold and garnet earring.

"A reason?" Charlie didn't have the strength to lie, not with the howling voices filling the room and the desperate effort it took to string a coherent sentence together. "I hear voices, Ms. Valentina. They come the most at night. My mind is like a dirty room that fights when I try to clean it out. My thoughts want to think themselves. I can't tell anyone what to do. And so when I read a book on history, James Madison gets mixed in with snowballs, and bugs, and the true relation of pi to the South China Sea." Charlie's breath hitched, and she managed to stop before any more words spilled out of her chapped lips. "It is hard to focus ... with all that."

The Headmistress' eyebrows peaked. "I can imagine. As a matter of fact, I'm very pleased with your ability to hold up despite your condition."

"My condition ..." Charlie bit the inside of her cheek, eyes burning with tears. She knew by Ms. Valentina's compassionate expression that she was not successful in holding her tears back. "Paranoid schizophrenia: thought disorder, hallucinations, poor emotional response, and disorganized speech and thinking."

"You forgot paranoia and delusions," the commanding woman reminded. Charlie let loose a disjointed, hyena-like laugh that she had to stop by clamping a hand over her mouth

"Oh no," Charlie said, shivering with cold and suppressed, uncontrollable laughter. "Oh, no, I didn't forget. But paranoia is fear and anxiety taken to irrational levels, and delusions are false beliefs based upon inaccurate or refutable information."

"And you don't believe you ever have such beliefs or feelings?" the Headmistress posed, fingering a fine black ballpoint pen.

"I know I have," Charlie answered, and a window of clarity opened in her mind just enough to allow her to answer. "I know I believe I'm being monitored, and believe I've been experimented upon, and believe I'm part of a conspiracy where I am being controlled and used for other purposes."

The Headmistress' lips twitched. "And so what makes you not paranoid or delusional?"

"For it to be a delusional belief," Charlie said, "it has to be false."

"I feel like we should have a drink if it's our last night here."

"Yeah? Of what exactly?"

Melvin shrugged, leaning back against the crumbling fireplace of the abandoned house and patting the dying walls almost fondly. "I don't know. Maybe the lake water, once we get there?"

"I ain't drinkin' that shit," Anthony said, shivering and rubbing at his arms as if he could feel all the strange effects which would result from imbibing the lake water. "Got no idea what could be in there. Parasites ... leeches ... Loch Ness Monster's ghetto-ass twin. Uh-uh."

"I still can't believe Ann and Joseph ... tested it out," Melvin said, waggling his eyebrows dramatically.

Lieutenant pushed off from the rotten bench she was leaning against and strolled over to her friends, snorting. "Them two crazy kids would fuck in a barn on fire and not notice 'til they burned as black as me if the mood hit 'em, best believe."

"We heard that, and y'all will prepare to pay," Joseph's voice rang out, followed by the man himself as he wedged open the door and held it so Ann, Charlie, and Toni could crawl inside. "We demand respect, yo."

"Well, I do. You can mock him all you want," Ann said with a toss of her hair, yelping when Joseph hoisted her up from behind in his arms. Lieutenant shushed them.

"How'd the scouting mission go?" Melvin asked in a sleazy voice, and Ann gave him the finger.

"I could draw you a diagram," Joseph said thoughtfully, yelping himself when Ann pinched his cheek.

"Seriously, seriously," Lieutenant demanded.

"I mean, it's kinda hard to get to," Joseph said honestly. "We're gonna hafta be careful if we wanna get back inside our houses without 'em noticin' dirt and mud and shit on our clothes."

"We've been able to do that so far," Toni reminded them. "I don't know ... are we all planning to swim in it?"

"We gotta scope it out," Lieutenant asserted. "If we could do it without dyin' or collapsin', I'd say try it, just to see how far across it is."

"I don't think anyone knows how deep it really is," Melvin said. "Nobody really visits it much. It's not like a scenic spot or anything." He turned to Ann. "Katrina would probably know about it. She probably did experiments there."

"I'll see if I can get anything out of her about it," Ann confirmed.

"Care-ful-ly," Lieutenant emphasized. "We gotta be so sly about this shit."

"Never let your right hand know what your left is doing," Charlie muttered, backing into one of the more shadowed corners of the house. "The game will be up if she catches us, but if she *thinks* she has caught us, well, it can go on and on, the show, throwing down, yes ... yes ..."

"Charlie? Are you okay?"

The skinny girl continued to mutter in a low, unintelligible voice, bumping her shoulder lightly against the wall. Toni cautiously stepped towards her friend and put a hand on her thin back. Charlie jerked away, her eyes wide and terrified.

"Charlie, it's just me," Toni said slowly. Behind her, Ann shifted, and Joseph looked away.

"Just me," Charlie repeated, cocking her head and peering at Toni's round face as if deciphering some foreign script. "Me ... Toni!" Charlie blurted out brightly, her face fairly alight with pride in the dark. Toni had to dig her nails into her own wrist to keep from screaming. "Yes, it's me. Your friend."

"Friend." Charlie nodded and crept over to play with Toni's abundant curls, smiling wide like an entertained child, her cracked lips bleeding at the edges.

"We have got," Toni said, forcing her words through gritted teeth, trying not to shock the fragile girl twisting her dark hair with dirty fingers, "to get out of here."

"We gotta move carefully. We rushed last time, and look how that turned out. I ain't havin' Seth get the last word on me again."

Toni winced inwardly, and Lieutenant turned at the sound of the deeper voice, looking her friend up and down. "Anton?"

Anton nodded, his dark, veiled expression and half-hooded eyes so different from Anthony's wide-eyed look and easy grin. "Yeah."

"How does that . . . work?" Ann questioned, leaning into Joseph, who rubbed her shoulder while scanning the tall boy. "I just . . . Anthony was just here. Now he's gone. Is there a . . . system, you guys use, ya know? I mean, who decides who . . . comes out, and when?"

Anton shifted, folding his arms and gnawing on his tongue as he considered. "I talk to Anthony sometimes . . . I know most a' what he knows. Sometimes he'll tell me what's goin' on with the . . . others, sometimes not."

"So . . . where are you when you're not . . . here?" Joseph asked, feeling Ann's heart rate increase in time with his own. The floor-boards creaked as the members of the group shifted in their respective spots. The wind whistled through the cracks in the walls, stinging their faces.

"At school," Anton answered. "At my supervisor's house. Here with y'all."

"No, I mean . . . when *you're* not here," Joseph said, almost unable to finish the question. "You know, when you're — "

"I know what you mean," Anton cut him off. Charlie trembled, her fingers slipping from Toni's curls and moving to pick at her own ears. "I'm tellin' you," Anton said. "I'm here. I'm at school. I am wherever I am, and then I'm . . . somewhere else here. At the school, and then out here. In my bed, then at the gym." Anton's black and white eyes ran through each member of the group. "I still don't get how y'all take so long to tell me and Anthony apart. We ain't look anythin' alike."

Lieutenant's thick, rapid breathing was audible to everyone.

"So . . . are you like . . . the one in charge?" Melvin broached, rubbing his red nose and sniffing casually. "The head personality?"

Anton pursed his lips and shrugged. "Guess so. Ain't been too many blackouts since I been here. I know all of y'all, I can figure my way through class . . ." He shrugged again.

"What about Antoine?"

Toni heard her voice, overly loud, practically echoing around the collapsing house. "You know, Antoine. He's your original name. That means he's the host personality. Where is he?"

Anton rubbed his hands together, smoothed his knuckles, and threaded and unthreaded his fingers. "He ain't here."

"He has to be," Toni insisted, taking a step forward and causing Charlie to emit a sad low sound and slink off into the corner. "He's the host, your real name."

"He's gone, Toni."

"Maybe you've never "met" him, but —"

"I met him, but he's gone," Anton said definitively. Toni put up her hands. "Okay, okay, I didn't mean to push . . ."

"Push? Push?" Anton's voice rose.

"I'm not —"

"*She* pushed. She pushed him down the stairs." Anton's eyes moved back and forth as if seeing the scurrying of rats upon the decomposing floorboards, his hands still clenching and unclenching. "Had him cleanin' the bathroom floor with a toothbrush. Kept him at it for hours, so your boy got tired. Stopped. She —" Anton motioned over his shoulder with one large, unsure hand, his face tight and drawn, struggling. "She came at him from behind. Picked him up and threw him down the stairs. Almost cracked his head open, 'cept there was full laundry basket at the bottom. She followed him, dragged him out, dragged him down to the door in the floor . . ." Anton spread his hands out over the floorboards to indicate its width as he stood. "She took him down, and I couldn't stop her . . . I remember the screamin' and then . . ."

Anton looked up, eyes wide with revelation, his chest heaving. The others waited, leaning forward, for him to finish.

"What?" Toni asked at last. "What then?"

"He stopped." Anton let his hands fall and dropped down into a crouch, placing his elbows on his knees and his head in his arms. "He was just gone."

"So is that why Antoine don't come out?" Joseph questioned, looking to Toni for confirmation. Anton shook as he chuckled. When he looked up, Charlie let out a rattling, scared moan.

"No," she supplied. "That's not why. He can't ever come out."

"But he's the first," Toni argued. "The host personality, the original. He's the whole reason this happened. People develop this disorder to try and protect the mind from all the pain. Antoine is the one who's suppose to be protected. He's the center identity, he's —"

"Dead, Toni," Anton declared, his voice as hollow as his statement. "Antoine is dead. That's why he don't come out." He stood, taking a step forward and looking down the faces of his friends with raw eyes. "She killed him, that night, down in the room under the floor. It was more'n he could take, and we couldn't get there in time. She killed Antoine, and now we the only ones left."

"Oh." Toni crossed her arms allowing Charlie to nuzzle into her side, ignoring the other girl's unpleasant smell. "I'm sorry. That's just . . . different."

"Makes sense though, don't it?" Joseph offered. "I mean, all of us are wrong and weird somehow, right? Why wouldn't our own fuckin' illnesses not obey the rules as well?"

remember

"WOULD YOU PASS THE MILK, ANN?"

"Sure, Kit-Kat. Here ya go."

Katrina smiled broadly as Ann passed her the milk carton over the small vase of sunflowers decorating the pinewood table. The sunlight streaming in through the frosty windows made Ann's tired, sensitive eyes ache though she grinned back. The two girls continued to give each other sweet, adoring looks until the ornery, oversized cat growled in the next room, and their supervisor, a portly, middle-aged woman named Lorena Fosset grunted and struggled against her own bulk to stand up and meander out of the kitchen to attend to it. Once Lorena's heavy steps were no longer audible, Katrina's smile dropped as if by the force of gravity.

"You're laying it on *way* too thick," she snapped at Ann, who rolled her eyes and tossed her blonde hair over her shoulder. Ann winced as the bruises from her last Discipline visit rubbed against the scratchy cotton of her ill-fitting blue sweater.

"C'mon, we're good little reformed angels — a credit to our totally awesome Academy," Ann reasoned, crunching her cereal with the curved end of her spoon. "Everyone smiles and gives each other cute nicknames here."

"The only one who gives me nicknames," Katrina began, dropping her voice and looking around to be certain their supervisor wouldn't hear, "is my boyfriend. You are not him, so please, refrain."

"Mmm-hmm," Ann responded, letting her lips spread into a seedy smile. "So, how are things in paradise?"

"Are we such good pals that we're sharing now?" Katrina asked skeptically, twisting her sun-kissed brown hair around her fingers and playing with the neckline of her pastel pink top. Ann wrinkled her nose against the onslaught of perfume and scented oils emanating from the older girl.

"Sure, why not?" Ann suggested wryly. "We're clearly more alike than we thought before. Maybe we're even similar when it comes to sex."

"It's not all sex," Katrina said instantly, her voice rising. Ann's eyes widened in warning, and Katrina clamped her mouth shut. Both girls waited, completely alert, for any sign that Lorena had heard them. After a few minutes, Ann sighed and resumed grinning slyly at the lean, carefully made up girl opposite her.

"Oh, don't tell me there isn't sex." Ann scoffed, crossing one leg over the other and winking across the table. "You're the one lending me the pills."

"I didn't say there wasn't sex, just that it isn't everything," Katrina mumbled, and when she blushed Ann's smile became less of a sneer and more of a soft, answering grin.

"Yeah." Ann nodded, flicking the fringe at the edges of her placemat with slightly shaking fingers. "Yeah, that's true."

Katrina's eyes shot up and narrowed, her look hawkishly appraising. "Huh."

Ann shifted, and glared back, going on the defensive immediately. "What?"

"You actually love him, don't you?"

Ann's stomach tightened as if readying for a blow, and she tried not to regurgitate her breakfast. "Is that such a shock to you?" she snapped as quietly as possible. "The big town slut might actually have feelings for someone? Is it funny, or something?"

"*No.* I wasn't even thinking of that. God, everything is always so extreme with you," Katrina noted. "I was just asking."

Ann bit back another nasty reply, fighting against her ingrained response to go on the offensive to release the tension building in her body through a violent screaming match. "Okay, okay. Sorry," she said, as roughly and nonchalantly as possible. Katrina waved it away, and went back to working on her toast. Ann took a sip of her orange juice, laid her glass carefully to her right side, and leaned forward on her elbow. "I actually ... we're thinking we need to find new places to meet. Change it up so they have less of a chance of catching us."

Katrina gave her a sidelong glance and continued to chew as she listened. "Uh-huh?"

Ann rubbed at the edges of her porcelain bowl, letting the condensation stick to her forefinger. "We wanted to find a place where we could be loud without ... ya know, the obvious consequences." She moved her soggy leftover cereal from one end of the bowl to the other with her spoon. "We were thinking of swimming across the lake and trying out the other side."

Katrina hiccuped, swallowed her toast, and grabbed her glass of water. Grasping it with one hand and holding a finger up toward Ann with the other, she finished with a gasp and shook her head. "No. That would be a stupid fucking idea."

"Language," Ann reminded her, and Katrina laid both her palms flat on the table, her french-manicured nails almost touching Ann's arms.

"No, seriously. Not only would you probably die of hypothermia and drown trying to get across, but that lake is ... I mean, c'mon, you've lived here all your life. No one goes to Lake Amiszi."

"Yeah, and people here don't rock climb or throw orgies," Ann dismissed. "This place is boring."

"It's more than that," Katrina continued, her eyes alight now. "There's no fish in that lake — at least not any we could find. The plants that grow around there shouldn't in this area. There's no birds, and the only animals that don't avoid it are frogs, and the frogs don't even ..."

"So, you've studied it?" Ann prompted. Katrina shook her head, delicately brushing a strand of straightened hair from her eyes.

"Not nearly enough. We still don't understand what the hell is wrong with it. It's like it's a dead lake, only not. And there's gases coming from that area, and the water . . ."

"The water . . . ?"

"It was weird," Katrina declared, pursing her lips into an expression Ann had never seen before. *I guess this is her 'science genius face'*, Ann reckoned. *It's kinda like the one Joseph has when he's drawing, or Charlie when she's plotting. Or, well, just about all of our friends have one except me and maybe Melvin.*

"Just stay away," Katrina was saying, and Ann refocused. "Nobody understands what is up with that lake, not even the Headmistress, and if she doesn't know, I'm definitely not gonna risk it. If you wanna try, go ahead, but I don't think I have a pill for whatever might happen after."

"Duly noted," Ann agreed, hiding the thrilling surge of excitement and fear running up and down her spine. "That's really important to know."

I can do this. I can. Put your poker face on, Toni. No, not even that — believe it. Believe you have nothing to be ashamed of, and nothing to hide.

Toni slid into the seat next to Seth with as much nonchalance as she could muster, placing her books down neatly on the library table, and pulling out her history notes. The blonde senior beside her continued carefully copying from the large reference book in front of him, every now and then swinging his head to push a strand of hair away from his eyes. Toni cast him multiple quick, subtle looks for over ten minutes before finally turning to her own work.

"You know, a very, very small part of me almost thought you wouldn't come."

Toni's eyes flicked up and over, but Seth frowned, and she turned back to her notes. Around them the library buzzed with the low hum of hushed chatter as students studied, read, or worked on projects together. The loudest discernible noise in the building was the printer as it emitted pages for a line of students. Carefully modulating her voice so that it wouldn't carry, Toni rested an elbow on the desk and, twirling one of her full curls, whispered back, "Yes, I'm sure there are some very, very small parts of you."

"Oh, touché," Seth whispered back, surprising Toni with his genial response to her rough attack on his manhood. "See?" he said out of the corner of his mouth, picking up on Toni's train of thought, "I can appreciate some spice in a girl."

"I didn't come to flirt," Toni said shortly. "I —" She fell silent as another student passed their table, waiting until he was a ways down the nearest book aisle before barely mouthing, "I just came to find out what you actually meant before."

"Oh, I think you know," Seth answered, lifting a page of the reference book with a ringed finger and squinting at the lines of text. "What you want to know is how I plan on doing it."

"Okay, fine," Toni replied, scratching her right ankle against the leg of her chair. "How do you?"

Toni could almost feel Seth's smile next to her like the bite of a sharp breeze. "I don't really think we should discuss it here."

"I hope you don't think I'm running out to meet you somewhere at night to discuss it," Toni shot back.

"How would we do that, with all the cameras?" Seth probed silkily. Toni's nerves screamed, and she had to jam her toes into the carpeted floor to release some energy and give herself time to compose her face and lie.

"I assumed you would have a way," Toni said, retracing some of the letters in her notes so that she would still appear to be focused should anyone be watching. "You're the one trying to tell me you can break us out."

"Was I?" Seth taunted. "What a big jump to make, Miss White."

Toni rolled her eyes and started pulling her notes back into a stack. "You know what? Thank you for confirming what an awful idea this is, really. Clearly this is just a replay of last time, with you playing the entrapping cop."

Now please, take the bait, take it, don't let me leave . . .

"Wait." Seth put his hand down over the edge of her notes.

Thank you.

"What?" Toni said, but she was already sinking back into her chair.

"So much hostility," Seth whispered morosely. "What do I need to do to earn a little trust?"

"I would say you could try honesty, but I think your skin might sizzle with the effort."

"We can get out of here," Seth said, his baritone deep with seriousness. "You and me. If we work together, we can get out of here, away from this school, and into the wide blue yonder."

Toni pushed away the shame she felt at the gleeful skip in her chest. "Just you and me?"

"Just you and me."

"No one else?"

"No, of course not."

"Of course not?" Toni asked. "Why of course not? Why not anybody else?"

"Your *friends* —" Seth said the two words with utter disdain and pity. "Your friends, I'm sorry to say, are not invited. They would be . . . liabilities."

"Liabilities?" Toni bristled. "How?"

"Let's just count the ways." Seth laughed caustically, ticking them off on his fingers. "Your little friend Charlie is schizo and would probably break down, start screaming about the devil coming after us, and get us caught before we got ten miles away. Lieutenant plays it like she's together, but she'd snap under the pressure and throw a manic fit. Anton — " Seth paused to smother giggles. "Anton might run off and turn into Ant or who-the-fuck-knows-else and tell the Headmistress again, and Melvin is already half-way into his own grave without any help from me."

"What about Joseph?" Toni fielded. Seth's handsome face contorted, and Toni had to force herself not to pull away at his brief, violent expression.

"Joseph?" Seth snorted. "C'mon, even if he was willing to travel with me, he can't last in the outside world. This school is just the last stop between him and prison. He's lucky to be here. Ann might've been good to have, once, but now she's panting after him like a bitch in heat," he noted disgustedly.

"She loves him," Toni felt compelled to reply. Seth turned to give her a cruel, winning half-grin.

"Yeah, well, we all have our faults. I'm trying not to judge."

Toni bit her lip, and looked down, becoming very interested in her shoes. *Here goes nothing.*

"So do you actually have a plan to get out, or not?"

Seth scowled, irritated. "No, but between the two of us I figured we could concoct something that might work. We almost managed it before."

Yeah, before you betrayed us like a sniveling, fucking, two-faced—

"The lake."

"Huh?"

Toni rumpled the edges of her notes, the crinkling sound of the paper nearly drowning out her words. "We could cross the lake, couldn't we? They'd expect us to use the roads going away from the town, but if we swim the lake we'd throw off the scent of dogs, and soon we'd be practically in the mountains, and then we could make a run for the border. I mean, across the lake is north, right?"

Toni stopped talking, her heart racing, worried that her voice might have risen. She cast a glance around the room, checking to see if anyone appeared to have heard her. Seth was quiet at her side for another few minutes.

"That is an idea," Seth said at last, and Toni tried to keep her relief from her face. "Yeah, maybe. We'd have to find a way to get out there. And we'd be taking a chance if we went through the mountains. Plus, we have to get past border patrol ..." Seth played with a chunk of the reference book as he mused.

"But it's a possibility, right?" Toni prompted.

"Oh, definitely," Seth replied, his cold blue eyes searching out her own hazel-green ones. "Yeah. It's an idea."

C'mon, c'mon . . . s'almost twelve fifteen, girl. Dammit, where is you? Joseph scanned the cafeteria again, white-knuckling his tray as he searched for Ann and practically jumping at any glimpse of blonde hair. Students milled around, whispering, laughing, scraping plastic utensils against Styrofoam plates. Aides patrolled the aisles, and every now and then a teacher would escort a class into the dining hall or usher another out.

Fuck it Ann, don't tell me you got in trouble again, please.

"Maybe you'd better sit down."

"Maybe I —" Joseph bit back his sharp response when he recognized the subtle, drawling voice. He swallowed hard as he slipped into the bench besides the muscular black girl.

"Checkin' for Blondie?" Lieutenant asked out of the corner of her mouth, stirring her soup with her left hand as her right rapidly scrawled words haphazardly across an already full page.

"Ooh, Debbie Harry," Melvin mused, a rare smile making an appearance on his wide face. "If I was straight, that's the kinda woman I could go hard for."

"Well we should all praise Jesus you gay then," Lieutenant muttered, grinning at Melvin's supremely offended look.

"We probably shouldn't be sittin' together," Joseph murmured, tearing into a crust of French bread with his hands. "Right?"

Lieutenant shrugged, her braided hair swinging as she rolled up the sleeves of the white shirt she wore under her drab black sweater in an attempt to make the outfit more stylish. "Headmistress already knows we up to somethin'. She'll just assume we're plottin', and she'll be right."

"Yeah, I guess," Joseph acquiesced, pursing his lips and crumbling up the bread in his left hand.

"You . . . and Ann. Did you have another fight?" Melvin broached delicately, turning his fork and biting into a soggy glazed carrot when Joseph's amber eyes shot up.

"Fight? Nah, no. We're fine. It's all good."

Lieutenant nodded. Melvin nodded.

"Seriously, it's fine you guys," Joseph asserted.

"Sure," said Lieutenant.

"Of course," said Melvin.

Joseph bit the inside of his cheek. "We're good, okay? Yeah, we fight a lot, that's us. It's whatever. She's just got . . ." He rubbed his palms against his jeans. "Just got . . ."

"Issues?" said Melvin and Lieutenant.

Joseph gave a brief, wry laugh. "Yeah."

"Well, but I mean, we've *all* got issues," Melvin pointed out. "It's kinda the whole deal here. As a group we pack some serious, high-level damage."

"Yeah, but . . ." Joseph shook his head. "Nuthin', nuthin'."

"But what?" Lieutenant asked kindly. "C'mon, we're all friends here."

"Yeah, exactly," Joseph responded with the speed of someone releasing something long held inside. "We're friends. And she's my . . . what isn't she tellin' me? Why *can't* she tell me?"

Lieutenant chewed on her thick lower lip, resting her elbow on the table. "I don't know. What do you think she isn't telling you?"

Joseph's smile was raw and knowing. "C'mon you guys. We're friends 'member? I ain't the smartest person in our little Scooby gang, but I'm not an idiot neither. Help me out here. I —" He swallowed, the veins in his throat constricting painfully. "I'm scared for her."

Lieutenant sucked at her teeth, head weaving as she deliberated. "I mean . . . what specifically is the thing you're worried about? I mean, Ann's always been Ann. Is she gettin' worse? Less blonde bombshell, more . . ."

"Bombshell?" Melvin offered. Lieutenant tried to keep her eyes from hitting her forehead as she rolled them, but nodded. "Yeah, that."

"She's throwin' herself in their faces," Joseph explained, his voice lowering so that the others needed to lean in to hear. "Fightin' other kids, attackin' aides ... she's covered in shock burns, and she don't even tell me half the time why she's gettin' 'em. It's like she's ..." He wrung his hands, tongue running over his teeth as he searched for the words.

"Punishing herself."

Lieutenant and Joseph turned in unison to Melvin, who was folding his arms over his ample chest.

"You got an insight, Dr. Stavos?" Lieutenant prompted.

"I didn't really know her before high school," Melvin began, chipping away at the edge of his Styrofoam plate with the tines of his fork. "I would just see her around sometimes, but it was *always* with her sister. I think her name is Callie. They were inseparable. They'd even do the matching outfits thing some-times, like they were twins. By middle school Ann was already getting her —" Melvin winced in advance at Joseph's reaction. "Um, *reputation*, but Callie seemed to be just a normal kid. I think Ann was really protective of her. I ... don't know if she's been able to see her since being put into STARE."

"Fuck," Joseph swore, pressing the cross tattoo on the inside of his wrist. "She hasn't. I know she hasn't. Damn it. She told me before that she felt guilty 'bout leavin' her sister there. Shit, and I been askin' her 'bout family like it was nuthin.' Now I really wish I wouldn't a' did that. I'm so fuckin' stupid." Joseph nearly brought his fist down on the table, only abandoning the action with effort. "*Fuck.*"

"She's runnin'," Lieutenant confirmed, fiddling with her dog tags. "Shit's bad at home, and she wants to get out, but lil' sis gets left ... she's runnin' from hurt *and* guilt. That's deep."

"So what do I do?" Joseph pressed his thumbs to his temples. "How do I get her to stop?"

Lieutenant sighed. "You ain't gonna like the answer, Smart One."

"I'm a semi-grown man," Joseph asserted. "Hit me."

"Look, I've been there," Lieutenant reasoned. "I didn't want to admit I was . . . sick like I am, for a long time. I wanted to go places, and I didn't need this holdin' me back. I had enough to deal with family-wise. I had to end up on the floor of a jail cell for a night before I just gave up and accepted what I had. It looks like Ann's got the same deal. She's gonna keep rammin' her head into that brick wall until she hits brain, unless she can face up to what's ridin' her."

"So what do I do?"

Lieutenant looked at Melvin, and Melvin looked back at the boy with the pleading, amber eyes.

"I don't know, doll," Melvin said helplessly. "All I can say is to be there for her."

Joseph suppressed a growl. "That's not enough."

"She loves you," Lieutenant said, placing a hand on his shoulder and squeezing quickly. "Trust me — it's enough."

These hands aren't mine.

Charlie spread out her fingers, eyeing the short, dirty nails and red joints distrustfully. *How do I keep them from knowing that I know they replaced them?* Charlie bit her lip, trying to think through the fog of strangeness, to hear her inner dialogue over the symphony of whispers crowding her brain. *I must keep the secret. As long as they don't catch on, I can stall them.*

"Charlie? Would you mind helping me with the dishes?"

Charlie stared at Mrs. Carter's elegantly made-up face, the older woman's burgundy lipstick drawing Charlie's gaze as she tried to uncover the secret significance of her wearing so dark a color. "No. I don't mind. Mind . . . I don't, you know. I would really, but my hands aren't my own, you know, and I can't get them to do what I want anymore. They don't listen."

Mrs. Carter opened her disapproving mouth to speak, and Charlie tensed up, her half-emaciated body preparing with what little strength it could muster. "Shocks, shocks, she will be punished," whispered the voices. If Charlie's hands had been her own she would have clapped them over her ears to keep out the mocking sound.

The burgundy lips twitched. Mrs. Carter's chest rose and fell deeply under her navy button-down shirt. Charlie winced at the grating sound as the principal pulled out the chair on the opposite side of the kitchen table and sat across from her.

"Your hands still seem to be attached to your body, Charlie," Mrs. Carter said calmly, her own laced together and resting firmly on the soft, blue-and-white cotton tablecloth.

"They do, but seeming doesn't make it so," Charlie answered earnestly. "They did things I would never approve of, that's the rub, it is, really, really. I couldn't stop them, I was ordered."

Mrs. Carter raised one well-trimmed brow. "Ordered? Ordered to do what?"

"To press buttons. To write answers to questions. To touch things and do things . . ."

"Charlie." Mrs. Carter spoke in a voice that Charlie, until now, had only ever heard the principal use towards her own daughter. "I know sometimes you may think and feel things that to you seem real. But what you have to try and remember is that these things cannot harm you. You are safe here."

Charlie ground her teeth together to keep from laughing in the woman's face. "I'm not safe. Never safe. They took my hands, and now I don't know what these ones will do. They don't do what I tell them!"

"If you are hearing voices but you cannot see them, then it is a good way to know you should not be listening to them," Mrs. Carter said, tapping her forefinger on the table.

"But I do see them," Charlie said, blinking. "The voices don't tell me what to do. She does."

Mrs. Carter's brow furrowed. "She? What do you mean?"

"She tells me what to do," Charlie continued, her eyes drifting, micro-expressions that had no apparent connection to the blank tone of her voice flitting across her face every few seconds. "She tells me where to put my hands, what to say, what is needed for science."

"Charlie, who are you talking about?"

"And then she has her take it all down, notes, notes, notes," Charlie pressed on, her hands gliding back and forth over the table cloth like tentative spider's legs. "All for the sake of science. And so I have to do the experiments, you know."

"Charlie, who conducts these experiments?"

"If I tell she will be most displeased, seized, I'll be brought to my knees, the bee's knees, the crux of the issue, the heart of the problem, the problems calls for —"

"Charlie!"

Charlie's dazed eyes rolled unsteadily back to meet the intense, demanding ones of the principal. "I can't tell you."

"Who orders these experiments?" Mrs. Carter inquired urgently, hunched forward, her steady demeanor quite gone. "Hmm? Charlie? Who has you perform these experiments?"

"Can't tell you, I can't. Consequences, actions will be taken . . ."

"What has she made you do?" Mrs. Carter's voice was sharp now, her nails rasping at the tablecloth and pulling it towards her. "What happens in these experiments? Where does she perform them?"

"She'll know if I tell." Charlie nodded, almost sagely, at the nearly undone woman across the table. "She'll know."

"I need to know. If she's hurting you . . ."

"It all goes in the file. All of it. Every little thing, your thoughts, your reactions . . ."

"Wendy, Mrs. Waters?" Mrs. Carter grasped. "She's there too, isn't she? She takes the notes?"

"We're all in her files," Charlie said, voice lilting as if she was losing focus. "All of us."

"Where are these experiments taking place? When? What does she have you do?"

"The files have all the information. The nanobots send her signals."

"Charlie, answer the question, please."

"Your file is probably full of questions too."

"I — my file?"

Charlie let her head drop to the left to rest on her shoulder, half of her unevenly growing hair draping across her face. "It was almost as big as mine. I know it's full of questions and answers, graphs and drafts. They can interpret the signals, we wouldn't understand, that's why we can't see."

"Where is this file? What do you mean by 'mine'?" Mrs. Carter's bottom lip jutted forward and the table itself seemed to be preventing her rigid body from lunging forward to shake the young teen into giving more coherent answers.

"Your name was right there," Charlie said, not meeting the hungry eyes that tried to seek her out. "Evelyn Carter. Printed and packaged. All clear."

"Where? Where was this file? When did you see it?"

"In the morning . . . in the evening . . . I don't remember."

"*You —*"

Charlie face remained impassive but her body cowered as the principal shot to her feet. The dark-haired woman paused in her fury at the sight of the trembling teen below her with her ankles wrapped around the leg of her chair as if she feared being dragged away.

"It's all right, Charlie," Mrs. Carter said, closing her eyes and smoothing down her bangs as she composed herself. "I'm not angry with you. Why don't you go . . . wash your hands?"

Charlie peeked through her hair at the principal and nodded, once, twice, almost rodent-like, before shuffling to her feet and making her way over to the sink. Fumbling at the faucet, she thrust her hands under the cold water and willed herself to wake up and dissect the exchange which had just occurred.

"You did it, now didn't you?" said one of the mocking voices which always sounded as if it was coming through an old Dictaphone. "Now she thinks the Headmistress and Mrs. Waters have files on her. Now she's scared like you are. What a dirty game to play, fit for a dirty, rotten little swine like you."

"Shut up," Charlie whispered, splashing her hands in the water to distract herself from the mocking laughter that she couldn't turn off.

"Liar. Liar, liar, liar . . ."

"Am not," Charlie mumbled once Mrs. Carter's heels had clicked away into another room, and the sound of a door slamming confirmed she was alone. "I am not."

Oh, but am I? Am I lying? Charlie's head swum and the strangeness seemed to overwhelm her, like a menacing sort of déjà vu. She tried to recall which of the things she'd said was true, and which was simply her part of the plan to set Mrs. Carter against the Headmistress by weaving suspicion between the two women. *Am I lying? Or am I telling the truth? Or is the truth telling me? Maybe it's a living thing, just like us?*

Maybe just like us, it wants out.

"Leeches. Fuckin' leeches. I swear to God, if I come outta here with my ass covered in leeches . . ."

"Calm down, Anthony. Trust me, I have spent quality time in this water, and, look, here I am, completely leech free."

Anthony stared Joseph down, his stern expression intermittently visible in the patches of moonlight glinting off the quiet lake. "I'ma hold you to that, 'cause if I come outta here with even one of them things on me . . ."

"I ain't pullin' leeches off your ass, man." Joseph laughed. "Sorry, but we ain't that close."

Anthony turned to Lieutenant with puppy-dog eyes, and the tall girl snorted. "Uh-uh," she refused, folding her muscular arms over her chest, her dog tags rattling. "Don't you look at me with that face. Everybody deals with their own little bloodsuckers. I ain't pickin' bugs off of anyone else's parts. No, no, no."

"Leeches aren't so bad," Charlie mused, wiggling her toes in the cold mud at the water's edge. "They're hermaphrodites, you know. Little girl leeches are also little boy leeches. They still use them in medicine sometimes, for microsurgeries." Anthony shivered all over, and Lieutenant winced.

"Don't say that. Please don't say that," Lieutenant pleaded, putting a palm over Charlie's mouth. The little girl crossed her eyes trying to stare at it. "We already got one kinda bug in us, don't give our dear Academy any more ideas. Last thing we need is them borrowin' more ideas from the fuckin' Victorian era."

"I don't *think* there are leeches in here," Ann considered, her gaze sweeping out over the wide, dark body of water as a few strands of blonde hair escaped her tight ponytail to swing in the fine, cold breeze. "But then we didn't really go that far before."

"Oh, I'm pretty damn sure we went all the way before," Joseph bragged, smirking over at Ann with hooded eyes. She cupped a hand around her right ear and bit the tip of her tongue, as if listening.

"What's that? You never, ever want to have sex again? Hmm, that seems drastic."

"Aw, don't be mad," Joseph cooed, hopping through the mud to wrap his arms around Ann from behind and burrowing his face into her neck. "See, I promise if you get covered in leeches, I'll pick 'em all off for you."

"That is real love, right there," Toni noted, trying to remind herself that mud was supposed to be good for the skin, as she felt herself sinking in almost to her ankles.

"I love all you dolls just fine, but when it comes down to creepy crawlies with no spines, it's every man for himself," Melvin informed them all, tossing his head.

"Gee, I feel so much more confident 'bout doin' this wit' y'all now," Joseph deadpanned. "This can only end well."

"If we're gonna do it, we gotta do it now," Lieutenant asserted, eyes narrowed with determination as she surveyed the expansive lake. "We gotta give ourselves plenty of time to make it across."

"So..." Melvin whistled. "This will require us to all be naked, yes?"

Lieutenant rolled her eyes. "My Jesus. Yes, our clothes do

have to come off."

"Everybody just turn around, and let's go one by one," Anthony suggested helpfully, demonstrating by turning around and covering his eyes. "Down the line, and you call out when you're in the water."

"Be honest," Lieutenant threatened as she turned her back. "If I get blinded, I will hunt you down by smell alone."

Charlie turned around with the others, and then realized she was first. "Oh ... okay." She looked down to her feet and then remembered that they'd already removed their socks. They'd placed them at the edge of the woods, a precaution against tracking back any tell-tale mud. She swallowed, pulling off her shirt and pants with trembling hands. "Where do I put these things so I, um ... we don't want them to get dirty ..." *Dirty, unclean, filthy, bury yourself in the mud like the worm you are, leech, leech, there's been a breach!*

"Toss them to me, FunSize," Ann offered. Charlie complied, and Ann caught the pair of baggy black pants and grey sweatshirt as they soared over her head. She threw them the extra foot to the grassy clearing at the edge of the woods. There was a splash and then a yelp.

"Charlie? You okay, Tiny?" Anthony questioned.

"Yesss," Charlie hissed through rattling teeth, moving her pained limbs through the water in an attempt to keep from going numb. "I'm in!"

"My turn," Ann announced. "None of you had better turn around."

"Oh no. Oh dear. Oh God. Whatever will I do? I am missin' out on so much," Joseph stated robotically. "How will I live when I cannot see something I have so clearly never seen before?"

He felt warm breath contrast with his cold neck and bit back a yelp of his own when something wet and hot which was definitely not a leech, brushed his shoulder. "It must be really, really hard for you," Ann purred.

"Always for you," Joseph whispered back, and Melvin and

Lieutenant groaned.

"Get in that damn water," Anthony said, cackling. Ann and Joseph muffled the sounds of their laughter with each other's mouths as they pulled off their clothes. They tossed them aside and dove into the icy lake.

"Make sure all of your eyes are closed," Toni requested self-consciously, pulling off her sweater quickly. Her sensitive body protested when she started on her underwear. "Nobody needs to see all of this hanging out and have nightmares."

"You shut up," Lieutenant ordered flatly. "You are a beautiful, hot, sexy mama. None of these idiots *deserves* to see you, that's true, but I won't have any of my people gettin' down on themselves for no reason."

"Not in your squad, huh commander?" Melvin teased.

"You damn right," Lieutenant confirmed. There was a gentler sound as Toni made her way into the water up to her neck. "Mel, your turn."

"Shit, shit, shit it's fucking cold!" Melvin pulled his clothes off and hurled them away as quickly as possible. "I am ashamed of nothing!" he decreed as he plunged into the lake.

"You next, L."

"I can count, Anthony. Van, two, three, ah, ah, ah, remember?"

"Okay, okay!" The tall boy threw up his right hand, his left clamped over his eyes as Lieutenant disrobed and grinned. "Yo ... you ever think maybe some kid watchin' *Sesame Street* saw The Count and thought the number after three was actually 'ah, ah, ah'?"

"No, I think that was just you."

"Hey, be careful of my tender feelings." Anthony pouted as Lieutenant scurried over to lay her clothes down neatly on her shoes.

"Be careful of your tender head. I think it's been dropped one too many times," Lieutenant mumbled as she headed for the water.

"Yeah, you probably right 'bout that one," Anthony acknowledged as he undid his belt, shimmied out of his pants, and yanked off his sweater and T-shirt. "A'ight, if your eyes ain't closed, it ain't my fault what'chu see!"

"Wait, if everyone's eyes are closed, how will we know if—"

Toni and Ann shrieked, Joseph laughed, and Charlie yipped as the wave made by Anthony's entrance sent her wheeling out into deeper waters.

"Whoa, whoa! A wild Charlie is headed out to sea," Melvin commented.

"We all are," said a decisive voice. Lieutenant glanced over at the boy wading beside her and raised a regal brow. "Anton?"

Anton nodded. "Yes, ma'am. You gonna debrief us?" Lieutenant held his gaze for a few minutes before swimming out in front of the others.

"Everybody stay together," she instructed, water churning around her as she worked to keep her head afloat. "Last thing we need is for anybody to get lost at the bottom of Applegate Lagoon. We make for the opposite bank. We got a path from the moon, so let's head out."

"We're following you," Melvin answered, and when Lieutenant pivoted in the water and thrust forward with a steady breast stroke, the rest of the group did the same.

For a few minutes the only sounds as the little band make its way across the lake were the water brushed aside by their strokes and the sound of chattering teeth as they fought back the cold.

"Yo," Joseph said, coughing a little with the water in his mouth. "Ain't it better if we put our heads under?"

"You wanna try that, go for it," Lieutenant offered. "I am not gettin' my hair any wetter than I have to."

"Really?" Ann dove under the water and came up, shaking out her wet ponytail like a mermaid. "It feels great."

"For you maybe." Lieutenant grunted. "I get pond water all up in my hair, it'll take me a hot minute to get it back to base."

"Exactly," Toni confirmed in between huffs of breath, her arm muscles prickling sharply as she used them to keep her head as far above water as much as possible. "Thus, my ponytail."

"I hate swimming. Can I just say that?" Melvin grumbled, his stroke smooth and powerful, despite his words, as he pulled abreast of Lieutenant and Anton. "The only place I could ever practice was at the YMCA, two towns over, and it was a cesspool."

"You mean to say that it *wasn't* fun to stay at the YMCA?" Ann questioned. Melvin flutter kicked in her direction, and she dove under again and swam closer to Joseph.

"Yo, any idea how many miles across this is?" Joseph posed, breathing heavily. Ann frowned.

"Are you okay?"

"Yeah, yeah, m'fine," he assured her. "Just wonderin'."

"Less than the miles it takes to walk around it," Toni supplied, twitching at what she hoped was nothing more than the waves from the others rubbing against her bare legs. "We get ... across this ... and we have a clear shot to Canada."

"That's all I need to know," Melvin murmured, speeding up and passing the others, his head bobbing in the moonlight.

"Wait — Charlie! Where's Charlie?" Ann asked suddenly. "Charlie? FunSize?"

"Don't yell. Sound carries over water," Lieutenant warned. "Charlie?" she whispered. "Everybody stop, now!"

The party came to a halt, and the teenagers whirled around in the water, desperately trying to locate their youngest member amidst the pitch black waves. "Charlie?"

With a splash the small girl emerged from the water, shaking her hair out like a dog, a brilliant grin visible on her face by the moonlight.

"Tiny, where were you?" Anton demanded.

"I can hold my breath for a really long time," Charlie volunteered.

"What the hell were you thinking?" Ann chastised. "We thought we'd fucking lost you!"

"But I was listening," Charlie explained. "There's nothing on the upper layers of the water — no fish, no turtles, no bugs. But if

176

I listen, I can hear other things even lower down. Not everything is dead in this lake."

The friends exchanged glances which they could barely register in the dark. "Let's get across this as fast as we can," Anton said finally. "Break."

They recommenced swimming in an uncomfortable quiet. "Yo." Joseph laughed, trying to liven up the mood. "If we really do —"

He broke off with a pained yell, grabbing at his chest and falling under the water.

"Joseph!"

Ann dove towards her boyfriend, propelling herself below the surface, and grabbing for him in the murky depths. Gasping, she shot to the surface, eyes wide with panic. "I can't find him!"

"Ann, wait —"

She dove beneath again, and Lieutenant growled as she forced herself down as well. The others whirled around in confusion and terror, blinking out into the dark.

The water bubbled, and then the three teens exploded to the surface, Lieutenant and Ann dragging Joseph by his arms, and fighting to stay above water.

"What is it? What happened?" Anton demanded. "Joseph? Joseph, you okay?"

"There's . . . something wrong with his heart," Ann gasped, balancing herself under Joseph's right arm with one hand on his back and the other over his chest. "It's beating weird. We gotta get him outta here, now."

Anton sized up the panting boy, lips blue at the edges, head lolling, and nodded to Lieutenant, who was situated under Joseph's other arm. "Okay, keep his head outta the water, and let's swim fast."

"You, you sh-should try and get him on his back," Toni recommended, her mouth nearly frozen with cold and panic. Ann nodded, and together with Lieutenant, they rolled until Joseph was floating on his back. He labored visibly for breath, and Ann swam hard, salty tears burning down her freezing cheeks.

"Joseph? Joseph, c'mon keep breathing, we're almost there. It'll be okay, just keep breathing, in and out, in and out . . ."

"What is it?" Melvin asked as they plowed on back towards the shore. "Is it hypothermia or something?"

"Maybe it's the pills," Charlie said. Her eyes were riveted to her gasping friend as she side-stroked. "They lower body temperature, and now we're in cold, cold water . . ."

"But then why . . . why didn't we collapse too?" Lieutenant panted, speaking with extreme effort when coupled with dragging a body through the water.

"His power." Toni spit out the water which kept finding its way down her throat. "It's about . . . temperature . . . it must have something to do with —"

"How the fuck do we fix it then?" Ann snapped, her voice high pitched and hysterical. "Guys, guys, I don't know if he's breathing . . ."

"We're almost there, Blondie," Melvin soothed. "Calm down . . ."

"Do not tell me to calm down!"

"You will calm down," Anton barked. "'Cause if we ain't calm, we're all gonna die, startin' with your boy." Ann's gaze was lethal, but she was too busy fighting for breath to fight back.

"Here . . . we're just about there," Charlie called out as she felt her feet touch the sandbank. Ann and Lieutenant doubled their efforts, and as soon as they could stand, they hauled Joseph to his feet and ran with him to land. The little pebbles and stones cut into their feet as they made for higher ground and then collapsed on the sand. Ann scrambled to the gasping, groaning prone figure.

"Joseph? Joseph, are you okay? God, you better not be dying, or I'll fucking kill you."

Joseph coughed, spat out some water, and then chuckled, breaking off in a whimper of pain. "Love . . . you too, baby," he murmured.

"If you can joke, it means you're going to be fine, and if you're going to be fine, it means you're ready for a slap for scaring me," Ann warned. The others crowded around, the sand sticking to their wet bodies. Anton knelt down near the other boy's head. "How you feelin'?" he inquired.

"Fuckin' awful," Joseph rasped. "My insides burn, my legs and arms is numb, and I got a naked man swingin' inches from my face."

Anton grinned. "Yeah, I think he ready for that slap now, Ann."

Ann glared fiercely, but her actual blow was light and quickly followed by a round of kisses.

"Okay, okay," Lieutenant cut in. "The boy needs heat, but you over stimulate him *that* way and his heart gon' explode right out his chest, and we get painted with his insides."

"Hey, it's my heart," Joseph countered. "I get to choose how I go."

"I'll go get his clothes," Toni offered, extracting herself from the huddle to run off and fetch them.

"Yes, I think clothes would be a good thing," Melvin deadpanned, and the others joined him in exhausted, relieved, awkward laughter.

"So . . . how far you think we got?" Joseph asked when Toni returned. Anton met the other boy's amber eyes, and then let his own travel slowly around the circle to lock with each and every one of the others.

"We made some progress. It's a start. Definitely a start."

CHAPTER THIRTEEN

FOCUS ON THE PLAN. IGNORE THE FLAW IN REALITY.

Speak, speak, speak...

"Charlie? Are you finished with your toast?"

Charlie looked up at Mrs. Carter's face, and even through the twist in the fabric of time, which made it seem as though she saw everything through warped glass, Charlie could see the signs of extreme stress in the principal; the drawn mouth, the bags under her eyes, the developing acne visible even through the heavily applied foundation.

"Finished." The word felt strange on Charlie's tongue, and it came to her that secret messages were trying to make themselves known, important causes of drastic events needed to be unraveled, and it was her job to see it done. *But why can't the anagram come clean? Finish, I shed, I shed fins, shine, dish ... fine, fine ...*

"Fine," Charlie said aloud, and felt a surge of glee at having come out with the right answer. Becky, Mrs. Carter's daughter and star J. Alter pupil, cleared her throat, neatly stacked her molasses-drenched plastic utensils on her plate of half-eaten French toast, and downed the last of the orange juice in her glass. "Mom, is it okay if I check my messages? It'll just take a second."

"Sure honey, go right ahead," Mrs. Carter allowed, and Charlie shrunk down closer to the table in an attempt to minimize her small size even more as the perfumed teenager passed.

"You don't need to be afraid of Becky," Mrs. Carter said with a touch of irritation, brushing some crumbs from the table into her hand and tossing them into the trash. "Good friends are an important way of staying grounded, which would help you very much."

Friends, friends ... remember the mission, and don't fuck it up, be subtle, be careful, be as sly as a mouse in a house full of traps ...

"She wouldn't want me telling you," Charlie whispered confidentially, glancing from side to side before leaning in closer to her supervisor. "But they were talking about you, and I thought you had a right to know. I know how bad it is to deal with people" — Charlie swallowed — "with people — people who whisper, and laugh, and pass little notes, and keep records, and don't let you ever see."

Charlie held herself as still as her overstimulated body would allow as Mrs. Carter stared her down, clearly attempting to discern if Charlie was speaking from madness or memory. Charlie's hands twitched, and she made no effort to stop them, all her energy concentrated on not letting the lies on her lips split her bedraggled mind even further apart.

"What exactly are you talking about Charlie?" Mrs. Carter asked with supreme composure, precisely picking a stray hair from her beige turtleneck.

"I couldn't tell what they said," Charlie said, her heart thumping shallowly against her thin breastbone, and a dull ache bothering her ribs. "But I knew it was about you. 'She might prove a problem,' that's what the scientist said, Mrs. You-Know-Who. 'I can handle her,' is how our redheaded lady responded. And I knew, I knew it was about you."

"Are you sure you heard what you thought you heard?" Mrs. Carter's voice was hard with icy control. "What makes you think they ... what you thought you heard was about me?"

"It wasn't in my head," Charlie promised. *Liar, liar, liar, set the heretic on fire.* "It was at a ... session, and they were hushed. They were talking about who might make them stop, about making sure she didn't find out what they were really up to, because she could put an end to it. And I knew it could only be you. You're the only one with that power."

Charlie had to bite her lower lip to keep from smiling as she watched her final words exact the desired effect. Mrs. Carter's expression softened, then became one of stern resolve. "Charlie, I think you should go and make sure you have packed all of your supplies properly into your back pack."

Charlie nodded, her sweaty palms almost unable to carry her plates to the dishwasher. *Don't drop them,* she pleaded with her hands, which she knew to be a part of the conspiracy. *I know you aren't my real hands. I know you're part of the second reality they want me to believe exists, a member of the Unreal Contingency, but please — don't give this all away. All of my friends are depending on me. I have to lay down the scent for Mrs. Carter to follow, and people are so much harder than dogs, you can't just wave a piece of clothing in their nose. I promise,* she thought at her hands as hard as possible as she doused her plates with steaming hot water, *I promise I'll keep your secret if you help me keep mine.*

Joseph touched the tip of his tongue to the side of his lip, concentrating. Bent over his desk, his right hand lay splayed out on his heavily corrected test, his left carefully copying letters as his amber eyes switched rapidly between the two. There was nothing odd about what he appeared to be doing. He was supposed to correct his test and deliver it back to Mrs. Waters before the end of class.

I'm just a good little student, makin' my corrections, and not at all copyin' my teacher's handwritin' for a forged note. Nope, nope, I'm good, I'm chill, I'm not suspicious at all.

Joseph traced the upturned end of Mrs. Waters lower case 'e' as steadily as he could manage. *Well, it ain't gonna fool the FBI or no shit like that,* he mused, narrowing his eyes as he tried to gauge the slope of his science teacher's *i. But if I can get our principal to buy it, then —*

Mrs. Waters stood up from her desk and stalked around the classroom, moving down the rows to inspect her students' work. Joseph slipped the yellow sticky note under his actual page of corrections. Mrs. Waters moved slowly down the line, peering intently, and frowning or smiling slightly depending on the content.

Shit, hurry up, Joseph swore inwardly, his right elbow boring into the edge of his desk, and his left hand scribbling and then erasing words, trying to conjure up an example of a naturally occurring sugar. *Just fuckin' get it over with, go back to your damn desk ...*

Mrs. Waters turned down the edge of one row of desks and up the other. Two students now separated her from Joseph. He could see her as a haze of tweed and orange nylon if he glanced behind him, out of the corner of his eyes.

No, man, don't look behind you. Focus on your work. You'll be fine. Agitated, he nearly ripped his paper with the force of his pencil strokes. *Hurry up, hurry up, hurry the fuck up!* Irritation was building into fury, anxiety furrowing his brow. He could sense a sharp twinge traveling up his right side, making its way to his chest.

Hurry up, God dammit, hurry up, hurry —

"Ah!" Joseph exclaimed, clasping a hand to his chest, clutching at his side.

"Joseph?" Mrs. Waters moved into his field of vision. "What's wrong?"

"Nuthin'," he forced himself to say, massaging his ribs. *Fuck no, not here.* "Nuthin', I'm fine."

"You should see the nurse."

"Nah, nah, just wanna finish my ... corrections." He smiled up at the older woman weakly, and her hook nose wriggled, the lines about her mouth creasing.

"You don't seem to have made much progress." She tapped his correction paper. Only a single, thin sheet prevented her from touching the yellow sticky note. Joseph bit the inside of his cheek, hard. "Are you sure you wouldn't be better able to concentrate if you went to the nurse?"

"No, really, I'm good. Just . . . just tryna finish before the time is up."

Mrs. Waters pushed her glasses up with her pinky and blinked between Joseph's taut face and his paper. "You had better hurry. Class is almost over." She gestured with her fine black pen toward the clock, and Joseph had to fight off another painful attack of panic.

Shit, she's right. She don't even know how right.

"I can do it," he assured her. Mrs. Waters raised her eyebrows skeptically, but continued on down the rows. Joseph felt as though his heart was waiting to beat between breaths as she moved away. He pulled his papers more towards the center of the desk and waited two whole precious minutes before pulling out the yellow sticky note again.

Don't rush it, he reminded himself as he slowly blocked out the final letters. *No point in rushin' and messin' up now. Make it work. Make it look real.*

He let out a low sigh of relief as he dotted the last period and slid the sticky note back under his corrections. He quickly filled in his final answers in time for the bell ring, and he shoved the note up under his long shirt sleeve. His muscles tight and sore with holding in all the tension of his masquerade, he deposited his test and corrections on Mrs. Waters desk beside her cherry red apple paperweight. He gave what he hoped was a non-committal, non-guilty, quick half-smile, and headed for the door.

"Mr. Valdez?"

Fuck no. Please fuckin' hell, no.

"Yeah?" He pivoted, swinging his backpack over his shoulder, his nails digging into the mesh fabric of its strap.

"I still think you should consider going to see the nurse."

Joseph nodded, his mouth dry, and the ache in his right side refusing to subside. "I honestly might do that."

Mrs. Waters nodded, her mess of brown, flyaway hair bouncing. "Good."

"See ya," Joseph offered, but she had already turned to grading her pile of papers. Half-stumbling, his legs suddenly leaden, he managed to make it out the classroom door just as another class was passing by. Shifting as minimally as he could, he waited for Lieutenant's arm to brush his, and as deftly as he was able, passed her the note.

Ann turned in toward her locker mirror and rubbed her lips together. She felt naked without her dark lip gloss, but with all of her current punishments for bad behavior she'd had just about every privilege she'd ever had at the Academy taken away.

Oh if they only knew *how bad I really was*, Ann considered with a deeply satisfied smile, *they would have me in a full straitjacket twenty-four seven.*

Ann exchanged her mathematics textbook for her English notebook and closed her locker just in time to lock eyes with Ariel who still sported bruises in the shape of Ann's hand. The other girl scowled fiercely at Ann. Rachel and another of Ariel's friends joined her, whispering loudly in support.

Rachel put her arm around Ariel's shoulder. "Don't let her get to you," she advised her friend."If she tries anything we can just call for security. Don't let her intimidate you."

Ann rolled her eyes obviously dramatically. The other girls made disgusted sounds and huddled closer together. Ann blew Ariel a loud, vicious kiss.

"The hell do you think you doin'?"

Ann grimaced, speaking out of the side of her mouth as she bent down to adjust the straps on her backpack. "Just cementing my well-deserved reputation as the bitch to be feared in these parts."

Ann could hear Lieutenant suck her teeth disapprovingly behind her. "Sometimes I swear . . ."

"What?" Ann snapped as quietly as she could. "Swear what? You've known who I am for long enough now."

"Yeah, long enough to know when you straight up forcin' the bad girl act," Lieutenant murmured.

"Excuse me? I don't remember —"

Lieutenant pushed a small piece of sticky paper into Ann's hands from behind. "C'mon, Blonde Bitch, don't bite my head off," Lieutenant whispered, making the hairs on the back of Ann's neck rise. "Just callin' it like I see it 'cause I care. You're my friend. Don't want anythin' to happen to you if I can help it."

Guilt pooled in Ann's stomach, then slid its way up her throat, trying to spill past her lips as truth. She swallowed it. "It's my choice if I help it or not."

Ann could feel Lieutenant tense behind her, and then shrug. "Fine. You right, 's your life. Your mark is at ten o' clock. Time to use those skills."

My skills? Ann scratched her right arm, hard, willing blood to flow. *My mark?* She glanced over her shoulder and then flattened out the piece of paper in her hand. *Oh. Those skills. That mark.*

Ann hoisted her backpack over her shoulders and palmed the sticky note. She started down the hall, holding her copy of *The Great Gatsby* out in front of her as if she was reading it.

She judged Mrs. Waters' steps by sound at first and then used the excuse of her book to glance to the side. The science teacher clipped along beside her, heading toward her office. Ann waited until the woman drew just ahead of her to cast a glance over at the science teacher's bag. She quickly located the black bound notebook Charlie had described.

Ann waited until Mrs. Waters was just about to turn before making her move. She swung her arm back and forth, establishing a rhythm. Then, smoothly, Ann glided the sticky note onto the cover of the notebook, just far enough inside the bag so that it wouldn't be too readily visible, so long as its owner simply gave her belongings a perfunctory glance before setting them aside.

Ann held her breath as she waited for Mrs. Waters to turn. The woman pivoted away as if she had felt nothing, and Ann continued walking on at the same pace.

Bingo, Ann thought, almost laughing aloud at the sensation of release that adrenaline always provided her. *My skills, my mark. Now we just have to wait and hope she takes the bait.*

Toni judged the time by the drip-drip sound of water from the bathroom faucet pinging around the small, tiled room. She bit her lip and strained, listening closely for the telltale sound of the door opening just outside and a few meters to the right of where she stood.

I can't keep standing here, Toni reminded herself anxiously, wiping her hands off carefully with the rough paper towels and buying time. *Another minute and it's gonna look suspicious. Find the damn sticky note already!*

Toni smoothed out her royal blue button-down and pushed her brown silk headband further back, examining herself in the mirror and playing for time. She was scheduled for lunch around this time, and a free study period beforehand, so she wasn't part of the groups being shepherded from one end of the Academy to another. Still, if she were seen on the cameras going into the bathroom and not coming out for a while, it would be noticed and would raise suspicion.

Maybe I should just go, Toni reasoned, pulling her backpack slowly over both of her shoulders, her muscles happily relieved to be free of the skin shock device which had been removed two weeks ago for good behavior. *If she found it, she found it. My knowing doesn't really matter, right? I mean —*

The sound of the door swinging open was minimal, the hinges squeaking ever so slightly. Someone was leaving Mrs. Waters' office. Toni moved towards the bathroom door just as it opened. Mrs. Carter stepped inside. Her face was pale, and her hands tightly fisted.

"Toni, what are you doing here?"

Remember, she's guilty, not you. "Just going to the bathroom. I'm headed to lunch," Toni replied, as innocently as she could.

Toni made her face open and blank, her sharp eyes taking in the principal's uncharacteristically mussed hair and the beads of sweat dotting her gently rouged cheeks. *She's just come from sneaking into another teacher's office, and she isn't even supposed to use the student bathrooms. She's not used to being guilty, and it shows.*

"Well, I think you should go there right now," Mrs. Carter ordered in a tone brooking no disagreement.

Toni nodded. "Yes, ma'am." *Seem cowed but not too afraid,* Toni reinforced, walking at a quick but measured pace around the dark-haired woman and to the door. *You're not guilty of anything, Toni. Of course you aren't. So no need to run, but get out of here before she associates you in her mind with what she's just seen. Just head out that door, and don't look back.*

"Toni?"

Breathe.

"Um, yes?" *You're not guilty. Just turn around and look confused, but not scared.*

With tightly controlled fingers, Mrs. Carter pinched a lock of her hair and tucked it behind her ear, her diamond earring blinking in the harsh, florescent bathroom lighting. "You haven't been called up to the Headmistress' office recently, have you?"

Shit, shit, shit. How do I play this? Should I lie because the Headmistress wouldn't want me to tell? Or should I be honest? Should I look nervous and secretive? But then will she suspect me of planting the note?

"Not this week, no," Toni replied, blinking with eyes she hoped appeared curious, but not overly so. "Am I ... am I supposed to?"

"No!" Mrs. Carter paused after her abrupt answer, schooling her face into a more composed demeanor. "No, but if you are, please report it to me."

Toni nodded. "Of course, Mrs. Carter. Is there ... anything else?"

Fuck, should I have said that? Was that suspicious? Toni's lower stomach constricted, and it was everything she could do not to double over with the force of her nerves. Mrs. Carter swallowed, but her eyes on Toni were distracted.

"No, that will be all. Thank you. You may go to lunch."

Toni nodded, turning. Her sweaty hand was slick on the handle as she opened the door. She passed over the threshold, walking away from the bathroom and out into the wide hallway even though she longed to run.

"What if she doesn't bite?"

Charlie had turned her head ever so slightly to the side and directed her whispered question over her shoulder to the table behind her, where Joseph and Ann were conspicuously eating their sandwiches. Lieutenant and Melvin occupied the edge of the table across the row, and could hear Charlie if they both leaned slightly to their left. The friends fell silent when anyone passed their small triangle, so they communicated in fits and spurts.

Lieutenant shook her head, twisting her paper cup of ice water back and forth between her long hands. "I'm more worried about her just findin' it. It's *if* she picks up the right notebook, and *if* she sees the note, and *if* she reads it. That's a lot a' ifs."

"What if Platelets finds it first?" Charlie considered, using the codename they'd designated for Mrs. Waters. "What if Mrs. C— *White Cell* doesn't take it with her?"

"Yeah, and what if she *does* see it," Melvin piled on, "and it's so obvious that she thinks it's planted?"

"C'mon you guys," Joseph whispered, rubbing his forearms against the metallic edge of the cafeteria table. "A little optimism here ain't gonna kill us."

"I don't know," Charlie muttered, waiting as an aide patrolled past on her right. "If there were ever a place optimism might get you killed, it's here. Or, you know, in a war zone. Or West Virginia."

"I'm with Joseph on this one," Ann said, sifting through her wilted lettuce with vigor, her fork plunging in and out of cherry tomatoes practically reverberating with enthusiasm. "There's no point in worrying at this point. Either Mrs. C— *White Cell* catches on and lights us up like a white trash family's Christmas lights in June, or she doesn't. Nothing we can do now, so we might as well just sit back and relax."

"Yes. I feel so comforted. I will now commence relaxation," Melvin intoned, casting a sidelong glance at the other table. He noticed Joseph's hand sneak out to squeeze Ann's leg and earn a playful swat. "Aren't you two, like, forbidden to see each other?"

"And?" Joseph raised his brows in a challenge to Melvin, but looked away when two loudly chatting girls passed through the row between their tables.

"And," Lieutenant said when the coast was clear, "as romantic as I'm sure y'all two find kissin' away the shock burns you get from bein' busted, the last thing we need is to raise any suspicion."

"Thought our lovely H— Red Cell already knows we're sneakin' out?" Joseph shrugged, unable to keep from shooting Ann a heated glance as her fingers found his under the table.

"But White Cell doesn't," Lieutenant said. "That's the whole point. 'Member the point? The one where we tryna make our principal suspicious of our other teachers and *not* us? As cute as you two lovebirds are, if you mess this up and get us caught, I will dump y'all at the bottom of the lake."

Ann and Joseph shared a sympathetic, pitying look. "Honey, I think we need to get Lieutenant laid," Ann postulated.

"I agree. Hey Mel," Joseph said. "Take one for the team, eh man? I promise it's really not that bad."

Lieutenant tapped the edge of her cup delicately. "Melvin, where did you put my hatchet again?"

"In your — oh, look to twelve o' clock. It's Toni," Melvin whispered.

"Where?" Joseph looked over his left shoulder.

"Not your twelve o' clock, my twelve o' clock." Melvin rolled his eyes then looked down at his bowl of minestrone soup as another group of giggling students past by.

"Yo, can we just use directions?" Joseph pleaded. "Clocks scare me. My mom used to have one a' them cat clocks where the eyes moved. I had nightmares about that clock."

"Wow. And here I was actually going to have sex with you, ever again." Ann shook her head forlornly, then caught her breath when she felt a clever finger slide up the inside of her thigh.

"You'd stay away from me forever?" Joseph whispered, his voice dropping two octaves. Ann swallowed, glad she had an excuse not to meet his burning gold eyes.

"Maybe . . . not forever," she relented. "Oh, I see her. There's Toni. Is she giving the sign? Charlie, can you see?"

Charlie leaned forward, blinking. "I . . . I think so," she mumbled. "I . . . can't be sure." *Because I never know if what I'm seeing is real or not anymore. Because my eyes are another part of me that the Unreal Contingent is experimenting on, and no one else knows that, not even the Headmistress with her bells and whistles and thistle down . . .*

"She is," Lieutenant confirmed, pulling on her vest in response to Toni's seemingly innocuous hair curling. "White Cell swallowed the virus."

"Here's hoping she rots with it," Melvin toasted, downing his apple juice fervently.

"She really didn't know," Charlie informed the others softly, poking at her sandwich and making indents in the malleable white bread. "Know what the H— what Platelets and Red Cell were doing. It's been going on right under her nose the whole time, and she never even suspected. She feels . . . blindsided."

"Hey, as long as it's her blindsided and not us," Joseph stated, taking another bite of his sandwich.

Where are you?

Toni shivered. The nights were only getting colder, and she hadn't had a chance to hide her black sweatshirt under the covers before slipping out of her room. The breeze off of the lake went right through her, and her chattering teeth were almost as loud as the rubbing together of the bare branches of the trees.

C'mon, hurry up! Toni hopped a little at the edge of the woods, wincing at the way the twigs and leaves dug into her heels even through her socks. *If I get caught because I have to report to the nurse with frostbite . . .*

The trees rustled with movement not caused by the wind, and Toni whirled around. Her heart thudded with relief and fresh anxiety as he stepped out into the open, the light cast from the waning crescent moon just barely allowing Toni to make out his wide, winning grin.

"You look surprised?" Seth baited, moving slowly but inevitably closer to her.

"I wasn't sure if you would show."

Seth skipped three times, bringing himself inches from Toni. "There's that trust issue again. We are really going to have to work at that."

Toni crossed her arms and raised her eyebrows. "We?"

"It takes two," Seth murmured, his bright eyes traveling up and down her body. "To . . . run away together, you know."

"Yeah, of course. I know," Toni fumbled, and when Seth's grin widened, she quickly proceeded. "So, what were you able to find out about what's beyond that lake?"

Seth slipped his hands into his pajama pants pockets. "There's a town, ten miles through the woods to the west. The main highway passes through it, and then it's another sixty miles to the Canadian border. Or we could trek through the woods and try not to get eaten by a bear or caught by Mounties."

"And once we're in Canada?" Toni asked.

"I can get cash," Seth assured her, the wind playing with his blonde hair, which appeared almost white against the backdrop of the night sky. "We can last on that for a while before we go to the press with our story, or we can use the wonders of the internet to try to find someone to get us fake IDs and start all over." Seth kicked at the dirt as he took a final step forward, his chest radiating heat all along Toni's upper body as he cocked his head and stared down at her. "Of course, you'd have to stick around with me for that to work."

"Are you really that bored?" Toni questioned. "What, no other girls willing to get close to you? All your boys run off?"

Toni waited for Seth's face to morph into the blood-chilling visage she knew he could summon when infuriated. Instead he snaked his arm around her waist, pulled her into the warmth of his body, and covered her lips with his. When she gasped, he used the opportunity to skillfully insert his tongue into her mouth, the firm grip of his right arm around her belied by the gentle way he used his left hand to smooth her hair and tilt her head back. She shoved against him, and he broke away, panting and grinning.

"What the fuck was that?" Toni demanded.

"You talk too much," Seth said arrogantly, laughing. "I'll have the money we need. You decide when you want us to go."

With one last laugh, Seth turned and jogged off, robbing Toni of the focus for her fury, and leaving her growling, her body enlivened by anger and treacherously roused blood.

CHAPTER FOURTEEN

THE UNREAL CONSPIRACY ISN'T REAL. OF COURSE NOT.

That's what they want you to think. No, no, it really *isn't real.*

"This is unreal."

That's what I said! It's just a symptom of a schizophrenic mind — my mind. But . . . I know it's real. And I'm the only one who can see it. But I know it's not real. How? How do I know that? How do I know anything?

Charlie bit back a whimper as her mind warred against itself, one side desperately trying to hold onto sanity, the other just as insistently pulling her toward delusion. It was already dark outside the window. Her hand trembled around her pencil, and her feet pressed against the black coffee table as she leaned over it, pretending to do her homework. Shivering and shaking with the effort of keeping her battle contained, it took Charlie another minute to realize the voice she'd heard was that of Mrs. Carter.

"Twelve years, Wendy. We have worked together for twelve years. We've known each other for almost twenty. When we got these jobs we made a promise to ourselves and the children. Do you remember that?"

"Evelyn, you're worrying over nothing." Even through the phone Mrs. Waters' voice didn't sound convincing to Charlie, and from the glance she stole through the cracked door into the kitchen at Mrs. Carter's blanched face and tight expression, Charlie gathered the principal felt the same.

"I do not like to be patronized within my own school." Mrs.

Carter's tone was that of barely contained fury.

"Who's patronizing you?" Mrs. Waters countered. "But Evelyn, you're making accusations with no basis in reality, and that isn't like you."

"No basis in reality?" Charlie wondered what Mrs. Carter's hissing response sounded like through the other end of the phone. "What are you insinuating, exactly?"

"Look, all that I am saying," Mrs. Waters declared slowly, as if calming an angry child, "is that we are dealing with students who have proven to be manipulative and who have attempted to perform all kinds of sabotage, and so it's natural that we have heightened suspicions and are . . . overly vigilant. But we can't turn on each other, or, you know . . ."

"What?" Mrs. Carter snapped. "What do I know? Because you seem to be telling me I don't know anything, and for me not to know anything, at my own school, is a very, very serious problem."

"I only meant that we can't allow ourselves to become torn apart by suspicions of each other based upon personal insecurities or stress, or hyper-vigilance, or fears founded in the worry that we're not in complete control. We have to be the adults in this situation in order to take care of the children, and to fulfill our promise. Remember that it is these children who are at risk. Let's not concern ourselves withour own personal sway or standing."

There was a long pause. *That was it,* Charlie recognized, even through her disorganized haze. *That was the line. She crossed it. Now take it, take the bait, be offended, let it push you over your own line, snap, snap, snap . . .*

"How dare you."

Snapped.

"Evelyn . . ."

"No, how dare you try and insinuate that this is about a petty power-struggle. This is about the children, and what is best for them "

"Evelyn, Sophia has always had her own visions of what this

school could mean for the future of education and science, but she would never harm or put our students through anything unethical to do it." Charlie thought it sounded like Mrs. Waters might have been reciting from part of a speech she'd practiced before, almost as if she were trying to convince herself, as well as the angry woman on the other line.

"So you are admitting that you and Sophia are performing . . . acts of which I am unaware of on our students? Is that it?" Mrs. Carter pounced. "Experiments of some kind?"

Charlie could hear a hitch in Mrs. Waters' breath through the phone. She wondered if Mrs. Carter had as well. "Evelyn, do you really want to cause a ruckus between you and Sophia, and jeopardize the leadership and stability of our school, especially one that contains such volatile students, all over . . . what, exactly? Do you have any evidence, proof, any reason to believe the Headmistress and I are engaged in something we would feel the need to hide from you?"

The click of the principal's heels on the floor as she tapped her toes felt like little gunshots against Charlie's sensitive ears, but she waited, swallowing hard, for Mrs. Carter's answer.

"No," Mrs. Carter answered softly, with an undercurrent of bitterness and malice so subtle Charlie didn't believe it could be detected over the phone. "No, and I certainly don't want to accuse anyone without proof."

"Well, of course not," Mrs. Waters replied with audible relief. "Look, I'm sure Sophia would be more than happy to schedule a meeting with you to clear this up and define exactly what should go into the treatment and lesson plans for our students."

"Certainly," Mrs. Carter responded silkily. "I didn't mean to be abrasive Wendy, but you know it's my job as principal to make sure everything being done at the school is done with the best interests of the children as the paramount objective."

"And you know I agree with you Evelyn, one-hundred percent," Mrs. Waters said, eager now. "Completely."

"Good. Good night, Wendy."

"Good night, Evelyn."

The principal clicked off her phone and waited for two or three minutes before slowly stalking out of the kitchen and into the adjacent bathroom, pulling the door shut with more force than necessary.

Like a rope thrown to a drowning man, Charlie's mind grasped onto the implications of Mrs. Carter's statements. Replaying the conversation over and over internally, stimulated and occupied, Charlie felt her head clear as her next move steadily crystallized. With a surge of glee, Charlie found herself finally able to focus, to think. She let out a long, slow breath and began to plot.

"I like this house."

Joseph lifted his head off of the rough, chipped floor of the abandoned house to raise one eyebrow at the barely-visible blonde curled into the crook of his arm. "You like this raggedy-ass, cold-as-fuck, broken-down house?"

Ann narrowed her eyes at him. "Yeah, I do, boy. That a problem?"

"You're a problem. A serious problem. You need serious help, and —" He broke off into low laughter when she smacked at him, catching her wrists in his hands. Ann stuck out her tongue.

"Oh, real mature."

"Like you can talk." Ann shrugged, shifting on the floor to avoid a stray nail. "No, but I mean . . . obviously I want a real house someday, but I like abandoned, quiet places. I guess I like not knowing the whole story behind a place and having to guess about the people who used to live there."

Joseph's hands trailed up from her wrists to her palms, his fingers working their way into hers and slowly entwining with them. "Yeah, I can see that. So what do you think happened to the people who used to live here?"

Ann tilted her head to the side, the movement of the strands of her hair just visible to Joseph in the dim moonlight that managed to fight its way through the cracks in the boarded up windows. "I don't know. It's been abandoned since before I was born. I feel like maybe ... something sad happened here. And the family just left because they didn't want to remember it. But they didn't sell it either, because the good memories were all mixed in as well, and maybe they wanted to have it still here to hold them."

"Wow. That's deep."

"Oh shut up," Ann grumbled.

"Nah, I'm serious," Joseph insisted, playing with her hands gently. "That's real beautiful. When we get outta here, we should look for an abandoned house to live in. I mean, it'll just be so romantic when the roof falls in on our heads, and they find our naked corpses crushed under —"

Joseph laughed as Ann tried to pull away, catching her around the waist and tugging her back. "I'm playin, I'm playin' ... if my girl wants an abandoned house, I'll get us an abandoned house. Hell, I mean, it's probably the only place we could live in on the run."

"I'd want a real house eventually," Ann said, and Joseph could tell by her voice that she was pouting. "But please, continue mocking me. I was only sharing my hopes, and dreams, and feelings."

"I would never mock your hopes, dreams, and feelings," Joseph promised. "I mean, not really."

"Yeah, but your stuff is ..." Ann shrugged, and Joseph could just detect the motion.

"My stuff is — what?"

"You know, you have all these talents and if you wanna be a graphic novelist or ... or paint or whatever you can, and me —"

"You could be a ventriloquist," Joseph suggested. "Yo, you could do magic shows, or haunted houses, like work on throwing your voice to make it seem like people are comin' from other places ..." Joseph stopped. "Don't give me that look."

"What look? You can't see my face."

"Yeah, but I can feel that you givin' me a look," Joseph asserted.

"Oh, what, you're psychic like Charlie now?" Ann tried to divert.

"Yup. Now I wanna know why I'm gettin' The Look when I'm tryna be the good boyfriend and talk about your dreams."

Ann pursed her lips. "Because you're being patronizing, acting like my talents are actually . . . you know, talents. Let's be honest, the only thing I'm really good at is, you know . . . not a real talent."

"Now I beg to differ," Joseph said, as sleazily as possible.

"I'm being serious," Ann argued.

"No, you're not," Joseph said firmly. "'Cause if you was, you wouldn't be gettin' down on yourself like this and talkin' like you're one a' them bimbos from the rest a' the school. You got plenty of skills that ain't have shit to do with sex. You're smart, and funny, and as tough as a kick-to-the-balls, so stop bein' stupid and accept it."

Ann narrowed her eyes, and then dove down to nip at his nose.

"Ow!" Joseph informed her. "And violent too. Did I mention violent?"

Ann grinned and nipped at his nose again, then at his cheeks, then his lips. She felt his body still beneath her and his mouth react when she bit him again, carefully, lingeringly. Her next bite turned into a kiss, and then another, and she felt heat rise against her abnormally cool body. She pulled away, listening to his deepened breathing. She knew from previous experience how golden his eyes would look in his current state, but she could only just make out the contours of his body.

"I really wish I could see your eyes right now," Ann confessed, her fingers running up and down the taught muscles in his neck, rubbing against the stubble on his chin, finding his cheekbones and searching for his hair. She felt hands drift up her back.

"Feelin' is mutual," Joseph murmured, swallowing as Ann fitted her body to his, her hands coming up to grip his shoulders. In the dark he sought her mouth, found her neck, her pulse point, her chin, her nose. Fumbling, shaking, he felt wet heat and finally captured her lips.

Ann clutched at Joseph's neck, every inch of her body becoming suddenly supremely sensitive, and aching with insistent pain as her mind surrendered to primal emotion. Everything felt desperate, everything felt real, everything felt good, and Ann moaned as Joseph ran his arms up and down her back.

"God, I wish I could see you," Joseph rasped between passes on her mouth in a voice which had dropped several octaves. He lifted his arms as Ann yanked off his sweater, his mind too giddy to really register the scratches on his back from the splinters of wood that made up the floor. He undid the buttons on her shirt as she started removing the rest of his clothing. "You ... are so ... so beautiful."

"Mmm ... I love you," Ann gasped back, heady and dazed by a raw, physical experience of happiness that surged through her like a fever.

"Yeah?" Joseph's voice was hot, burning. It practically hurt her ears, and Ann didn't want it to stop.

"Yes."

"Good, 'cause I fuckin' love you too." He growled, driving his hands into her hair and rolling them over. Ann couldn't see, and it made every other sense seem new and exciting. She inhaled his scent, familiar, and comforting, and stimulating. She heard his pants, his gasps, his whimpers. She tasted his mouth. She could feel his skin, his hands, his chest. *Hot, hot, God it feels so good ... it's hot ... so hot ... it's like burning ...*

No, really, it's burning ... I'm burning —

"Ow. Ow. No, ow, no! Stop, that hurts!"

Joseph came to a complete stop mid-kiss and pulled back immediately, trying desperately to read Ann's face. *Fuck, I can't see her,* he cursed the dark. "What, what is it?"

"I'm ... I feel like I ... skinned myself maybe?" Ann gasped. "My chest and my arms, they feel ... burned."

"Is it from your burn scars from your last shock treatment?" Joseph questioned, wincing as he moved away from Ann and

200

pushing himself up with his forearms.

"I . . . I don't know," Ann said through gritted teeth. "I can't see . . ."

"Here, gimme a sec . . ." Joseph felt into his sweatpants pockets and pulled out his plastic lighter, flicking it on easily. He held up the tiny flame with his left hand, illuminating Ann's scared, confused face. "Where does it hurt? Can you see what it looks like?"

Ann glanced down at her exposed upper body. "I . . . I feel it here." She placed a hand in between her breasts.

"Here?" Joseph met her hand with his, and Ann hissed. "Sorry, sorry!"

"It's okay, it's okay . . ." Ann trailed off, and Joseph could see her eyes widen by the firelight. "Joseph — your skin."

"What about it?" Joseph frowned, looking down at his own bared chest.

"You're burning up," Ann murmured, pressing the pads of her fingers to his chest and then yanking them back. "Joseph, you're practically on fire, what are you doing?"

"Nothing, I swear, I feel fine!" he promised loudly. "I didn't mean to do anythin'. I just . . . oh, fuck!" Joseph spat. "The fuckin' pills musta wore off!"

"Wait, wait, I have extra. I took what I had for the week with me," Ann assured, crawling over to where her shirt lay and fishing in her pockets. "I kept it on me, thank God. Here, you can take another one."

Ann reached out her hand and Joseph started to grab for it and then paused. "You . . . I don't wanna hurt you again."

"Fuck that," Ann dismissed. "Take it, c'mon. You're practically burning me from way over here, just take it."

"Ann!"

"Take it!"

Joseph picked at the pill with the tips of his fingers, careful not to touch Ann's hand. She watched him as he swallowed the pill dry. Joseph swallowed a second time to keep from regurgitating at the bile that rose in his throat while closing her shirt.

"Ann, I swear, I didn't mean to … I just …" Joseph trailed off helplessly. "You … maybe you should try to … come up with an excuse for them, and go to the nurses's tomorrow."

"These will heal," Ann dismissed. "I'm not worried about me. I'm worried about you. Does it seem like you're getting … like this is happening more?"

"Yeah, and there's fuck-all I can do about it," Joseph said bitterly. "I'm just gonna end up killin' someone someday, unless I'm lucky enough to burn myself out first."

"That is not an option," Ann declared. "We just have to find a way to fix this. Maybe the pills are even helping, you know, by lowering your body temperature some of the time?"

"Yeah, maybe," Joseph said, trying to convince himself as the flame from his lighter made shadows dance around the walls of the dilapidated house.

Homeless Shelters in the United States.

Toni typed the search term into the computer and waited for the results, knowing already that they wouldn't be specific enough. *Patience,* she told herself, glancing around the library. No one was looking toward her with any interest. The three nearest students were absorbed in their own research, and the librarian was answering someone's request for a specific reference encyclopedia.

Just take your time, Toni told herself yet again, pinching the eraser on her pencil with sharp, filed fingernails. *You're not doing anything suspicious.*

Toni had been patient for the last twenty minutes. She had searched 'homeless statistics for the United States'. She'd looked up 'average age of homeless person in the U.S.' and 'homeless on the streets tn the U.S.' Now she amended her search terms, adding the words 'for Teens'.

The screen blinked and then filled with results. Toni pretended to examine them, clicking on a few sites and even taking down some notes. There was nothing suspicious about a project on homelessness for her Social Studies class. Her teacher had displayed no reservations when Toni had requested the assignment. *Patience. I can do patience. I can.*

Toni turned a page in her notebook to give herself more space to write as she entered the terms, 'homeless shelters in Canada.' Again she clicked on a few sites and took down some notes. She lingered on one site in particular, taking down the name of the place for future reference. *Okay ... now.*

Toni's lower stomach clenched with excitement and the sense of arrival as she finally typed in the terms for the results she was actually seeking.

Homeless shelter in Canada for teens.

She had to remind herself again not to look around or over her shoulder as she clicked on a site. No one was looking for her. She'd covered her tracks as well as she possibly could. *Why wouldn't I want to compare statistics to shelters for teens in the United States and Canada?* Toni rationalized, blowing a curl out of her face as she took slow and steady notes on multiple sites. *It's perfectly normal.*

Toni clicked her way through as many hits as she felt she could without seeming to be wasting time, and then she glanced down at her list of Canadian teen shelters. *Perfectly normal.*

Toni stared at her dim reflection in the computer screen for a few moments, composing her rounded face, staring down her own hazel-green eyes, and preparing.

Then, neither quickly nor slowly, she typed in 'Canada Map' and changed her search preferences to images. Quickly now, she began eyeing towns and cities listed near the Montana border, glancing down at her list, writing, matching.

Patience. I can do patience. I can play the long game, I can lie, and I can hold out until I have all the final pieces.

Okay ... now.

"Fuck it's so cold!"

"At least it ain't snowin'," Joseph soothed, wrapping his arms around Ann, pulling her back to his front, and kissing her hair. "Could be worse."

"Actually, snow insulates," Toni said. She shifted back and forth to keep warm. She envied Ann for more than just the insulation of Joseph's arms as the rough wind off the lake raked harshly against her skin through her woolen pajamas. "So it would actually be less cold."

"Not good for us though," Melvin supplied, staying close to Lieutenant, who was pulling bits of leaves out of her hair. "Once it starts snowing we'll leave tracks for them to find us by."

"Then we better get our plan movin' fast," Anton said firmly. "A'ight, circle up." He motioned the others inward. "'Kay, where are we on money?"

"I can get it if I go home," Ann said and felt Joseph's arms tighten around her. "I know where my Mom keeps the extra cash."

Lieutenant and Melvin exchanged rapid looks.

"I'll do it," Melvin offered. "I know where my parents keep cash, and since I actually live there, I can get it easily."

Anton nodded. "That's your call. If you sure . . ."

"I'm sure."

Anton nodded again. "A'ight. That's our money. Clothes we can handle. Food, that's on L."

"I got a pretty good idea of what to take," Lieutenant confirmed, tugging on her dog tags, her brow furrowed. "My uncle gave me some advice on how to deal in the woods, but I never been there myself."

"Charlie." Anton gestured to the smallest member of their company who was almost invisible nestled in between Toni, and Joseph, and Ann. "You lasted a while out in the woods before they caught you. You think you could help us with that?"

"I . . ." Charlie shivered. "I can't really . . . remember much. It's all . . . I didn't know what was going on, and it's hard to remember . . . I . . ." She dug her nails tightly into her wrist.

"Hey, hey, it's okay," Anton promised.

"I ... I know," Charlie said through gritted teeth. "I'm just ... working on being sane. It ... hurts, sometimes."

"I can talk to Katrina about edible plants," Ann assured brusquely, saving the pained Charlie. "She'll probably know all about anything like that around here."

"Good, good." Anton nodded. "Where are we on our safe house once we in Canada?"

"I found a homeless shelter right over the border in a town called Colmar, that takes teens," Toni stated. "I was able to sketch a basic map of the general area, with the towns, but it's gonna take some work to find it, 'cause you can't know for sure what area you're gonna come out at when you get over the border."

"I've run away before," Melvin assured her. "Once you know how, you can usually find the place you're looking for if you ask in the right way and pay attention. Getting through the woods and over the mountains — the big issue there is staying on the right track."

"It's straight north the whole way," Toni said. "If you can follow the North Star you should stay on course."

"Follow the North Star to the safe house in Canada," Charlie said, almost wonderingly. "It's like the Underground Railroad."

"Why's it gotta be the Underground Railroad, huh? Just 'cause black people on it?" Anton teased.

"No!" Charlie protested. "Because of Canada, and, and ..."

"Don't let him tease you, BiteSize," Lieutenant instructed, punching Anton lightly in the shoulder.

"Ouch," Anton informed Lieutenant. "You a mean woman, you know that?"

"I do. What's important is that you know it," Lieutenant retorted smartly.

Anton shared a commiserating glance with Joseph, then continued. "Okay, so for now it seems like we on track when it comes to Mission A, and we got a little more to work on before we go through with those plans. What about Mission B?"

"The time is right now for that," Charlie said, drawing in a deep breath as all eyes turned towards her. "Mrs. Carter is going to try to steal the files on her from Mrs. Waters office tomorrow night."

Anton raised one eyebrow. "You sure, Tiny?"

Charlie's nails dug deeper into her wrist, but she nodded. "Yes. I overheard her talking to Mrs. Waters. She didn't confront Mrs. Waters directly about the note, but she asked about experiments and was all mad about not knowing what was going on. Mrs. Waters tried to convince her she was being paranoid, but it was easy to tell she was lying and hiding something. Mrs. Carter snapped, just like we need. She's gonna go for it."

"You really sure she's gonna gonna go for it now?" Joseph questioned gently. "I mean, based on a forged note that just said 'E. may suspect, recommend we suspend all activities until situation is fully handled'?"

"*Yes,*" Charlie insisted, her jaw set. "You have to build and build," she explained. "First it was her being suspicious in general of the Headmistress. I could smell that on her ever since I heard them talk the first time. Then she heard my stories. Then the note, and then the phone call. They're all little things, but when you're scared and in the dark they become big things, because they throw shadows, and things you don't understand and can't see are always scarier than things you can. Once you get into that state of mind, it only takes the little things to crack it all open. It's like . . . mind-Jenga."

"Okay, so Mrs. Carter gets in, takes some of the files, and then we get in right after and take what we need," Anton reviewed. "Mrs. Waters and the Headmistress suspect Mrs. Carter, and they right, so we slip by."

"Assuming she does go for it and breaks in. What if she takes her file plus the ones we want, before we do?" Ann asked.

"Then Charlie can just take 'em from Mrs. Carter at home," Lieutenant said with a shrug. "Right, FunSize?"

Charlie nodded. "Yeah, I . . . I think I can. Sometimes she

leaves her office door unlocked, when she thinks she knows I'm downstairs. It would take time, but I — I *think* I could do it."

"What if Mrs. Waters confronts Mrs. Carter about the break-in when she finds 'em missin'?" Joseph said.

"And admit that she's been keeping a file on her boss because of her other boss's orders?" Toni raised her brow. "No. She'll run and tell the Headmistress first."

"Won't the Headmistress confront her?" Melvin asked. The circle fell silent.

"They are circling each other," Charlie remarked, eyes half-glazed. "Looking for weaknesses and matching their strengths. They won't want to move to confrontation *too* fast. They're still gathering, gathering, and sizing each other up."

"It's gonna come to a head eventually," Ann reasoned.

"Eventually we can deal with," Anton determined. "By the time eventually come around, we'll be ready. What we gotta do is deal with what we got now."

"Okay," Lieutenant began, kneeling down and picking up a stick. As the others joined her, she started to sketch in the dirt. "I know it's hard to see, but try and follow along . . ."

"Mrs. Carter."

Mrs. Carter nodded to the security guard who greeted her as he opened the front door to J. Alter Academy. He made no sign of surprise at the principal's late night visit and held the door open for her courteously as she pulled a second key out of her purse.

"John," Mrs. Carter said, and John the security guard stood up straighter.

"Yes, ma'am?"

"I'll be doing some checks of the cameras tonight, which may result in certain cameras being temporarily disabled, so needless to say you would be advised to keep everyone on alert," Mrs. Carter stated, buttoning the top button on her tailored black coat.

"You want me to radio and let everyone know about it, ma'am?"

John offered.

"No, that's fine," Mrs. Carter said measuredly. "No need to worry anyone. It's just a note for you."

"Is this check of the cameras going to replace the scheduled check two weeks from now? Or is it in addition?"

"In addition," Mrs. Carter replied briskly. "We want to make very sure we don't have to deal with any surprises this semester."

"Understandable," John acknowledged. Mrs. Carter pulled her collar higher and entered the school. The guard let the door swing closed behind her as a faint owl call sounded somewhere over the grounds.

Huddled together in the small staircase by the entrance to the boiler room, Toni, Joseph, Ann, and Charlie stilled as they heard the imitation bird cry. Anton cocked his head and then grinned, his white teeth flashing off the dim light emanating from Panther Field.

"Two slow hoots, one long," Anton explained Lieutenant's signal quietly to the others. "Mrs. Carter's in the buildin' at the front entrance."

"How long does that give us to get to Mrs. Waters office?" Joseph questioned as Ann opened the boiler room door with the first of their lifted set of keys.

"From the front to the teachers' offices?" Toni frowned. "About five minutes."

"Then we gotta hustle people," Anton whispered, opening the door to the lower levels. "Let's move."

Mrs. Carter nodded toward one of the guards who paced the school's hallways, his flashlight pointed towards the ground. Ever since the break-in the principal had insisted upon having security inside of the building as well as around it, as an extra precaution.

The guard nodded back as Mrs. Carter turned the corner into the section containing the offices of J. Alter Academy's teachers, his flashlight bobbing along as he continued his rounds.

As the tramp of heavy boots faded into the distance, Joseph and Ann leaned out of the shadowy alcove between the end of one set of lockers and a classroom door that they were wedged into. Crouching close to each other, their arms brushed, and when Ann let out a small breath of relief at the cool temperature of Joseph's skin, he stilled. Ann tried to catch his eye before realizing he was counting. Reminded of their mission, she waited until she could detect a faint light shining off the gleaming metal water fountain at the opposite end of the hall.

Squeezing Joseph's shoulder with a trembling hand, Ann moved aside as he retreated back into their hiding space. The two teens pulled up the respective black hoodies they had hidden in their bedcovers to wear for just this occasion. They kept their heads down, trying so hard not to breath, and not to move, as the sound of the guard's feet drawing ever closer vibrated down the polished marble hallway floors.

We're not here, we're not here . . . you don't see us, just keep moving past . . . we're not here.

The footsteps were loud now, echoing just a few inches away. They seemed for a moment too slow, the rhythm less staccato, and Ann felt a familiar terror invade her body, paralyzing her limbs and making the area below her waist cramp up in a weak attempt at self-defense.

Oh God, I'm not here . . . I'm not in the closet, or under the bed, so go away, because I'm not here, go away, don't see me . . . it's dark you can't, can't see me . . . I'm small, I'm so small . . .

Ann felt Joseph's cold fingers squeeze hers softly, breaking the hold of the memory on her body and mind. Her heart resumed its shallow beating.

We're not here, you don't see us, just look straight ahead . . . we're not here . . .

The pace picked up again and the sound began to decrease as the boots migrated down the hall, until even Ann's oversensitive ears could not detect it. Joseph raised his head and she looked away, forgetting that the dark could hide the pallor of her face. She looked back as he leaned out and raised four fingers for the four minutes it took the guards to rotate around and back.

There was movement further down the hall, and then three shadows emerged from another alcove, sliding their way on stocking feet toward the teachers' offices.

Mrs. Carter hoisted her purse over her shoulder as she selected the key to Mrs. Waters' office. As the principal she had access to every office save that of the Headmistress. Shooting a glance down the carpeted hallway toward the door labeled 'Sophia Valentina, Headmistress', Evelyn Carter's arm shook causing her to scrape the copper key loudly against Mrs. Waters' doorknob.

Starting only slightly, she paused, then in a swift series of actions, she inserted and turned the key, turned the knob, pushed the door open, and stepped inside.

The office within was sparsely decorated and consisted of a closet, desk, chair, and a series of shelves on the back wall that were neatly stocked with books propped up by a number of river stones. Mrs. Carter's hand moved toward the light switch. She reconsidered, instead removing her phone and using its surface light to examine the premises.

Mrs. Waters' computer was absent, as was her notebook, most likely at home with their owner. Mrs. Carter frowned in consternation, and then she stepped around to the back of the desk to Mrs. Waters' locked desk drawers. Rifling through her set of keys by minimal light, Mrs. Carter tried out a number of small, rounded ones before she was finally able to open the first drawer. It contained some packets of gum, erasers, a broken watch, and various colored rubber bands.

Closing and re-locking the drawer quietly, she moved around Mrs. Waters' chair to the other end of the desk and opened the second drawer with the same key. This drawer was so tightly packed with files that the principal had to exert a certain amount of brute strength to pull it out enough to shine a light on all of the carefully labeled tags detailing their contents. Mrs. Carter's eyes narrowed as she read off the names of nine of her students. Angling her phone towards the back of the drawer, Mrs. Carter spotted a noticeably unmarked file.

Parsing it out of the others with her finely pointed nails, Mrs. Carter withdrew the collection of papers, stood up, laid the file upon Mrs. Waters' desk, and began to examine its contents.

Anton, Toni, and Charlie stood flush against the white plaster wall, waiting in perfect silence as the bump of a softly closing door and the rapid clicking of heels just around the corner sounded Mrs. Carter's exit from Mrs. Waters' office. Anton inched slightly out of the alcove, leaning his head out just far enough to glimpse the principal turn right, down a corridor that led to the front entrance of J. Alter Academy.

Anton squeezed Toni's shoulder with his left hand, and Toni passed the same gesture on to Charlie, who froze, and then remembered that it was the signal Lieutenant had taught them to use when they were ready to move. Across from them Joseph and Ann leaned out of their alcove, and Joseph raised four fingers — four minutes until the guard made another round.

Anton moved first, ducking around the corner and then into the hallway containing the row of teachers' offices. Toni and Charlie followed in quick succession, gathering outside of the door marked 'Wendy R. Waters'. Toni had the keys that Ann had lifted from Mrs. Waters' gripped tightly together in her hand to keep them from jingling. She carefully inserted one into the keyhole. Anton turned the knob slowly, smoothly pushing the door open and closing it quietly behind them once they had slipped inside.

"I can't really see," Toni whispered, blinking in the dark and just able to make out broad shapes. "Charlie, can you?"

"Yes." The small girl sounded oddly detached. "It's okay, it's right over here ... just take a few steps and you're at her desk."

Toni fumbled forward in the dark, wincing as her legs banged against something hard. "Found it."

"No computer, no notebook," Anton surmised, and Toni tried to gather the tall boy's general direction by the sound of his voice. "Most important stuff must be at home with her."

What, can they both see in the dark? Toni thought, angry at herself for the twinge of jealousy she couldn't help but feel rising in her gut. "So wait, do we not have anything then?"

"No," Charlie said softly. "Over here ... I can smell Mrs. Carter on this. She opened these drawers."

"You can *smell* her?"

"Toni, bring the keys over here," Anton requested, and Toni shuffled around the edge of the desk, using her hands to find her way and holding the keys out before her.

"*Ow!* My eye!"

"Sorry!" Toni said, pulling the keys back as Anton smothered a whimper. "I can't see!"

"Here, let me." Charlie's hand brushed up against Toni's, and the heavy girl tightened her fist before relaxing enough to relinquish the pointed bit of metal that had so injured Anton.

Toni could hear a soft rumble, and then the sound of grating hinges. "Find something?"

"Files," Anton answered. "Our files."

"Hardcopies," Charlie narrated as her tiny fingers sifted through them, pulling out and putting back printed forms, notes, and photos. "Not everything she has on us. She must keep her most important secrets close, close to her chest, close enough to keep constant watch."

"Yeah, but we don't need the deepest darkest secrets, Tiny," Anton explained. "Just keep lookin'."

Mrs. Carter was nearing the entrance to J. Alter Academy when she reached into her pocketbook for her phone. She frowned as she rummaged through it without success. Trying both of her coat pockets, she scratched against bare lint, and came to a sudden stop as she realized where she had left the missing item.

Closing her eyes and letting out a long, slow breath, Mrs. Carter pivoted and walked back towards the teachers' offices.

Toni waited impatiently, the knot in her stomach growing. She blinked in the dark, her eyes only slowly adjusting. "So is it there?"

Charlie withdrew several printed forms, a few photos, and a small packet of typed notes. Anton leaned over and joined Charlie in examining them.

"Okay," Anton murmured, squinting. "That's what we need. Now just try to find the specific one we want."

The arches of Ann's feet ached, and she twisted slightly, enjoying the feel of Joseph's heart thumping reassuringly near hers. For a moment the rhythm was so in time that she almost mistook the clicking for the combined music of their beating pulse. Then the clicking of heels against the floor drew closer, and Ann realized with a horrible shock that Mrs. Carter was returning.

Ann felt Joseph's heartbeat speed up in time with hers, and she didn't have to see his face to know he wore a look of shock and fear mirroring her own.

She's gonna catch them, Ann thought with dreadful, furious certainty. *They're still in there, and she's gonna fuckin' catch them. It's all over.*

"Bingo," Charlie chimed, and Toni suspected the little girl was smiling one of her unsettling smiles. Charlie handed Anton the documents. He folded them lengthwise and stuffed them into his jacket.

"A'ight, we got what we need, people," he announced. "Time to bounce."

Mrs. Carter's hand paused in the act of opening the door to Mrs. Waters' office, delaying her entrance as she listened. Eyes widening and face paling, she quickly turned the knob and rushed into the room.

Locating the general direction of the noise, she hurried forward, lips tightening with apprehension and fear. Blinking in the dark, Mrs. Carter moved in closer, and after a moment or two of observation, followed by understanding, she heaved a great sigh.

Picking up her phone, she accepted the call and raised it to her ear.

"Yes, Becky? Why are you still up at this hour, you should be in bed? Oh? Oh, honey, you know those old pipes . . . yes, we absolutely *do* need to get them fixed . . ."

Ann shivered at the sound of Mrs. Carter's voice, and she clenched Joseph's hand tightly. She felt him place a wild, desperate kiss on her cheek as the principal stalked back out of the office. Ann closed her eyes as she waited with Joseph for the inevitable.

"Yes. Yes, I'm sure. Becky, Becky, I know. No, of course I'm not angry, sweetie. These things happen. Yes. Yes . . . no, but we can work on that . . ."

Mrs. Carter disappeared down the hall. Ann shook her head in confusion, and continued to do so, when a few seconds later, three Anton, Toni, and Charlie shaped shadows rounded the corner and hurried back to their pre-office hiding places.

"What?" Joseph stopped as quickly as he'd begun when a light bobbed at the left end of the T-shaped confluence of hallways in which they were hiding. All of the teens kept their heads down and their mouths shut as the security guard made his scheduled patrol, pacing down the hallway to turn a sharp left, his flashlight bobbing along as he whistled loudly.

"They're takin' too long," Lieutenant whispered worriedly, chewing on her lower lip. Melvin poked his head up over the bushes behind which the two friends were crouched, and he scanned the front lawn of the school.

"No guard activity. Doesn't seem like anyone's noticed anything..." Melvin broke off as the front door opened. Lieutenant pulled him down sharply. Hands buried in cold dirt, the two peered at an angle through the bushes to glimpse the principal chatting quietly for a few moments with the door guard before setting off at a brisk pace towards the front gate.

"What ha—"

Lieutenant clamped a hand over Melvin's mouth as the security guard turned. For a few tense seconds the bulky man appeared to be looking for something. Melvin closed his eyes and dug his nails into the net of roots and twigs below him. Then the security grunted, stretched, and leaned back against the school's brick wall.

Melvin and Lieutenant let out sighs of relief that almost turned into screams when they each felt soft squeezes on their shoulders. Whirling around, the tall black girl identified her five friends, relaxed, and nodded. She motioned for Melvin to follow as Anton indicated for them to all head toward the back of the school. The reunited group set off in a series of sprints from one place of cover to the next, stopping to hide behind bushes, under arches, next to trash cans, and in alcoves during their journey to the side of the fence through which they had entered the school grounds.

Pausing to catch their breath in the shadows of the cafeteria just a few feet away from their point of escape, Joseph panted, "Mrs. Carter ... did she see you?"

"No, she —"

Anton cut off his answer as another guard paced past their fence. The group waited several more minutes in silence before racing out to the small, manageable hole and working their way under the bent wire.

"She came back for her phone," Anton explained swiftly to Joseph, Ann, Lieutenant, and Melvin as Charlie and Toni scurried under the wire and headed for the woods on the other side. "Tiny noticed her phone when it started buzzin' and had us all hide in the closet."

"You get what we need?" Lieutenant questioned as first Melvin and then Ann made their way out.

"We got it," Anton confirmed. "We keep playin' our cards like this, and we might even make it outta this alive."

"Let's pray we keep gettin' dealt lucky hands, then," Lieutenant agreed, following Joseph under the wire and holding it up for Anton as he shimmied through and followed them at a run into the night.

CHAPTER FIFTEEN

"I FEEL VERY, VERY CLOSE TO YOU ALL RIGHT NOW."

Lieutenant scowled at Joseph. His face, just visible in the dark, was merely inches from her own. Sitting where grass turned into sand, the seven boarder friends huddled tightly together against the brutal wind that roared, unopposed, across Lake Amiszi.

"Yo, you have a problem with the seatin' arrangements, we can do this Eskimo style, and send your ass out on an ice floe," Lieutenant warned dangerously, her right elbow hooked into Anthony's, her left into Melvin's as she kept her head down and out of the wind. Their icy clouds of breath mixed within the circle so that it appeared almost as if they were crowded around a small fire.

"You'd need to find an ice floe first," Charlie pointed out, her voice almost seeming disembodied with her head buried in Toni's chest.

"Senilicide wasn't always accomplished by ice floe either," Toni stated, rubbing her hands together for friction warmth. "And it was usually more like assisted suicide. When old Eskimos felt like a burden they would sometimes ask their younger relatives to kill them because inhabitants of many regions believed a better afterlife awaited for homicide, rather than suicide, victims. The person who was asked to help would feel bound to comply."

"See?" Joseph asserted triumphantly. "It's important to get all your facts straight 'fore you go makin' statements. I'd need to ask someone to kill me first, and if I ever *did* ask, I would expect y'all to argue and fight me on it, and tell me I got every reason in the world to live, just like the good friends you are."

"I don't know if you have every reason in the world to live," Ann posed, snuggling closer into Joseph's arms. "But I can think of . . . one or two."

"Okay, no," Toni said flatly. "We are definitely not close enough to start having hoochie coochie business all in a circle."

"Hoochie coochie business?" Melvin cackled.

"We got Muddy Waters up in here, y'all," Anton cracked, as Lieutenant shook her head and rolled her eyes in sympathy at Toni.

"Guys, I think we need to get Toni laid," Joseph drawled.

"Oh, yeah, because that's definitely going to happen here," Toni joked nervously. "I think I'm gonna keep my nightly appointments with Mr. Darcy in my dreams for now."

"Hey, hey," Anthony argued, "it's always important to be ready for Mr. Right. C'mon now, what's on your list of what you want in a man? Obviously for our Toni, he needs to be classy, intelligent, have good conversation . . ."

"He should have nice style," Lieutenant ticked off, playing with the end of the big French braid she had twisted out of her many tiny braids. "He needs to be able to dance."

"He should recycle," Joseph offered.

"Funny can be a cheap way of compensating for sexy," Ann said, ignoring Joseph's pinch of her arm, "but I think we can add it to the list."

"Gimme a second. I'm gettin' it all down," Anthony stated, holding up a finger.

"Yeah, where?" Melvin asked.

"One of us keeps the records," Anthony explained, still looking at his fingers as he recalled the different elements given. "He does homework, papers, and lists and shit for the rest of us."

The wind protested loudly, breaking the dead branches of trees and freeing them of brown, shriveled leaves.

"So, you have another . . . someone inside you who does a specific kind of work?" Toni ventured at last, trying to make her voice as clinical as possible. Anthony nodded.

"Some of us are good at different things, and since we can't all be out at the same time, some of us get shit done in the background." He grinned almost apologetically. "Turns out multitaskin' is easier when you got multiple people to do it."

"I thought you . . . you, um, guys didn't know when . . . someone else was there?" Joseph questioned.

"Some of us don't," Anthony explained, as Lieutenant ran her fingers through the gritty sand. "I didn't use to know what happened when Anton was out front, and there are still a lotta . . . blank spaces, fuzzy stuff. But lately people inside been talkin' to me more, 'cause I'm good at mediatin', you know, me bein' such a skilled listener and all. I'm kinda like everybody's confidant."

"So when you're . . . out," Ann said, her brow furrowing as she tried to understand, "talking to us here, there are . . . other people are still in there? How? Where are they?"

Anthony shrugged, a heavy lift and drop of his shoulders. "I wish I could explain it better, but things is still hazy. Not everybody wants to talk to me. I don't think I even met 'em all yet. I still get blackouts, and headaches, and not everybody in the house is . . . happy 'bout bein' woke up."

"Why not?" Toni asked. "Now that you know what you — what the issue is, you can work together more, and more of your, your . . . people can get a say."

Anthony tsked, meeting Toni's eyes with both brows raised. "Not everybody wants to hear what everybody has to tell, Miss Therapist."

Joseph coughed, and Ann reached up to wrap her hand around his neck and pull his head closer to hers. Toni felt Charlie shiver against her chest.

"I am not silent," Lieutenant said, her fist embedded in the dirty sand.

"I am a spinning, vicious light.
I curl up at the touch of the sun and taste the weight of darkness
in the night.
I can still feel ecstasy, you ain't beat that out of me.
You just made the fall that much deeper, and the holes that much
harder to see.
I feel around on my hands and knees like I'm blinded.
This is always what you wanted, to have me brought down to your
level.
You couldn't understand my aspirations, you wanted me defiled,
And tried to force me to make your deal with the devil.
I fought you tooth and nail, 'cause I saw what not to be.
So you shut me away, 'cause you couldn't shut me up.
You denied me my audience when I tried to speak.
I am not silent, but it don't fuckin' matter at all.
'Cause like a tree with no one to hear in the forest when it falls ... a
voice without a listener is just howling at the wall."

"That's depressing, L."

"I feel depressed, Mel."

"Aw, group hug you guys," Joseph suggested.

"We're *sitting* in a group hug," Ann pointed out. "If we got any closer we'd all just meld into one person."

"Yeah, I don't think I could deal with havin' all y'all inside me as well," Anthony admitted, chuckling. "No offense, but believe it or not, 's kinda crowded up in here."

"Yeah, and you ain't even met my split personality, Ralph," Joseph said with a shake of his head. "Dude is such an asshole, it's a problem."

"Is he the guy responsible for last night?" Ann teased.

"You shut up," Joseph grumbled, biting her shoulder playfully through her shirt.

"Aaannd that's the limit," Lieutenant stated. "That's when it gets too close for comfort."

And that's just it, Toni realized with an ache as they laughed together again, the sound drowned out by another gust of wind. *We're too close. We became friends so fast, got so close so quickly, and need each other so much 'cause of where we are that now if anything happens to one of us, it's like it happens to all of us.*

So if anyone crashes we're all going down.

"You're out, Cost. Go to the bench."

Ann rolled her eyes as she practically skipped off the court, wiping her sweaty hair off her forehead.

"I saw that, Cost. Take an extra ten minutes," Miss Saunders exhorted, frowning deeply.

Oh, no, Ann thought, grinning as soon as the gym teacher had turned her back and resumed coaching the rest of her class. *I'm so punished. Please, stop, don't. Have mercy.*

Ann pulled her ponytail tighter atop her head and pranced up the bleacher stairs, situating herself right on the edge of the bench closest to the walkway that divided the half of the seats reserved for the girls gym class with those set aside for the boys.

Seated on the bench to her left, Joseph leaned back and whistled softly. "You seem to get in trouble an awful lot, you know. 'S like every time I turn around you violatin' some rule and gettin' kicked off the court."

Ann didn't risk looking over at Joseph as she answered, "Yeah, and you seem to be fouling a little too much for someone who knows the rules to basketball pretty darn well."

"Can't help it," Joseph said casually. "There's somethin' over here that's way more interestin' distractin' me."

"Really?"

"Yes," Joseph said quietly, sincerely. "You know how you can't look at somethin' beautiful just once? Your eye just keeps gettin' drawn back? Well, especially as an artist, every time I try to focus on my game, I see this beautiful thing out of the corner of my eye, and I just have to try and get a closer look."

Ann swallowed. "Oh, yeah?"

"Yup."

"That's so gorgeous," Ann whispered, thankful that the need avoid suspicion by not meeting each other's eyes prevented Joseph from seeing the flush in her cheeks. "Really, it is. Now me, I'm focusing just fine. I just happen to suck at basketball."

"You know, why do I even bother with you?" Joseph muttered. "All my stunningly crafted romance just gets wasted."

"I guess I'm just too simple to appreciate you," Ann commiserated, struggling to keep a straight face, happy in the knowledge that he was doing the same.

"Honestly, though," Joseph said after a moment while playing with his fingers as a distraction. "If we keep doin' this, they're gonna start to notice. We should be more careful."

Ann bit her tongue and tried to buy time to think of an intelligent response, a way of agreeing with him, or some clever way of getting around the truth. "I don't care," she said instead, embarrassed at how low and desperate her voice sounded. "I don't fucking care."

Joseph started to look in her direction and then stopped himself, his face working with the effort. "Are you feelin' okay? You kinda look a little . . . I don't know, off."

"Thanks, you sure know how to make a girl feel special. What was that you said before about your expertise at the art of romance?"

"I was just askin', damn," Joseph responded. "Can't a guy ask his girl how she feels without said girl rippin' said guy's head clean off?"

"I didn't —" Ann closed her eyes. "I haven't been sleeping. At all."

"Nightmares?" Joseph fiddled with his sneaker laces.

"Yeah," Ann acknowledged, rubbing her bare arms and feeling cold now that the sweat had dried.

"Is this a new one?" Joseph asked carefully. "Or one a' the ones you told me you been havin' for years now?"

"A . . . new one," Ann said from between gritted teeth.

"You wanna talk about it?"

222

Ann fought the urge to drive her nails into her skin. "I'm . . . in a town."

Joseph nodded slowly. "What kinda town?" he prompted when Ann's pause lengthened into a silence.

"That's just it," Ann explained. "I don't know. I'm in a completely new town. I'm walking around and no one recognizes me. No one knows me."

"And is that what's scary?"

"No." Ann crossed her arms over her chest. "I walk up to someone, sometimes it's a woman, sometimes it's a man, and I ask for directions. I get them, I'm not sure how, but I kinda just walk around for a few minutes. And then I start to get so, so . . . so happy. Because I realize, no one knows me here. No one. I'm not Ann Cost, that slut, I'm not Wildcat, I'm not in STARE, I'm just some random girl. I realize, I can be anyone. I can just shake someone's hand and introduce myself, and I can be . . . nice. And maybe we'll be friends, and maybe I can be funny, and then that's all that he'll know me as, this nice, funny girl. I can be anyone, I can do anything, and it's *so* incredible, and then . . ."

"And then?"

"And then I see h— someone who recognizes me," Ann continued, pushing past the sick feeling of exposure, past the little voice warning her not to tell, never to tell. "And suddenly everyone just turns and looks at me. Everyone. Sometimes it's all at once, and sometimes it's bit by bit, like one person turns, and then they whisper to another, but they all end up looking at me, and then I realize I can't breath, and . . ."

"Slow down, slow down." Joseph's voice was soft, calming. "Breathe."

"That's what I'm trying to do!"

"Okay, okay!"

Miss Saunders turned to glance up at the bleachers toward the two teens. Ann and Joseph looked quickly away, pretending to focus on the games below until Miss Saunders put her back to them again.

"We're gonna get outta here, you know," Joseph said. "Ann?"

"Yeah, I hear you."

"No, don't just hear me," Joseph demanded, his voice firm with conviction. "I'm not just sayin' it to say it, or to make either of us feel better. We are *going* to get *out* of here. We are *going* to go to a place where we can leave all this shit behind us, and we are *going* to do whatever the fuck we want with our lives and forget all about the shitty fuckin' people here we hate. A'ight?"

"That a promise, huh boy?" Ann said, the edges of her mouth teasing a smile.

"Not even a promise," Joseph said, still serious. "A fact. We're gonna get outta here. We're gonna find a nice abandoned house and fix it up. We're gonna stay out dancin' until three, and sleep in until four, and eat French fries with hot sauce on 'em for breakfast, and use Seth's face for a dart board, and die fat and happy, period. Okay?"

Ann smothered a laugh with the back of her hand and nodded. "Okay. Sounds like a plan." Ann felt something within her fight against the words like a mental gag reflex, but this time she overrode it. "Joseph, I just want to tell you that —"

"Cost?"

Ann had to hit the back of the bench to keep from launching down toward the gym teacher and tearing her eyes out. "Yes?"

"You're wanted in the principal's office."

"It's okay," Joseph whispered, finally meeting Ann's eyes as she stood to descend the steps. "Whatever happens, remember — we're gettin' outta here."

Ann nodded, not caring if Miss Saunders saw. *I wanna kiss him*, she thought, her body screaming for her surrender. *I wanna put my arms around his neck, and kiss him, and hold on so hard that they have to call in security guards to rip us apart.*

"We're gettin' outta here," Joseph repeated. "Say it, c'mon."

"We're getting out of here."

"Cost!"

God, please get us out of here.

"You aren't avoiding me, are you?"

Toni felt a cold thrill run up her spine. A corresponding hot thrill coursed down it as Seth relaxed into the seat across from her, his vivid crocodile eyes narrowed into blue slits. Toni fought to remain composed, but by the handsome blonde's lazy smile, she knew she wasn't succeeding.

He likes it when I'm uncomfortable, Toni realized as she pushed her tray away knowing she had permanently lost her appetite for the day. *He likes it when he's making someone else feel strong emotions. Probably 'cause not having them himself makes him feel powerful.*

"You should be avoiding me," Toni responded, lowering her voice and glancing under her lashes around the busy cafeteria. "If you keep coming around like this, people might start to think I like you."

"Don't you?" Seth rolled his apple idly back and forth between two hands, but there was an insistence in his question that made Toni pause and examine the tension in his pale face.

"What are you doing?" Toni kept her voice soft to mask the searching confusion in her question. "Is this part of the game for you? Tell me you want to run and then see how far you can push me?"

"Not pushing," Seth argued, his self-satisfied grin returned. "Just giving you the little nudge that you need to . . ."

"To what? Come to you?"

"You make it sound like I'm asking you to jump off a bridge," Seth protested, twirling his apple by its stem.

"Yeah, because that's the equivalent," Toni declared. "You're asking me to stick my hand in the crocodile's mouth."

"No, I'm asking you to kiss the crocodile, which you don't seem to mind as much as you'd like to pretend you do," Seth shot back.

"Once, once," Toni said, pulling her brown overcoat across her chest as if covering her body might put an end to the pleasant, heated rush that persisted in spreading up from her center. "There are lots of things you enjoy once that you should never do again. Heroin is great that one time you do it, and then you do it again and suddenly you're broke, sprouting lesions, and have guys with names like Weasel and Big Shorty looking for you."

"But you —" Seth frowned. "Am I the crocodile, the heroin, or the guy named Weasel?"

"Never mind," Toni muttered, blushing and scowling.

"Okay, let's just stop with the mixed metaphors and be honest," Seth proposed. "You like me. I like you . . ."

"I do *not* like you," Toni practically spat, sinking down in her seat to hide the blush she knew was rising in her cheeks.

"You want me, and I want you, then," Seth amended, placing his elbows on the table and rubbing the apple with his thumbs. "I don't see the big problem. What is it about this that is so hard for you to believe?"

"You 'want' me," Toni asserted, putting the word in quotes with her fingers, "because you hate my friends and you like the idea of stealing me, because I'm not as easy to manipulate as the other people you've slept with, because I know what you are, which makes me a challenge, and because I'm one of the few girls in this school who's told you no."

Seth folded his hands over his apple. "And you're attracted to me because you like the idea of being wanted by someone you know is dangerous, because you know it would shock your friends, and because you wonder if maybe, just maybe, you think you could change me if you could just get me to feel something real." Seth cocked his head and shook one finger. "See, you're not the only one who can play doctor here."

"I'm not stupid enough to think I could change someone's essential nature," Toni argued.

"Oh, not this again." Seth scratched at the apple's skin. "C'mon, this whole reducing me down to just a sociopath is getting tired. I thought you had more imagination than that."

Toni opened her mouth to respond, and stopped. *Think, Toni. He wants sensation, he wants something exciting.* She tried to regain control of her breath, which was coming hard from the combined heat of anger and arousal. *He wants to feel something, but he could get* bored of you if you push him too far, and you can't do this without him.

"Satisfying a purely scientific curiosity," Toni began cautiously, "let's say I did have . . . imagination. What would that . . . entail?"

Seth's azure eyes gleamed, and his smile darkened considerably, setting the hairs on Toni's bare lower arms on edge.

"Well, you know what they say about imagination," Seth said, balancing the scarlet apple on the tips of his fingers and inclining it towards Toni, "it's pretty much unlimited."

"How have you been feeling, Charlie?"

"I've been well," Charlie said brightly, her euphoria allowing her to eye the stone-walled, lower level room she had been brought to with interest rather than fear.

"Why is that?"

Charlie opened and closed her mouth. She didn't know how the Headmistress would react if she explained that *everything* — the walls, the ceilings, doors, plants, the wind — and every person she came into contact with — were united in singing songs from Jefferson Airplane's *Surrealistic Pillow*.

But . . . if she's part of the symphony, shouldn't she know? Charlie felt the question cross her unusually serene mind like a dark cloud. *If I tell her, she might get mad at me for pointing it out, and then the music will stop . . . or she might start playing bad music.*

"Just a good day, maybe," Charlie said instead, and Ms. Valentina seemed to accept her answer, glancing over to Mrs. Waters, who was wheeling out an IV pole.

"Charlie, would you like to have a seat?" the Headmistress asked.

Charlie eyed the padded operating chair fitted with leather straps that the older woman indicated. Even in her rose-colored state, Charlie could tell that it was not truly a request. Sliding back into the chair with her feet not reaching the end, Charlie winced as the backpack she still wore to carry her shock device power source ground against her spine.

"Here, now sit up, and Mrs. Waters will help you remove that," the Headmistress said solicitously. Charlie smiled openly as the science teacher helped her remove the troublesome pack.

This must be why I was feeling good today, she realized, as the weight on her back eased and Mrs. Waters plucked the cool metal disks and connecting wires from her arms. *Something in me knew this was going to happen, and my head is pretty clear, and my mind, my mind is full of red ...*

Charlie twitched and blinked down at her arm, a full minute or so passing before she made the link between the straps being pulled tight around her arms and the understanding that she wasn't to be free of wires after all.

"How much do you understand about neurobiology, Charlie?" the Headmistress asked as Mrs. Waters proceeded to attach new shock disks to Charlie's arms and legs. The wires now ran to a computer on her right which fell just out of her sightline. Mrs. Waters tightened the strap around Charlie's neck.

"I ... I think a little, maybe?" Charlie ventured.

"Do you know what neurotransmitters are Charlie?" Ms. Valentina specified as she selected an IV bag full of a blue-tinted liquid from one of the shelves that lined the white room's back wall.

"We haven't really got to that section of biology yet," Charlie said lamely.

"Oh, it's about as simple as the name would suggest," the redhead dismissed. "Neurotransmitters are the chemicals that transmit signals from a neuron to a target cell across a synapse. They're the little busybodies of the brain, zipping around, influencing, and tampering, and whispering, and bringing you up and down. Too little of one of them in your brain, and you can be stuck in darkness and depression; too much of another, and you can become lost in delusions and hallucinations."

"Like me," Charlie said, her mouth twitching upwards into a smile that had no corresponding feeling of joy. "Too much or too little and you have a broken mind like me."

The Headmistress frowned. "You have an extraordinary mind,

228

Charlie," she said sternly. "It is not broken. Yes, you have painful and difficult symptoms due to a neurological condition that you cannot help, but you also represent a step forward for your entire species, as someone who is evolving to adapt to your condition and turn it from a weakness into a strength."

"I appreciate being able to help the species, if you think I am," Charlie said as politely as she could manage, "but I don't really feel all that strong. And to tell you the truth, if someone asked me if I would like to take a big leap for mankind or just have a nice, normal brain, I'd definitely go with the second choice."

The Headmistress smiled. "I appreciate your honesty. Unfortunately we're not usually given that choice." The red-haired woman lifted up the bag in her right hand and observed it musingly. "Being a scientist can so often try your patience. The work takes time and precision, and the results come so slowly. Sometimes a great thinker never sees the true fruit of their efforts in their lifetime. I'm not so very patient. This serum right here for example — like heroin, it takes only a few seconds after injection to create a feeling of pleasure." Ms. Valentina handed the bag off to Mrs. Waters who hooked it to the top of the IV pole, connected it to the IV line, and swabbed Charlie's arm as she readied her for the injection.

"I thought you were against drugs here," Charlie questioned, trying to distract herself from the sharp pinch of the needle.

The Headmistress chuckled shortly. "I am against dependency on medication. I am against the deadening effects it can have on the mind, especially a mind as special as yours. But drugs and chemicals have their uses. I take a direct approach to training the brain to perform to its full potential, and both direct pleasure and direct pain can be used to train the mind to reach new heights, which is what we are doing here."

Ms. Valentina nodded to Mrs. Waters, who placed a clamp on the IV line, preventing the solution from dripping into Charlie's arm. The science teacher let her right hand hover over the IV; the left hung above the keyboard of the computer hooked to the shock wires.

"Now Charlie, I am going to ask you a series of simple questions," the Headmistress proposed. "And I would like you to answer each one as best you can."

Charlie wet her lips. "Oh … okay."

The Headmistress smiled. "Good. Now." She placed both her hands behind her back. "How many fingers am I holding up?"

"Seven," Charlie said instantly. The Headmistress nodded to Mrs. Waters and the other woman released the clamp on the IV line. The unblocked solution streamed rapidly down the tiny tube into Charlie's vein, and she gasped when only seconds later an irresistible sensation of pleasure blazed through her, retreating slowly when Mrs. Waters clamped the IV again at a nod from her superior.

"Now." Ms. Valentina drew Charlie's attention back, her grey eyes dynamic in an otherwise impassive face. "How many fingers am I holding up?"

Eager for another rush, Charlie said the first number which came to mind. "Four."

The Headmistress shook her head, and Mrs. Waters pressed a key on the computer. The shock hit Charlie in her shoulder, the jolt even harsher for coming so soon after the previous positive feeling.

"Don't guess," the Headmistress warned. Charlie tried to catch her breath, feeling almost betrayed. "Focus. How many fingers now?"

Charlie tensed her muscles as she fought to conjure up the state which would allow her to see correctly. *But everyone is still singing!*

Charlie squinted, trying to read the answer in the sharp, blank face of the tall, lean woman.

The Headmistress tsked. "Come on, Charlie. None of that. You're using your eyes."

"I'm still using my brain," Charlie protested, shivering as much as her bonds would allow. "I'm looking for non-verbal clues. I'm, I'm making connections be-between …"

"You're afraid of failure," Ms. Valentina charged. "Don't be. You are absolutely capable of answering my questions. There is no reason to be worried."

You're not the one hooked up to a shock device! Charlie screamed inwardly, tears from the pain of not being able to voice her anger clouding her vision.

"Just try again," the Headmistress intoned, her speech calm and devoid of outward emotion. "What shape am I thinking of?"

Charlie swallowed, and it hurt against the worn leather of the strap across her throat. "You're thinking of a . . . a triangle."

"Is that a guess?" the redhead questioned, one ginger brow raised.

"No," Charlie said, the plastic material of the chair growing damp with sweat under her palms. "No, no, it's a triangle."

"And now?"

Charlie bit her lip, her head ringing. "It . . . it has seven sides. I forget what it's called."

The Headmistress' eyes turned to Mrs. Waters, and Charlie whimpered.

"A heptagon!" Charlie burst out.

The Headmistress smiled. Charlie felt her body forcibly relax as the IV lines surged with fluid and the warm, positive sensation made its way up the back of her neck, her headache receding.

"Very good," the Headmistress praised. "Now, let's move on to colors. What color am I thinking of now?"

Through the fading effects of the serum, Charlie could feel her anxiety and terror building again. The dizziness and roaring hole in her stomach felt like the sensation between the rise and dip of a roller coaster. She swallowed hard to prepare herself.

"Blue."

The Headmistress nodded to Mrs. Waters. Charlie felt another rush of pleasure, but it was laced with fear as the grey, kind, merciless eyes turned back to hers.

"And now?"

CHAPTER SIXTEEN

"C'MON, L, YOU GON' FREEZE. COME BACK IN THE HUDDLE."
Arms crossed tightly over her chest, Lieutenant shook her
head and paced rapidly back and forth in the dirty sand. Anton,
Toni, Charlie, and Melvin clung together against the wind in a
standing circle on the edge of Lake Amiszi. Joseph covered the
small fire of twigs he'd started with his lighter — the only reliable
illumination in the pitch dark, moonless night.

"You gotta keep your head," Lieutenant ordered, her voice clear
and commanding and certain. "'Cause losin' it and crawlin' into
a tiny ball will kill you faster than anythin' else out there, best
believe. You can't afford to get depressed when you makin' your
way through the woods. Depression is for people, and animals
can smell fear. But you gotta be realistic, really realistic. Stop and
look at what you have, don't try to do everything at once, breathe,
see what you got, and then make a plan, 'cause if you try to do
somethin' when you're panicking, or when you're confused —"

"L," Anton tried to interrupt. "I think we get the idea."

"'Cause if you just run at the problem," Lieutenant continued,
"you ain't gonna be able to really comprehend it, and that's when
you make mistakes." Words came out of Lieutenant in a battery
of sharp, demanding sounds, one sentence rushing over and
into the other as if the minute she formulated the words for
one insight, another presented itself. Despite her pacing she
seemed full of unreleasable energy, disturbingly and painfully

kinetic. "Mistakes, mistakes, mis-takes, takin' the wrong turn, missin' somethin'. You can't afford that. Not in the wild. You break your leg in the city, fuck it. It might hurt, but you can go to a doctor and prop your leg up, but break it out there?" She gestured broadly across the lake, a chaotic silhouette vibrating in the shadows cast by Joseph's fire. "All of a sudden you ain't got no medicine, no way of gettin' back, and you catch an infection, and like that!" Lieutenant snapped both her fingers. "You're fuckin' done. Or if you eat the wrong things, that'll fuckin' kill you, even if it doesn't *kill you* kill you from the poison . . ."

Charlie made a small noise, like a whine, accompanied by a twitching motion with one hand — her first reaction of the night, before returning to the glassy-eyed swaying silence in which she had come. Melvin and Toni exchanged looks as Lieutenant continued to rant, her voice rising and falling with no particular logic, as if she had lost the ability to modulate her own speech.

Joseph knelt down by his fire. Rocking back and forth, he glanced up and scanned the tree line with ever increasing frequency and anxiety.

". . . And water, water can fuckin' kill you. You gotta collect rainwater, can't drink from streams, 'cause that will just end you right there," Lieutenant's rant raced on, and she no longer paced in a straight line. The sand around her feet scurried and rose, and grew into a miniature sand storm. "You can go without food for weeks, but a few days with no water, and nope, you're done. You gotta find water, and you gotta make sure it's clean. You can boil it, but if you ain't got a pot that's no good, you can try straining it through your shirt, or a water still. And then you gotta find food . . ."

"L, we're going to get food, remember?" Melvin interjected. "We —"

Toni put a hand on his shoulder, and he ceased. Anton took a brave step forward. "Lieutenant, L, girl? You ravin' a bit right now. You wanna calm down?"

The small sand tornado around Lieutenant spiked, and she

turned on the taller boy. "I'm telling you all what you need to know to survive. Why ain't you listenin'? Seriously, severely, I speak but am not heard. The crowd sounds are explicit and foul, but I know my inner worth. I shall not let you make me mis-remember myself. I am the daughter of a proud race, I face you all and I do not bow . . ."

"Will someone calm her the *fuck* down?" Joseph snarled, standing up. By the firelight he could see Lieutenant's eyes, fanatical and furious. A blast of sand, not caused by the wind, hurled itself toward him. He covered his eyes just in time to avoid being blinded as the sand doused his tiny fire and left them in the dark.

"Yo, what the fuck?"

"Okay, calm down . . ."

"L? L, you okay?"

"This is bullshit. Ann's not fuckin' here, Charlie's catatonic or some shit —"

"Will everyone please calm down?"

"And I seriously do not have the patience or time . . ."

"L, hey, it's me . . ."

Can someone please . . ."

"Everyone, calm down and shut up!"

Toni's voice split the air, and the babble ground to a halt. Toni let out an audible sigh. "Thank you. Okay, Joseph, can you find your lighter?"

"The fire's out," Joseph responded glumly, his voice muted but still sullen.

"I know the fire is out," Toni said testily. "I asked about your lighter. We can relight the fire if you can find it, yes?"

"Possibly."

"Or we could just sit in the fucking dark then. Your choice."

There were a few clicks, and then the tiny flame of Joseph's lighter flared into view. He used it to guide himself to the sandy collection of twigs and brush he'd used to kindle the little fire.

"Okay," Toni said, turning to squint around at the rest of their group. "Is everybody okay? Lieutenant?"

234

"She'll be fine," Anton said, speaking for Lieutenant, who lay in a half-crumpled heap in the sand with her head down. "She just needs a few minutes."

"Melvin?" Toni questioned.

"I'm fine, for once," Melvin said, raising a hand. "Miracle, I know."

"And Charlie?" Toni blinked, searching for her friend at eye level.

"Down here," came the small girl's voice.

"Are you okay, Tiny?" Anton asked, his arm around Lieutenant, who was utterly still.

"Okay ... okay ..." Charlie contemplated the word. "No," she finally answered softly. "No, I don't think okay. No, not today."

"Yeah," Toni had to agree heavily. "Maybe we're not so okay."

It's coming. Oh God, it's coming. God? Is it working for God? Is it the divine monster of retribution, resolution, come to resolve me in a final solution? Or the Devil? D—evil, evil, D—vile, coming, coming, coming ... No, no, no ... quiet, quiet, quiet, so it can't hear me ...

Charlie shivered, her hands clasped over her mouth, as she balanced atop the toilet seat cover in the Academy bathroom. Leaning against the stall wall, her gaze turned up toward the ceiling, Charlie focused on the florescent lights as if they were a holy relic.

Light, light can keep it away, she thought with certainty. *Demons hate the light, it hurts their eyes, but people revel in the light because it provides safety and sanctity and sanctuary, it will protect me, I just have to hold onto it, stare at it, stare, prepare, pare and parse and purse my lips in prayer ...*

Charlie muffled a sob with her hands to keep from alerting the one hunting her to her presence. The air seemed full of discordant noises, like the music old black-and-white movies used to designate when something was wrong; loud, ostentatious, and jarring. Her terror kept her thoughts confined to similar themes,

235

the instinct of self-preservation just strong enough to overcome the sauce of unrelated emotions and beliefs which threatened to plunge her again into the daze of the past few hours. Charlie had barely been able to make her way to the bathroom, finding the well-traveled corridors of the school suddenly confusing and tricky, as if working together against her to get her lost. She pressed the left side of her face against the cool metal of the stall. The sound of her shallowly pounding heart echoed in her ear.

The sound of the hinges creaking as the entrance to the bathroom was opened went through the tiny girl like a gun shot, and an involuntarily yelp escaped her dry, chapped lips.

The demon, the Devil, the One, he's here. Charlie tried to shut off her breathing, but it only made her gasp more desperately for air. *He is come for me, three times three, making a beeline to the honeycomb, ready to sting, to kill, to drag me to Hell . . .*

"Hello?"

The Devil knows many tricks. Respond, and maybe you can trick him back, like the violin player in Georgia. "Hello?"

"Charlie? Is that you?"

Charlie swallowed, still alert lest the monster chasing her could change its voice. "Toni?"

There was a shuffle and another click as the other girl opened the adjacent stall and locked the door. Charlie bent down quickly to glance at the feet. She squinted, trying to discern hooves or claws. Instead she recognized the pretty pink flats as those Toni had worn a few days ago. Or was that weeks ago? Years?

"Charlie, how are you feeling?" Toni's voice was warm, firm, and Charlie felt something in her ease at the sound. It was as if she could relax against the other girl's strong center.

"It's following me, you know," Charlie explained. "The monster. I'm hiding here, because it's afraid of the light. You might be a trick though, so I shouldn't really be talking to you."

There was a pause, and Charlie blinked, wondering if now the Toni illusion would fall away to reveal the gaping horror beneath. Charlie's brain didn't conjure any images of what the true face of evil might be — there was greater terror in not having an reference, in knowing it would be awful, but not being able to conceive of its form.

"Okay, Charlie?" It was still Toni's voice. "I know that probably made sense to you, but I couldn't really hear what words you were using then. It sounded sort of like a jumble of maybe a couple of different ones and then some sounds. Do you think you could try and just say one sentence? Would that be easier?"

What is she talking about? Charlie tried to unravel the reason why Toni couldn't understand her. Unable to piece the puzzle together, she hit some kind of flimsy block just solid enough in her mind to be a barrier. *I used simple sentences, didn't I? Maybe she thinks I'm wrong about the monster, but she should be able to hear me, right?*

Then, like a returning boomerang, Charlie's words reverberated back on her inner ear. What in her own mind had been a collection of rushed but comprehensible sentences had come out of her mouth as a soup of phrases, words, and broken sounds. Charlie opened her mouth again to explain herself to Toni, and then realized sharply that she still might not be able to speak. Hot tears coursed down her cheeks.

"Charlie? Charlie, I just want you to know I'm right here."

"I'm ... can't talk ... Oh God ..."

"Okay, that I understood," Toni congratulated. "See, you can do this."

"I can't. I really can't. I'm ..." Charlie's cracked lips burned with the salt of her tears. "Sick. Sick, sick, sick, broken."

"Sick isn't broken," Toni said firmly. "If you're sick you can get better, and we will get you better."

"You can't." Charlie's despair was total. "I'm ... stuck here. Broken. Sick, and different."

"And we're going to get out," Toni reminded in a low but vital tone. "We are going to get you out, and get you good medication, and good therapy, and you can get better. I know it doesn't feel like it, but you can get well."

"I'm schizo." The shortened word made Charlie giggle. "Schizo, schism, snap, snap, snap."

"You are not schizo," Toni said, voice rising. "You have schizophrenia, yeah. But you are also smart, and clever, and adorable, and with some help and work you can make your own life. Trust your Therapist here. I've read lots of books and stuff."

"Then you know I won't be the same," Charlie murmured.

"What do you mean?"

Charlie licked at her burning lips, but her mind was cleared enough by pain to speak plainly. "I won't be the same," she repeated. "You should know that. No one ever comes back the same, after this. The girl I was when we met, the girl I was before I broke, she's never, ever coming back. No one ever gets to be the person they were really meant to be, not with this disease. I might do better, I might do worse, but I'm gonna live in this every single day even if we get out. I never get to go back, or even really forward. Ever."

There was a silence and Charlie closed her eyes, letting hope go and feeling the swell of relief that came with having no expectations.

"Okay, no." Toni's voice intruded on Charlie's trip into the comforting dark of depression. "No, you can't accept that. You're freaking psychic Charlie, and if that means one thing, it means that things are changing, that we don't know a bunch of things for certain, and if you can see into someone else's mind and tell what they're thinking, then I am damn skippy you can manage to beat this disease with some help. And since I'm going to help you no matter what, you don't have a choice in the matter, so you might as well just say thank you."

Charlie blinked. "Thank you?"

"Good. You are welcome."

Charlie wiggled her toes in her tattered shoes. "You know . . . if I was really psychic, I should have known you would say that," she offered, knowing her joke was weak even as it left her mouth.

"No," Toni said grandly. "That would require being able to enter a mind as complex, and fortified, and special as mine, and even for a psychic, I mean, that would take a lot of work. So don't beat yourself up over it."

"I won't then," Charlie said with a smile, the motion spurring the emotion that was usually its cause.

The bathroom door began to open again and Charlie grinned. "Ann!"

The door stopped midway.

"Hey, Ann. It's Toni and Charlie," Toni volunteered.

The door banged closed again.

Frowning, Charlie got down from her perch, opening her own stall as Toni did the same. Both girls surveyed the empty bathroom.

"Are you sure that was Ann?" Toni questioned.

Charlie nodded. "Without a doubt. I'm psychic, remember."

"Then why did she run?"

Charlie turned to face her friend. "She's scared. She has a monster following her, too."

"Admit it. You like having me around."

Toni took a deliberate bite out of her pear, using the excuse of food to collect herself under the forceful, penetrating power of Seth's gaze. The blonde senior's blue shirt matched his eyes, and Toni swallowed as he played with his straw with powerful fingers.

"You haven't got me to admit anything yet, so what makes you think I'll start now?" Toni challenged. Seth just smiled lazily.

"I'm wearing you down," he insisted. "You'll see."

Is he really that arrogant and sure of himself? Toni wondered. *Is it because all his life he's pretty much always gotten what he wanted from people? Or is it part of being what he is that he just expects everyone to do what he wants and can't imagine that someone wouldn't?*

Or is he right? Am I starting to like him in a way?

"Mind if I sit down?"

Toni was spared answering as Melvin, whose approach she hadn't noticed in the flurry of activity throughout the cafeteria, let his tray hover over the seat beside her. Seth raised his eyebrows at Toni, scratched the mole on the left side of his face, and shook his head. "Actually, yes. The lady and I were having a private conversation."

Toni glanced over at Melvin, who didn't meet her eyes. "Why?" Melvin continued, sitting down at the table firmly, his tray grating, metal on metal. "Do I make you nervous?"

"No," Seth said, irritated but still languorous. "Why would you ever, for any reason, think that?"

"Because I think people who know what you are make you nervous," Melvin confronted. "Because I think the sight of someone who knows your secrets makes you sick."

"Wow." Seth laughed, genuinely amused as far as Toni could tell. "Someone's desperate to start something today."

"I think he has a point, Melvin," Toni said significantly. *You are coming off desperate*, she thought. Melvin gave an exaggerated snort of dismissal in her direction.

"This isn't anything to do with you." Melvin waved her away and turned back to Seth. "This is about you and me."

"There's nothing between you and me," Seth chuckled.

"No?" Melvin said with simpering falseness. "You don't want anything to do with the town fag?"

"Your persecution complex thing is really tiring," Seth said, bored and chewing on his straw. "It's you who decided to come out in this town, and you who is constantly shoving it in everyone's faces. You just bring it on yourself, and then you get mad when people react. Why don't you take some responsibility for yourself?" Toni could see some of the nearby students eavesdropping out of the corner of her vision.

"Me take responsibility?" Melvin laughed bitterly. "Coming from the guy who takes his little girls *and* boys out by the woods

240

and down by the lake to mess around with in ways this flaming fag right here would never do?" Toni looked down and stabbed a potato with her fork. "I'm not the one who has to threaten people into hiding actual *scars* and then tell them to pretend they *fell* after I've had sex with them."

"I've never been out by the lake and done anything like that with boys or girls," Seth said clearly, with no hint of guilt or nervousness in any part of his face, or voice, or body, and with the exact same annoyed righteousness that Melvin displayed."I've never had sex with a guy, but neither have you from what I hear, and that's your problem. You're just projecting your own pathetic desires off on me. It's sad."

Toni blinked. Even knowing for a fact that Seth was lying, she found it hard not to believe him. He seemed in every gesture and expression to mean what he was saying.

"Am I?" Melvin taunted. "You don't seem to get it. You're slipping. It's not a secret you're in STARE now. It's not a secret you were part of The Incident. You think I'm just making this up?" Melvin shook his head, smiling now. "For some reason some of your friends seem a little more nervous about you . . . and a little more willing to talk to me."

Seth's eyes narrowed, finally revealing something akin to an emotion. Toni decided it was frustration, the recognition of a possible threat. "No one believes you," Seth insisted, still confident but without his former rock-solid certainty.

Melvin whistled. "You can keep telling yourself that, or you can look around at the people watching us now, and then tell me that like you mean it."

Seth's cold, sharp eyes scanned the tables nearby. Most looked away from his penetrating gaze, staring down or quickly creating conversations with other students. His fist tightened, knuckles cracking, and his expression when he turned back to Melvin was enough make Toni pull back.

"Seth, let it go," Toni said quietly. "Melvin, c'mon, leave it . . ."

"Shut up," Melvin snapped at her.

"Hey, don't talk to her like that," Seth barked, pulling the straw from his mouth and gesturing to Toni.

"Thank you," Toni said, surprised and warmed. Seth rolled his eyes and shot her an unguarded glance which turned her temperature almost instantly in the other direction. The handsome blonde's face betrayed annoyance and impatience with her, and a disdain and disregard that wove her insides together in a knot of embarrassment and shame.

It's like I'm a little dog that's yapping at his heels, Toni saw clearly. *He's not upset at how Melvin is treating me; he's upset that Melvin is talking at all to his possession. He's not upset at Melvin outing him for what he's done because he cares about being straight or gay, he's angry at the possibility of losing everyone's respect and fear.*

"I gave you a chance." Seth snarled, rising slightly out of his seat. "Now it's your own fault."

"What is?" Melvin baited, raising his voice and forcing Seth to respond louder in turn. "My fault you're going to bury me six feet under?"

"Melvin, be careful . . ." Toni warned.

"That would imply they might have a chance of finding your body," Seth practically growled, and Melvin's face paled.

"So, you're threatening me?" Melvin's voice trembled, but now it was high enough so that it attracted broad attention. Toni swallowed as several aides moved toward their table. *C'mon, c'mon, c'mon . . .*

"I don't need to threaten you," Seth snapped, and Melvin's hands shook.

"You just did! You just said they'd never find my body . . ."

"That's not a threat," Seth said as the aides closed in on them. "That's just the inevitable."

Melvin shot Toni a desperate glance, and Toni quickly looked around at the students who sat captivated by the fight. She could hear snatches of conversations and Seth's words being repeated and passed on.

"God!"

Melvin hissed and stumbled back as the shocks hit him, biting back groans of pain as the aides descended.

"See?" Seth said, biting back down on his straw. "You just bring it on yourself."

Where. The. Fuck. Is. She?

Joseph flicked his lighter on for the third time as he paced the old abandoned house. He held the flame under his right hand absently, feeling the heat build and ignoring the light scorching of his skin. The powerful night wind easily invaded the house, streaming in through the cracks in the walls and boarded up windows.

"C'mon Ann. Where the hell are you?" Joseph asked the empty house.

This is ridiculous, Joseph fumed, angry with himself and embarrassed at himself. *I'm just standin' here like an asshole when it's clear as fuck that she's not comin'. I should just go.* Joseph paced nearer the door but didn't leave.

There was a creak near the door and Joseph whirled around, holding up the lighter. He let out a heavy sigh as Ann pushed her way inside, pulling a leaf off of her pants.

"There you are," Joseph said, the tightness in his chest easing as she moved into the light.

Ann rubbed her shoulders and glanced at him. "Yeah, where else would I be?"

"Well, I mean you wasn't at the meetin' last night," Joseph pointed out. "And you weren't here the night before that, so . . ."

Ann frowned, shrugging defensively. "So, what?"

Joseph blinked. "So, I was wonderin' what happened?"

Ann tightened her ponytail. "Nothing happened. I just couldn't make it."

Now Joseph frowned, taking a step toward her. "If you couldn't make it, somethin' musta happened. Kinda the logical progression there."

"Or I just didn't feel like it," Ann said curtly, tugging on her ponytail.

Joseph paused, took a deep breath, and tried to make his voice non-committal. "Okay, where did you feel like bein'?"

Ann's eyes narrowed. "What is that supposed to mean?"

"I just —"

"Is that an accusation, Joseph?" Ann took a step forward. "Is there somewhere you think I was?"

"No, I just —"

"Because if you think something, okay, if you have something you wanna get off your chest —"

"Just hear me out for five seconds before —"

"Don't come at it from the side, asking about my whereabouts. Just fucking say it," Ann continued rapidly, her voice riding loudly over Joseph's attempts to speak. "Ask me what you really wanna know. Go ahead. Ask me if I was with a guy, because that's what this is, isn't it? You don't trust me. That's what this whole thing is, right?"

"I don't ask you about your whereabouts 'cause I don't trust you. I ask you about 'em 'cause you're my girlfriend!" Joseph finally managed to respond, his voice now considerably louder in his attempts to be heard. "God, what the fuck just happened?" He shook his head. *How do things always fuckin' spiral so damn fast like this? What did this conversation even start as?*

"Why are you so goddamn needy?" Ann snapped. "What, can't you make it a day on your own? Why do I have to tell you where I am? What, are you my supervisor now?"

"Will you stop?" Joseph exploded, his voice echoing around the house. "God, just shut up for five fuckin' minutes, and let me finish a damn sentence! All I was doin' was askin' where you were to make sure you was all right, but you've obviously decided to have a bitch day, so please, go ahead."

"A bitch day. Oh, that's real mature," Ann shot back, tossing her hair, her eyes blazing. "Didn't take long for you to drop the whole 'loving boyfriend' thing now did it?"

"Yo, I didn't stand *you* up just to come around two days later and act like a cunt for no fuckin' reason," Joseph responded nastily. "What's your problem? Was I bein' too nice? You want me to treat you like the whore everybody here is always callin' you?"

Joseph wasn't surprised when she slapped him; a part of him expected it. It was his own reaction to the sharp sting on his face that took the both of them off guard. His body took over, and he shoved Ann violently back, causing her to stumble and almost bang her head into the crumbling fireplace.

Fuck, Joseph thought, half in shock. *Fuck, what are we doin'?*

Ann's green-blue eyes met Joseph's, and for a split-second he could see the desperate pain and fear in them, before she hardened her jaw line and barreled towards him, shoving him back even harder.

"Go ahead!" she demanded, her voice rising and falling wildly, angry, hysterical, vicious, scared. "C'mon!" She shoved him again. "You wanna fucking hit me, then be a man and hit me!" Ann punched him in the shoulder, trying to force his hand. "Go ahead! Do it, you know you want to! Go ahead!"

Joseph dodged another blow and caught Ann's right hand. "Stop it, Ann, I don't wanna fuckin' hit you. I just want you to stop bein' such a fuckin' bitch!"

"You've known I was a bitch since you met me," Ann countered. "What makes you think you can get me to stop?"

"I'd be a fuckin' idiot to ever think anything could stop you from bein' a cunt," Joseph enunciated nastily.

Ann ripped her hands out of his hold. "So why don't you leave? Huh? If I'm so goddamn awful then leave! Why didn't you leave?"

"Because I love you, you bitch!" Joseph screamed, the raw cry ripped from the center of his aching, pounding chest. "Okay? Get it? I put up wit' your shit, and I actually care what the fuck you say, and I'm still here even after we have sex, and I fight for you, any time, any day, against anybody, but I am not gonna be your punchin' bag, or your puppy, or your bitch. You want me?

You gotta come clean, or I'm out."

Joseph waited, hot, furious, hoping, and sickened, as Ann's mouth worked, her face pale, eyes darting over his face as if looking for an escape route. "There's nothing to come clean about," she finally announced. "I just am what I am, and if you're not man enough to take me, then don't waste my time."

"Fine," Joseph snarled, his voice low and ragged. "Good. Then I guess we're done."

"Fine," Ann snapped back. "Then I guess you can just go."

"The door's right that way," Joseph drawled viciously, and Ann visibly swallowed before turning on her heel and storming out, her ponytail swinging.

"Good fuckin' riddance," Joseph told himself, his nails digging into his palms. *I'm fuckin' done, and I'm glad, it's over fuck it, I'm done, I'm d . . . I'm . . . I . . .*

A scream broke past Joseph's lips as he seized. He grabbed for something, anything to hold onto, before collapsing to his knees, gasping, heaving, and trying to fight off the pain in his chest from his too rapidly beating heart.

"Take your time."

The Headmistress' voice was relayed out from within the confines of the booth as she tapped the soundboard and observed the subject of the experiment through the glass. Mrs. Waters stood beside the redhead, monitoring the vitals of the boy strapped to the chair.

Anton stared forward, his unfocused gaze on the table where the device lay. The piece of equipment resembled an old fashioned radio; two antenna stood straight upwards from either end of its body, and a dial in the center was moving slightly back and forth.

The tall black boy strained slightly against his bonds as he glared through the darkened glass of the booth. Inside, Mrs. Waters tapped her pencil restlessly on her clipboard, nibbling on her lower lip as she examined the computer readings.

"There's no change so far ..."

"Wendy ..." The Headmistress let the name alone quiet her companion. The science teacher lapsed into an uncertain silence besides her superior.

Anton's fingers tensed against the armrests of the chair. His face seemed to ripple, his expression going first blank and then brightening. His features softened, and his eyes glazed in and out of focus.

The dial on the radio device shifted to the right, and the baseline graph on the computer before Mrs. Waters began to spike widely.

"It's —"

"Yes, I see," the Headmistress hushed.

The vein in the subject's forehead bulged, and as he blinked the dial veered almost wholly to the left. The computer's baseline became a series of tiny, jagged upshots.

The Headmistress leaned forward, placing both hands on the soundboard as she watched the student through the glass. The tight edges of her lip wavered as they began to spread into a triumphant grin.

Mrs. Waters frowned. "Wait, something is wrong."

The Headmistress' eyebrows shot up. "What? What's wrong?"

"Something is interrupting the readings. Another source of electric —"

There was a click and the sound of a key turning, and then the door to the lower level room slammed open. Mrs. Waters let out a strangled gasp, dropping her clipboard, and the computer's baseline went flat.

The Headmistress smoothed back her red hair as she exited the booth slowly, her grey eyes meeting the furious, shocked, and stunned brown ones of the woman who had interrupted her experiment.

"Well, Evelyn," the Headmistress said evenly. "I suppose it's time we had a chat."

CHAPTER SEVENTEEN

"WELL, DON'T FEEL YOU HAVE TO STAND," THE HEAD-
mistress proposed, pushing aside some of the papers cluttering
her desk and gesturing to the seat opposite her own. One of the
masks that normally hung upon her office wall was missing,
and the bookshelf behind her head appeared overfull, sporting
a number of new volumes. "Please, sit down."

"I feel I have to stand."

"Well, suit yourself of course. Would you like something to
eat? I always keep a packet of mixed nuts here —"

"Sophia," Mrs. Carter interrupted.

"Evelyn," Ms. Valentina responded equally. "Oh, come on. If
we're going to speak honestly, I don't see any reason why we
can't be civil."

"Oh, I can think of several reasons why we cannot be civil,"
Mrs. Carter said.

The Headmistress raised one bemused brow. "Can you?"

"What I just saw —"

"Was an experiment," the Headmistress completed, her voice
clear and unabashed. "Conforming to the highest professional
standards and utilizing —"

"An underage, non-consenting student," Mrs. Carter snapped.

"Most of our STARE students would inform you that they were
brought to this school without their consent," the Headmistress
noted dryly, tapping the top of her abacus.

248

"They are here for their own good," Mrs. Carter replied immediately, drawing herself upright, her short black hair swinging. "So that we can treat them and help them. Not so we can use them for our own personal amusement."

"Careful, Evelyn," the Headmistress warned, her voice dropping to a lower octave. "Be very careful."

"Of what?" Mrs. Carter questioned. "Of trying to protect my students?"

"They are my students as well," the Headmistress retorted with icy politeness. "Don't forget that. How exactly do you expect to help heal these adolescents unless we study them?"

"We have strict treatment plans and procedures already planned out," Mrs. Carter stated fiercely. "All strictly regimented, and all based upon the same guidelines —"

"And that is exactly where you go wrong," Ms. Valentina declared, planting her hands on her desk and leaning forward so that her eyes were level with those of the principal. "Mental illness is not strictly regimented. It is not the same. It varies not only with every disease but with every person suffering from the disease, which you would know if you spent more time actually trying to understand them."

"I understand my students perfectly well, thank you," Mrs. Carter defended, her face very nearly white with affront and rage.

"Oh, do you?" The Headmistress pursed her lips and nodded, considering, as she settled back into her chair and folded her hands. "And how well are you understanding and helping Charlie Persan?"

"Charlie is a very scared, very disturbed young girl," Mrs. Carter said rigidly, "and your experiments on her are only fueling her inability to cope with reality."

"On the contrary, I believe my experiments are the best thing for Miss Persan," Ms. Valentina challenged. "She is a brilliant, gifted young woman with powerful gifts, which I am helping her to realize. Once she is able to view herself as more than merely insane, she will be able to harness her abilities and not only live well in our reality, but better understand others as well."

"Charlie *is* insane," Mrs. Carter attested, shaking her head and looking at the Headmistress with wide, scandalized eyes. "You can't possibly think you can change that?"

"Now, Evelyn." The Headmistress tittered. "Here I thought you believed that behavior could be changed; isn't that the whole idea behind our use of aversives?"

"There is a difference between changing behavior and thinking you can, can re-program insanity into a skill!" Mrs. Carter argued, raising her voice. "These children aren't lab rats, Sophia! They are teenagers, vulnerable, volatile teenagers. Sick teenagers —"

"Yes, and these volatile, vulnerable, sick teenagers have outsmarted and outplayed your full-grown staff, time and time again," the Headmistress said in a voice matching the principal's for steel. Standing up and yanking open one of her drawers, she pulled out several files and slammed them down on the table with force. "All while dealing with demons, to which, quite frankly Evelyn, you have chosen to shut your eyes and cover your ears against understanding."

"Excuse me?" Mrs. Carter practically spat. "How dare you imply —"

"I'm not implying. I'm stating," the Headmistress declared, picking up one manila file and flipping it open. "If you'd had open eyes you would have long since realized that for all her brilliance in her schoolwork, Amina Jackson is working herself into a frenzy, and if we don't catch her soon we'll have a full-blown manic, psychotic episode in front of the whole school, and I can promise you that her break will do a considerable amount of physical damage to whatever is in the vicinity."

"Amina has been exemplary in controlling herself," Mrs. Carter began.

"Yes, exactly," Ms. Valentina said impatiently. "She's been bottling up all her mania, trying to hide it and avoid punishment, and all you see is a success story, while if you looked for even a second longer you would see the signs of an impending nuclear meltdown."

The Headmistress shoved the file at Mrs. Carter, who took it with surprised, shaking hands. The redheaded woman instantly whipped open another file.

"Melvin Stavos." Ms. Valentina snorted. "He's headed for suicide if he continues like he has." She tossed his file towards Mrs. Carter, who caught it clumsily, even as the Headmistress opened another.

"Joseph Nathaniel Valdez." The Headmistress shook her head, her fiery hair swinging from left to right. "He's headed for a physical collapse if I cannot find out how to offset his condition."

"His condition?"

"Yes, perhaps if you checked his vitals and the medical status report I wrote up after my most recent experiment, you would be able to better understand the immense danger one of *your* students is in," Ms. Valentina suggested, thrusting the new file atop the others that Mrs. Carter was attempting to balance in her arms.

"Oh, I see," Mrs. Carter snapped caustically. "So when they are put in danger it is of course my fault, and then they are my students?"

"When you put them in danger — yes," the Headmistress supported. "Ann's recent situation, and your handling of that, for example."

"Ann has been rapidly regressing," Mrs. Carter justified. "Clearly her current living arrangements are not helping, and —"

"And you then sending her back into the breach, back into what she has been trying so desperately to escape, will help?" the Headmistress asked.

"I don't know what you mean by —"

"Oh, wake up, Evelyn," Ms. Valentina snapped, rolling her eyes. "It's been completely obvious what the situation is with that girl from the very beginning. You only have to spend two minutes in her presence to understand exactly what is causing her behavioral problems. It's in her *eyes* for God's sake. The best thing you ever did for her was bring her into the STARE program and set her up in one of our houses."

"Yes," Mrs. Carter drawled. "Where she promptly had unprotected sex with another student."

"And all you saw in that was disobedience," the Headmistress murmured, her smile pitying and disappointed. Mrs. Carter swallowed, her arms full of files, the delicate blue vein in her neck throbbing. "I suppose you see nothing out of the ordinary with our Mr. Levant?"

"His teachers say he is doing exceptionally well in his classes," Mrs. Carter replied in a muted, brittle voice. "Except for his difficulty in responding to or sticking to one version of his name."

"Yes, well, having multiple identities can make these things so very confusing," the Headmistress said with silky venom.

"None of this changes the fact that if I reported your experiments to the police or any scientific board they would be found unethical and illegal," Mrs. Carter said in a voice pitched low to keep from shaking.

"Yes," the Headmistress agreed easily. "And they would come here to do a thorough investigation, and just imagine what they might think of *our* methods." Mrs. Carter's redhaired superior chuckled. "Oh, Evelyn, I can just see you up there defending us against the media scrutiny, explaining the therapeutic use of skin shock devices and food deprivation on tender young adolescents to eager reporters and human rights commissions, dealing with the deluge of emails and phone calls, preaching our specialized version of treatment to a world that might not truly understand."

Sophia Valentina tapped the very still principal gently on the shoulder as she headed for the door. "Why don't you just hang onto those files for now?" she suggested considerately

252

to the dark haired woman. "That way you can look at them at home, without having to come into my or Wendy's office for a copy." She smiled as Mrs. Carter turned slowly to meet her grey, knowing eyes. "After all," the Headmistress whispered, "we are in this together, now aren't we?"

"Ma'am, you mind if I sit with you?"

Toni grinned up at the tall boy who was holding a full lunch tray uncertainly. She searched the friendly smile on his dark face. "Sure . . . Anthony."

"Thank you." Anthony sighed as he lowered himself into the bench opposite Toni. He picked up his knife and fork with either hand and set to work cutting up his meatloaf. "Don' know about you, but it's like the nastier the food here gets, the more of it I eat. I'd even eat bologna at this point. Shows you how desperate I am."

"Yeah, it's like they expect us to all stay healthy and punish you if you aren't," Toni contributed. "And even when they . . ." Toni trailed off as Anthony scratched his shoulder, pulling up one of his sleeves inadvertently. She caught a glimpse of telltale white and bit her lower lip.

"Hey, Anthony, what happened to your arms?"

"Huh?" Anthony inserted another piece of meatloaf into his mouth and chewed heavily.

"You arms," Toni said again, loudly, trying to be heard over the din of the cafeteria. When Anthony continued to stare at her blankly, she reached forward and pulled both the sleeves of his grey, oversized turtleneck back, revealing large white bandages on both. Anthony gazed down carefully and raised one eyebrow as he took in his arms.

It's like he's just noticing it, Toni realized.

"Someone cut me," Anthony answered simply. "Yeah, those look pretty serious. Damn. Ouch."

"You don't remember what happened?" Toni questioned.

Anthony frowned, blinking. "Nah ... I guess I wasn't there."

"So you don't remember who did it?" Toni specified. Anthony frowned more deeply, scratching the back of his head.

"No, and that's weird too, 'cause normally I get told." Anthony rubbed his chin. "Communication is important, Toni. Make sure you have that in a relationship. When you pick a man, pick one who understands the importance of good conversation. Communication though, right? Not just game." Anthony pointed at her, nodding sagely. "Game is your man using a lot of words to tell you nuthin', you get a man who acts like a wordsmith and after twenty minutes he still ain't told you where he was last night?" Anthony shook his head. "Run, girl, run outta there fast, before you catch a disease or have the police at your door." Anthony continued nodding, and Toni swallowed.

"So ... do you think it was a man who cut you?"

"Cut me?" Anthony jerked and looked around. "What you mean? Oh, this?" Anthony registered his bandaged arms again. "Mmm ... only one I can think of who would do it is Seth."

"No," Toni answered slowly. "It couldn't have been Seth, I just had science with him."

"No? Damn, this is gettin' to be a straight up mystery," Anthony noted. "Feels like I'm in a middle of a damn film noir. People was classy in those films, talkin' 'bout "dames done me wrong" and rockin' the fedoras. We need more of that today. *The Maltese Falcon*, you seen that one? That is a strong movie. Got a good femme fatale, and that's always hot."

"Anthony." Toni leaned forward. "The cuts on your arms ... I think it would be hard for someone else to slash you from the outside and reach that far in unless you kinda held your arms out, and that doesn't seem likely."

"I'm sensin' you got a theory," Anthony prompted. Toni chewed on her lower lip, her mind working, and then she held out her own right arm and drew back her sleeve.

"See that?" Toni said, trying to keep her voice steady as with shaking fingers she showcased three long scars decorating her inner upper arm. "Those are from when I used to . . . when I used to cut."

"Damn." Anthony tsked in sympathy. "Why'd you do it?"

"I just kinda — hated myself," Toni explained abruptly, the pit of her stomach lurching dangerously. "I was ashamed and didn't like my body or what I'd . . . it was a bad time."

"See, you always actin' the therapist for everyone else," Anthony said. "But you probably need one for yourself too, especially dealin' with us."

"Yeah, that's the thing," Toni said, plunging ahead lest she lose her courage. "Your scars, they look like mine. Almost exactly like mine."

Anthony narrowed his eyes as he locked onto Toni's gaze, and then he pulled back.

"Oh, you sayin' you think . . . I did this?" Anthony twisted his head away, eyebrows high on his dark forehead.

"Maybe not *you*, you," Toni clarified. "But . . . one of . . . of you. Someone in there, in . . . an alter."

"Shit," Anthony whispered, slumping back into his seat, his arms resting limply on the table on either side of his tray. "Damn that's . . . if that's what's happenin' we got a problem. A real big problem."

"Yeah, I can imagine," Toni said.

"No, you really can't," Anthony asserted. "If someone inside is hurtin' us, if someone woke up and is angry, and I don't know? That means it's someone real deep."

"So this has never happened before?"

Anthony shook his head and then froze. "Only once. Damn, if this is . . . this means that someone is bein' reminded of somethin' bad."

"So you don't know who is being reminded of whatever it is that's so bad?"

Anthony gritted his teeth. "Somebody knows." His eyes darted back and forth, back and forth, making Toni's head ache as she watched. "Somebody was there. Somebody remembers. One of us knows . . . one of us was there. They just won't tell."

"Why not?" Toni asked.

As soon as the question was out of her mouth Toni felt foolish for asking it, and when Anthony didn't respond she didn't ask him again.

I need something sharp, something that can cut me. I'll do it, I'll fucking do it. God, I wanna do it. They don't think I'll do it. That's why no one cares. They think I'll just go back, that they can make me. He doesn't think I'll do it. That's why he broke up with me. Well, won't they be surprised when they find me dead and bleeding on the floor? And how will they feel then?

Ann paced in the tiny space of the bathroom stall. She pushed up the sleeves of her pink flower-and-heart printed shirt, scratching rapidly, uncontrollably at her arms. Her hair loose and stinging as it whipped against her face.

They won't care, she realized with perfect clarity, her stomach sinking. Ann had to bite down on her entire lower lip to keep the wailing shriek of despair inside. *They don't care. They hate me. Joseph hates me. All the others hate me too. They pretended to like me, but now, now they don't have to hide it. Well, fuck them. I hate them.*

"We don't hate you."

"Yes you do," Ann snapped. "You all do, you all fucking hate me, and you think I should die. Well, good, fuck you. I hate you all anyways." Ann took a breath and realized that she had spoken aloud. "Charlie?" she whispered.

"Hello," said Charlie in a lilting, little-girl voice from the next stall over. "We don't hate you. Not any of us."

"That's a lie," Ann snapped, pressing her hands against the cold stall walls and pushing against them as if she could knock them down by virtue of the rage coursing through her. "You all hate me, and I hate you, and that's just fine. You should. I'm disgusting, and sick, and a bitch."

"They tell me that, too," Charlie said, almost brightly, as if

256

Ann had just shared that she also liked strawberry ice cream. "You shouldn't listen, though. They like to lie to you and try to trick you."

Ann's throat seized up. "I'm not hearing voices in my head, Charlie," she said harshly. "I'm talking about how you all hate me."

"And who's telling you that?"

Ann gnawed at the inside of her mouth wishing she could make it bleed. "I . . . I don't need anyone to tell me that," she said quickly, tossing her hair out of her face. "I might not be fuckin' psychic, but I can tell when I'm not wanted, ya know?"

"No," Charlie denied. "I don't know. I've been trying to stay out of your head."

"Oh." Ann's heart slowed slightly. "So . . . is it . . . working?"

"Hmm? Oh, for thoughts and things, kind of. It's the feelings I can't make stop. Feelings are stronger than thoughts," Charlie rambled, her chirping voice both grating and soothing to Ann. "Your feelings are really loud and hard but all muddled together. They keep switching, switching, almost like Anton to Anthony to Ant—"

"I get it! I get it! Will you just stop!" Ann slapped her hands over her ears.

"I'll stop," Charlie barely whispered after a minute of absolute silence. "I'm sorry."

"Oh, no! No, I'm sorry ," Ann protested, suddenly contrite. "No, Charlie, it's not your fault. It's me. I'm such a bitch. I'm sorry, I just . . ." Ann braced both her arms on either side of the stall, trying to anchor herself, but still she felt herself pulling up, becoming weightless. "I always do this. I'm so bad . . ."

I'm bad. I'm so bad. Why would anyone love me? Well, there's an obvious answer — they don't. God, I'm such an idiot, I —

"It's okay," Charlie said, interrupting Ann's erratic flow of thoughts. "I accept your apology."

"No you don't," Ann shot back. "You're lying. You're just smarter about it because of your whole mind thing. It's not okay."

"Do you want it to be not okay?"

"What the hell is this? That's — that's turning my words around!" Ann's voice rose, propelled by fury. "Don't do that!"

"I'm sorry."

"I hate that — that twisting your words crap." Ann folded her arms, gripping her shoulders with either hand. "Joseph is always goddamn doing that. Twisting things around, making it seem like, like ... it's always "Oh, I love you, why don't you tell me the truth"? Like, hello? If I told you the truth you wouldn't, so just stop fuckin' askin' about it, ya know?"

"You think he'd stop loving you?"

"Oh, he doesn't love me." Ann laughed dismissively. "He just — just wants sex and someone to listen to his sob stories. He likes *having* a girlfriend." *Or ... he did.* "Whatever." Ann tossed her hair and laughed again, loudly. "He fuckin' bailed on me when it got rough, which I shoulda known he would do anyway. Whatever. He's pathetic. I was getting sick of him anyways. He's fuckin' clingy and whiney. He makes me sick to my stomach, ya know?" Ann felt a vicious delight at tearing into Joseph. *I wish he was here*, she thought ferociously. *I wish he was here. I wish I could tell him how much I hate him. I want to see his face. I want to look into his eyes and see him fucking cry.* Ann's hatred and disgust were absolute. She knew with complete certainty that she felt nothing for Joseph but spite. *I hate him. I'll always hate him.*

"Maybe he was just worried about you," Charlie piped in. "He worries about you a lot. Worry, worry, worry ... you can see it on his face all the time."

"Worry? He doesn't worry about me. Well, maybe worry that I'll cheat on him, but not worry about me, like, care about me." Ann scoffed, pacing again, scratching her shoulders again. "Worry about me — yeah, he worries about me, because he hates me and thinks I'm a whore. He's worried that I'll embarrass him."

"He loves you," Charlie said, simply, and Ann could hear the sound of the other girl rocking atop the toilet seat. "He loves you lots."

"No he doesn't. He hates me. He fuckin' left me."

258

"He'll be back."

"You don't know that." Ann's lower lip trembled. "You can't know that." *Oh God. Oh God. I made a mistake.* "You think so?"

"I know so. You don't have to be psychic. Love is easy to see. People are bad at hiding it," Charlie confided. "People think they can hide it, but it always shows. They glow, even when they're really sad. They glow with it. Like someone switched on a light behind their eyes. And then when they get heartbroken it's like looking at a drain: they're empty and they keep trying to suck things down and fill themselves up, but nothing is the same as before, and so they keep trying and they get all tense and strung out and thin, trying to move and run and distract themselves, and it's really uncomfortable looking at them. Or they just give up and curl into a ball and try to sleep, and go numb, and not feel."

Ann banged her back rhythmically against the left stall wall. "And which one am I doing?"

"The first one," Charlie answered. "It sounds painful."

"It is." *I love him. Oh God, I still love him. I'll always love him. And he's gone. I drove him off. I wish he was here. I need him to be here, now, right now. I'll never, ever hurt him again, God, just send him back. I promise, I'll be the perfect girlfriend, just send him back. Please. Make it stop, please make it stop.*

"Ann? Are you okay?"

"No." Ann chuckled, then winced as her body struggled between the opposing needs to laugh and cry. "It stings." The actual tears were slow in coming. Instead deep sobs ripped up through her chest and to her throat, racking her body, and Ann collapsed to her knees.

"Ann? Ann?"

Charlie's feet plunked down, followed by her knees as she knelt and laid her head against the floor. She blinked over at her weeping friend. "I'm sorry."

"For what?" Ann laughed through her crying, and it made it more painful. "I'm the bitch. It's my fault. I was . . . w was . . . aw . . . awful to him and he . . . he left . . ."

"He'll come back."

"Why?" Ann wailed, slamming her fist onto the tiled floor, feeling a surge of relief at the self-inflicted pain. "Why the fuck would he come back to me? I'm a fucking cunt."

"Because he loves you."

"Oh God." Ann stretched her arms out, flattening her hands against the cold, damn floor, putting her forehead between her knees. "I don't think I can breath, Charlie."

"Why not? Ann?"

"I . . . I can't breathe . . ." *Everything's dark.*

"Ann? Ann!"

"I'm . . . I need to get ou . . . out of here." *It's dark. I need to get under the bed. He can't find me there.*

"Ann, you should stand up, or talk maybe. Ann? Ann?"

"Can't . . . can't breathe . . ." *Coming, coming . . . where do I go? Oh God, I can't get safe, I can't get safe.*

"Ann?" Charlie scrambled to her feet, undid the lock on her own door, and ran to work on Ann's. "Ann, Ann! Open it, come on, open it!"

I can't get safe, where do I go? I need to crawl, where do I crawl?

"Ann!" Banging, someone was banging on the door.

Oh God, he's here. How do I get out? Do I scream?

"Ann!"

No. No, if I scream . . . I can't scream. Breathe . . . I can't breathe. Oh God.

Oh God.

The whistle blared sharply, and Joseph closed his eyes and bit his tongue.

"Valdez, traveling."

And I ain't even have to move for that call.

Joseph passed the basketball into the hands of one of Drew Zimmerman's stupidly grinning friends.

Yeah, play around with your fuckin' little minions, Joseph thought, falling back into the defensive line and pulling his shirt away from his sweaty chest. He caught Mr. Protus glaring at him from the sidelines and considered giving the burly, balding gym teacher the finger.

Nah, he's not fuckin' worth it, Joseph decided. *None a' them are worth it.*

Despite his best attempts at control, his gaze still shot momentarily up to the bleachers where Ann was seated, having been benched by Miss Saunders for another foul.

What, does she expect me to fuckin' foul out and go over and sit with her? Joseph scoffed to himself, zigzagging across the gymnasium to block his mark. *Fuck her. Fuckin' bitch can just sit up there till she falls through one of the cracks and hits the floor.* Joseph saw the pass coming and leapt up to smack away the ball, propelling it towards one of his scrimmage teammates who promptly used it to score a basket.

"Hey, he grabbed my arm," the boy Joseph had blocked claimed loudly.

"You're a fuckin' liar." Joseph spat, then hissed as the shock hit him on the back. "Fuck!"

The second shock hit him on the left arm, and Joseph whirled around to glare at Mr. Protus.

"Blue team's ball," the heavy-set man announced, and Joseph's teammates protested loudly.

"Get back, get back," Mr. Protus bellowed. Joseph searched for sympathy in the faces of the other red-team boys, but most of them were glaring at him too.

Oh, that's great, Joseph thought, boiling. *Like it's not hard enough runnin' in this damn shock backpack shit, but now when I get blamed, even when they know it's not my fault, I become the bad guy.*

Again I say — fuck 'em all. God, and they wonder why bullied kids go crazy and off themselves.

Joseph pulled back once more — and zeroed in on Zimmerman who stood consulting with his friends.

Yeah, buddy, don't think I don't see what's goin' on here, Joseph said silently, narrowing his burning golden eyes at the cackling sophomore. *Think you real clever, playin' the "Let's See How Many Times We Can Get The Ghetto Boy Shocked" game? Fine, man. Just remember you started this.*

Joseph kept his head down as he covered the pimply freshman who made no real attempt for the ball. He bided his time until Zimmerman came into range. Turning away so that he wouldn't be seen to be looking at Zimmerman, Joseph made a pretense of waving his arms in front of the freshman's face and shoved his elbow out, hard.

Ouch. That was a crack. Joseph had to struggle to hide his smile as Zimmerman howled and fell back.

"He attacked me!"

"Oh, man, I'm sorry," Joseph placated, looking down at the fallen Zimmerman, who clutched his bleeding nose. "Here, lemme help you."

Joseph extended his hand. He had judged correctly that Zimmerman would believe Joseph was trying to avoid another shock. Zimmerman's glance was wary, but he reached for Joseph.

Joseph took the tips of the other boy's fingers and pulled just enough to lift him, before yanking his hand away and letting Zimmerman thump back on his backside.

"What was that?" Zimmerman growled, jumping up and shoving Joseph in the chest as the other boys circled around.

"Aw, gee, I'm sorry man," Joseph drawled, waving his hand. "Slippery fingers."

"You —" Zimmerman began as he got back on his feet.

"What? What?" Joseph challenged as the other boy drew in. "Gonna whine and cry, and pretend I hit you again?"

"What is it with you out-of-towner freaks?" Zimmerman said. "Can't you leave?"

"And what, go back to the hood I crawled out of, right?" Joseph supplied.

"Hey, you can take the home grown trash with you too," Zimmerman snarled, gesturing up to the bleachers where Ann sat.

262

"Bring the slut back with you, and I'll pay for your ticket myself, and you can —"

Joseph grabbed Zimmerman by his blue jersey and pulled him into the punch, decking him first in the face and then delivering a knee solidly to the other boy's groin. The huddle around him converged as soon as Zimmerman hit the ground, and Joseph felt arms go around his neck. He slammed his shoulder up in response and found himself rewarded with another boy's groan and the ability to breath once more.

A fist connected with his face, and Joseph kicked out wildly, catching someone in the leg. Hands were all around him, trying to pull him backwards. He struck out blindly but forcefully, jabbing someone in the neck with his left hand and jerking his head back to collide with another boy's chin.

The shocks hit his legs, his back, his arms, his chest, and Joseph shrugged them off—they simply blended into his adrenaline. When someone tried to drag him down by his shock system backpack, Joseph ran backward into his unseen assailant, tripping him and delivering a low back kick to the boy once he was down.

"Break it up, break it up!"

Joseph shoved, and smacked, and punched, and laughed as his heart beat in his ears like machine gun fire, and when he felt the feverish rise in temperature he rode it out like an energy surge until he finally collapsed. His vision went black as the guards rushed in, a collection of thumping feet and shouting voices, all low and buzzing and indistinct save for the one female sounding one that was screaming his name.

CHAPTER EIGHTEEN  take

TONI WAS STANDING IN THE AISLE OF THE LIBRARY

dedicated to science books, flipping purposefully through a book on evolution, when she felt the breath at the back of her neck.

"Learning anything interesting?"

Even when I know he's there, even when I'm waiting for him — I'm still never ready for him.

Toni kept her gaze on her book, not meeting the ice blue eyes. "Yes, actually. It's about the benefits of social structure, and why we evolved to need them."

"Hmm."

Toni instantly regretted her jibe. *Don't be an idiot, Toni,* she reminded herself fiercely. *This isn't the time to piss him off. We're too close for you to start being snarky and clever.*

Toni heard the senior heave a large, overdrawn sigh, and she shivered.

"Cold?" Seth asked solicitously.

"Something like that," Toni agreed.

"Am I making you nervous?" Seth didn't both to hide the amusement in his voice, so Toni didn't bother lying.

"Yes. You always make me a little nervous."

"Yeah, that's what attraction is like though," Seth explained confidently, his voice the soft, mesmerizing tone of practiced seduction. "The constant nerves, the excitement . . ." He moved in closer, and the heat from his body warmed Toni's back. "The need and the desire."

So did he read romance novels to understand how this works? Read through articles on dating sites about "How To Know If You're Truly In Love" to find out how real people feel? Toni wondered cynically as she focused her gaze on the book's glossy picture of a smiling nuclear family sitting around a table. *Or maybe he didn't have to. Maybe he just watched enough girls — and guys — go through it that he noticed the signs. I mean, he's been watching us since he was born. He probably knows how we operate better than we do.*

Oh God — I better hope not.

To Seth she said, "Yeah, that's about right."

"So you've decided to stop fighting it?" Seth asked casually.

Careful. "No, I'm still kicking and screaming," Toni said wryly, tossing her hair to let him know the game was still in play. "Just … screaming a little less."

"Oh, screaming can be its own kind of fun," Seth noted with laughter in his voice. Toni kept her feet firmly planted, bravely resisting the powerful urge to flee. *Yeah, I bet screaming is just truckloads of fun for you.*

"Do you …" Toni had to stop and swallow to keep her voice from cracking. "Do you have what we need?"

Seth sighed and tittered. "Always straight to business with you just when things get interesting. Tsk, tsk."

Seth moved to Toni's right, his perfectly carved profile finally coming into view. Toni felt something in her relax, some inherent animal instinct calmed now that she could at least see her predator.

Seth handed her a worn, peeling copy of *On The Origin Of Species*. "Old Darwin's a good friend of mine too," he said calmly, tapping the cover of the book to draw her attention to where his index finger was buried between the pages, marking out a specific part. "There's something interesting on this page."

Toni couldn't avoid touching Seth's hand as she slipped her finger in beside his to hold the marked page as she accepted the book, any more than she could avoid the pleased grin that he allowed her to see.

Toni let her hand travel down the page, her fingers touching leaves of paper that definitely didn't belong. She inched them outwards, glancing quickly around the aisle to make sure no one else was present, before leaning in to examine them.

Five exact copies of Benjamin Franklin's face stared up at her, and Toni felt inwardly pleased that she didn't gasp aloud.

"You got this all from your supervisor?"

"Yup," Seth said easily, flicking aside pages in a large paperback on marine biology. "Poor old girl just had it hanging around in her underwear drawer. If she didn't want it stolen, she could have put it somewhere safer. Stupid bitch, some people just need to have their stuff taken, just to show them how careless they are. You gotta feel sorry for people like that."

Toni blinked rapidly as she tried to absorb the mix of sympathy and derision jumbled into Seth's conflicting statement. "She probably thought her underwear drawer wasn't a place anyone would look."

"Well, yeah, judging by how ugly the bitch is, who'd want to?" Seth snorted.

"Won't the cameras catch you going through her drawer?" Toni asked, defiantly resisting the urge to slap the smug expression off that handsome face.

"No, they all shut the cameras down in their rooms. Don't want anyone watching them while they sleep," Seth said quickly.

"What if she notices the money's gone today?"

"She won't suspect me," Seth asserted boldly, cavalier. "She loves me. Thinks I'm like a second son. Can't understand why my family would ever give up a bright, promising young man like me. Thinks they're crazy. I won't get caught."

Toni nodded. *Of course you think that. And you're probably right most people probably would never suspect you, and if they do confront you, you'll just sweet talk and lie, or threaten and lie, and they'll back off.*

And I've made myself your partner.

"There's one more thing we need." Toni rolled the money up

266

into her hand and shoved it down between her breasts, under her bra, as she pretended to adjust her shirt. When she looked up, Seth's eyes were still on her chest.

Well, at least there he's still like a normal guy.

"What?" Seth raised his eyebrows.

"We're gonna be out in the woods," Toni reminded. "We're gonna need to survive against animals, hunt . . ."

"I can do that," Seth affirmed.

Yeah, I know. "So we're gonna need a way to do all that," Toni said, knowing she was spending too much time beside Seth for it not to look suspicious on the cameras. "We're gonna need a knife."

Seth was silent for a long moment, drawing out Toni's obvious tension. "And do you trust me with a knife?"

The air abandoned Toni's lungs. "No," she confessed. "But we don't have a choice."

Seth chuckled. "Okay then. I can get us a knife. I'll have to break into a locked drawer though, and they'll notice that."

"But by tonight we'll be gone," Toni promised.

Seth nodded once, his smile now wide, anticipatory, and satisfied. "Yep. Gone."

"Are you awake?"

Unfortunately. That means that I'm not lucky, and they didn't actually manage to kill me. Oh well, maybe next time.

Ann blinked, opening her eyes sullenly, her body still aching from the long round of shocks. They widened slightly when she recognized the scarlet haired woman sitting before her, but she could only summon up enough energy to turn her head forward to better meet those intensely focused grey eyes.

"I guess," Ann mumbled in answer when it become clear the Headmistress expected one. "I'm not exactly *up*, if you know what I mean."

The Headmistress scanned the heavy straps that bound Ann flat to the steel bed, and she smiled briefly, just enough to show that she registered the joke. "Well, I would be tired too. You gave our security more than a bit of a run around in trying to keep them from Mr. Valdez."

"A run around?" Ann narrowed her eyes, and Ms. Valentina lowered herself into the chair beside the shock table, careful to avoid stepping on any loose wires.

"Yes, that is how one might put it," the Headmistress said, adjusting her shirt cuffs.

Ann almost smiled, her face hurting with the attempt. "I punched Mr. Protus, and I'm pretty sure I fractured his nose before I turned around and kicked one of the guards in the balls."

The Headmistress raised one gingery eyebrow. "So what would you call your display?"

Ann rolled her eyes, shrugging as best she could through the heavy restraints. "I don't know . . . a violent meltdown, a fight, an 'exercise in willful disobedience' . . . what would you call it? That's all that matters, right?"

"Perhaps I'm interested in what you think your reasons were," Ms. Valentina offered. "Did you simply want to attack guards wantonly? Rise up against your oppressors? Exhibit this 'willful disobedience' and violence?"

"No," Ann said derisively, looking down at her bruised left hand. *Maybe. Maybe part of me is just looking for a reason to snap, and hit, and do damage. It would explain a lot.*

"Then you must have had a reason. Something must have motivated your attack."

Ann glared up into the infuriatingly calm face of the other woman. "I think it's pretty clear what motivated my attack, and I'm really not in the mood to play word games right now."

"A very refreshing stance," the Headmistress commended, leaning forward, her elbows on her knees. Her broadly-cut pantsuit made her appear almost lanky. "So. You jumped into the fray to help Mr. Valdez."

"He was on the ground! He was just just lying there, on the ground, collapsed, and they were just shocking him and dragging him away for more, like that was gonna help? I mean — they were gonna punish him for it and keep shocking him until he really passed out and d—" Ann stopped her tirade, the meaning catching up to her words. She clamped her mouth shut and hardened her jaw.

"Yes, more shock treatment like what you received might very well have had severe consequences," the Headmistress agreed and watched a little color come into Ann's pale, drawn cheeks. "Luckily I was able to recognize the symptoms of his condition before it was too late."

Ann tried to jerk her head up off the plastic pillow and winced as the strap around her neck ground into her flesh. "So he's, um … I mean … you're saying he's alive, right? He's okay?"

Ms. Valentina smiled and answered softly. "Yes, he is most certainly alive. And awake."

"Oh." Ann colored even more, biting at the tip of her tongue. "Well, that's good."

The Headmistress continued to smile. "Would you like to see him?"

Ann's eyes narrowed again. "Why would you let me do that, after all I did to your guards?"

The Headmistress tilted her head, her ginger brow raised once more. "*My* guards?"

Ann opened her mouth and then closed it quickly, breathing and thinking. The Headmistress allowed the silence to extend for a few minutes and then asked again, quietly, clearly, "Would you like to see him?"

Ann nodded, biting her lower lip hard, the strap grating against her sore neck. "Yes."

The Headmistress briskly removed Ann's straps herself, and Ann cooperated with the tall woman, slipping on the shock pack without protest.

"Oh, you won't need that," the Headmistress informed her. Ann left the pack and its collection of wires in a heap on the metal table as she followed the redheaded woman out of the

Discipline room.

The Headmistress took her up back stairs and through passageways that mostly avoided the main halls. Huffing slightly as she tried to keep up with the tall woman's brisk pace, Ann was glad when they arrived at last at the nurse's office.

The Headmistress extended her arm and pointed Ann past the first two beds. Ann swallowed and made her way, step by halting step, toward the figure behind the curtain surrounding the third bed.

Joseph lay back against the sea green hospital bed, propped up on his elbows, his shirt, shock pack, and wires piled in a corner, the small burns covering his chest still visible, along with a number of rapidly darkening bruises. His eyes fluttered open as Ann rounded the curtain fully and came into view, their liquid gold half-obscured by hooded, suspicious lids.

"You look like crap," Ann began conversationally, challenging him in the hope that he would do more than just stare.

"Oh . . ." Joseph said slowly, as if remembering, nodding to himself. "Yup . . . that's why we broke up."

Ann sucked on her lower lip. Her eyes darted over to the Headmistress, but the redhead stood at the other end of the station, talking quietly with the nurse. "Joe, I . . ."

"No Joe, I hate Joe," Joseph whined, pouting. "You know I hate Joe. It's Joseph, or nuthin'."

Ann had to smile. *He's like a little boy sometimes.*

My boy.

"Yeah, well, I told you not to call me Annie, and you do it anyway," Ann said, her smile twitching when Joseph didn't respond. "Um . . ." Ann shrugged. "Are you alright?"

"Yeah, I'm just dandy. Can't you tell?"

"You don't have to be nasty. I'm only asking 'cause I care," Ann snapped. Joseph raised one dark brow, and the irony of her words slapped her in the face.

"Do you?" Joseph shifted slightly on his elbows, wincing. "Thought you didn't want me 'wastin' your time'?"

"Yeah, and I thought —" There was a noise from the other end of the office, and Ann lowered her voice. "Um, Joseph, I ..." Ann swallowed. *Oh, just fucking DO it!* "I'm sorry." Her voice came out very small.

Joseph's eyes widened somewhat at that. "Oh, yeah? That's nice."

"Oh, don't do that," Ann said, frustrated and starting to pace. "I'm trying to explain myself here. The least you could do is listen."

"Oh, I'm listenin' just fine," Joseph drawled, spreading his hands. "Go ahead, you got the floor."

Ann closed her eyes and rubbed her hands against her pants to remove the sweat. *I'll just talk. I'll just talk, and keep talking, and I won't stop until it comes out.*

"You know the other day, when we were talking in gym?" Ann waited a moment for some kind of reaction from Joseph and then plowed ahead, knowing if she waited too long she wouldn't be able to continue. "When I got called away? Well, it was Mrs. Carter. She had me go down to her office, and obviously I thought it was gonna be that I'd done something wrong, and I guess in a way it was, but ..."

Ann worked her thumbs into the sore muscles of her arms as she paced. Her eyes studied the ground as she roamed the tiny space in front of the bed, every now and then casting brief, nervous glances over at Joseph.

"Anyway, she sat me down, and started to talk about my 'progress', or the fact that I haven't made any, that I've been 'steadily regressing'." Ann made quotes with her fingers. "So I was just waiting for her to say she's gonna let them shock me more or take away my food, and I remember just thinking, 'Whatever it is, just punish me and get it over with. Just do it.' But ..." Ann smoothed a bit of hair behind her ears. "But then she starts talking about family, and how important it is, and how she's been talking to my parents about what might help me stop backsliding so I just waited. I had no idea what she was talkin' about, until finally, finally she just comes out and says it, says, 'Your parents and I have agreed that you can best recover from home'."

Ann paused. Joseph opened his mouth to speak, but Ann began again.

"So I'm like, 'What do you mean, 'recover from home'? You mean take me out of school?' And Mrs. Carter, she says, 'No, just remove you from the supervisor program and reinstall you in your parent's home.' And then, then she smiles at me, like I should be happy, like she's just given me a fuckin' Christmas present, and I should thank her or, or lick her boot or something, and I say 'How are you supposed to monitor me from home?' And she looks confused, like, why would I ask that, and I guess that makes sense. I mean, no one else would, but she says 'Your parents believe they can provide a stable environment without the need for such close monitoring.'" Ann started to giggle, her nails digging into her arms. "She really said that, 'A stable environment.' Like she has no idea. And I said to her, 'Ya know, I don't think I'm really ready to go home,' and she looked at me like I was insane, or, ya know, more insane than usual, and she said it had been decided. Just decided, like that."

Ann stopped pacing and stared at Joseph, her breath coming in heavy bursts.

"But . . . isn't that good?" Joseph questioned finally. "I mean, you won't be monitored. You won't have to worry about sneak—" Joseph glanced forward and lowered his voice. "Worry 'bout sneakin' around. I mean, I know your parents suck, but you can stay away from 'em at school and come out at night, with m wit' the rest of us."

Ann laughed loudly and then covered her mouth with both hands, shaking her head erratically. *He doesn't understand. Well duh, of course he doesn't fucking understand, I never said it. Oh God, I have to say it.* "I know, right?" Ann said, nodding, biting her lip. "It should be great. It should make everything easier, but I . . ." Ann tapped her fist against her thigh. "And I should go home. I should. Because Callie's there."

"You don't want to see your sister?" Joseph frowned.

"Of course I wanna see my sister!" Ann exclaimed. "I hate that

I never get to see her, and I hate myself for leaving her, but I was scared, and we both know I'm a selfish bitch —"

"Selfish? How are you selfish?" Joseph demanded. "You selfish for gettin' put in a house that's monitored? For gettin' shocked?" Joseph indicated his own burned, bruised arms and chest. "For —"

"For leaving her! I'm selfish for leaving her!" Ann forced the words out of her raw throat. "Because I left her there, all alone with him! And with me not there, I worry that he . . . that he's doing to her what he did to me."

"What he did to you? Like hitting you?"

Ann looked away shaking her head.

"Ann?"

Ann turned back to Joseph, meeting his eyes with her own, her breathing heavy and pleading. "Please."

Joseph widened his eyes in open question, frowning at her stricken expression. "Ann?"

Ann's eyes grew red, and her mouth worked. "Please," she whispered.

Joseph held her gaze, realization coming slowly. He began to shake his head. "No." He bit his lower lip, squeezing his eyes shut. "No." He put his hands over his face. "No, don't tell me that." He turned on his elbows, half burying his face in the pillow. "No, don't tell me that. God, don't fuckin' tell me that."

"I'm sorry," Ann whispered. "I didn't mean to disgust you."

"No, no." Joseph pushed himself up on both hands, his burning eyes finding Ann's watery aquamarine ones. "No, I didn't mean . . . Ann, why didn't you tell me . . . before?"

"What, play the abused girl card? Joseph, I had a way out and I took it, and I left my little sister there," Ann said through gritted teeth. "I don't have the right to..to play the victim, to . . ."

"Bullshit you don't," Joseph said stubbornly. "God, why . . . when did it —" He swallowed. "When did it happen?"

Ann kicked at the legs of the wooden chair that was a few inches from the bed before slumping into it. "Started when I was nine. Stopped when I . . . got out."

Joseph's throat muscles worked as if he were swallowing

something bitter. "Why . . . your mom —"

"She said I was lying." Ann smiled, feeling the vein on her left wrist with her other hand. "I always lie, so why would she believe that? She said I was trying to 'destroy her happiness out of a misplaced jealousy'."

"Fuckin' bitch," Joseph snarled. Ann shrugged.

"I don't know . . . maybe I would say that same thing in her shoes," Ann muttered, picking at her nails.

"No you wouldn't," Joseph said firmly. "Yeah, sometimes you lie, and yeah, sometimes you're a bitch, but you would never let anyone get away with doin' something like that."

"How can you know?" Ann asked wryly. "How —"

"I know, Ann," Joseph interrupted with steel in his voice, and she looked up. "I know you. I . . ." Joseph looked at her helplessly. "I'm sorry."

"For what?" Ann smiled sadly. "You did nothing wrong."

"I coulda asked you." Joseph growled, fisting the blankets of the bed. "I coulda fuckin' . . . *suspected*, I coulda not pushed you "

"Don't," Ann demanded, and Joseph stopped. "Don't. It's not your fault. I'm the one who didn't tell you."

"*Why*?" Joseph questioned, shaking his head again. "Why didn't you?"

"Because I wanted you all to myself," Ann whispered. "I didn't want you to — to look at me like you are now. When we have — have sex I wanted you to be able to do . . . anything, without thinking, 'Oh I shouldn't do that be-because' . . . I . . . I just wanted to be able to be normal with you, to be the me I always wanted to exist. I . . . wanted to have good things when I was with you. I wanted my life to be *mine* when I was with you, to have something that wasn't infected with this like everything, *everything* else in my life is." Ann bit her lip. "I wanted you all to myself."

Joseph nodded. "That . . ." He wet his lips, his chest muscles still contracting, as if he was fighting the urge to lash out. "That . . . makes sense, I guess. But Ann —"

"Please," Ann begged, breaking off.

274

"Please what?" Joseph began, before they froze as the sound of steps signaled the arrival of the Headmistress and nurse.

Ann met his eyes, her voice barely a whisper. "Please don't be afraid to kiss me."

"Time to go, visit's over," the nurse said curtly. Ann looked up, searching the Headmistresses' face, but the redheaded woman didn't contradict the nurse. Ann stood, slowly. She felt Joseph gently catch her wrist.

"Come on, time to go," the nurse said again.

"Ann?" the Headmistress prompted, trying to catch the attention of the girl whose blue-green eyes were locked onto the golden ones of the boy.

"I'm not afraid," Joseph whispered, a promise, his fingers entwining with hers.

"Thank you," Ann mouthed back, her cold hands warming in his.

"It is time to go," the nurse intoned.

"Charlie, could you come over here and help me with the dishes?"

"Yeah, yes, Mrs. Carter."

Charlie got up and carried her plate to the sink, slipping it into the soapy mix Mrs. Carter had already created, and picking up a sponge to scrub away the remains of dinner.

"Charlie," Mrs. Carter asked, drying off the dishes Charlie passed her. "Do you think you're special?"

Charlie paused, her hand warm and wet as she clutched a spoon. *Is this a trick? A trial? A tantalizing trap?* "What do you mean?"

Mrs. Carter briskly wiped away a spot of sauce Charlie had missed. "Well, everyone has their gifts. My Becky is brilliant with math, and she's always been a great athlete, one of those girls who loved hockey and soccer ... And I hear that you're very perceptive, that you have a, uh, a sense about people."

Charlie started to shiver and plunged both hands into the soupy water to keep the principal from detecting. "Well, I mean

275

". . . I guess I . . ."

"The Headmistress," Mrs. Carter began in a voice so controlled only some rigidness at the edges told Charlie that the redheaded woman was the real subject of their conversation, "she seems to think you have an almost extrasensory perception when it comes to other people's minds."

"She's been testing me," Charlie revealed. "She's been testing me, and having me guess things, tell things . . ."

"And can you?"

Charlie hesitated. *How much do I tell?* she wondered, trying to use the temporary clarity of mind she'd been reveling in all day to gauge what to say.

She wants to know about the Headmistress, not me.

"I'm not sure," Charlie said, adding some more dishwashing liquid to the sink. "She has me do so many tests, but she never tells me what I get on them. I . . . I never know whether I'm right or wrong, if I'm doing what she wants . . ."

"It's all right, Charlie," Mrs. Carter said soothingly, taking a glass from her and rubbing it with her towel. "You're safe here."

Charlie looked down and worked on cleaning the dressing from a bowl.

"Or at least you were supposed to be," Mrs. Carter murmured, wringing out the towel harshly. "That was the purpose of this school, or at least it was *my* purpose. Clearly you were the true purpose for her, all along. She simply . . ."

Charlie glanced up at the older woman, then away, but the principal did not miss her this time.

"What do you think, Charlie?" Mrs. Carter asked, opening the cabinet to her right and beginning to put away the glasses and cups. "Is the Headmistress interested in my school? Or is this school simply the bait to draw you and your boarder friends here? A safe little place to perform her —" The principal swallowed, and abruptly stopped, fumbling at her wrist to remove a silver charm bracelet dripping with water and foamy with soap.

She's said too much, Charlie judged. *She didn't mean to confide in*

276

me. But she did, and now she's made my trap that much easier to lay. Or . . . is it spring? Spring a trap? Spike a trap? How do you trip a trap?

"I heard her talking with Mrs. Waters about the lake," Charlie offered, her heart pounding. *Carefully, carefully.* "About it being special. Being something different."

Mrs. Carter nodded to herself. "They used to say that. That it might be the reason behind our . . . previous behavioral problems. That the kids used to go down to the water, and swim in it, and drink it, and they said it made them . . ."

"It makes the plants different," Charlie prompted. "There are no animals there."

"So we were just in the right place for her," Mrs. Carter stated wryly, closing the cabinet with a snap. "We lived in a town near a lake, and she knew . . . somehow she knew, or thought she knew what it meant . . . then she exploited us," Mrs. Carter decided. "She saw our trouble and she . . ."

Mrs. Carter stopped, and for a moment she seemed frozen save for her over-bright eyes. *The wheels are turning,* Charlie thought. *I can see right through them to the gears and bells ,and when she finds the idea I'll know because —*

"Thank you, Charlie," Mrs. Carter said, breaking the silence. "I think I can handle things from here."

Charlie swallowed and nodded, shaking the water off of her hands and trying to shake herself free of the seductive spiral of her thoughts.

I need to stay sane for just a little longer, Charlie told herself, repeating it like a mantra. *I just need to stay a little sane for a little longer. Just long enough to get through tonight.*

"Are we sure this place ain't bugged?"

"Joseph, *we're* bugged. I think that's enough."

Joseph shrugged and leaned back against the dusty fireplace of the abandoned house. Though cold, there was no real wind. The night outside was almost perfectly silent. "Hey, I'm just tryna make sure we don't get caught out at the last minute."

"Last minute's here," Anton stated flatly, looking over at Joseph, then to Ann, who leaned on his shoulder. Melvin crouched in the corner, his hands balanced on his knees while Toni hovered near him, her hands arranging and rearranging her mass of curls. Charlie seemed even smaller than usual as she shivered against herself, but she met Anton's eyes when he focused in on her. To his right, Lieutenant stood with her arms folded, her eyes hard, glittering and ready.

"Last minute's here," Anton repeated. "This time, we make sure they get caught in *our* trap."

CHAPTER NINETEEN

THE PHONE RANG FOR THE THIRD TIME, AND MRS.
Carter rolled over in bed, rubbing her forehead. She reached over to her bedside table and accepted the call. "Yes?"

"Mrs. Carter?"

"It is one o' clock in the morning, Andrews . . ."

"It's a security issue."

Mrs. Carter pushed herself upright, shivering as she slipped free of her comforter. "Yes, what is it?"

"We received a call from a supervisor who says she heard a loud noise downstairs, and when she went to investigate she found her silverware drawer broken into, as well as some personal items missing. Her boarder is gone."

"Which house is this?" Mrs. Carter inquired, still trying to rouse herself.

"House 5B, ma'am."

"House 5B . . ." Mrs. Carter frowned, blinking rapidly to wake herself up. "That's . . ."

"Seth Dryer is the student under watch there."

Mrs. Carter's eyes shot open, and fear acted like a potent dose of adrenaline as she tossed her blankets aside and flipped on the light. "What exactly was taken from the house?"

"A large butcher knife and some pieces of jewelry, ma'am," Andrews reported.

"Jewelry . . ." Mrs. Carter bit the tip of her tongue, thinking as she changed quickly from her sleep shirt into black pants and a heavy white sweater. "Expensive?"

"She definitely wants them returned, and . . . okay?" There was a pause as Andrews' voice grew faint.

"Andrews?"

"Yeah, sorry. She's just reported that cash was taken as well," Andrews supplied.

"He's running," Mrs. Carter surmised darkly, pulling her belt tight around her waist. "Andrews, take everyone who's been trained for an escape attempt and create a ring around the east woods. I'm going to call Officer Mills."

"Yes, Mrs. Carter."

"Oh, wait," Mrs. Carter said quickly. "Do the cameras show any other boarders out of their beds?"

"One minute . . ."

Mrs. Carter waited as Andrews called out on the other line. "Ma'am?"

"Yes?" Mrs. Carter asked impatiently.

"No, no one else out of bed."

The seven friends moved quickly through the forest, staying close. Anton led the group, his white-and-black eyes held wide as he guided them around fallen trees and away from stinging thorns. Charlie ducked and wove easily through the underbrush. Joseph and Ann stuck close together, linked at the hands, while Toni and Melvin blinked at the dark, fumbling as Lieutenant brought up the rear.

There was a sound like a sharp break of a twig. Lieutenant gave a low whistle, and everyone dropped to the ground. Charlie closed her eyes and kept her mouth shut, feeling wet dirt against her lips. She tried to make her breathing small and shallow.

Why is everyone else so loud? Charlie wondered. *Can't they hear? They need to try and make their hearts sound little, like rabbits. Toni's heart is all heavy, beating loud like a bass drum. Melvin's is fast, rattling like a snare. Joseph and Ann are making a blended beat, Lieutenant has a steady kettle drum beat, and Anton . . .*

"Clear."

Charlie rose with the others at the sound of Lieutenant's voice, searching out Anton with her night acclimated eyes.

His heart keeps changing, Charlie realized. *From fast to slow, deep and heavy to shallow . . . switching, always, always switching.*

"We almost there?" Joseph asked, dusting dead leaves off his shirt and helping Ann over a stump.

Lieutenant sniffed the air. "Yeah, lake's close. You can smell the water."

"Maybe you can," Melvin muttered, adjusting his grip on the backpack thrown over his shoulder. "Some of us don't have X-ray vision or . . . a mutant nose."

"Mutant ears," Charlie murmured, freezing. "Someone else is coming."

The others froze, frantically searching out faces that they could barely distinguish in the dark. Only Anton's deep eyes found Charlie's. "You sure, Tiny? I don't hear any feet."

"Not feet," Charlie explained softly, lowering her voice. "Heartbeats. There were only seven."

"But now?" Joseph prompted.

"Eight," Charlie whispered.

"Where?" Anton mouthed, a motion only Charlie would be able to see. She raised her hand and pointed.

Anton squinted in the direction Charlie indicated, licked his lips, and then put one hand on the smaller girl's shoulder. With the other, he made a fist, and then splayed his fingers as he gestured behind his back. Charlie nodded her understanding as she carefully placed one foot behind the other, backing away into the trees. Anton padded off softly towards Lieutenant, pressing a hand to her shoulder and signaling her to climb the dying oak to the left.

Charlie let the bark of her own large tree rub into her back as she slid down to kneel in a tangle of bushes. Covering her mouth with both hands, she watched Anton direct each member of their company off to a hiding place, finally disappearing himself into the black until only Toni was left.

Mrs. Carter waved her hand across her face as if she could brush away the ache behind her eyes caused by the blinking red lights of the cars lining the street.

"Mrs. Principal? Did you need something?" Officer Mills asked, breaking away from his fellow cops lingering at the road block.

"No, no," she dismissed. "No, wait. Are you sure you haven't seen Seth approaching any of the roads? He may have been scared off by the lights, and be waiting in the woods nearby."

"I don't have enough people to comb all the woods and hold the roads . . ." Officer Mills explained apologetically, and Mrs. Carter waved her hand again.

"No, no, I understand, of course." Mrs. Carter pursed her lips and tapped her nails together. Officer Mills cleared his throat, and Mrs. Carter raised an eyebrow. "Thank you, Officer. You know how much this is appreciated."

The rotund little man stood for another minute as if waiting for a more definite expression of thanks, before smiling thinly and turning on his heel to return to his car.

Mrs. Carter tented her fingers, glaring at the two cars blocking the road. Tenting became tapping, and the principal was moving on to cracking her knuckles when her phone rang.

"Carter," Mrs. Carter answered, tapping her black flats against the cement road.

"Mrs. Carter?" Andrews asked on the other line.

"Yes, Eric, when I answer *my* phone generally I am here," Mrs. Carter snapped, rubbing her temples.

"I'm sorry. I —"

"No, no, it's my fault," Mrs. Carter interrupted, taking her phone away from her ear to let out a heavy sigh before continuing, "I shouldn't have snapped. Did you find Seth?"

"No, ma'am."

"No." Mrs. Carter chipped one of her well-painted nails on the edge of her phone.

"No, but we did get a call about another missing student!" Andrews spoke quickly. "Just a few minutes ago we got a call from the parents of Melvin Stavos. He's also missing."

"Melvin ..." Mrs. Carter murmured.

"Yes, Melvin Stavos," Andrews repeated, the eager pride in his voice evident. "So, we sent the alert out to the rest of our people in the field to be on the look for Melvin as well. I ... made sure to call you as soon as it was done."

"Good, good," Mrs. Carter said absently. "Are you sure there was no one else? Just Melvin?"

"No, no one else was seen on the cameras. Mr. Stavos' parents heard a noise downstairs, and when they went to investigate they found the door opened and his backpack missing."

"His backpack missing ..."

"Yes, ma'am. Could it be they're running away together?" Andrews postulated.

"Melvin and Seth?" Mrs. Carter couldn't keep the disbelief out of her voice. "Hardly."

"Well, you know your students better than me. I just monitor them," Andrews surrendered, sounding sullen.

"No, no, it is possible there is a connection," Mrs. Carter thought aloud. "Tell everyone to look for both boys individually, but also keep eyes out for both of them together."

"Yes, of course, definitely." Andrews replied. Mrs. Carter rolled her eyes at the excitement in his voice.

"And are you going to contact the Headmistress?"

Mrs. Carter raised her eyebrows. "The Headmistress? Yes, she'll be very interested. Thank you, Andrews. I'm going to head back over to the school. Call me immediately with any news."

"Yes, Mrs. Principal."

Mrs. Carter let the call end and then searched her phone for her contacts. She scrolled down until she came to Sophia Valentina. She let her thumb hover over the name for a few seconds before pocketing the phone.

The whistle consisted of three sharp, piecing notes, and Toni froze when she heard them sounded behind her.

"There you are."

Toni turned around, blinking in the dark, her eyes focusing on the tiny flashlight the handsome figure held in his right hand. He waved it around the clearing, toying with it, as if it wasn't necessary.

Can he see in the dark too?

"Toni." The tone was overly warm and seductive. "Toni, it's me."

"Oh." Toni swallowed, knowing she needed to give more of an answer, but her tongue stayed firmly in knots.

The flashlight clicked off, and Toni whipped her head around wildly, feeling out in the cold air with both arms, even more blinded after the temporary bright light.

There was a rustle, heat at her front, and then Seth clicked the flashlight back on. He'd placed it right under his face, grinning. "Boo."

"Not funny," Toni whispered, putting a hand over her chest. "God damn it, you fucking scared me."

"Aw, bad mouth," Seth chastised, biting his lower lip and stepping in closer, inclining his head slightly so that he was inches from Toni's front. "Very bad mouth."

"Yeah, well —" Toni fumbled for words. "That's why we're leaving this fucking school."

"Excited to be gone?" Seth ran a finger down Toni's bare collarbone, and when she shivered, he seemed pleased.

"Yeah, aren't you?" Toni proposed, her stomach muscles clenching when his roaming hand made its way from her collarbone, around to her back, and down to her waist. "No more rules, no more shocks, no more punishments . . ."

"Definitely no more rules," Seth agreed, looking at her sideways, his pale eyes glinting like melting ice. *He really is insanely good looking,* Toni admitted to herself. *I mean, part of his charm is probably because of what's wrong with him,* she immediately justified, immediately reminded herself. *He's like a snake with those eyes, like a crocodile, a predator . . .*

"Is there something wrong?" Seth asked the question lightly, but his eyes were starting to narrow.

"No. Why, is there something I should be worried about?" Toni countered. "Did you bring the . . ." Her throat constricted. "The thing we agreed on?"

Seth licked his teeth, and Toni felt her insides contract as an ancient fear bred deep in her genes demanded she run. The urge only grew as Seth withdrew the long, shining butcher knife from the backpack slung over his right shoulder.

"Think this'll work?" the older boy questioned. Toni nodded slowly.

"Yeah. Yeah, it should be fine."

"Is there something wrong?" There was a hissing undertone to Seth's question.

You're losing him. Do something. Do something. Good, sweet, pastry-tasting Jesus, Toni White! DO something!

"No." Toni breathed deeply, closing the distance between them with another step and sliding a hand up around Seth's neck and into his hair. "Nothing but this."

Keeping her eyes open, braving the knife, and going against every basic message her body was sending her but one, Toni met Seth's lips with her own.

"I know how to start a fire."

"I never said you didn't! You don't need to be so fuckin' touchy!"

"Will you just be —" Joseph bit his lower lip and held his tongue. *You can do it, man. You love her, right? You wanna live with her the rest a' your life? Well, then you gonna hafta to learn to zip it up and not call her out on every bitchy thing she does, mutherfucker. That's just what love means.*

"Be what?" Ann demanded, but in a whisper now. She stopped pacing through the dirty sand and knelt down beside the small pile of twigs and sticks Joseph crouched behind.

"Just ... I need to focus, please," Joseph requested. He flicked his lighter on again and carefully inserted it into the small teepee he'd created on the driest part of the sand he could find. The water lapped steadily at the lake's edge only a few feet away.

Like the shit's fuckin' mockin' me. Fuck nature, I swear.

"I think it's working," Ann offered, as a few leaves caught on, followed by the lighter twigs.

"Gimme a minute," Joseph said, raising the index finger of the hand not holding his lighter as he leaned in to blow on the steadily growing blaze. The fire dwindled, and then reversed, spreading eagerly to the larger sticks.

"You got it," Ann praised, but Joseph shook his head.

"Nah, that was the easy part. Now comes the part where I gotta concentrate."

"Can you do it?" Ann asked softly.

"'Course I can do it," Joseph said sharply.

"I just meant —"

"I know what you meant! I just — I'm sorry." Joseph headed off Ann's rebuttal. "I'm sorry, I just ... I can do it. I can."

I have to.

Joseph let his hands drift forward, feeling the heat and teasing his fingers with the edge of the dancing flames. Biting the inside of his cheek, Joseph narrowed his golden eyes and focused.

C'mon, higher. You can do this. Higher.

The fire perked up slightly, but then ebbed back down. Joseph gritted his teeth.

Higher. Burn. C'mon, fuckin' burn. You did it all them times before when I didn't need it, well, do it now!

Joseph's hands were beginning to curl into fists when the fire started to crackle louder, its heat growing, the flames leaping higher as a line of smoke funneled upwards.

286

"Joseph," Ann said. "Joseph, we've got smoke. I think it's good."

Joseph nodded, his eyes still riveted to the fire. It roared again as if doused with kerosene, the heat scorching Ann's face and hands. She stumbled back until she touched colder sand, and when another burst shot the fire higher she covered her eyes.

"Joseph, stop, it's done!"

Coughing, gasping, and scrambling down over wet, muddy ground, Ann circled around the fire to where Joseph still stood, transfixed.

"Joseph!"

He twitched at her scream but didn't move.

Hell no you don't. Ann steeled herself as she bit her lip to keep in her screams and ran towards the burning heat. *No, no, no . . .*

Ann grabbed Joseph by his flimsy night shirt and yanked. His lack of resistance sent them both careening down the bank, toppling over each other until they landed painfully in the sludgy edge of the lake.

"What" — Joseph said, coughing and shaking his head — "the fuck was that?" He knelt on the smooth lake rocks.

Ann shoved Joseph as she turned over onto her backside, pulling pondweed off her face. "That was *you* having a mutant moment, and *me* snapping you to your fuckin' senses!" Ann snapped, Joseph wincing as she splashed him. She hurried to her feet. "Thank you very much."

"You're welcome very much," Joseph grumbled as she pulled him up by his hand. "Think maybe you could snap a little softer next time?"

"Nope," Ann said, smiling brightly. "I specialize in tough love. Deal with it."

"As long as it is love."

"It is," Ann said, pulling Joseph's hand more gently as she urged him back up the embankment. "And don't forget it."

"I don't think I could, the bruises I got," Joseph said slyly, earning him a laugh from Ann, who tugged him towards the woods. Joseph started to follow her and then stopped, gripping her wrist.

When she turned he pulled her roughly to him and kissed her. Ann kissed him back, laughing against his lips, laughing even more when he hoisted her up by the waist and swung her around, the tips of her feet kicking up sand. They broke apart gasping and immediately grabbed each other's hands once more, fleeing, already out of breath, into the woods.

"There's no one here, Mrs. Principal."

"Well keep looking, they ran away to go somewhere!" Mrs. Carter snapped, running her nails roughly through her short hair as she turned away from her security and headed out the door.

"Where are you going?" the ever interested Andrews called after her.

"For some air, Andrews!"

Mrs. Carter shoved open the front doors of J. Alter Academy with brute force, relishing the slap of cold wind to her face.

"Where are you?" she asked aloud, glaring out over the grounds of the school, looking from one pinprick of light to the other, the signs that guards were still searching for her missing students. "Where did you run off to?"

Mrs. Carter squinted as a few pin pricks started to coalesce, and raised voices carried over the windswept lawn. Frowning, the principal started towards the grouping guards. She winced as her shoes sunk into the wet, cold ground with every step.

"What is it? What's going on?" Mrs. Carter bellowed, her voice making the chatter cease as she drew abreast of them. "What is it?" she repeated, blinking at the flashlights.

"That, ma'am," said one of the guards, pointing behind her, to the back of the school. Mrs. Carter pivoted.

A line of smoke rose steadily from the west, a challenge to the sky.

"Think it's a wildfire?" one of the guards asked.

"If it is, the police will pull back some of their people to contain it," the principal griped.

288

"It shouldn't get far," a guard with a voice she almost recognized put in. "That over there is right near the lake."

"The lake . . ."

"Ma'am?"

Mrs. Carter rounded on the guards, and some of them pulled back instinctively.

"All of you, head around to the back of the school, near the west gate," Mrs. Carter instructed. "Be ready to head through the woods."

The guards stared at her, waiting for elaboration, but Mrs. Carter was busy dialing her phone.

"Andrews? Yes, get everyone you can together and head them off to the west, through the woods. I think I know where we'll find our missing boys."

Seth's mouth was practiced, skilled. His hands were assertive and demanding, carrying Toni along, and she went with the tide because there was no alternative.

But something's wrong.

For all of Seth's skill and enthusiasm, and his clear talent for seduction, the only fluttering Toni felt in her belly was from fear. The danger which had both frightened and attracted her, the allure of this gorgeous boy wanting her, even if she knew he would never care for her, seemed to turn to dust in her mouth as he actually kissed her. His hands on her back and her waist, stroking her, didn't excite her at all.

I'm not safe, Toni realized. *And I know it. My whole body knows it, and it's not gonna let me do this.*

Seth broke the kiss, and Toni could have sworn that every hair on her skin raised as those cold blue eyes searched hers.

"What's wrong? Moving too fast?"

Toni shook her head trying to think of a response, but all her glib comebacks seemed to have vanished along with her lust.

Seth sniffed, and for one insane moment Toni wondered if

he could smell fear. *It wouldn't surprise me. It would make perfect, perfectly deadly sense.*

The vivid eyes left hers to stare over her shoulder and widen. When the smell reached Toni's nose, she understood what the sociopath had seen.

"Fire," she whispered, and the eyes shot back to hers. Toni took a step back.

"Probably a forest fire," she proposed. "We should ... should hurry."

"Oh?" Seth advanced on her, and Toni stumbled over a broken branch as she backed away. "Got that answer all ready, huh?"

"What do you mean?" Toni tried to make her voice as innocent and confused as possible.

"What do *you* mean?" Seth questioned, his shoulders hunching up like the haunches of a big cat. "Don't treat me like a fucking idiot little girl. I know when someone's lying to me."

If you did I never would have gotten this far. "I'm not lying. I don't know what you're talking about, and if there's a forest fire we need to fucking hurry before police come!"

Seth seemed to pause at the honest fear in Toni's voice, as if assuaged by it. Toni swallowed as Seth glanced up again, finding the smoke. Toni risked a look around the clearing.

The pit of her stomach dropped into her feet when she looked back at Seth and found his unsettling eyes glued to hers.

"What'cha lookin' for?" he asked softly.

"Nothing. I mean, fire," Toni fumbled verbally.

Seth nodded slowly, giving Toni a moment's hope before he said quietly, awfully, "You didn't come here alone. Did you?"

"No." Anton stepped out into the clearing. "She didn't."

Seth spun around, and Toni used the distraction to try and put more distance between herself and the furious boy.

"No, don't you move!" Seth shouted, pointing at Toni with the butcher knife, his gaze still on Anton. "Don't you dare more."

"Or what?" challenged Melvin, stepping forward and forcing Seth to turn to the left. "There's five of us and only one of you.

Even you can't kill us all and get away with it."

"Watch me," Seth raged, baring his teeth like a fighting dog, eyes darting between the four. He moved his flashlight around the clearing with one hand, the knife held firmly in the other. "Five of you? I only see three."

"Maybe there is something wrong with your eyes," Charlie intoned, and Seth whirled again, trying to find the girl in the dark.

"Where's Big Joseph and his little whore?" Seth sneered, his eyes narrowed. He kept the knife up and angled out as he slipped his backpack off the opposite shoulder, spreading his legs apart and getting ready.

"They got a different part of the mission," Anton said obscurely, and Seth gestured with the knife in the direction of the stack of smoke.

"What, setting the fire? Planning to burn down the forest this time?"

"Sorry, Seth," Toni said with mock sympathy. "But this time? You're not in on the plan."

"You be quiet!" Seth seethed, shooting Toni a look that accomplished his command. Gone was any appeal to his bright blue eyes, which now appeared overly wide and demented, and Toni finally understood what Charlie had meant when she said she could see in them a single goal.

He's going to kill me. Toni swallowed and tried to remember how to form a proper punch. *He's going to kill all of us.*

"So ..." Seth chuckled, a crazed, sickening sound. "This was all a little game for revenge? And now what? Now that you've got me out here, in the woods, with a weapon — what?" Seth licked his teeth. "Four against one?" Seth smiled and gave Toni a taunting wink that froze her entire body as surely as if he'd encased her in ice. "You're gonna need better odds."

"How 'bout five, mutherfucker?"

Seth jerked his head upward just as Lieutenant swung down from the overhanging branch, smashing her feet into the boy's face and sending him careening backwards. The muscular girl

291

slapped the ground and rolled to break her fall. She made it to her feet just in time to avoid a nearly fatal swipe from the butcher knife.

"You." Seth spat, throwing aside his flashlight and gripping his left eye. "I'm gonna enjoy carving you up like a pig and throwing you in the gutter, you filthy fucking cunt."

"Oh." Lieutenant grinned nastily. "You gonna make my breakin' that pretty lil' face just *too* easy."

Seth sliced the knife through the air menacingly, before lunging forward and trying to plunge it into Lieutenant's side. Lieutenant skipped back, and Seth barked a laugh.

"Not so ballsy now, huh?" Seth sneered, only noticing Anton coming up behind him at the last minute. Seth kicked out, hitting the tall, thin boy hard in the chest, moving into an uppercut with the blade, and just missing Anton's throat as he too skipped out of range.

Seth prowled slightly between his two foes, switching the knife from one hand to the other. When he stopped, Anton and Lieutenant tensed, and the blonde's face expanded with a delicious, disturbing smile.

"No one's running," Seth noted softly, his snake's eyes also moving to Toni and Melvin. "And Toni here was so specific about me bringing the knife, weren't you, baby?" Seth tossed the butcher knife lightly from one hand to the other. "So that must mean this is what you all want, hmm?" Seth waved the blade back and forth in his right hand, the flashlight glinting off its steel edge. "Don't worry," Seth promised, eyes wide. "I'm gonna give it to you. Oh, yeah. I'm gonna give it to each and every one of you, starting . . ." Seth twisted his left arm across his chest and over his right shoulder, glancing behind him towards Anton. "With you."

In the single, dim light of the dying flashlight, Seth was almost a blur to Toni as he jumped for Anton. Catching the taller boy in the temple with the handle of the knife, Seth gave a swift kick to Anton's chest, forcing him onto his back. Seth quickly straddled the other boy's shoulders with both knees, bringing the knife to his throat.

"Anton!"

Seth twisted his upper body, tossing a handful of dirt into Lieutenant's eyes as she came at him, temporarily blinding her and throwing her a look of annoyance before turning back to his prize.

"Look at me," Seth ordered, pressing the tip of the knife to Anton's nose. "I want you to watch every piece as it comes off."

"But I said my prayers," a small voice spoke through Anton's lips. "You said no more 'til next Sunday."

Seth coughed a disgusted sound out of the back of his throat. "You're so fucking crazy." He lifted the blade. "You should thank me for this. It's practically an act of mercy."

There was a crack and Toni blinked. Suddenly Seth was howling and rolling away from Anton, who flipped to his feet with feline grace, shaking his head as the heavier, stronger boy hurried to stand while clutching a dangling left arm.

"Don't try that shit with me," Anton warned, advancing on Seth despite the other boy waving the knife erratically to ward him off. "I learned a long time ago what mercy meant."

"You can learn about pain then," Seth threatened, his voice hoarse and unbalanced.

"No," Anton said, his voice calm and in control. "It's been past time that someone schooled you."

Seth emitted a cry like a wounded animal as he swung wildly at Anton. The taller boy simply skipped back deftly, leaving the way open for Lieutenant, who ran at Seth, leaping into the air and delivering a solid flying knee to his chest. The blonde boy stumbled back and hit the ground hard, losing his grip on the blade. It soared into the air and then fell, heavily, to the ground.

There was a frozen moment where everyone in the clearing sought out the silver gleam in the dark, leaf-strewn ground. In the next moment Seth was crawling madly towards the blade, panting and spitting, as Anton and Lieutenant immediately dropped down to catch him, stopping him inches from the blade's lethal edge.

"Charlie, get the knife!" Anton grunted, struggling to hold down Seth's flailing right arm with both of his own arms while Lieutenant pressed her elbow against Seth's neck.

Charlie glanced at Toni. *Move!* Toni's mind screamed. *Help! Do something!*

"Charlie, Tiny, c'mon!" Anton hollered, punching Seth's reaching hand and tugging his fingers away from the knife.

Charlie shot one last look at Toni before scampering forward, picking up the knife by the handle with two hands, and scurrying over to Melvin, handing him the weapon.

"Get off me!" Seth bellowed. "Get off me!"

Anton nodded to the huffing Lieutenant, and both teenagers sprang back from Seth in unison, allowing him to rise, fuming, to his feet.

"You think I need a knife to kill you?" Seth yelled as Anton and Lieutenant joined Melvin and Charlie off to his right. "I can break you with my bare hands, tear out your God damn eyes —"

"Then do it!"

Toni felt adrenaline break the icy spell on her body as she spoke up and took a step toward the wide-eyed, cold-blooded blonde.

"You're all talk," Toni asserted, putting as much derision into her tone as she could manage, willing herself not to watch as the others slipped quietly away, back into the woods. "Yeah, your blood is cold enough to kill, but doing the actual deed is a problem for you, isn't it?"

"What did you just say to me?" Seth whispered.

"Oh don't. You heard me," Toni said, gaining steam. "But for the hearing impaired, I'll repeat. I just implied you have performance issues." Toni gave Seth's body an up-and-down glance and then smirked. "Of one kind or another."

"That's rich coming from you, you fucking slut," Seth said spitefully. "Grinding against my hand and panting like a bitch in heat. You want me, and you would have let me fuck you —"

294

"But I didn't, did I?"

"You would have," Seth repeated. "There's not a bitch in this town I couldn't have if I chose to."

"I've got four witnesses here who can confirm that there's one bitch you can't have," Toni snapped back. "I may not be able to teach you compassion, Seth, but if there's one thing you should learn? For every man who thinks he's irresistible, there's a woman who walks away."

"Walk away?" Seth licked his teeth as he advanced on Toni, his voice lowering as the speed of his steps increased. "Walk away? You think you're gonna walk away from me?" His voice was a low whisper, and the relaxed, sing-song quality sent a jolt of energy to Toni's legs. She backed away, stumbling, starting to run. "You're gonna walk away, run away?" Seth's voice stayed almost dazed, gentle, as he picked up the pace. "You're gonna run away? Don't run away. Don't run away. Don't you run from me, Toni. Don't you run from me you little bitch. I'm gonna catch you. I'm gonna catch you and kill you. I'm gonna kill you. Don't you run from me! Don't you run away!"

The raging, screaming voice followed Toni as she ran, ran, ran, crushing leaves and twigs beneath her feet, her pounding heart the constant reminder that the monster she fled from demanded her blood.

"Should we call the police?"

"The police are off blocking the roads, and this may only be one student. Besides, they wouldn't get there in time," Mrs. Carter dismissed, gritting her teeth as she shoved aside another branch. Around her, fifteen odd guards cut their way through the surrounding woods. "We need to get there while they are still around the fire."

"Are you sure the students started the fire?" Andrews asked, holding a thorny vine away from the principal's face as she stepped surely over a log.

"No, I'm not sure of anything anymore," Mrs. Carter stated

bluntly. There was a buzz at her hip, and she withdrew her phone. The screen identified the caller as Sophia Valentina, Headmistress.

"Is it important? News?" Andrews asked.

"No." Mrs. Carter ignored the call, re-pocketing her phone. "No one important. What's important is getting everyone to push faster. Hurry up! Move!"

Move!

"I'm gonna kill you, you little bitch."

Seth's voice behind her was almost conversational and genial, and it spurred Toni to run even faster. Sprinting over uneven ground, she smacked aside vines and branches, vaulted over logs, and splashed through freezing puddles.

"I'm gonna kill you with these two hands, and while I'm choking the life out of you, I'm gonna take everything else as well," Seth continued, the heavy pants in between his words becoming laughter. "I'm ... oh, I'm gonna fulfill your deepest wishes. I'm gonna be your perfect man, Toni. It doesn't have to hurt, if you just stop. I can kill you so nice, so nice and sweet, there's really no point in running!"

Run.

Toni cried out as she hit the trunk of a fading? tree, shaking away bark shavings and stumbling on. *Can't stop. Don't stop. Run, run. C'mon, Toni, run.*

"Toni? Toni, are you hurt Toni? I don't want you to hurt. I don't want you to hurt, baby, not until I'm hurting you. 'Cause I'm ... I'm gonna make you scream, you bitch, gonna make you beg for that mercy you think I don't have, and you'll pray I do. You'll pray for it, you cunt!"

Toni choked for breath, the terror propelling her forward while warring against the pain in her chest and the plea for her to stop, just stop.

"Stop! Just stop and end it now! End it now, you bitch, and I'll make it only last a few hours. Just give up! Give up so I can give you what you need, you bitch!"

Don't stop. Never stop. Keep moving. God, stop saying my name. Just stop saying my name.

"I'm gonna fucking kill you. I'll kill you! Don't run from me! Come back and just let it happen. It's gonna happen anyways. You're gonna die, you bitch, you bitch . . ."

Block him out. Toni ignored her eyes, almost useless in the dark, and followed her nose, racing towards the scent of smoke.

"Come back here you little bitch! Come back, and let it happen, let me kill you . . ."

Block him out. Block him out and run.

"Alright, I want you to block off that half of the woods, and —"

Mrs. Carter jerked her head up with the others, as a dozen flashlights roamed through the trees, trying to find the source of the screams.

"You fucking bitch! Don't you run from me!"

Mrs. Carter shivered, opening and closing her mouth, as the men around turned to her, waiting.

"Don't keep making me run after you!"

The principal winced again at the vicious scream, and then forced herself to muster her strength?. "That . . . one of our students is clearly out here. Let's get moving. Faster, come on!"

"Come on, don't hide from me!"

Seth's voice grew triumphant as he saw the glimmer of flame up ahead. Growling and shoving aside the last of the vines and branches at the woods' edge, Seth emerged onto the beach, scanning the lakeshore for Toni.

The dying fire illuminated the empty beach, the slap of the waves against the shore the only sound besides the cracking of burning sticks.

"Where are you, you little bitch?" Seth muttered, kicking up sand as he moved down to the water's edge. "Where are you?"

The water lapped at Seth's shoes, and he frowned, squinting down at the spreading stain. Pulling back into the light of the fire and narrowing his eyes, Seth bent over to examine the sneakers, touching them with his right fingers. He brought them to his nose and his eyes widened.

The woods behind him rustled, and Seth whirled. "What is this, you bitch? What did you do?"

"Seth?"

"What did you do, you bitch?" Seth screamed.

"I really do *not* take kindly to my students using that kind of language, Seth," Mrs. Carter said loudly as she stepped through the trees. "Or to threats toward other students."

Seth's neck almost snapped moving back and forth as he watched the guards emerge from the trees.

"Where is Melvin, Seth?" Mrs. Carter demanded as the flashlights caused Seth to cover his face with his unhurt arm.

"Melvin? What the hell are you —"

"Language," Mrs. Carter barked, pulling away Seth's arm and staring him down. "Where is Melvin?"

"Melvin, what about Melvin?"

"We heard you screaming," Mrs. Carter stated. "We heard you threatening him."

"I wasn't threatening that fag," Seth snapped, and then bit his tongue as Mrs. Carter's eyebrow popped. "I wasn't! I was —"

"Ma'am!"

Mrs. Carter turned as Andrews walked over carrying something wet and dripping in outstretched hands.

"We found this in the water, ma'am."

Mrs. Carter took the item and held it up to the light.

"Oh my God."

Blood dripped from the shirt, mingling with the water, coursing down to stain her shoes. Shaking, Mrs. Carter turned to Seth.

"What did you do?"

CHAPTER TWENTY

"SO. YOU HEARD THAT TWO STUDENTS WERE OUT AT
night, both of whom you knew had deep animosity towards
each other, one of whom had a weapon, and never once did you
think to call me."

"I was handling it."

"And then you found one student standing over the bloody
clothes of another by a deep lake, the other student missing, and
still you did not call me."

"Sophia . . ."

"It was only when the police arrived on the scene, having
been spread so thin protecting the main roads that they could
not respond to the fire which led you to the student, that you
chose, at long, long last, to call."

Mrs. Carter gripped the edge of her desk as the Headmistress
came to a stand-still before the principal and clasped her hands
together.

"So."

"So, what?" Mrs. Carter said heavily, her eyes resting blankly
on the many memos, files, and documents littering her desk.

"So what is your plan?" Ms. Valentina questioned. "I assumed
the reason you finally called me was that you had thought of
a brilliant scheme for damage control, which you intended to
share with me."

Mrs. Carter raised her dark-rimmed eyes to meet those of the bemused redhead. "No. I do not have a contingency plan for this."

The Headmistress raised an eyebrow, and the edge of her thin mouth twitched. "Well, we certainly need one."

The principal chuckled humorlessly as she propped her elbows up on the pile of papers and rested her head in her hands. "I can't see the use. We have one student missing and presumed dead at the hands of another, grieving parents, thousands of dollars worth of missing property ..."

"Have a drink, Evelyn," Ms. Valentina said as she settled into the chair opposite Mrs. Carter. "It will help you clear your mind."

"This will spur a whole investigation," Mrs. Carter muttered, rubbing her temples. "The press will focus on the school, on our response, and whether or not we are legally to blame. The court of public opinion will most definitely find us guilty, or at least questionable enough to shut us down —"

"Calm down, Evelyn," the Headmistress said, rolling her eyes ever so slightly. "You did call me for a reason."

Mrs. Carter's head shot up, her tired eyes squinting fiercely at the other woman. "You can't stop an investigation."

"Of course not!" Ms. Valentina exclaimed, shaking her head reprovingly at the black haired woman. "Perish the thought. Of course we want to find out what has happened here more than anyone else, save of course the grieving parents and Ms. Daley. An investigation will certainly be conducted. *Our* investigation. And when we have discovered the true nature of the situation, *we* will remedy it to the best of our ability, and ... " The Headmistress leaned forward " ... at our discretion."

Mrs. Carter huffed a laugh, half disbelieving, half hopeful. "And you can guarantee that this will all stay a ..." Mrs. Carter waved her hands, searching for a way to match the other woman's delicate phrasing. "A family affair?"

Ms. Valentina pursed her lips, drawing out her answer. "Who can guarantee anything in this world?" she said enigmatically. "All we can do is count on our friends and associates to remember our many kindnesses to them in their own times of need and remind them of their many promises and obligations in the hours of ours."

"I suppose not all of those promises and obligations are ones I am aware of?" Mrs. Carter responded with bone dry cynicism.

"You are the right hand of J. Alter Academy, Evelyn," the Headmistress said with an elegant shrug. "That makes me the left. You know how the saying goes."

"I very much doubt *He* had *this* in mind when he said those famous words," Mrs. Carter noted.

The Headmistress' wry little grin gave way to a true smile. "Who can say?"

"It's been six hours, and I have to say it doesn't look good, ma'am."

Mrs. Carter folded her arms, tugging her windbreaker close to her body as another bitterly cold gust whipped around the coats of the officers managing the boat. The tip and sway of the craft forced her to reposition her feet, giving her more time in which to answer the detective.

"It is a large lake, Detective. You can't possibly have searched it all yet."

"That's not the issue, ma'am," Detective Nichols began to explain in a patient tone, the grey sky behind his head washing out his sun-damaged skin. "We could search this lake for days, from dawn till dusk, and we still might never find the body, even if it is here. The quality of the water, and the depth, is such that even if we sent divers down they might never find him, even if he was staring them in the face."

Mrs. Carter eyed the men leaning over the bow of the white boat and extending what looked like a heavy black wire deep into the waters. "And what about the very expensive equipment the school has lent you to aid you in your search?"

Detective Nichols raised his hands in badly concealed frustration. "We appreciate you lending it, but so far even when it isn't goin' haywire, it just doesn't seem to be able to find anything about a body, just a lot of readings that say the lake's deep and there's somethin' funky about the water."

"Something funky about the water," Mrs. Carter repeated absently, gazing out over the lake's dark expanse, its surface churning and rippling with the wind that buffeted the small boat.

"Our best bet is still hoping he washes up with the current. We can map out where the boy might've been deposited based on where we found the blood, and going from there . . ."

Mrs. Carter let Detective Nichols continue to speak, his voice mixing in the back of her awareness with the groan of the boat engine as she scanned the cruelly impassive surface of the lake.

"I didn't kill him."

The Headmistress balanced one elbow on the armrest of her chair while rolling her pen between her fingers. With her other hand she pushed a photograph of blood-stained shoes toward the boy who sat in the chair opposite her, his hands firmly cuffed. "It doesn't look good, Seth."

"It doesn't matter what it looks like," Seth snapped. "What matters is I didn't do it."

"Oh, I'm afraid it matters very much what it looks like," the Headmistress informed the fuming teen. "And it looks like you lured Melvin out into the woods, stabbed him, and pushed his body into the lake."

"I *found* the clothes. I had just gotten to the beach when I saw what was there —"

"And why were you at the beach?" the Headmistress interrupted, watching Seth's throat muscles constrict, an ugly expression pulling his face tight. He didn't answer. "Why were you at the beach, Seth? Why were you out at night, after having stolen five-hundred dollars from your supervisor, as well as a considerable amount of jewelry?"

"I didn't steal her jewelry," Seth denied, using the same tone of voice and widening of the eyes as he had to deny the previous assertion. "She must have misplaced it herself. She's got bad eyesight. She'll probably find it a week from now, if she hasn't already. She's just lying to make me look guilty."

The Headmistress raised one brow. "And why would she want to do that?"

"Because that's what all of this is!" Seth declared, tightening his hands into fists and rattling his cuffs. "This is all designed to make me look guilty. I'm being framed."

"Do you also deny breaking the lock on the drawers in Ms. Daley's home to steal one of her butcher knives?" Ms. Valentina questioned.

"Yes," Seth hissed.

"So someone else broke the drawer and took the knife? Ms. Daley herself, perhaps?"

"Maybe. She probably thought it would help her story," Seth proposed.

"Mrs. Daley has a broken wrist, Seth."

The Headmistress watched Seth grind his teeth for a moment before continuing. "You did have an altercation with Mr. Stavos in the cafeteria only a few days back, yes?"

"Yes, but I never —"

"And you were heard to be screaming all sorts of violent epithets and threats when you were found by Mrs. Carter."

"They probably heard wrong," Seth put forth boldly, shifting in his chair, his eyes narrowed. "They didn't really understand."

"Mrs. Carter says she heard you call her a bitch."

"She misheard," Seth stated. "I wasn't calling her a bitch. I was yelling for someone else."

The Headmistress' other eyebrow popped. "Who?"

"Toni," Seth whispered, his entire body tensing. "She was one of the ones who set me up. She asked me to go with her, to run away with her. She was there. They were all there."

"They?"

"Anton. Lieutenant," Seth pronounced scathingly. "Charlie. Melvin. Joseph and Ann were out there too, but I didn't see them."

"So you did see Melvin that night?"

Seth's knuckles cracked as he opened his fists, his hands clawing at his legs. "He was alive when I saw him. He was alive. He was a part of it. They all were. They lured me there. They told me to bring the knife. Toni told me to bring it, it was her idea."

"So you admit to bringing the knife?" the Headmistress specified.

Seth barely blinked at being caught in the lie. "Yeah, I brought the knife, but I didn't use it. It was Toni's idea to get me out there, and then they jumped me, all of them."

"Why would Toni ask you to bring a knife?"

"To frame me!" Seth said, leaning forward. "They're all in on this. She told me to bring the knife, she called her friends out, and Melvin? Melvin's probably halfway to Canada with the money Toni told me to steal, and laughing at me."

"That's a very elaborate story," Ms. Valentina noted. "And you are known for your elaborate stories."

"Give me a lie detector test," Seth demanded. "I'll pass it."

"Yes," the Headmistress agreed. "With flying colors, because those tests were designed for those who find lying emotionally and mentally difficult. For those burdened by pangs that you will never feel."

Seth's sapphire eyes gleamed, and his upper lip twitched. "I didn't kill him."

"Which is exactly what you would tell me if you had."

Seth licked his front teeth, eyes narrowed and calculating. The Headmistress rolled her pen.

"I understand that this is difficult for you both, and that you've done this once before with Detective Nichols, but we just need to go over this one more time. Is that alright?"

Mrs. Carter waited, hands resting on the granite kitchen table as Mr. Stavos placed his shaking arms around his seated wife's shoulders.

"How many times do we need to do this for you all to be satisfied?" Mrs. Stavos demanded, her heavy frame straining against her checkered, magenta dress as she needlessly pushed her already bound hair away from her plump, red face.

"The school just needs your statement for our records, Mrs. Stavos."

"Oh, the school! Let me tell you, the school can just —"

Mrs. Carter raised her brows, and Mrs. Stavos broke off with a visible gulp. The principal waited patiently for the other woman to consider her next words.

"What statement do you need?" Mrs. Stavos' asked, her down-turned mouth opening just enough to mutter her reply.

Mrs. Carter gave the couple a moment before laying the photograph on the table and pushing it towards them. Mrs. Stavos' face crumpled, and Mr. Stavos squeezed her shoulders.

"Can you identify this shirt, Mrs. Stavos?"

Tears slipped out of the corners of Melvin's mother's eyes as meager little dots, blotching her overdone makeup as she looked down upon the blood-soaked image.

"Yes." The mother pulled the photo closer and then yanked her hand away quickly, as if burned. "That was one of his favorite shirts. He bought it when he was out . . . with me." Mrs. Stavos' full lips curved into an excruciating smile, and more watery dots dribbled out of her brown eyes. "He always kept it so clean. He always kept all of his things so clean. He would never have . . . have wanted those big holes in it . . ."

Mr. Stavos tightened his hold on his wife's thick shoulders as she drew her fingers over the sharp cuts in the shirt, shuddering. Mrs. Carter glanced over at Detective Nichols, who leaned, arms folded, against the doorframe.

"Mr. and Mrs. Stavos, the night your son disappeared, he took his backpack," Mrs. Carter reminded, rubbing her ankles together under the small table. "You've also reported that many of his clothes were missing, along with a substantial amount of food. Can you think of anywhere he may have been intending to run? Were there any relatives he mentioned recently, did you see any evidence of maps, or anything that would hint at a destination?"

"You think he might have gone somewhere?"

Mrs. Carter angled herself backwards, pulling instinctively away from the hungry desperation in the mother's eyes. "We're just trying to put the whole picture together."

"But if he hasn't been found, and if he was planning to run..." Mrs. Stavos roused herself, sniffling back tears. "If he was then maybe he is at a bus stop somewhere, or in the woods. Or looking for a hotel. Maybe he's at some other police station. You should call them, call the other towns. Put out an alert, he might call."

Mrs. Stavos cast her starving eyes from Mrs. Carter to the detective who was adjusting his stance uncomfortably on her right. Both looked away from her attempt to enlist them in her new hope.

"Maybe he just cut himself?" Mrs. Stavos rubbed the gold cross that dangled from her neck. "You think? Maybe, maybe he was running and he cut himself, and he ch-changed his shirt. Maybe he's really just lost. Maybe he's not gone, he ... he's just ... he's just ..."

Mrs. Carter cleared her throat softly as Mrs. Stavos dissolved into silent, body-racking sobs.

"Thank you for ..." Mrs. Carter let her voice trail off as Mr. Stavos embraced his now moaning wife. "Thank you for your time."

"This is a waste of time," the tall black girl stated.

The Headmistress calmly waited while Lieutenant slid her hands up and down the sides of her chair. The black girl squinted at the masks on the back wall and then slumped further into her seat, staring down at the fringe of the rug under the desk.

"What is a waste of time?" Ms. Valentina asked patiently.

"This." The girl waved one ebony hand dismissively, her baggy blue shirt slipping down to reveal the dog tags nestled between her breasts. "Searchin' the lake, askin' me questions. Pretendin' there's hope."

"You don't believe there is hope?"

Lieutenant's long lashes half-obscured her almond eyes as she dully examined the array of photographs before her. "Look at it." She shoved one of the photos back towards the redhead's side of the desk. "Look at the cuts in that shirt, the *stab marks*," the teen enunciated. "Check the blood. That's not an accident. That's murder."

"And you believe Seth did this," the Headmistress elaborated.

"He was the only other one out there," Lieutenant stated.

"Well, he tells it differently," the Headmistress began.

"Yeah, I'll bet he does," Lieutenant mumbled.

"He insists you were there, Amina." Ms. Valentina watched the girl's long face closely.

"Don't you think if I saw him stab Melvin that I would have *done* something?" Lieutenant asserted, the sturdy muscles in her arms visibly tensing under her shirt. "Don't you think I wish I was there?"

"Seth said you were," the Headmistress insisted. "He says you were there, along with your friends; Anton, and Charlie, and Toni, and Melvin. He thinks you planned this to set him up."

"Planned what?" Lieutenant's voice rose. "*Planned* my friend's murder? You think I would plan for my friend to die?"

"No," the Headmistress conceded. "I don't think you would ever plan for that. But perhaps things didn't go according to plan."

"Oh, they went accordin' to a plan." Lieutenant scoffed, her eyes fixed on the photograph of a certain scowling, handsome blonde. She shoved it towards the redhead. "*His* plan."

"I just didn't think he was capable of something like this."

"Ms. Daley, you were aware when you took in a boarder that he was being supervised because of behavioral problems, yes?"

"Oh, yes, I know," the nervous, honey-blonde woman simpered as she continually touched the cast on her right wrist with her fluttering left hand. "But he was always so well behaved, he always cleaned his room and helped with the dishes, and asked me about my day, and when I broke my wrist he became invaluable around the house."

"Yes, Seth can be very skilled at making himself of use," Mrs. Carter noted dryly.

"He was always so sweet," Ms. Daley continued, her willowy frame swaying as if from a light breeze despite the stuffy quality of her small bedroom. "I just have a hard time understanding why he would do this."

"Did you notice anything unusual about Mr. Dryer's behavior prior to his fleeing the house?" Mrs. Carter said in a polite tone which masked her reduced expectations.

"No," Ms. Daley said, winsomely. "He was just as helpful and calm as ever. Even after I called to report him missing and noticed the money and the jewelry were gone, it was still hard to ... to really think he had done it."

Mrs. Carter could barely conceal her exasperation as she asked, "Did you see or hear anything in the weeks leading up to the theft that suggested plans to run? Did he ask you about roads or hotels or towns, did you find any maps or signs he was packing?"

"No, not until that night," Ms. Daley said immediately, and then her round eyes lit up. "Wait. He did ask me once about whether I had been across the border, to Canada. When I said no, he changed the subject, but ... that's all I can really remember."

Mrs. Carter engaged her considerable willpower and resisted rolling her eyes. "Did he ever mention Melvin Stavos, or any other student with animosity, or make any threatening or angry comments towards any other students that you can recall?"

"No." Ms. Daley shook her head, her bangs rustling. "He mentioned eating lunch with friends, and hanging out with friends ... he said he got along really well with all of his classmates."

"Of course he did." Mrs. Carter summoned up a comforting smile. "Well, Seth is safely in our custody now, and the police are doing everything possible to recover your property."

"Thank you, Evelyn," the other woman said exuberantly, causing the principal to stiffen. "It's so horrible about the other boy, and really, I don't need anyone worrying about me and my money or property when there's still a child missing. They were only some old sentimental pieces I had from my mother anyway. It's nothing that'll break the bank."

Mrs. Carter stared at the delicate, swaying, aging other woman.

"Rose, how did you break your wrist?"

"Oh, this." Rose Daley laughed at herself as she looked down at her cast. "It was all my fault, completely my own clumsiness. When I wake up in the morning, because of my blood pressure and my eyesight, it's always hard for me to really see until I have my coffee and an hour or so to adjust. Anyway, one morning a few weeks ago I end up tripping right over three books and tumbling right down the stairs. It was my own fault of course. I didn't remember doing it, but I must have left those three books there, right in front of the steps."

"I don't remember."

The Headmistress tapped her pen against the crystal sphere on her desk. "You don't remember? Or you weren't there?"

"I don't remember 'cause I wasn't there," Anthony clarified, his speech carefully paced as he hunched his tall back, as though he didn't know what to do with his considerable height. "I was asleep."

"You were asleep," the redhead repeated.

Anthony nodded in a bobbling motion. "I went to bed around nine, fell asleep at ten, and then I woke up the next day and I heard that..." Ms. Valentina watched the black teen's chest rise and fall to a staccato rhythm, his sharply black and white eyes full and round in honesty. "I wasn't there. You gotta believe me."

"I've got to believe you?" the Headmistress specified.

"No, no, I mean you don't got to, don't have to believe me," Anthony corrected, his imp-like beard twitching nervously with his chin. "But I swear, ma'am, it's the truth."

The Headmistress clicked her pen again. "Oh, of that I have no doubt."

"And you're sure?"

Mrs. Waters shook her head, her frizzy salt-and-pepper hair swinging about her madly. "I wish I wasn't, but I tested the blood from the shirt against the sample we have for Mr. Stavos and it is undeniably his DNA."

The Headmistress let out a harsh breath, like a runner at the end of a race. Her tight grey eyes surveyed the tiny lower level lab with its walls lined with shelves on all sides, before coming back to the steel table on which the series of vials and DNA profile sheets lay.

"So are we to determine from this that the cause of death for our student was blood loss?" Ms. Valentina murmured, separating out the two identical DNA profiles and examining the alleles.

"Not necessarily," Mrs. Waters put forth, removing her blue latex gloves. "The blood is certainly Melvin's, and yes, there is a lot of it, but not a lethal amount." The science teacher met the taller woman's eyes. "There is a chance he's still alive."

"His tag went offline, Wendy." The Headmistress lifted one of the vials up to the light and peered at its viscous content.

"Meaning . . . ?"

"Meaning it was crushed, smashed," the redhead explained impatiently, loudly. "If it hadn't been, we would have found his body by now. We should have found his body by now."

"Maybe it was damaged somehow?" Mrs. Waters offered, watching the subtle changes in the metallic face of her superior.

"The tag was imbedded in his back."

Mrs. Waters nodded and looked down at the many angled photos of the blood-drenched shirt. "There was a stab to the back," Mrs. Waters noted quietly.

The Headmistress drew herself up, adjusting the waistband of her sailor pants and pushing one of her copper tendrils behind her ear. "As far as the police are concerned, this still has the possibility of being a missing persons' case. I see no reason to disabuse them of that notion."

Mrs. Waters nodded and then blinked, looking up as she realized what was being said. "Aren't we going to tell them?"

"Tell them what?" Ms. Valentina prompted. "That the blood on the shirt is Melvin's? They will come to that conclusion in their own time, and I am sure they will follow your reasoning that the blood was not enough to be assuredly fatal. They will then follow whatever leads they can identify in the search for the missing boy and ultimately conclude that his whereabouts cannot be determined. The case will go cold. Melvin's parents may cling to hope, or they may assume the worst, and whenever they decide to hold the funeral we will be there to offer condolences for their loss."

"But if we know from the . . ." Mrs. Waters trailed off at the redhead's steady grey gaze. "That poor kid," she finished simply.

"That poor kid."

"The poor kid is terrified. I just didn't have it in me to hold her down and force the examination."

"You know you can call in extra security if you need help restraining her."

"That isn't the issue, Evelyn! She was still as the dead when I took a blood sample, not a peep, but the minute I tried to get her to take her clothes off for the pelvic exam she screamed bloody murder."

"Not the best choice of words at the present time, Teresa."

"Look, all I am saying is that in my professional opinion? The girl shows every sign of a very *specific* type of trauma. Regardless of whether she lets me do the physical exam or not, regardless of what I find, I do believe it is safe to say that the girl has been damaged."

Damaged.

The whispered words filtered into Ann's awareness as the principal and the nurse continued their badly suppressed conversation on the other side of the curtain. She tightened her arms, locking her legs even closer to her chest. Her knees rubbed against her chin, and she shivered in her bare feet, shaking out her hair so that it fell around her face, making its own curtain against the rest of the room.

Okay, so fine, I'm damaged, Ann thought flatly, emptily. *I'm a broken doll. Whatever. I can deal with it. But what the fuck does that bitch nurse think she's gonna accomplish? She could give me a hundred baths and I'll never get clean, she could shoot me up with bleach and my insides would still be shit, so why doesn't she fucking leave it alone?*

"I've contacted her parents," Mrs. Carter was saying on the other side of the curtain. "Hopefully they can help with the situation."

Ann had to bite the black material of her pants to keep in a harshly mocking laugh.

Oh yeah, so helpful. Mom will be just so excited to talk about what a problem her little angel became when she married Rick, how much she loves her precious girl but Ann, oh she is such a liar. She has a real problem with jealousy and trying to manipulate other people. Oh, and sex? Yes, she is promiscuous, loose, easy, and it's just a trial to deal with her. I didn't raise her like this, I swear. I don't know where she gets it.

"You think she'll do better once she's back in the home?" the nurse asked.

"I'll only know once I speak to the parents," Mrs. Carter answered.

Sure, send me back, Ann thought fiercely. *They'll be so happy to have their little girl home. I know Rick will just roll out a welcome mat. He's always so happy to play Daddy.*

Ann felt a rush of fear put a crack in her frozen indifference.

Callie's at home. He's been Dad for Callie. But he never . . . liked her like he liked *me. He always said he didn't.*

But then he never had a problem with lying either.

"Try to get her to do the exam, if possible. It's important to know if she's recently had sex," Mrs. Carter instructed the nurse.

Oh, of course it is. Ann felt another inner-ice crack. *Because if bad, bad Ann had sex, then it means she's just a lying little slut trying to play victim. It means she's telling lies again, because that's just what girls like her do, to try and cover up . . .*

Ann drew in a stiff breath.

If she finds out I had sex, she'll trace it back to Joseph.

"Alright Evelyn. But I'm not going to push her."

Well, you'll have to, bitch, if you want me to strip for you. I might be a whore but I'm not that easy.

Mrs. Carter's heels clipped out of the room, and as the door closed the nurse pulled the curtain aside. The old woman's wrinkling face stretched into a semblance of a smile.

"Hun, I really need to check you out, just to make sure you haven't been hurt. I can promise you I will make it as painless as possible, and it'll be over just before you know it."

Ann brushed her hair aside as she looked up. She stared into the nurse's kind, understanding, sympathetic face.

"Go to hell."

"You really could make this easier on yourself, Joseph."

"Yeah, well, guess I ain't the *easy* type a' guy," Joseph snapped at the redhead who stood to the left of him while Mrs. Waters inserted an IV into his strapped arm. He struggled against the full body bonds which held him to the operating bed — a useless gesture, as the leather straps dug into his bare chest.

I'm not gonna make it easy on 'em, Joseph told himself once more as he blinked up at the stone ceiling.

"Would it make any difference if I told you this is for your benefit?" the Headmistress said wryly, as Mrs. Waters monitored the cherry red liquid dripping from the IV bag, down the tube, and into the prone boy's arm.

"Oh, it's all for our benefit, right?" Joseph drawled. "Them skin shocks are there to help us too, huh? Yeah, I can really feel those benefits." He glanced down as far as the neck strap would allow him, staring pointedly at the burn marks on his chest. "So what's the treatment with this, Doc?" he directed at Mrs. Waters who had moved to his right side and was pressing her fingers to his wrist, taking his pulse. "Is it some serum to make me nice and ... friendly? Take away my sparklin' personality and replace it with a good little boy's?"

"It is a solution designed to lower your internal body temperature," the Headmistress replied, placing both hands on the operating table near Joseph's head and boring into his amber eyes with her own. "To prevent you from collapsing and dying of heat stroke. I was actually worried we wouldn't be able to develop it in time. Your prognosis was such that I expected a crisis to present itself much sooner."

The Headmistress smiled. "Luckily, something seems to have been staving such a crisis off for the past few weeks, almost as if you already had a means of cooling internally before now."

Joseph stared the grey eyed woman down, his lips firmly closed.

"I wonder what that could be?"

Joseph shrugged as best he could. "I guess I'm just a lucky guy. Blessed, you know?"

The Headmistress smiled. "*I know. You're* about to find out."

"Firstly I want to thank you both for coming here on short notice. Things have been in an uproar for obvious reasons, but I felt it very important that we should meet."

Mrs. Carter smiled at the two adults on the other side of her desk. Cheryllynn Cost had clearly bestowed both her blonde hair and her belligerent manner on her daughter — the tall woman was tending towards overweight, and she sat in the chair as if eager to leave it. Her husband was tan-skinned and solidly built; he fiddled with the silver band on his index finger as he eyed the principal.

"As you know from my reports, Ann has been backsliding behavior-wise," Mrs. Carter said, her thumbs balanced against either side of the file in her hands. "She has had increasing bouts of violence towards both authority figures and other students, and there have been a number of instances of self-harm, though these seem to be more attempts for attention than attempts on her life."

"That's always been a problem," Mrs. Cost said in a grainy, grating voice. "She will do that. She will do things just for attention. I used to drive myself crazy trying to keep up with all her stunts, until I realized that it was just what she wanted, just what she wanted."

"Yes, I understand things were hard for you at home," Mrs. Carter opened.

"Cheryllynn tried," Mr. Cost explained. "And I love Annie like any father loves his daughter, but it's been really hard on the both of us, dealing with her problems."

"You and your stepdaughter got along well?" Mrs. Carter posed.

"He tries, he really does," Mrs. Cost answered. "He does perfectly well with Callie, Ann's sister, but Ann, she just refuses to behave for him. Well, you've seen how she is. When she doesn't want to listen, she doesn't listen. She just refuses to accept him as an authority figure, and, well, I mean, you've seen it!" Mrs. Cost waved a hand jangling with bracelets towards the principal.

"Yes I have," Mrs. Carter agreed. She shot a swift, calculating glance at each adult. "You know, when I brought up the possibility of a change of living space, Ann wanted to talk to me about the . . . conditions in your home."

Mrs. Cost paled, throwing her many facial blemishes into

relief, before hurriedly rolling her eyes and asserting, "Oh, Annie loves to tell her stories. As I said when we first enrolled her, as I said to you, you remember, I *said* she lies." Mrs. Cost threw up both her arms in a grand, helpless gesture. "She lies. She is always looking for a way to manipulate others to get her own way. I swear, I don't know where she gets it, but she does. She has an absolute talent for it, and she will spin tales for you for as long as you listen."

Mrs. Carter nodded and threaded her fingers together on top of the file. "And is there anything you think she might have lied about or exaggerated in her comments to me?"

Mrs. Cost drew in a few quick, intense breaths and flicked her eyes towards her husband who was examining his ring.

"She really can't deal with a male figure like Rick. She has discipline issues, as I've said," Mrs. Cost offered rapidly. "She has *always* had it out for Rick, and she likes to elaborate and create these scenarios where she's a victim. She loves being the center of attention, and when she's not, well, you know, she'll do anything to get it, anything for sympathy. She's one of those girls," Mrs. Cost said, lowering her voice confidentially.

"Those girls?"

"You know," Mrs. Cost said with a knowing smile. "The girls who want everyone to feel sorry for them, the ones who make themselves the — the star of their own little play. Ya know, the ones who don't ever wanna take responsibility so they want to blame everyone else for their problems. The girls who have . . . issues with men. You know. You've seen her."

"I have," Mrs. Carter said again. "Well, as you may know, she's been presenting with a lot of extreme crises recently, and we feel Ann needs specialized help."

"You want to send her home," Mrs. Cost stated.

"Not at all. In fact, nothing could be further from my mind."
The mother frowned. "What?"

"I have no intention of releasing Ann back into your care," Mrs. Carter said with a calm smile. "I would no more send her back into your home then I would throw her off a cliff."

"Excuse me?" Mrs. Cost gasped.

"I believe I was clear," Mrs. Carter said, the upper left corner of her mouth threatening to break into a smile. "But take all the time you need for it to sink in."

"You're way outta line," Mr. Cost snapped, looking up from his ring.

"Oh, am I?" Mrs. Carter posed delicately. "Ann will remain in the school's custody, in a home where she may be appropriately monitored, and you," Mrs. Carter said opening the file in her hands and rotating it towards the two adults, "will agree that your daughter may remain with the school until such time as we decide she is ready to reenter society — regardless of whatever feelings you may have to the contrary in the future."

"You can't force me to sign my daughter away," Mrs. Cost protested, her bloated face florid.

"I am not forcing you to do anything," Mrs. Carter countered. "You are voluntarily relinquishing custody. Force is what will be used by the police if your daughter is taken by the police on suspicion of child abuse, which is exactly what will happen if I hear even the slightest complaint as regards your younger daughter."

"You can't do this." Mr. Cost growled. "We'll sue."

"You will lose," Mrs. Carter certified, one eyebrow arching dismissively. "As you may have noticed in the recent commotion, we have very close ties to law enforcement here at J. Alter Academy. Would you like to see if those ties also spread to the other arenas of our justice system?"

"You bitch," Cheryllynn managed.

Mrs. Carter tilted her head. "Ah. There it is."

"There's what?" the angry mother snapped.

"The family resemblance," Mrs. Carter responded.

"You —" Mrs. Cost fumed. "You listen to me —"

"No." Mrs. Carter stood and stared down at the two adults before her. "You listen to me." Her voice dropped into a low, velvety, deadly tone. "I don't know which one of you perpetrated the abuse, or if it was both of you in conjunction, and I don't much care. My job is to protect these children, and I intend to do my job." Mrs. Carter adjusted the lapels of her coat. "No matter who I need to protect them from."

Mrs. Carter deposited the file in Mrs. Cost's lap as she collected her purse. "Now, if you will both follow me, I will be happy to see you out."

"Where are we goin'?"

The Headmistress did not answer, and Joseph winced, rubbing his arm, as he followed her up another flight of stairs.

She can say that stuff was just to keep me from burnin' myself up all she wants, he thought. *And I bet some of it's even true. But there's definitely more to it than that. There's always more.*

The Headmistress turned a sharp left and pushed open a door. Joseph blinked. They were in the nurse's waiting room. Ms. Valentina stepped aside and Joseph's eyes widened.

Ann looked up from her seat and swallowed, staring at him fearfully as the Headmistress went over to confer with the nurse. Joseph opened his mouth to speak and then remembered that he couldn't.

They'll catch us. Fuck! That's probably what happened. That's what she meant. They found out 'bout us, and now . . .

Fuck.

The conversation between the Headmistress and the nurse ended abruptly and both teens gazed intently at the floor.

"Well, this isn't exactly a good sign," Ms. Valentina appraised. "You can't be very good housemates if you don't look at each other."

Joseph frowned at the pink and white squares below him. *Housemates?* He raised his head slowly and found the redhead wearing a bemused smile.

"What do you mean?" he asked.

The Headmistress elevated both gingery brows. "Katrina

Vaglienty's living arrangements are going to change this week, and Ms. Nearson had decided to retire from our program. Ms. Fosset has kindly agreed to take on the both of you."

Ann and Joseph couldn't keep from looking to each other.

Why the fuck would she do that? Joseph communicated to the blonde girl without having to speak. Ann glanced mutely at the nurse, and Joseph's mind slowly began to put the pieces together.

She knows, he thought grimly. *She knows we been sneakin' out, and she knows what we've been doin' when we do. Shit, she's probably figured out Katrina's been helpin' us. That's why her "living arrangements" are changin'. This way, we're together, where they can monitor us, and Katrina isn't, to keep us from workin' with her.*

"Is there a problem?" the Headmistress asked, and Joseph looked again at Ann who was now watching him with mingled fear and hope.

"Nah, no, no," Joseph answered, as Ann shook her head in agreement. "No problem."

"Lovely. Now, there is one last thing." Ms. Valentina motioned for Ann to rise, which she did, on shaky feet. "Ann, I believe there is someone here to see you."

Ann swallowed, scared eyes searching out Joseph's, and he moved as close to her as he dared in support. Ann looked to the door, and her chest jerked forward as she took a step back, as if dealt a blow. Joseph almost cracked his neck following her sightline.

The young pre-teen in the doorway was very nearly a miniature version of Ann: the same blonde hair, the same dominant nose, the same full lips. She held herself in the same manner as the taller girl across from her and stared at her with the same mixture of fear and elation.

The tears ran down Ann's cheeks and wet her mouth as she opened and closed it, finally managing to choke out one word.

"Callie?"

"Mrs. Carter?"

"Yes, I've been listening," the principal assured the man who sat before the sea of screens which monitored the whole of J. Alter Academy proper and the residences which housed the students enrolled in STARE. "And it's all very fascinating, Norman, and I would appreciate a full report on my desk by next Monday, but as of now what I really need to know is whether any of the students I listed left their beds on the night in question."

"I can definitely say that they did not," Norman answered and swiveled his chair to the right to point out a specific screen. "Right there is Mr. Levant's room, and that heat signature, right there? That's him. He spends all his night in bed, just like all the others you wanted pulled up."

"Are you sure nobody missed anything on that night?" Mrs. Carter quizzed. "No one went up for a bathroom break and missed them sneaking out? The door, see, the door is left ajar."

"But he never leaves the room," Norman attested. "Look." He sped up the image, and Mrs. Carter stared as the heat signal continued to glow in rippling red and orange. "He fluctuates a bit when his temp drops as he falls asleep, but that's perfectly normal, and he's right there until he wakes up in the morning."

"But the door was left open," Mrs. Carter muttered again, gazing at the thermally portrayed image.

"Even if it was, he never could've gotten to it without us seeing," Norman stated flatly.

"And you're sure no one has been able to get into your records?" Mrs. Carter asked.

"No one," Norman insisted. "Mrs. Principal, I can promise you that we had this place on lockdown the minute we spotted Seth up and about."

"And yet he swears he saw the others that night, up and about as well," Mrs. Carter murmured, examining the time stamp on the footage.

"Maybe he did," Norman allowed. "He does have mental issues, right?"

"What? Oh yes," Mrs. Carter confirmed, rubbing her temples.

320

"Well, there you go," Norman said confidently. "Kid like that could very well have *seen* the other kids all dancin' around him, taunting him, tellin' him to run after them. He could very well have *seen* it. But him seeing it doesn't mean they were there."

"You're asking me if I've been seeing things."

The Headmistress placed the palms of her hands together and pressed them to her lips. "Have you?"

"No," Charlie answered, feeling as though she were swimming in the chair opposite the grand mahogany desk. "No, not really seeing things. Hallucinations aren't common though, are they? Visual ones? The most common ones are auditory."

"Have you been hearing voices, Charlie?"

Charlie swallowed and pushed against the chair's cushion to prop herself up against the chair's back. "No, not really. Not too much. I can ignore them."

"Can you?" The copper eyebrow went up. *Up, pop, hop on Pop, Dr. Seuss, loose, loose association, another typical symptom . . .*

"If I try," Charlie said, her response coming out louder than she'd meant it to as she focused on making sure she was saying what she intended. *Meaning, my life has meaning, feeling, once more, once upon a time, a time to kill is meaningful if you insert it into the wheel, whirring like a clock . . .*

"So you believe you can control your symptoms," Ms. Valentina interpreted. Charlie's wrist jerked, and she leaned on it.

"No, I don't . . . I don't know." Charlie slipped her thigh over her roving wrist. "You're the one who thinks I'm psychic," Charlie countered. "Why don't you tell me if I can control it?"

"Well, that was a bit hostile," the Headmistress said, and Charlie sank back into the chair.

"I'm sorry."

"Are you?" The Headmistress didn't bother waiting for an answer. "Schizophrenia can be likened to a very specific kind of labyrinth. It is complicated and scary, it has all of these traps and pitfalls, and finding your way through it can take a very,

321

very long time."

"Do you?" Charlie asked, making the redhead pause. "Do you find your way through it? I thought the idea was to find a way to live with it."

"For most." Ms. Valentina's pale lashes hid her storm colored eyes for a moment, before she fixed them firmly on Charlie. "But not for you. I don't think I have to tell you the story of Ariadne and the labyrinth."

"No. I mean, you can, if you want," Charlie said, and the Headmistress smiled. "So, am I Ariadne?"

"You have a string," the Headmistress said gently. "The very fact that you have any measure of control over your symptoms is proof of that." Ms. Valentina leaned forward. "But now you are in a very delicate position, Charlie. You must walk a very, very fine line, between trusting your abilities, and being seduced by your mind's . . . pitfalls."

"And you think I can?"

The Headmistress considered the small, mousy girl with the over-bright eyes. "I think you have the potential to become something very different."

Charlie's nose twitched. "Different from what?"

"That's exactly the question we'll have to answer," the Headmistress proposed, smiling.

Charlie looked down. *Golden girl. Good little girl. So she doesn't know? No, how could she? She isn't psychic. I am. Powerful. Am I powerful?* Charlie blinked. *Not now . . . am I? Maybe . . . maybe I will be.*

And if I am, once I am, she might not think I'm so golden.

"I hope I don't disappoint you." Charlie said, looking up at an angle at the redheaded woman.

Ms. Valentina's brow creased. "How do you think that would happen?"

"I don't know," Charlie said. "Maybe by not being as smart as you need me to be."

"I think you are far smarter than you give yourself credit for," the Headmistress soothed, beginning to smile, then pausing. "Or maybe not," she noted. "Maybe you're smarter than I give you credit for."

"I don't think so," Charlie assured aloud. *I don't think so,* Charlie repeated inwardly. *I know so. You designed this labyrinth, but I found the trap door.*

And if I opened it once, I can open it again.

"We can reopen the case later, but at this point I think we're hitting a dead end. So far all our leads turned up cold. We barely know any more about what went on here then we did when we started . . ."

"Then you're giving up?"

"Do you want me to give up?" Detective Nichols demanded, scuffing his leather shoes against the floor of the Headmistress's office. "Huh? You?" He turned toward Mrs. Carter, who stood to his left. "Isn't that what this is all about?"

"We're not trying to impede the carriage of justice, Brian," Mrs. Carter said calmingly. "If Melvin is out there, alive or otherwise, we want him found, and we want this solved."

"Yeah. Without press attention," Detective Nichols reminded smartly, his boyish face drawn in a sardonic half-smile.

"Who needs to care about one case in a million in a small Montana town?" Ms. Valentina asked rhetorically. "You said yourself we don't really know what's happened here. I don't see much of a story."

"But there is a case, and you're all wrapped up in it," the detective judged. "Now, I don't care about making a name for myself, or stirring up . . . whatever. But if you're holding out evidence . . ."

"Everything we know that is pertinent to your case we've given you," the Headmistress asserted, spreading her hands. "Along with extra information we thought might have been useful. We want Melvin found, Brian."

"Quietly. Quietly you do." The detective wiggled his finger back and forth between the two women. "Which one of you convinced the Stavos' not to press charges on Dryer?"

Ms. Valentina raised both eyebrows almost to the roots of her copper hair. "I thought you had, considering we have no murder weapon, no body, and no proof of death. What kind of outcome could they get? On what evidence could any jury convict Seth?"

"And you're just gonna take him back into your school, aren't you?" Detective Nichols fitted his hands into his pants pockets and shook his head.

"Where else would he go?" Mrs. Carter asked pertly. "We have the technology to monitor him and keep him in line."

Detective Nichols laughed pleasantly, patting his legs. "Yeah, good job."

"You think he'd be any better handled in prison?" Mrs. Carter demanded curtly. "He won't get the kind of treatment he needs there."

"I interviewed the kid," Detective Nichols stated. "He's a psychopath. What kind of treatment do you think is gonna work on him?"

"How perceptive of you," Ms. Valentina praised. "Yes, Seth is a psychopath, or sociopath. As to his treatment, since that does not concern your investigation, I'm afraid it will remain on a need-to-know basis."

Detective Nichols laughed again. "You've got one hell of a polite way to jerk a guy around by the balls. Okay. I see what my part of the deal with the devil is here."

"Then you accept the terms?"

Detective Nichols scoffed at the principal. "Don't ask me like I got a choice."

"Oh, there's always a choice, Brian," the Headmistress stated. "If there weren't, our lives would all be much, much simpler."

I did this.

"I have no idea."

I knew exactly where this would end up.

"You are sure?"

I have to stick to the story. If I deviate, if I look like I know too much, or too little, we're all going down.

"If I knew what happened to Melvin, I would tell you so they could arrest Seth."

If I told you what happened you might arrest me.

"How could you know Seth was involved, if you weren't there?" Grey eyes pierced her green-hazel ones, and Toni was careful not to swallow, and not to blink, but also not to look too calm or together.

Your friend is dead. He's gone, or dead. You don't know what happened, but you think Seth does because they found him out there.

Just like we planned.

"I don't *know*, obviously," Toni said, keeping her hands in a ball in her lap as she sat, leaning slightly forward, at the edge of the Headmistress's desk.

"Obviously?"

Toni turned towards Mrs. Carter, who stood at the redheaded woman's right hand. "If I knew, then Melvin would be ... be here, and I would ... maybe he'd ..."

Cry, damnit! Cry!

Toni sniffled as she forced the tears out, pinching the insides of her thighs for help. Mrs. Carter watched the thin line of tears trickle down Toni's cheeks and glanced over at the Headmistress.

"So you think he's dead?" Ms. Valentina asked, and Toni shrugged heavily.

"I don't know. I don't ... want him to be, but that's ... that's what it looks like," Toni murmured.

"Yes," the Headmistress agreed. "That is what it looks like. And we, both of us," the redhead said, indicating Mrs. Carter, "have looked over the facts again and again. But just looking at facts doesn't answer anything. The facts have to tell a story. And we have two different stories."

Toni didn't swallow. She felt a moment of pride for that, and then squashed it thoroughly. *You might have blushed. She could have noticed something else. Don't get cocky.* "Yeah?"

"Yes." Mrs. Carter spoke now. "On the one hand, we have the

story of two boys who go out into the woods. One has stolen money, jewelry, and a knife. The other has taken some clothes, and some food. While in the woods, one stabs the other with the stolen knife, pushes his body into the river, and is then caught."

"Can you see the problem with this story, Toni?" the Headmistress questioned.

Yes. "No?" Toni tried to mold her face into the picture of innocent confusion.

"These two boys hate each other," the grey-eyed woman narrated. "So, while it makes sense for one to kill the other, it doesn't seem plausible that they would be running away together."

Toni waited for Mrs. Carter to pick up the story and then offered, "Unless they weren't running away together."

"No? Just on the same day then?" The Headmistress's eyes crinkled.

Toni did swallow now. "Melvin ... every time I saw him he always looked unhappy. I could see him trying to run. The last time I talked to him he was saying how much he hated it here."

"And when was that?" Mrs. Carter interrupted.

"About two weeks ago now. At lunch. He didn't want to talk much," Toni stated, then her words came slowly, as if only now realizing, "But ... maybe Seth got him to talk. Seth could always ... he kept trying to talk to us," Toni continued. "In science class. At lunch. I couldn't figure it out, because I knew he didn't like us, but he ..."

"So Seth finds out when Melvin plans to run," Mrs. Carter said, picking up Toni's line of thought, "and decides that he'll run as well. And he plans it to coincide with Melvin, just so he can ... why?"

"Because of who he is," Ms. Valentina supplied. "Because it is exactly something that Seth would do."

Toni almost nodded. *Careful,* she warned herself. *Don't look guilty. Why would you be guilty? You're grieving. Be grieving.* "I should've done ... something, I ..."

"Yes, that is one story." Ms. Valentina gave her bemused half-grin. "The other has more characters and is slightly less neat. In it, seven friends decide to frame a boy for murder. They lure him out into the woods, they take the knife from him, and they goad him into running to the beach. There he finds planted evidence that implicates him in the possible murder of one of them."

"Is that Seth's story?" Toni didn't have to feign her disgust and dismissal.

"It does sound less plausible, doesn't it?" The Headmistress leaned forward. "But there's something about it ..." She tsked. "It *would* explain why the knife, and the jewelry, and the money Seth took still haven't been found."

"How?" Toni asked. *Play dumb. No, not too dumb. She knows you're not dumb. But you're disoriented, you miss your friend.* "How does that explain anything?"

"Well, if Melvin is still alive," the Headmistress said, "then he may have taken them with him."

"With him where?" Toni demanded. The redheaded woman inclined her head, and her nostrils expanded. *Shit, shit, shocked, be shocked, be grieving ...*

No. Be hopeful.

"You think Melvin's alive?" Toni said, making her voice light and breathy. *Yes, good recovery.*

"Do you?" Mrs. Carter asked harshly.

Toni ran her left thumb over her right palm. *I'm sweating. Do they see me sweating? It's okay to sweat, right, I mean, if I think my friend is dead? And now he might be alive?*

"I don't know, I don't know. I want him to be, but ..." Toni turned her focus to Mrs. Carter. "They showed the picture of his shirt, and there was all that blood. Are you saying he survived that?"

"*I'm* not saying anything." Sophia Valentina captured Toni's gaze and held it. "I am asking you. Is. Melvin. Alive?"

"I don't know, I wasn't there," Toni repeated.

"No?"

"No, I wasn't there!"

"Then tell me what you think!" the Headmistress demanded, her voice striking out like a whip. Toni shuddered and stilled, that same primal instinct causing her to freeze.

Ms. Valentina froze as well, her eyes squinting, recalculating. Mrs. Carter stepped forward, bent down to place a hand on the desk, and met Toni's eyes.

"Do you think Melvin is dead?" Mrs. Carter asked quietly.

Toni looked up into the warm brown eyes of the principal and mother.

"Yes," Toni lied. "I think Melvin is dead."

Mrs. Carter continued to hold her gaze, and Toni returned it until the older woman broke. Toni turned to look at the Headmistress, but the redhead was already standing, her face to her office window. "Thank you, Toni. I believe you have classes now."

Toni rose, stumbling as she dragged her backpack up and around her shoulders. She followed Mrs. Carter, her head downturned, and caught a glimpse of the Headmistress at the window, her vibrant hair shadowing her expression.

"Come on."

Toni had to shake herself, and as she tailed Mrs. Carter, she felt herself unwinding with each step. With every turn of a corner she could feel the tension and fear that had become almost commonplace to her over the past week rolling off her shoulders like water.

"Here you are."

Toni's eyes ran blankly over the faces of her classmates. *Classroom, this is my classroom,* she had to tell herself. Toni nodded, her neck aching, as she pushed past the principal and inhaled the scent of rosemary as she did.

Toni couldn't understand what the teacher was saying. She knew eventually that part of her brain would reassert itself once the terror had fully evaporated from her mind.

We did it.

The knowledge came slowly. First as a relaxation of her body, and then as an expansion of her lungs, and then as hard, glittering, breathtaking victory.

We did it. We. Did. It. It's done. We did it. We got away with it.

Toni shook down her hair, hunched over her paper, and let the smile come, a glory on her face.

We did it.

One down. Six to go.

ACKNOWLEDGMENTS

Thanks to my amazing editor Mary Vitas, without whom this book would have been pretty darn messy.

Thanks to Nina Terhune for crucial emotional support and strength when yours truly was truly out of it. I will deal with many-legged buggies for you any day!

Thanks to my dear old Ma (sorry, Mom) for invaluable proofing and sharing of your immense knowledge as a doctor.

Thanks to my incredible and bumfy designer Joshua Langman, who has always gone above and beyond to help this rather silly and jumpy author in making this all possible.

Last and not least, thanks and praise to Ganesha, Remover of Obstacles, for making the path to this book clear, and to Inanna-Ishtar, for strengthening my will with Hers. Nin-Me-Sara, Lady of countless cosmic powers. ॐ श्री गणेशाय नम, OM Sri Ganeshaya Namah.

ABOUT THE AUTHOR

Aubrey Coletti is the twenty-one-year-old songwriter, dancer, and author of the Academy series novels *Altered* and *Shattered*. She is currently working on the third book in the Academy series.

www.ingramcontent.com/pod-product-compliance
Lightning Source LLC
Chambersburg PA
CBHW020333180626
46012CD00001B/180